By DON TRAVIS

BJ VINSON MYSTERIES
The Zozobra Incident
The Bisti Business
The City of Rocks

Published by DSP PUBLICATIONS
www.dsppublications.com

THE
CITY OF
ROCKS

A **BJ VINSON** MYSTERY

DON TRAVIS

DSP PUBLICATIONS

Published by

DSP PUBLICATIONS

5032 Capital Circle SW, Suite 2, PMB# 279, Tallahassee, FL 32305-7886 USA
www.dsppublications.com

The City of Rocks
© 2017 Don Travis.

Cover Art
© 2017 Maria Fanning.
Cover content is for illustrative purposes only and any person depicted on the cover is a model.

ISBN: 978-1-63533-154-7
Digital ISBN: 978-1-63533-155-4
Library of Congress Control Number: 2016958594
Published July 2017
v. 1.0

Printed in the United States of America
∞
This paper meets the requirements of
ANSI/NISO Z39.48-1992 (Permanence of Paper).

To my late wife, Betty, and my two sons, Clai and Grant, who suffered through my compulsion for writing.

Acknowledgments

TO MY critique buddy, Joycelyn Campbell, for her stern eye and steady guidance. And to the members of Wordwrights, the writing class I coteach, for their willing contribution.

THE
CITY OF
ROCKS

A **BJ VINSON** MYSTERY

DON TRAVIS

Prologue

M Lazy M Ranch in the New Mexico Boot Heel
Wednesday, July 9, 2008

THE THIEF froze as a string of sharp yips hammered the quiet night. He'd darted both big Dobermans that were now sleeping soundly out at the fence, so this yapper must be a house pet. A light flashed briefly as the back door opened. A fur ball with pointed ears bounded down the steps and made straight for him. The feisty canine latched onto his pant leg and whipped it back and forth, growling furiously. A growl was preferable to a bark, so he dragged his dog-impeded leg like a zombie in some old Hollywood movie.

As he reached the poultry pen, all hell broke loose. A single quack built into a raucous caterwauling. Someone must have flipped a switch up at the house because brilliant light suddenly flooded the enclosure. He reeled backward, stunned by a sea of white. Ducks. Dozens of ducks. Hundreds. How was he going to find the right one?

The dog attached to his pant leg shifted its grip and closed on his ankle. Cursing, he gave an involuntary kick, sending the pooch over the fence. The ducks scattered, opening a circle of dark earth around the confused mutt. The pup transferred its attention to the birds and began a joyful chase, dashing this way and that, parting its panicked prey in dizzying waves of undulating white, creating a living kaleidoscope of shifting shades and shapes.

Then he saw her. In a coop all by herself. Like she waited to turn into a swan or something. A clamor from the house galvanized him into action. He vaulted the fence, threw open the cage door, and dragged her out by the neck. He ignored the claws raking flesh from his forearms as he fled through a horse corral at the back of the pen. He made it to the cover of some shrubbery before the ranch came alive. Moments later a woman's agonized wail rose above everything.

Remembering he needed to deliver the duck alive, he loosened his hold on the feathery neck. The bird immediately set up a loud protest that could have awakened the dead but wasn't enough to overcome the clamor of the hundred or so other birds. He turned and headed for his pickup. Best get out of there before Millicent Muldren's drovers filled him full of lead.

Chapter 1

Ten days later, Albuquerque, New Mexico

I JERKED the cell phone away from my ear and looked at it as if it had lost its mind—or its chip. Del Dahlman, a local attorney, wanted me to drop everything and run down to the UNM Emergency Center to interview a man named Richard Martinson. When he told me why, I assumed he was kidding. He had to be.

"You want me to go question a ducknapper? There's no such thing. He's just a plain, ordinary chicken thief."

"Whatever," Del said. "I need you to catch him before he leaves the emergency room."

This was simply too good to let go. "Have you called in the FBI yet?"

"Don't be an ass," Del snapped.

"Donkeys now? What is this, a menagerie run amok? Who did it? The pigs? Good Lord, it's Orwell's *Animal Farm* come to life."

"Dammit, Vince, I'm serious. *This* is serious. I need you to get over there right away."

I stared at the bright blue sky on this cloudless Saturday afternoon and considered hanging up on Del. I stood on the fourth tee of the golf course at the North Valley Country Club with Paul Barton. Although we lived together, it was a rare occasion when Paul and I could share the daylight hours. Between my confidential investigations business and Paul's schedule—UNM grad school summer courses and an aquatic director's job at the country club—we were the proverbial ships passing in the night.

I resented Del's intrusion, but he and I went back a long way—some of it sweet, some of it bittersweet, and some downright sour.

"You need to get a move on," he said. "You've got to get to him before they let him go. His name's Richard Martinson, but... but they call him Liver Lips." Del didn't like playing the straight man.

"Liver Lips? Calves' liver or…. No, don't tell me. Let me guess. Goose liver."

"You're wasting my time, BJ." He always called me Vince, a carryover from the days when we were a couple. Anytime he resorted to addressing me as BJ like the rest of the world, he was pissed.

"Hey, you called me. Right in the middle of my backswing, as a matter of fact."

"Are you going to do it or not?"

I sighed. One of my better clients, Del commanded my attention. "Okay. Give me the details. There's really a lawsuit on this thing?"

"No, it's not actually a suit… yet."

"Then why is your firm involved? More to the point, why are you involving me?"

He went defensive. "We're New Mexico counsel for the Greater Southwest Ranchers Insurance Company or GSR, as they liked to be called, and the VP handling their problem and I are old friends. At this point I'm doing this as a favor to him. At any rate, the missing bird's name is Quacky Quack the Second. This—"

"Quacky what?"

"Shut up, Vince."

I snickered through the rest of his briefing, hung up, and turned to my golfing companion. Paul got as good a laugh out of it as I had. In fact, we both broke up a couple of times during the retelling.

I DO not like walking into a situation I don't understand, and I damned well didn't understand this one. But I had no trouble locating Martinson in the waiting room at the hospital. *Liver Lips.* The young man's nickname described him perfectly. His thick, purple-hued oral projections drew my eye like a magnet. Only later did I notice he was skinny, seedy, and carried a generally disreputable air. Gray eyes darted here and there as if he were constantly searching for a bolt-hole. The man's scalp glistened through thin strands of frizzy blond hair. Whether he was talking or listening or simply idle, his dark tongue periodically snaked out to wash those heavy lips. Seldom had I been so thoroughly repulsed by another's physical appearance.

He looked at me blankly after I handed over my card and introduced myself. "A private eye, huh. What you want with me?"

"I need to ask you a few questions." I nodded at the bandages covering his forearms. "What happened?"

"Had a fight with a thorn bush. Frigging bush won." He went for humor, glancing up through thin, colorless lashes to see if it had worked.

I pointed to the red veins snaking up out of the white bandage on his right arm just short of his elbows. "Thorn bushes didn't give you that infection. That's blood poisoning. How'd you get it?"

"Tangled with the wrong bush, I guess. Then didn't get it treated. Turned bad on me, I guess."

"Come on, I'll give you a ride down to my office where we can talk in private."

"Ain't got time. Gotta get outta here. I been here six frigging hours."

"Okay, I'll call Lt. Eugene Enriquez down at the police department, and we'll have this talk at APD."

He blinked rapidly three times. "No cops, man. Don't need no cops. I ain't done nothing, so leave me alone."

"What are you doing up here? You live down in Deming, don't you?" I drew on the thin biography Del had provided.

"Ain't no law against a man visiting the city. I guess that's what they do all that advertising on TV for. You know, to get me to come up here and spend my money."

"You want to tell me about it?"

"About what?" He seemed genuinely perplexed by my question.

"About stealing a valuable... bird." If I'd said "duck" I'd have burst out laughing.

"Don't guess I know what you're talking about."

"You do a lot of guessing, Richard. But I don't think the sheriff of Luna County would have sicced me on you if he was just guessing."

"Hidalgo," he blurted.

"What?"

"Sheriff of Hidalgo County."

"Okay, now that you've admitted you know all about the theft, tell *me* about it."

"Didn't admit nothing."

"You know where the abduction... uh, theft took place. Stop wasting my time. What did you want with a prize duck named...." I stopped, unable to call a bird by that ridiculous name.

"Quacky Quack the Second," he said. "That's what old Mud Hen calls her. Ain't that a hoot?"

"Mud Hen?"

"Millicent Muldren. Everybody calls her Mud Hen."

"She's the duck's owner?"

"Yeah. She's run the Lazy M Ranch since her old man died."

"Why'd you steal her duck?"

"Who says I did?"

I improvised. "About everybody in the countryside. Police chief, sheriff, Mrs. Muldren. There's a warrant out for your arrest. Talk to me, and maybe I can do something about that."

Old Liver Lips wasn't as dumb as he looked. Those blood-suffused appendages quivered a couple of times before he squared his thin shoulders. "Ain't nobody gonna arrest me for nothing, I guess. Who'd press charges on something like that?"

"Well, Mud Hen for one, and the insurance company for another."

"Insurance company?"

"You didn't know the owner had insured her property?"

"Shoot, I guess there ain't no insurance company in the world that'd insure a frigging duck."

I didn't know much more than he did, but I couldn't let up on him now. "Then you'd guess wrong. They'll insure soap bubbles if you pay the premiums."

Liver Lips wiggled in his chair, looking distinctly uncomfortable. "Uh… you said something about a warrant?"

Flying totally blind, I had no idea if a warrant existed for this character. In fact, I didn't even know why he was suspected of the theft. Or how Del found out he'd be at the UNM Emergency Center today.

"Yes, but I can deal with that if you give me what I want."

"Like what?"

"Like what have you done with Qua… with the duck?" His eyes slid away as he opened his mouth and licked his lips. I held up a hand. "Don't bother to deny it. You're caught flat out. Man up and admit it. Where's the duck?"

"Dunno." The word came out in a whisper.

"Why not?"

"Somebody took her."

"Yeah, we've already established that. You took her. What did you do, pluck her and eat her? You like roast duck, Liver Lips?"

His shoulders twitched. He did that rapid blinking thing and twisted his neck to loosen it up. A bead of sweat worked its way through thin tendrils of blond hair and trickled down his forehead. It looked muddy by the time it reached the corner of his eye. "Hell, I didn't eat her. I give her to somebody."

"Who?"

His pale gray eyes clouded over. "Just somebody wanted to play a trick on Mud Hen."

"Who was this somebody?"

"If I give up his name, he'll get me in trouble. And he can do it too."

"So can I. A world of trouble. You've already given me enough to report to the insurance company. You're the chicken thief, Liver Lips. And they'll come after you hard. You have any idea how far they'd go to keep from paying out all that money?"

"How much money?" His attitude changed. If Liver Lips had a crafty side, this was it.

"More than you can ever repay in your lifetime." I built on the fiction I was spinning. "They'll see you prosecuted for grand theft. What does your record look like? Probably penny ante, right? Well, you made the big time with this."

"For stealing a duck?"

I stared at the raunchy-looking man. Was this an act? "Answer my question. Who hired you to steal the duck?"

"Hired?"

Jeez. The guy hadn't even been paid. He'd done it as a favor, or else someone had leverage on Richard Martinson.

"Who told you to take the duck? Who'd you give it to?"

"Her."

"Her?"

"It's a her. The duck, I mean. Quacky—"

"Yeah, I know. Who'd you give her to?"

Liver Lips crossed his arms over his chest and hugged himself tightly. "Oh shit! I hurt, man. They supposed to be getting me something for the pain. And the infection too. I gotta go check on it."

"Okay, we'll go together. Maybe I can help."

"I can do it." The words came out as a whine. "I ain't no kid that needs babysitting."

Despite his objections, I trod on his heels as he walked toward a counter. They'd made some big-time changes at the UNM Emergency Center. It was now housed in a new building called the Pavilion. But I was pretty sure this wasn't the outpatient pharmacy. Liver Lips appeared ready to make a move. He did, but it wasn't the one I expected; probably not the one he anticipated either.

He turned a corner and bumped squarely into a burly Albuquerque cop. Backpedaling, he held out his hands in a plea. "Sir, this here guy won't leave me alone. Can you make him stop pestering me?"

The six-foot-two officer transferred his irritated look from Liver Lips to me. The shoulder microphone for his radio unit belched static, but he ignored it. "What's going on?"

I took a quick peek at his name tag. "Corporal Hines, my name is Vinson, and I'm a licensed PI. I'm going to reach for my ID, okay?"

I whirled as the outside door crashed open. A man and a woman rushed inside with a little girl nursing a bloody hand wrapped in stained towels. Hines brushed by me to see if his help was needed. This momentary diversion was all Liver Lips needed. He'd vanished. I made a quick sweep of the hallways, but he had disappeared. Maybe Liver did have a crafty side after all.

Muttering under my breath, I headed for the parking structure to get my Impala. On the way I hit the speed dial on my cell. Del wasn't pleased with the interview results, and I couldn't blame him.

"So to sum it up," he said, "you're convinced Martinson kidnapped—excuse me, stole—the duck. You think he did it at the behest of someone else and has turned the bird over to that party. Other than that, the only thing you learned is that Millicent Muldren, the esteemed daughter of an old-line New Mexico ranching family, is called Mud Hen behind her back."

"That about covers it. What do you want me to do now?"

"Nothing. I'll let the client know Liver Lips is running. Probably back to the Deming area. He doesn't seem to have personal ties anywhere else. Go back to your golf game, Vince."

"Too late for that. And thanks, by the way. Today was the first time Paul and I have had any time together in a month."

"The two of you still making it okay?"

"Smooth as silk. Except for our schedules. We seldom manage to meet up except at night."

"That's probably why it's still working." He hung up.

I was out of sorts, probably for the rest of the day. Paul's schedule had reclaimed him, so I left the UNM parking structure and headed west on Lomas. The office was closed, but I'd been in the field working on a case since yesterday afternoon, so Hazel Harris, my office manager, had likely left a pile of documents for me to review and sign. Might as well get that chore over and done with instead of waiting for Monday.

Hazel and Charlie Weeks, the retired cop fast becoming a full-time investigator for me, had wrapped up a couple of cases. Charlie was not only a godsend to my business; he also kept my mothering, smothering office manager off my back. The two were becoming quite a pair around the office, although they continued to believe they hid the relationship well.

I settled down at my desk and reviewed the reports they'd left for me. After signing off on the documents, I went through the mail Hazel had left that required my attention, made a few notations, and dictated an answer or two before snapping off my desk lamp.

Still vaguely disgruntled, I swiveled my chair to the windows behind my desk and allowed the vista beyond the glass to slowly calm my nerves as I came to grips with my ill-defined sense of unease. It was not Del interrupting my pleasant afternoon with Paul—although that was a factor—as much as a sense of failure. Of leaving a job unfinished, a goal unattained. Liver Lips had outfoxed me, and that did not sit well.

A pleasant evening with Paul finally laid the thing to rest. Until the telephone rang at one fifteen in the morning.

Chapter 2

THE CALL, which interrupted a pleasant dream about finishing the afternoon's golf game, pissed me off, and Del's voice didn't do anything to improve my disposition. Then I sat up and snapped on the table lamp.

"What? Say that again."

Paul turned over and looked at me through sleepy brown eyes.

Del sounded tired. "Liver Lips Martinson is dead. Went off the road in his pickup. Apparently killed him instantly."

"How do you know?" The words came flying out of my mouth. Still half-asleep, I guess.

"Hank Grass, a VP for Greater Southwest Ranchers, called me."

"Where?"

"A few miles west of Las Cruces on Interstate 10."

"He must have started for home as soon as he gave me the slip at UNM. Anyway, thanks for waking me out of a sound sleep to tell me that."

"Come off it. I need you to get down there and be my eyes on the ground."

"Why me? There are a couple of good investigators in Cruces."

"I know you, and I trust you, Vince."

"What's so special about this? I don't understand all the flap."

"How about a quarter-million-dollar insurance policy."

My reaction was similar to Liver's. "On a duck?"

"Duck royalty, I gather."

"What makes a royal duck worth two hundred fifty thousand dollars?"

"I don't understand the economics either. But Hank Grass at Greater Southwest Ranchers says that's the amount of the policy. How long will it take you to get down there?"

Las Cruces lay 250 miles or so to the south, but this time of night the traffic wouldn't be bad. Of course, I'd have to watch out for Saturday-night drunk drivers. "Say six hours or so, so I can have a shower and breakfast."

"The state cop in charge down there is Detective Manny Montoya."

"Why a detective?"

"I gather there's some question about whether it was an accident."

After Del gave me a few more particulars, I hung up.

"What now?" Paul's long arms thrown akimbo took up most of the bed. The small, dark dragon tattoo on his left pec glittered in the lamplight. He was amazingly tolerant of Del Dahlman, the only other man with whom I'd had a meaningful relationship, but after today he had about reached his limit.

I filled him in on the conversation.

"So why is it your problem? Let him get somebody down there to handle it for him."

I started to deliver a stock reply: it was my job, my duty, my responsibility. Instead I gazed at his smooth tan features for a moment and gave him an honest answer.

"I agreed to do a job for Del and then let him down. I feel... obligated, I guess. I have a few contacts in that part of the state, so I have as good a chance of finding who Liver gave the duck to as anyone."

He shook his head. "A sense of honor. Anyone tell you how old-fashioned that is?"

The question didn't call for a response, so I reluctantly got up and headed for the shower. "Have you ever thought about learning to fly?" I asked over my shoulder.

"Nope."

"Well, think about it. If I'm going to keep running all over the state, we might as well buy a plane and learn to fly it."

LAS CRUCES, a city of around seventy-five thousand and the county seat of Doña Ana County, perched on the Chihuahuan desert flats of the Mesilla Valley. This floodplain of the Rio Grande boasted pecan orchards as well as onion, chili, and other vegetable fields. The city was also a rail center and the home of the state's only land-grant school, New Mexico State University. The stark, striking Organ Mountains rose abruptly to the east.

I parked in front of the East University Avenue headquarters of State Police District Four around 8:00 a.m. I wanted to follow protocol and have dispatch let the officers on the scene know I was on the way.

Twenty minutes later I pulled in behind a swarm of activity. Emergency flares blocked the westbound lanes of the highway. The fact they were still diverting traffic on a major freeway this long after Liver's wreck told me the state police felt this might not be an accident scene. I pulled up to the uniformed patrolman diverting traffic to the eastbound lanes and identified myself. He used his shoulder unit to announce my arrival and then waved me over onto the side of the road. It looked as if the crime unit had about finished with their work. In the distance I could see a banged-up black Dodge Ram pickup lying upside down, snug against the corridor fence. A man in civilian attire detached himself from a small group and started for me as soon as I got out of the car.

"Mr. Vinson?" I nodded. "Dispatch told me a PI from Albuquerque was on the way."

"Detective Montoya? Good to meet you. I suppose the medical investigator's already taken Martinson away."

"Yeah, OMI's come and gone. They took him a couple of hours ago. Forensics is wrapping things up now."

"Why are they here? I thought this was an accident."

"In my opinion it's a crime scene. The investigating patrol unit spotted a second set of tires and what they thought might be foreign paint on the pickup."

"Forced off the road? Are you thinking homicide?"

"That's exactly what I'm thinking, but I don't know if it was negligent or intentional. The stray paint's hard to spot because it's black too. But it was enough for the patrol division to call us in on it."

The detective was a small, neat man with swarthy skin and piercing black eyes who looked as if he'd be more at home in a uniform. I judged him to be a couple of years older than my thirty-five. I'd be willing to wager he'd spent his entire adult life in the service—probably the military before going over to the state police.

"What's your interest in Martinson?" he asked.

"He was suspected of grand theft. I questioned him briefly in Albuquerque yesterday afternoon. When my client called me last night and told me about the wreck, I came down to see for myself. Uh… did you find anything unusual in the pickup?"

That got his interest. "Like what?"

"This is going to sound nuts, but he's accused of stealing a duck. A very valuable duck, as it happens."

"Quacky? He's the one who swiped Mud's bird?" He didn't crack a smile. Apparently they took ducknapping down here a little more seriously than I did. Of course, a homicide tended to wring the humor out of it—whether or not Liver's death was connected to the duck.

"You know about that? I thought it took place over in Hidalgo County."

"Yep, but the news is all over this part of the state." The radio unit in his left hand blared. He spoke into the thing and then turned to me. "They're removing Martinson's vehicle now. They'll be releasing the crime scene after that. You can walk it with me if you want."

Black rubber on the shoulder marked where Liver's vehicle had left the interstate. It appeared to have gone airborne for a short distance before landing hard and rolling a couple of times, coming to rest against the fence. The detective pointed out a second set of less noticeable skid marks on the shoulder.

"I figure this is the vehicle that forced him off the road. Either that or some heartless SOB stopped after the accident and didn't have the decency to call for help or try to render assistance. Of course, it wouldn't have done any good. Martinson died before the pickup stopped rolling."

Montoya led me over the verge and halted at a dark spot in the grass. "Martinson was ejected and landed here. Probably traveling at a pretty good rate of speed. I noticed his right forearm was bandaged."

"Yeah. The duck scratched him up pretty good—gave him a blood infection. I interviewed him at the UNM hospital yesterday. What time did the accident happen?"

"Probably sometime after dark, but nobody spotted the wreckage until around midnight. Nobody mentioned a duck with a broken neck, but I'll check with the forensics people."

Montoya got on the radio and determined the criminalists had found no sign of a duck or a feather or anything else indicating a bird had been in the pickup. When he finished the conversation, he asked me to go back to Cruces and make a formal statement.

DESPITE THE paucity of information I had to offer, Montoya's interview lasted over an hour and a half. The first part of the questioning was sort of arm's length, but midway through it someone walked in and handed him a slip of paper. After that, Detective Montoya—or Manny, as he prompted me to call him—began sharing information as well as gathering it. Apparently his check with APD let him know I was cop friendly. I'd been a law enforcement officer for almost thirteen years, if you counted my four with the US Marine Provost Marshal's Office as an MP. I likely would still be an Albuquerque policeman if I hadn't caught a bullet in the right thigh in May of 2004.

Apparently well known to several southwestern New Mexico jurisdictions, Liver Lips had been in scrapes over domestic violence, on the receiving end as often as not. A few DWI arrests and petty thefts… and carried the reputation of a pothead. Manny suspected he'd occasionally helped smuggle some of it into the area, although there was never any proof of it. But he'd made the big time with the theft of a domesticated duck. Even Montoya acknowledged the irony of that.

Just before we broke up, a technician came in to confirm foreign black paint had been found on the driver's-side door panel of the wrecked Dodge Ram. It would take a little more time and effort to learn anything from the scrapings. It was enough, however, to fuel suspicions of foul play.

"Tell me, Manny. Why did you wake up an insurance honcho in the middle of the night to tell him about Martinson's accident?"

"Fellow by the name of Grass apparently has some pull. We got an all-points bulletin late yesterday afternoon. When I discovered whose truck it was, I called Santa Fe. Somebody above my pay grade woke up the honcho."

I CONTACTED Del, who said he needed to consult with Hank Grass in El Paso, the friend calling in a favor. I asked him to find out if they had a copy of the police report on the theft. If they did, that would save me a trip to Lordsburg. As I finished a cappuccino at a local Starbucks, he got back to me on my cell and asked me to continue on the case and said he'd e-mailed a copy of the incident report. My assignment now? To interview the owner of the stolen property and locate the missing duck. This was a case that would never be posted on my website, even in the unlikely event I managed to successfully rescue Her Royal Duckness.

I headed for Deming, hoping to locate some of the dead man's family or familiars who might be able to give me a lead, before driving to the M Lazy M Ranch. The sixty-mile stretch between Las Cruces and Deming was relatively flat and dominated by creosote, honey mesquite, and yucca. An ungodly amount of cacti and spiked plants of every size and description lived among these anchors. Except, of course, the tall, stately saguaros the entire world associated with the American Southwest. To the best of my knowledge, those grew only in Arizona.

Roadkill revealed the makeup of the local fauna: jackrabbits, desert terrapins, kangaroo rats, and the occasional rattlesnake. Reminded me of trips Del and I used to take—which reminded me of Paul and set off a longing I tried to ignore. The desiccated carcass of a coyote hanging over the fence bordering the interstate diverted me from that line of thought. Of course, in the Cooke's Range to the north, there would be cougar and black bear and mule deer. The nearby Florida Mountains boasted ibex and mountain sheep with occasional unconfirmed sightings of the Mexican jaguar. I know this because I'm a confirmed history buff, especially the history of my native state. God, I love this place!

On a hot day beneath a blue-flame sky, the temperature probably hovered around a hundred degrees. But like we're fond of saying down here, it's a dry heat, so it doesn't hurt much, especially at an altitude of three-quarters of a mile above sea level. Dark, menacing thunderheads hovered south over Mexico, but the monsoon hadn't yet taken hold.

Deming, with a population of around fifteen thousand, was the county seat and principal town of Luna County. It is also located in rock hound country. A good part of southwestern New Mexico and southeastern Arizona is a paradise for rock and mineral collecting. Most of the old mines are closed now, but on public land it's legal to collect bits and pieces of once treasured rock. Geodes. Fire agate. Jasper. Quartz. Azurite. Even turquoise chips can often be found in old dumps.

I checked in at the police department to let them know I intended to poke around in their jurisdiction and to see what they knew about the late Liver Lips Martinson. Officer Bill Garza, a heavy, mustachioed man, gave me the same story Manny Montoya had with a little more emphasis on pot smoking. He suspected Liver Lips of a tenuous connection with a marijuana gang across the border but could never find enough evidence to nail him. Garza did not seem seriously distressed by Martinson's passing. He showed neither mirth nor curiosity when I told him my interest centered around investigating the theft of the M Lazy M property.

LIVER'S SHACK in a dilapidated neighborhood of wood shanties and bare-earth yards on the south side of town looked about ready to give up the ghost and simply collapse. More buildings in the area looked abandoned than occupied, but then so did Liver's from the outside.

Although Officer Garza had told me Martinson lived alone, a woman opened the paint-starved door when I knocked.

"Yes?"

Probably around twenty-five, she had a pretty face and a voluptuous body now thickening around the waist. Pregnant?

"I'm looking for Richard Martinson."

"Not here." The brevity of her answer and the slight accent told me she was probably Mexican. Not too surprising. The border lay only a few miles to the south. Even with a slightly bloated belly, she still looked a couple of cuts above Liver Lips.

"Mrs. Martinson?"

She shook her head, making the multiple metal hoops strung through her earlobes jingle. "No. Not wife. Friend."

"Are you aware he had an accident?"

She nodded. "Yes. Last night. Who are you? What you want?"

"I wonder if I could come in and talk to you for a few minutes? My name is B. J. Vinson. I'm a confidential investigator." The stoop had no porch or overhang, and I needed to get out of our benevolent dry heat before my collar wilted.

"Don't know nothing. Can't tell you nothing."

"You don't know what I want," I pointed out in a reasonable tone.

"Don't know nothing." She started to close the door, but I blocked it with my foot.

"All right, just tell me who his friends were so I can go talk to them. Otherwise I'll have to come back with a policeman named Bill Garza."

"Lopez," she said. "Go see Elizondo Lopez."

"Where do I find him?" I asked the question even though Garza had already provided me with Lopez's name and address.

She shrugged and managed to get the door closed.

I sat in my car for a few minutes to see if she left or showed her face again, but she didn't. So I started the Impala, turned on the air conditioner, and headed off to find Lopez's place, which turned out to be only a couple of blocks to the west. His shack was as weather-beaten as Martinson's. I eyed a big clump of ocotillo in the corner of the dirt yard and wondered how many rattlesnakes lurked in the shade of those meandering, spiny tendrils.

A Latin clone of Liver Lips jerked open the door to my knock. Well, not a clone, really, but the general impression was the same. Skinny, a good four inches shorter than me. Thick black hair that hadn't seen a comb in a while and actually appeared to be dusty. His lips, however, were normal—thin but normal.

"Elizondo Lopez?"

"Who wanna know?"

"My name's B. J. Vinson. I talked to Robert Martinson up in Albuquerque, and we agreed to meet down here and talk some more. But he got himself killed before we could do that."

Lopez must have heard about the accident because he showed no surprise. "Who are you, Mr. B. J. Vinson?"

"I'm a confidential investigator."

"How come you talking to me?"

"Thought you could answer the questions I didn't get to ask Liver Lips."

I'm not certain how he managed to swagger while standing stock-still, but an excessive amount of machismo leaked through the tattered screen door. "Liver Lips ain't gonna talk to no PI. He run the other direction." He gave a half smile, stretching a faint, black smear of a mustache even thinner. "That's what he done up in Albuquerque. He run off, no?"

"Why would he do that, Elizondo? I offered to get him out of trouble in exchange for some information."

"Name's Lopez. We ain't on no first name basis. Lopez."

"Okay, Lopez, but answer my question. Why would he run away when I tried to help?"

The man's shrug emphasized the hollowness of his chest. Although the rest of him looked soiled, the bright sleeveless undershirt he wore was spotless. "He don't like cops."

"I'm not one. Can you tell me who the woman over at his house was?"

"Woman? He didn't have no woman."

"One answered the door. Hispanic. Pretty, but carrying a little too much weight around the middle." The description earned me a blank stare. "Probably from across the border. Had an accent."

"Shit, everybody around here got accent."

"You don't know her?"

"Nope. But I know one thing. She don't have no business in Liver Lips' place."

Chapter 3

LOPEZ SURPRISED me by agreeing to go check out the mystery woman. Within two minutes we were at Martinson's front door. No one answered our knock. Lopez fished around underneath a rock beside the step and came up with an old-fashioned skeleton key. You wouldn't catch me sticking my hand down there. Might find something beside a little scrap of metal.

The two-room shack was deserted. Liver Lips apparently had done his furniture shopping at the local dump. A ripped and worn sofa. Dingy, once-white stuffing spilled out of both pillows. Threadbare arms ten shades darker than the rest of the couch. A sagging chair and an ancient boom box on a listing, unpainted table completed the décor. Nothing on the bare planking of the walls other than a big calendar still turned to last December.

The bed was the only piece of furniture in the other room. At first I thought the mysterious woman hid under the covers, but the lump proved to be the mattress piled with a jumble of old clothes.

While I looked for something that might tell me why the late Liver Lips stole a duck, Lopez searched for something else. After a few minutes, he stood in the middle of the almost-bare living room and swore in Spanish. Then he turned to me.

"Ain't no woman here. Sure you seen her?"

"Talked to her standing right there in the doorway. What were you looking for?"

"Liver always had a little weed stowed away."

"Maybe the woman took it."

"Dammit, I coulda used that."

I didn't associate emaciation with pot smoking. Liver Lips and Lopez both looked more like meth users to me, and I told him so.

He cut his eyes at me. "No way."

"I don't really care. I need to figure out why Liver Lips would steal Mrs. Muldren's duck."

Lopez gave a mirthless laugh. "That what this is about? Old Mud Hen's duck? That's rich."

At least someone besides me saw the ridiculous side of this affair. "Why would he take her?"

"Who said he did?"

"He did. Told me that yesterday afternoon. Said he'd given her to somebody who wanted to play a trick on Mud Hen. But it scared the hell out of him when I asked who wanted him to steal the duck."

Lopez's nod was almost imperceptible. "Yeah. That sounds right."

"Does that mean you know who put him up to it?"

"Don't mean nothing. Nothing except Liver Lips afraid of his shadow."

"I hear Mud Hen's a tough old bird, but he wasn't afraid to go after her prize duck."

"Look, man. What you want from me? I don't know nothing about it. He stole her, that's his business."

"I just want to know what you can tell me about him."

"Me an' Liver hung out some, you know, to smoke now and then, but he done his own thing. And I don't know nothing about no duck stealing. Now I got to go. You coming?"

"Yeah. Nothing else here. Unless...." I glanced through a filthy window. An unpainted shack stood at the rear of the property. "Unless you want to check out that shed."

"Might's well. But he didn't never use it."

The shed, merely a bunch of boards thrown together and placed on the bare ground without a foundation of any sort, was empty except for a block of wood with an axe imbedded in it. Nonetheless, Lopez was wrong. Liver Lips or someone had used the place recently. There were white chicken feathers on the ground near the bloodstained block. At least I took them to be chicken feathers.

"Well, shit." Lopez grinned. "Guess you found old Mud Hen's duck. Leastways, what's left of her. Good eating, I bet."

I examined the feathers more closely. "These look like chicken feathers to me."

"You sure?"

"Pretty sure."

"But not all the way sure?"

The skinny little bastard mocked me. "Ninety percent." I pocketed a couple of the feathers.

"Could be, I guess. Liver didn't buy stuff in the store if he didn't have to. He'd boost a chicken now and then."

Despite what he'd said about needing to leave, Lopez didn't seem to be in any hurry now, so I pressed him on what he knew about his dead friend. They met when they were both kids harvesting pecans over in one of the Las Cruces orchards. Liver Lips—he had already picked up that nickname—was so skinny and weak-looking he had trouble finding regular work, although Lopez said he was stronger than he looked.

"Could keep up with me any day."

Taking in Lopez's concave chest and bony shoulders, I wasn't certain how much of a recommendation that was. According to him, Liver Lips hadn't finished high school and bummed around doing the best he could to scrape together a living. He worked part-time on some of the area ranches—on both sides of the border—but for the last year, he'd put in some hours at the R&S Auto Repair.

"He okay guy," Lopez finished, and again I considered the source. Suddenly he laughed. "Let things get to him, though. You know, under his skin."

"Like what?"

"Loco things. Things didn't have nothing to do with him. One time he read about a woman up in Montreal, you know, Canada. She in a bar, and the damned ceiling fell on her. Killed her dead. That shook old Liver. Said a man didn't have nothing to say about his own *destino*. Things slap a man upside the head without no warning. He kinda quit struggling after that." Lopez laughed again. "Waiting for ceiling to fall on him, no? Guess it did too."

"Anything else?"

"Well, like that president got hisself elected a while back. Liver claimed whole thing rigged. That *hombre* Bush lost *la gente*, you know, the people, but that didn't make no matter. Big court up there in Washington give it to him anyway. A man ain't got no chance unless he was born up there in one of them families. You know, with money."

"I see. Tell me about his connections across the border."

"Don't know nothing about them."

"Don't give me that. If you've known him since you were kids, you know who his contacts were. Where he got his weed or meth or whatever. Give me a name, Lopez. Somebody I can go see."

"You go see, you liable to end up like that Canada woman. Something drop on your head."

"I'll take the chance."

"Uh-uh. You get Lopez killed too."

"I want a name," I insisted.

"You already got one. Told you he work at R&S Auto. Go see Zack Rybald. He know Liver as good as anybody. But don't tell him I give you his name. You gotta promise that."

I dropped a nervous Lopez off at his shack and headed back downtown. I'd had the feeling in the hospital emergency room that Liver Lips wasn't paid to steal the bird. But maybe his meth source threatened to dry up on him if he didn't do the deed. The same could be true of the pot source, but somehow that didn't ring true. It was a lot easier to score weed than meth.

FROM THE outside, R&S Auto Repair didn't appear to be a mechanic's shop. The tall wood-framed windows gave it a retail atmosphere. When I entered, however, the shop took on its true definition. Three big vehicle bays opened out onto a wide alley at the rear. Despite the fact it was a Sunday, the place was busy.

Zack Rybald peered across the counter at me through a pair of granny glasses. He hadn't reacted when I introduced myself as an investigator and stated my interest. I had the feeling he chose to deliberately misunderstand my inquiry, but he understood perfectly when I asked if I could record our conversation.

"You punch that button and there ain't gonna be no conversation." Rybald was a stout man in the old-fashioned sense of the word: heavy but solid.

I put away my portable recorder. I wasn't above some surreptitious taping—and it's legal in this state—but the client was an insurance company, and they were always particular about things like that. They wanted everything consented to and documented so it couldn't be challenged if things went to court.

Apparently satisfied everything was copacetic, he started answering questions. "Liver Lips Martinson? Yeah, he works here off and on. But he ain't here. Hell, he ain't anywhere. Checked out in a rollover on I-10 east of here last night, I hear."

"I understand that, Mr. Rybald, but I'm trying to get a handle on the man—who he was and who his associates were."

"How come? Nothing but a mediocre mechanic and a worthless human being. What else is there to know?"

So I invested a few minutes outlining my interest.

"Old Mud Hen's raising hell, is she? Well, she sure knows how to do that. And she's got the muscle to do it too."

"Actually it's an insurance company who's raising hell. Do you have any idea why Martinson would steal a duck?"

"To piss Mud off would be my guess. They didn't get along. Liver Lips used to work for the Lazy M."

Rybald reaffirmed Martinson's reputation as a loner and said he knew of no woman in the man's life. In fact, he showed more curiosity over the identity of the female who answered my knock this morning than why a rancher would insure a duck.

"Hell, I don't know," he said when I posed the latter question. "Mud does things her own way. Always has, always will. She ran that ranch even when Ren was alive. Ren—that was Reingold Kurtz, her husband."

"Kurtz?"

"Yeah, Muldren's her maiden name." He chuckled. "Hard to picture Millicent as a maiden. At any age. She went back to it when old Ren got stomped to death by a bull ten years back."

"You seem to know a lot about the family."

"Hell, everybody in this part of the country knows about that family. Ren was a state representative for twenty years before the accident. There ain't nobody over thirty who hasn't gone to him for one thing or the other up in Santa Fe."

"Tell me about Martinson's connections across the border."

He reacted like I'd poked him in the eye. His head reared back, and he squinted through his ridiculous glasses. "What do you mean? I don't know nothing about that."

"Liver Lips worked for you, and he didn't strike me as the sort of man who held his cards close to his vest."

"Some of them, he done. Otherwise he'd find himself in a pickle."

"Like being run off the interstate?"

"What? You mean that accident wasn't no accident?"

"Don't mean anything of the sort. Just trying to make sure I understood what you meant."

"Look, fella, there's some things a man don't talk about out loud down here. And what goes on along the border is one of them. I got work to do. You want that Impala out there on the street tuned up, you come back. Otherwise, leave me alone."

Chapter 4

EVERY TIME I talked to someone about Liver Lips Martinson, the subject of the M Lazy M invariably came up. Of course, the ranch's prize duck had been stolen, so maybe that was natural. Nonetheless, time now to go get some answers from old Mud Hen herself—Millicent Muldren. But first I wanted to see if Officer Garza could tell me anything about Rybald. The mechanic had closed down awfully fast when I asked about Liver's across-the-border associations.

I flagged Garza down on the sidewalk in front of the Deming Police Station. He waited with the usual frown on his face as I got out of the Impala. When I asked about Zack Rybald, his swarthy face went even darker.

"I'm gonna lasso that SOB one of these days. I figure he's a big part of the drug trade around here, but I can't lay a hand on him."

"He's protected?"

"That's some of it," he admitted. "He's careful, but he'll trip up one of these days. If you run onto anything, let me know."

"Deal."

He looked over my left shoulder and waved. I turned and saw a tall man exiting the café directly across the street. "Somebody you oughta meet." He whistled and beckoned, offering no explanation until the man crossed the street and walked up to us.

"Glad I saw you, Bert. Mr. Vinson, this here is Bert Kurtz from down on the Lazy M. Bert, Mr. Vinson's a private investigator asking about Liver Lips."

"What's your interest in Liver?" Kurtz asked in a pleasant baritone. He plucked a battered black Stetson from his head to run his hand through a shock of curly brown hair. A lanky, good-looking man of around thirty, he had reddish-brown eyes my mom would have called autumn leaf.

"I've been asked to look into the theft of your mother's prize duck."

"Go shake Liver Lips until his teeth rattle, and he'll give her up." He gave a lazy smile. "Or point me in his direction, and I'll do it for you."

"Ain't had a chance to tell him yet," Garza said.

"That won't get us very far," I said. "Martinson's dead." I told him about the wreck west of Las Cruces but didn't let on it was a suspected homicide.

"Well, crap. I guess that puts an end to that." Bert slapped his hat against his leg and set it back on his head.

"Makes it harder, at any rate. I need to talk to your mother and see the setup down there. I intend to drive down to the ranch tomorrow."

"Sure. You'll be welcome. Plan on spending the night. We'll give you a meal and a pillow, especially if you're trying to find Mom's pride and joy. Or you can come back with me now. I've finished my business in town. Gonna head out pretty soon."

"Thanks, but I'll get down there on my own. Probably tomorrow morning. Did your father build the ranch from scratch or inherit it?"

"Neither. Mom's family started it at the turn of the last century. Her grandfather, old Rudolph, and his brother started building the spread when New Mexico was still a territory. Muldren family legend says Rudolph's brother, Yancy, *was* the lazy M. Anyhow, my grandfather was Rudolph's son. He inherited the ranch and built it up some. Mud's added to it since she got her hands on it."

Mud. So even her family used that nickname. "How big is the spread?"

"A little over a hundred fifty thousand acres. It takes a lot of territory around here for a cow/calf operation."

That meant the Lazy M maintained a permanent herd of cows and heifers to breed and produce a spring crop of calves to put up for sale. Some other rancher raised the calves and sent them to a feedlot to be fattened up for slaughter.

"What kind of security do you have?"

"A couple of big, mean Dobermans patrol the place at night. Other than that, not much. Some intruder lights over the garage and front entrance. A thirty-thirty beside the bed and a revolver under the pillow."

"No cameras, alarms, that type of thing?"

"No, although some of the vehicles are alarmed."

"With everything that's going on down on the border these days, you might want to think about beefing things up," Garza said.

Bert shook his head. "It may come to that, but there's never been trouble at the headquarters… day or night." He thought that over a moment. "Well, except when Liver Lips stole Quacky."

"Is the ranch a crossing point for illegals?" I asked.

"Oh yeah, big-time."

After reassuring me I'd be welcome, Kurtz excused himself and left. I tarried a few minutes longer to pick Garza's brain about the man.

He told me Bert Kurtz was well known to the DPD, and not just because of him being an important rancher in a neighboring county. He was also a brawler. Apparently, Bert didn't even need to get drunk in order to mix it up. When the mood took him, the man just liked to fight. When I suggested he should have taken up boxing instead of ranching, Garza informed me Kurtz had been a local ring champion while at NMSU getting his degree in ranch management. He also confided Bert had been picked up for speeding and DWI a couple of times in his jazzy Corvette. His money and Mud Hen's influence had gotten him off with only a couple of slaps on the wrist.

I SPED down Highway 11 toward Columbus. It wasn't the quickest route to the Boot Heel country, but the town had once played a dramatic part in a clash between two nations, and as a history buff, I couldn't resist the opportunity to sop up some of that flavor. Besides, it was getting late in the day for a drive over into Hidalgo County to the M Lazy M. I planned on remaining overnight in the little village named for Christopher Columbus just north of the border across from Palomas, Mexico.

The Impala breezed south over a landscape reminiscent of the drive between Deming and Las Cruces: flat, high desert terrain broken by blue-shadowed mountains in the distance. Heat waves rising off the asphalt were pleasantly hypnotic.

Columbus was an official twenty-four-hour POE—Point of Entry—between the two nations, although it sits about three miles north of the actual demarcation line. Border City is where the crossings actually occur. Its proximity to the Mexican state of Chihuahua is what gave the place its brush with history.

The actual story is long and convoluted, as well as highly controversial. Two revolutionaries, Venustiano Carranza and Francisco Villa, better known as Pancho, tossed out a dictator named Victoriano Huerta and then turned on one another. A Columbus merchant and arms dealer by the name of Ravel supposedly sold defective ammunition to Pancho Villa. When the guerilla demanded a refund, the merchant reputedly told him the Ravels no longer dealt with Mexican bandits.

On the morning of March 9, 1916, one of Villa's generals attacked Columbus with more than 500 men. The twenty-four-hour invasion burned down a significant portion of the town and killed fourteen American soldiers together with ten residents. Another eighty or so revolutionaries were dead or mortally wounded. Various claims were made, so no one will ever know the true extent of the casualties. The raid led to General John J. Pershing's punitive expedition deep into Mexico.

Today Columbus initially appeared as a disruption astraddle the flat, monotonous highway. After entering the town of mostly one-storied adobe affairs—some painted in brash colors of green or pink—I found a bed-and-breakfast and registered for the night.

My carcass taken care of, I set out to tend my gullet. A hand-lettered sign reading Lupe's Cocina drew me onto the porch and through the door of what could have been a residence. A tall woman with jet-black hair in a white peasant's blouse and a dark midcalf skirt approached and bid me welcome. Her smile looked genuine—as opposed to commercial.

She seated me at a small table in the corner next to a rough wall of whitewashed plaster hung with colorful serapes and lace mantillas, introduced herself as Teresa, and handed me a menu. As she left to get my Dos Equis, her tall, tortoiseshell combs reminded me of Hazel's, before my secretary's recent transformation from dowdy plain to dowdy chic.

I scanned the menu and settled on a bowl of menudo—a traditional Mexican soup of tripe, hominy, and chili paste—and a couple of pork enchiladas with a side of black beans and rice. After giving Teresa my order, I sat back and sipped my beer, tuning in on the Spanish, Spanglish, and English conversations swirling around the small dining room. The two men at the table next to me spoke in English. The words "Mud Hen" caught my attention. Apparently, Quacky Quack's ducknapping was the talk of the border country.

Teresa brought my order, and I went to work on the food, blocking out everything until I heard one of the men at the next table say he thought swiping the duck was a warning.

"Maybe old Mud Hen got herself mixed up in some across-the-border doings," he said.

"She do seem to have plenty of money, even when the wells run dry," the other one allowed.

Maybe my penchant for local history had paid an unexpected dividend.

Chapter 5

RANCHERS, LIKE farmers, generally rise with the sun, so I got on the road early Monday, breezing west along Highway 9 over a landscape dominated by creosote, locoweed, and wildflowers. Scattered clouds dotted the bright sky. The blue silhouette of the Cedar Mountain Range shadowed the horizon.

The weathercast this morning had predicted a high of ninety-nine degrees, but the temperature had not yet climbed to that point as I drove into the country that once sheltered the likes of Curly Bill, Old Man Clanton, and Dick Gray, desperados who hid out in the caves and canyons of the Boot Heel. Somewhere ahead of me stood a black oak with large knotholes where the outlaws left messages for one another in what is still called Post Office Canyon.

I passed a sign noting I crossed into Hidalgo County, a landmass of about thirty-five hundred square miles populated by fewer than five thousand residents. I smiled inwardly. I knew people back east who couldn't conceive of such large ranches and small human populations this part of the country sported. Of course, they didn't understand the meager carrying capacity of a single section of land. Sometimes just one cow/calf unit. The Gray Ranch, now called by its original name of the Diamond A, boasted 321,000 acres—a staggering 500 square miles. Alongside that, the M Lazy M was a piker.

I turned south on Highway 81. The ranch lay a fair distance from Hachita, the closest town, and as I had a considerable amount of work to do, I phoned Del to let him know I intended to take Bert Kurtz up on his offer to remain overnight. He wanted to clear it with the insurance company to make sure they wouldn't consider it a conflict of interest should Mud Hen be involved in any sort of scam. He promised to call me back.

The M Lazy M lay hard against the Mexican state of Chihuahua just short of the Big Hatchet Mountains in the upper reaches of the Boot Heel. A cattle guard, flanked by a tall adobe arch bearing the ranch's brand—two capital Ms, the second one lying on its side—marked the main gateway to the spread.

I stopped to snap a photo of the entrance before heading down a well-graded gravel road toward what I assumed would eventually lead to the ranch house. I snapped several pictures of the road and anything else of interest. Like crime scene investigators, PIs can't function without loads of photos.

I traveled another ten miles with no sign of habitation, although white-faced cattle grazing in the distance identified this as a working ranch. At the end of the road, I encountered another fence, behind which loomed an odd-looking structure, one that appeared to have grown from a modest home into something of a monstrosity as succeeding generations of Muldrens left their stamp on the edifice, building first with wood, then with fieldstone and brick. The latest addition was adobe.

The place reminded me of Gothic novel cover art, although the graceful cottonwoods and sycamores scattered about the broad yard softened the effect. Even so, their towering presence on this landscape of stunted bushes and twisted piñons was almost as bizarre as the building itself. They had obviously been carefully nurtured by the first Ms, possibly even the Lazy M, until they dwarfed every other living thing within sight.

I parked in the gravel circle before the house between a late-model gray Lincoln and a vintage blue-and-white Corvette. Two big Dobermans trotted up to the car and regarded me solemnly. Just then the front door opened. Bert stepped over the threshold and greeted me with a wave. I rolled down my car window a couple of inches.

"Don't worry, Mr. Vinson. Bruno and Hilda won't bother you unless I put them on guard. Now the ferocious beast in the house, I'm not so sure of."

"Right." I cast a wary eye at the large animals and stepped more briskly than usual toward the broad, shaded veranda. I offered Bert a hand. "Most people call me BJ."

He accepted my shake with a smile, casting an indulgent eye on the dogs. "BJ, I hope you had a pleasant ride. Missed the hottest part of the day, anyway. Welcome to the M Lazy M Ranch, or as most folks call her… the Lazy M."

As he ushered me through the door, I took a good look at the Lazy M's manager. According to my information, he was born in Silver City and raised on the Lazy M. Single but with a reputation for playing the field. Although Bert carried the reputation of a hard drinker, he was credited with running a good ranch.

A small, hairy bundle of energy with sharp, pointed ears and equally sharp teeth greeted us in a foyer laid with rough flagstone. The feisty beast emitted an endless series of sharp yips as it raced in circles around the life-sized wooly calf cast in bronze dominating the entryway.

"That's Poopsie, Mom's terrier. Eventually she'll run down, but it takes a while."

For a moment I thought I'd been transported to the Middle East, where affluent families purposely hid opulent interiors behind ugly exteriors. The living room, a high-ceilinged, rough-paneled expanse, probably comprised the entire original house. A bank of twelve-foot windows looked out over a green lawn extending all the way to a group of buildings and fences about a hundred yards distant.

Poopsie, who had transferred her attention from the bronze calf to my host's boots, lost interest and wandered away. Kurtz pointed out a few things in the big common room: the mounted head of an antelope his father had killed, the rug made from a huge bear bagged by Granddaddy Muldren lying between a pair of heavy, overstuffed couches, and a board of mounted arrowheads he'd collected as a child. Rare pieces of Mimbres pottery, found on the ranch, lined a big fireplace mantel. I sized up Kurtz as someone easy to like and even easier to underestimate.

He knocked on a solid oak door and entered without waiting for an invitation. Two massive walnut desks, facing one another across a red-and-black Navajo rug that should have hung on the wall, dominated a room almost as large as the living area.

Poopsie scurried around us and jumped into the arms of a woman as she rose from the desk nearest the windows. I figured her at five ten and about one eighty. Big-boned, she was not fat despite the weight she carried. Millicent Muldren must have been in her early fifties with graying brown hair worn short in no particular style I could discern.

"Nice to meet you, Mr. Vinson." She acknowledged my introduction with a firm grip. "I hear you and Bert met in Deming yesterday." She touched her lips to the little dog's head. "And this is my precious Poopsie. I hope you had a nice drive. You missed the hottest part of the day."

Apparently finished with chitchat, she directed me to a black leather, brass-studded barrel chair and bluntly asked what I could tell her about her missing duck.

"Not a lot at this point, but you can answer a question for me." I reached into my pocket and pulled out two white feathers. "I found these in a shed at the rear of Richard Martinson's place, but I don't believe they're duck feathers."

She snatched them from my hand and swiveled to the windows, holding the feathers to the light with shaking fingers. A large diamond set in a heavy gold ring caught the sun and sparked shards of multicolored light. Her hands clenched involuntarily.

"No. These are chicken feathers, thank God. Did you talk to that scaly lizard before he ran off the road and killed himself?" She handed the crushed white feathers back to me. "Sorry if that sounded crass, but they tell me I am crass."

"I spoke to him in the emergency room at UNM hospital. He was being treated for some bad scratches. He'd developed blood poisoning, I believe."

"Good for her!" she exclaimed. I deduced she meant Quacky for getting in her licks. Then the room momentarily went quiet except for the ticking of a clock, made preternaturally loud by the silence. Somehow I didn't think this was in honor of Liver Lips Martinson's memory.

"My poor baby!" Millicent's cry shattered the moment.

A man was dead, and she worried about a damned bird. Well, to be fair, it was a $250,000 bird.

She leaned forward over the desk and fixed me with a pair of opal eyes. "You find her for me. I'll pay you. Find her and bring her back home."

I removed a tape recorder from the clip on my belt and laid it on her desk. "Do you mind if I record this interview?"

"No, of course not."

"Bert?" I asked.

"Okay by me."

I turned on the machine, stated whom I was interviewing, where and when, and had them repeat their agreement to be taped.

"Just to set the record straight, I'm working for the insurance company. If they want me to find the duck, then I'll look for the duck. But I can't work for both of you."

"That's okay." She smiled. "They'll tell you to find her. I'll make sure of that."

I briefly related the results of my abortive meeting with Martinson. "I'm convinced he took the duck, but he wouldn't say why. Before I could talk to him again, his truck rolled over and killed him."

"Shit!" she exclaimed.

"Who would want to steal the duck? Let me rephrase. Who would want Martinson to take the duck from you?"

"No one. At least, I can't think of anyone. Can you, Bert?"

"Not offhand."

"Have you been contacted for ransom?"

She let out a throaty cry. "You think they took her for ransom? Oh Lord. I hope so." She looked at her son. "Has anyone called? Anyone at all?"

Bert shook his head. "Just a couple of business calls."

"Is there anyone who would want to do you harm, Mrs. Muldren?"

"Call me Millicent," she said. "And I'll call you...."

"BJ. The world calls me BJ."

"Well, the world calls me something else, but I'm an oddity. I like my name. Millicent. It has a good sound, I think." She absently scratched a patch of white fur at Poopsie's silky neck. The animal squirmed contentedly, her button eyes half-closed.

"That it does. But back to the question."

"Half of Hidalgo County and half the state of Chihuahua across the border. And that doesn't even include Grant and Luna Counties. And then there's a few folks up in Santa Fe don't like my politics. I'm an old-fashioned Republican. Notice I said 'old-fashioned,' not the kind we got up there now. That means both sides of the aisle would probably like to see me kicked over the hill. But to steal my baby? I don't know anyone who'd do that."

I glanced at Bert, who sat behind his desk. He had no reaction to his mother's comments, so I led them through a series of questions about the ranch. The Lazy M not only ran cattle, it also bred and raised ducks as a commercial venture. The birds were sold for meat and eggs but were mostly prized for down. According to Millicent, Lazy M ducks were unsurpassed for down feathers.

Sometime after nightfall just shy of two weeks ago—Wednesday, July 9, to be exact—Poopsie had been making such a fuss that Bert put the little Yorkie out, presumably to do her business. Later he heard a clamor from the duck pen out back. When he and Luis Rael, the ranch's groundskeeper, who also tended the domestic livestock, checked on it, they found the dog happily racing around herding ducks first one way and then the other.

They were mystified as to how the small dog had gotten through the fence until Millicent came out and discovered her prize duck missing. Someone had let the dog into the pen when they took Quacky. Despite an immediate search of the area, they found no sign of the intruder or the missing bird. They did, however, find the two Dobermans sound asleep near the front gate.

"The vet said it was tranquilizer darts," Bert explained.

That meant the theft was planned. "Why didn't you just race down that long road out front and cut him off at the gate?" I asked.

Bert's Adam's apple bobbled a couple of times. "I did send somebody down the road, but there are several ways off the property. Liver Lips was long gone before we found out what was going on."

So far everything matched the Hidalgo County Sheriff's report Del e-mailed me. "How did you know it was Martinson?"

"Didn't at the time." Millicent's deep, rough voice seemed uncertain, tentative… yet forceful enough to command attention. "But it had to be someone familiar with the setup out here, and he'd worked for us off and on over the years."

"Wouldn't anyone familiar with the place know about the Yorkie too?"

"We've only had Poopsie for about a year. Liver hasn't worked here in almost two." She clasped her hands on the desk and absently twirled the square-cut diamond on her left ring finger. It looked like a man's ring. Her late husband's?

"How did you narrow it down to Martinson?"

Bert chuckled, which earned him a look from his mother. "Liver Lips never could keep his mouth shut. He told someone who told someone who told someone else he'd helped play a trick on Mud Hen." Bert looked sheepish. "The whole countryside calls her that."

"Certain elements of it, anyway." She leaned back in her chair and ruffled her short hair. Poopsie looked to be asleep in her lap. "Eventually word got back to us."

"Did you report this to the sheriff?" There had been no mention of it in the report I had.

Bert shook his head. "Didn't bother. He'd have heard it already. So I went to see Liver. Found him in that run-down shack he lived in. Shook him up pretty good when he saw me, but he went dumb. Scared speechless, probably. I should have hauled him back to the ranch and got the truth out of him, but one of his neighbors showed up right then. It wouldn't have been hard to squeeze the worthless son of a bitch. He wasn't only liver-lipped, he was yellow-livered too."

Given Bert's penchant for fighting, it's amazing there hadn't been bruises on Martinson when I saw him in the emergency room. Probably because of that neighbor. "When did this happen?"

"Let's see. This is Monday. That would have been a week ago today."

I turned back to his mother. "What makes a duck worth two hundred fifty thousand dollars? That's what you have her insured for, right? Frankly, I didn't think an insurance company would take that kind of risk."

"If you saw the premiums we pay on this place, you'd damned well know they're going to insure anything I want them to." Millicent rubbed her eyes with her thumbs. "Even though they watered down the policy until it was practically useless. As to what makes her worth that, come on and I'll show you."

She placed Poopsie on the floor and bounced out of her chair. I grabbed my tape recorder and followed Bert out the door. Millicent moved easily despite her bulk. I examined her as she led us across a pebble-encrusted concrete channel disguised as a creek bed on a decidedly out-of-place oriental-style bridge. Her back and shoulders were built like a man's, a hefty man's, but her broad hips were all female.

We were still ten yards from the fence when a cloud of white and orange rushed forward, emitting loud quacks and squawks and hisses. The Lazy M's herd… gaggle of ducks.

Millicent halted at the fence and waved a hand over them. "I've been raising ducks since I was six years old. I bred this flock to give the best down feathers in these parts. I did that. Me. Without any fancy degree from a college that costs too much."

I took that to be a backhanded swipe at Bert and NMSU.

"Quacky's the best of the lot. I breed her with a special drake, and she gives us ducklings that grow up to be the best."

"But surely their offspring give the same quality down," I said.

"You'd think so. They give us good ducklings, but not great ducklings. Not like Quacky."

"I think I heard somewhere that she's the second Quacky."

Millicent nodded. "Quacky Quack the Second. She came from another duck just as good as she was at giving quality offspring. When we found she did as well as her mama, we started to hope there'd be another duckling somewhere along the line that would do as good as she did. You know, a Quacky Quack the Third."

"But you hadn't found that duck yet?"

"Not yet. Close, but not yet. I'll find her, but I need my precious to give me a few more clutches of eggs, another couple of generations from different drakes."

"And that makes her worth a quarter of a million dollars?"

"Every dime of it."

"May I take a look at the insurance policy? I can get a copy from the company, but it will save time if I can look at yours."

"Sure. Let's go to the office."

As we walked back to the house, I thought over the past few minutes. Bert was pretty straightforward. His mother, on the other hand, puzzled me. I felt as if I'd just met two different women. The bluff, forceful Mud Hen who'd demanded I find her duck and the duck farmer who'd shown me her gaggle and explained the down business fit the mental image I'd built of the woman from what I'd heard about her. Yet, in the middle of the interview, Millicent turned nervous… almost hesitant. What was going on?

Once we were seated again, Millicent handed over the policy on Quacky Quack II—and that's exactly how the damned thing read. It solved the mystery of how to identify one specific duck among many by citing a serial number branded into the duck's bill. The policy was so watered down, about the only events covered were disappearance by theft or death by vandalism or malice. One clause excluded natural death. Fishy—or more appropriately, foul. On the face of it, the policy was worthless unless a human hand committed mischief.

At my request, Millicent called in Luis Rael and his wife, Maria— the housekeeper and cook—for interviews. Both were plump and rosy-cheeked, courteous but shy. They had worked on the ranch since legally emigrating from Palomas in 1999. Both claimed to know nothing about the theft of the duck. Luis confirmed the details of the discovery of the crime the night Poopsie had put up such a fuss. I learned they had a son named Paco who apparently lived on both sides of the border. On occasion he helped out with the spring and fall gatherings—which is what I'd always called roundups. He was expected to show up at the ranch sometime this afternoon.

Luis took me back to the duck pen, where I tried to ignore all the quacking while I snapped several photographs, including one of the coop that had held the stolen property. Then he drove me around the ranch in a pickup so I could take pictures of various points of entry and exit. While he had no proof, Luis believed Liver Lips had been the thief, probably to get back at the señora for firing him.

"Why did she fire him?" I asked.

"Couldn't count on him. Show up one day. Gone the next. Wasn't much of a wrangler. Liked to cook, but Maria, she's our cook." Luis gave me a shy look out of the corner of his eyes. "Liked to smoke funny cigarettes too."

About that time, Del called on my cell to say the insurance company had reluctantly agreed I could remain on the premises overnight. He made it sound as if he'd had to do a selling job to get their okay.

THE FOOD was good and the conversation noisy at the table that evening. If we ate Lazy M stock, the ranch raised prime cattle. Maria also served potatoes and string beans with a chili side for everything.

Millicent, looking more handsome than pretty in a plain white muslin skirt and a blouse adorned by a heavy Navajo squash blossom necklace and matching turquoise-and-silver earrings, dominated the room. She seemed less nervous than when I'd interviewed her earlier, but she constantly fiddled with something—the silverware, the stem of her glass, a napkin, the big square-cut diamond on her finger. Yet she met my eyes frankly, and her body language was open. I decided she was one of those human dynamos who couldn't sit still.

Bert would be equally at home chowing down from the back end of a chuck wagon out on the range or gracing the State Dining Room at the White House. On occasion he vied with Millicent for dominance of the small group.

The Lazy M sat a democratic table; the help ate with the masters and liberally voiced their own opinions. Maria kept popping up to serve another course or refresh some depleted platter.

The Raels' son, Paco, had shown up as expected just before everyone sat down at the table. My impression was that this was nothing more than a social visit.

In his mid- to late twenties, Paco was olive-skinned and sleek. Small framed, he stood around five eight. Quiet, he glanced away every time I looked at him, which, of course, caused me to look at him more. An evident bond of friendship existed between him and Bert, one likely forged on the anvil of shared work, whiskey, brawls, and the pursuit of willing women.

When a couple of cowhands came in from the range and plopped down into vacant chairs, the tenor of the table changed. Excellent fare became simply grub as the hungry men shoveled it down to the obvious embarrassment of absolutely no one. As soon as the two were finished, they headed out the door with big helpings of peach cobbler in hand.

After the group around the table broke up, I managed to get a hasty interview with Paco Rael and the cowhands in the bunkhouse, where I interrupted a poker game. Away from the big house—or perhaps because his parents weren't present—Paco was more direct. He seemed comfortable in the bunkhouse. He spoke easily about his work on the Lazy M but grew less clear about what he did on the Mexican side of the border.

The cowhands gave me their version of the night of the duck theft, punching it up with some of Mud's colorful language. One of them claimed he learned a new cuss word that night. I didn't pick up anything new but earned an invitation to join them at the card table. I didn't think the client would approve of that, so I declined.

LATER, IN the privacy of my bedroom on the second floor, I crawled between the crisp bedcovers and mulled over whether a duck could really be worth a fortune because it produced ducklings that gave the finest down known to mankind. Ranchers bred cattle and horses to accomplish certain ends, so was it unreasonable to believe the laws of biology allowed the same sort of fiddling in a duck's gene pool? I didn't know, but I'd check it out.

Somehow the whole thing didn't seem to hang together. Something was wrong with the picture. While I investigated a murder up in the Bisti Badlands country of northwestern New Mexico last year, the sheriff's detective in charge kept getting diverted by a dogfighting ring. Could there be *duck*-fighting rings? I sat up in bed. No, but they had duck races. I'd seen posters advertising the Great American Duck Race in Deming, coming up later this month.

That made more sense. Maybe Quacky was a champion waddler. Or did ducks swim their races? At any rate, Millicent struck me as the kind of gal who wouldn't hesitate to back her favorite with a high-stakes bet. Was Quacky well on her way to winning the web-foot equivalent of the Triple Crown before she disappeared?

Had I covered all the bases? Hazel was checking the appropriate records—police, DMV, credit, Dun & Bradstreet—anything to flesh out a picture on the people I'd run into. I was especially interested in any "known associates" on Liver Lips Martinson's sheet.

I had collected a lot of taped interviews, so I'd need to overnight them to Hazel for transcribing when I reached Deming tomorrow. Sometimes when she got the words on paper, something jumped out that went over Charlie's or my head at the time of the interview. On more than one occasion, Hazel picked up something from a transcription that we'd missed.

Tired of thinking about a stolen duck, I dialed my home phone. No answer. I decided against trying Paul's cell. Line dancing at the C&W, I suspected, so he wouldn't hear the ring over all the noise. I opted to leave a message on my home voice mail telling him how much I missed him and his various parts… enumerating some of those sexy parts in graphic detail.

I snapped off the light and tried to sleep. But escape from this crazy world of heavily insured ducks with pretentious names, a large woman who owned a big ranch and doted on a tiny dog, and a "ducknapper" with a name like Liver Lips—who was dead and probably murdered—was slow in coming.

Chapter 6

BY THE time I crawled out of bed around six, everyone else had already eaten. Maria kept a full-sized breakfast warm and waiting for me, so I felt obligated to devour every delicious crumb. As I polished off the last buttermilk biscuit, Bert stuck his head into the breakfast nook.

"I'm headed out to check on things. You want to ride along?"

"Thanks, but I'd better get on the road. Your mom might not take kindly to me sightseeing instead of searching for her duck. You don't seem too torn up by the bird's disappearance."

"Not as much as Mud. I run the beef end of the business. The ducks are hers."

"So that makes it her problem."

"Yeah. Don't get me wrong. I feel bad for her, but I don't have time to fret over it. Too bad you're in your car. I could get you back to Deming in nothing flat." He touched the brim of his hat in a farewell gesture and left.

What did he mean by that? Did he have a secret trail through Mexico that cut the trip in half? When I heard a racket outside, I understood. The small helicopter pad located well away from Millicent's duck pens had escaped my notice until I glanced out the window and watched him warm up the machine, an old Bell chopper with a molded plastic bubbletop called a fish bowl and an open tube-work tail boom. It reminded me of the whirlybirds on the TV program *M*A*S*H*. Within minutes, Bert cleared the ground and clattered off to the west.

"Horses still have their places." Millicent's deep voice took me by surprise. I hadn't heard her approach. "But that threshing machine sure comes in handy. It chases brush cattle out of the chaparral better'n any cutting horse. I just wish it wasn't so damned noisy. It upsets my ducks."

She shook her head as her gaze followed her son's rapidly disappearing machine. "It's a shame. In the old days, labor was easy to come by. My granddaddy hired Mexican cowboys—vaqueros, they called themselves—

but ever since they passed the Immigration and Control Act back in '86, it's illegal to hire undocumented workers. Bert's mechanized the place as much as he can to overcome that problem. That blessed chopper's part of it."

"Everything cuts both ways, doesn't it?" I said. "One part of the population considers something a solution while another classifies it as a problem. I assume they've built the big fence we've all heard about along your border."

That brought a grimace. "Down around Columbus and east to El Paso, yeah. Over along the Arizona-Mexico border, they're building like crazy. Around here, no. Not even the electronic kind. You know what that does?"

"My guess is it sends the illegals your way." Was that what those two men in the Columbus cantina had meant about Mud being involved in across-the-border doings?

"Like driving them into a cattle chute. Flushing them through a spillway." She started as if waking from a trance. "Anyway, it's caused some problems."

I thanked Millicent for her hospitality and apologized for eating and running. I needed to get instructions from Del and then presumably start back over Martinson's trail.

"That's all right, BJ. You go find my Quacky, hear?"

TALKING ON a phone while driving is illegal in parts of New Mexico unless you have a hands-free phone. Rather than trying to keep up with where it was and wasn't legal, I always used a mounted cellular phone while driving. On the way back to Deming, I punched my speed dial and contacted Del Dahlman at home. He spent thirty seconds grumbling about the early hour and then promised to contact Hank Grass, the GSR vice president, and learn all he could about Millicent's financials.

It was pretty clear GSR stood in jeopardy. Someone had stolen the insured property, one of the few events that put the company at risk under the terms of the policy. Two things might negate their liability: recover the duck or prove Millicent Muldren had a hand in her disappearance. Of course, before they paid, someone would have to examine a gaggle of identical white ducks on the Lazy M to look for a particular serial number branded into one of the bills. In any case, Grass should be motivated to cough up some details to Del.

I next called Det. Manny Montoya. When the dispatcher finally ran him down, he confirmed that Martinson's crash had been caused by a side collision with another vehicle. It wasn't clear yet whether it had been deliberate or accidental, but the other car fleeing the scene was a criminal act regardless of intent.

An analysis of the paint found on Martinson's wrecked pickup had them on the lookout for a black 1996 Pontiac Firebird with damage to the passenger's side. I was a bit dubious they could pin down the exact year from a paint sample, but his lab boys knew more about that kind of thing than I did.

My first stop when I hit the city limits was the Deming-Luna County Chamber of Commerce on West Pine. The converted residence had an old train caboose sitting alongside it to remind tourists of the town's long railroad history. I introduced myself to a helpful gray-haired lady with a name tag reading Mabel who gushed an exuberant welcome.

"The Great American Duck Race? Oh yes. We're famous for that nationwide. Worldwide, I imagine. This will be the twenty-eighth annual race. But you're too early. It doesn't start until August the twenty-first. That's a Thursday, and it runs through the weekend, ending Sunday afternoon with the racing finals."

"Explain how that works."

"Well, there are two types of races: a dry track and a water track. Each is run—" She tittered. "—or swum on an eight-lane, fifteen-foot track. So they run those until all the entrants have competed, and the winners of the dry track and the wet track are advanced to the quarterfinals, and so on until the championships on Sunday afternoon. It's not too late to make a reservation at one of the local inns. I'd be happy to call around for you."

"Thank you, but that won't be necessary. I assume there are prizes for the winners?"

"Oh yes. Each winner gets a prize of ten dollars. Since it costs only five dollars to rent a racing duck, the entrant has a chance of doubling his money. The final winners split whatever's left in the pot. Sometimes that's as much as $700 or so."

There went my prime theory up in smoke. "That's not exactly on a par with a steeplechase, is it?"

"Oh no. It's purely a social event. Tourists come from all over to enjoy the occasion. The people who put it on just hope to break even. If they do make a few dollars over and above their costs, it goes to charity."

"Is it necessary to rent a duck, or can someone enter his own?" Perhaps I could salvage something from this train wreck.

"Heavens no. There's a woman who breeds and raises ducks specifically for the Great American Duck Race organization."

"A woman in Hidalgo County?"

Mabel wrinkled her powdered nose. "She's local."

"I see. There must be some side betting going on. Otherwise the only people profiting are the local restaurants, innkeepers, and merchants."

She smiled broadly. "You've put your finger squarely on the mark. The duck races are a promotion for the City of Deming and Luna County. As I say, it's purely social for the general public. Of course, I'm sure there's a certain amount of friendly wagering. Among friends, you know."

"No one handicaps the races?"

"Good gracious, no. Not ours."

My ears perked up. "There are other races?"

"Oh yes. I'd guess there must be two or three hundred of them throughout the United States. Some of them could be more… uh, sports oriented, I suppose."

I left laden with brochures extolling the virtues of the area— heavy emphasis on the railroad history and rock hound potential—plus the names of a couple of those other duck races. As I examined the old railroad car outside, my phone rang. Del with instructions to locate the missing duck or find out the perpetrator behind the theft. Easy enough for him to say.

"What did you learn about Muldren's financials?" I asked.

"Because of the size of the coverage, the insurance company requires annual financial statements. The principal asset is the ranch. They own around a hundred thousand acres, but they lease another fifty thousand or so from private owners and the government. And then, of course, there's the inventory of livestock and ducks. They have over 200 ducks, Vince."

"I know. I've met them all. Personally. They swarm over a big duck pen like white ants."

"What keeps them from flying away?"

"They don't have flight feathers. They can get off the ground, but they can't sustain flight."

"Oh. Well, the ranch makes money… generally. Like all such ventures, it depends on outside circumstances—weather, outbreaks of disease, beef prices, and the like. When the son, Albert, became foreman, things started to look better. He's kept things profitable. Marginally so at times, but profitable nonetheless. Even the damned ducks usually make money. Apparently the M Lazy M is known for its ducks. They sell the eggs, the ducks, the down. They've got a fine reputation for the down and foie gras their birds produce."

"No sign of financial distress?"

"Not really, but last year was an exception. They reported a loss because of some extraordinary expenses. Had to replace a lot of fencing. Quite a bit of fencing, actually. And their rustling losses were unusually high."

"Why?"

"Grass didn't know. Fencing is a continuing expense. Despite the size of the pastures—some of them are as big as twenty sections—there's a lot of wire strung around the ranch. The livestock losses were attributed to hard economic times. Plus they're on the border, and Grass guesses some M Lazy M beef ends up in Mexico."

There wasn't much else Del could tell me, but he had unleashed me on the world of ducks and duck racers, duck down, and duck pâté de foie gras to make mischief as I saw fit.

I made calls to the Hidalgo County Cattle Growers' Association, the New Mexico Cattlegrowers, the Better Business Bureau, and the Attorney General's office in Santa Fe, hoping to add to my store of knowledge about the Muldren operation. Mud Hen—a name widely used among her peers in the beef industry—had a reputation for tough dealing. While she was willing to push the envelope, nobody openly claimed she was crooked or even unethical. Nonetheless, I got the feeling everyone kept an eye on the pocketbook when she was involved.

The ranch was, and always had been, a mother cow operation, and over the years their cattle had been bred to deliver good strong calves. Bovine TB had hit the ranch last year, and a small part of the herd had to be isolated and destroyed. That probably contributed to the unusual "rustling" losses Grass had mentioned to Del. Chances were good GSR didn't know about the TB outbreak, and I wondered what their reaction would be if they learned of it. That, of course, came under the heading of none of my business.

Nothing Del had provided got me any closer to Liver Lips, so I decided on another visit to Officer Garza at the Deming Police Department. I was in luck; he was in the station. Still only semifriendly, he nonetheless told me a little about one of the bit players in my little drama—Paco Rael. Sometimes Rael came to DPD's attention alongside his buddy, Bert, but he was perfectly capable of stirring up things on his own. Drunk and disorderly, speeding, and fistfights were his thing—no DWIs. He probably let Bert handle the driving.

"I understand he helps out at the Lazy M during roundups... uh, gatherings, but what does he do the rest of the time?"

"I'd surely like an answer to that question." Garza removed a toothpick from between his lips and pointed it at me. "You find out, you let me know."

"That's a promise. What do your compadres from across the border say about him?"

"Not much. I got a guy over there on the Palomas police force who usually exchanges some tidbits with me, but he's mum on Rael."

"That's interesting. Any known associates other than Bert Kurtz?"

"He went to school in the Deming school system down on the border at Columbus, so he knows lots of folks around here."

The Columbus Elementary School was part of the Deming Public School District and prided itself on its nondiscrimination policy. A fair percentage of its students lived across the border.

"He knew that guy you asked about the other day. Martinson."

"Liver Lips? Did Rael run around with him?"

"Not exactly. Got him into trouble is more like it. He used to talk the guy into doing stupid things that got him a bang on the head or a night in the pokey. Him and that kid, Lopez—they used to keep Liver Lips in hot water all the time."

Aha. An across-the-border connection with ties to both the Lazy M and Martinson, but that alone didn't mean much. In this remote part of the country, most people were probably interconnected. Nonetheless, it was something to check out.

Just before leaving, I remembered the woman who had answered Liver's door the day he died. Garza's face remained blank when I asked about her.

"Don't know who that coulda been. He didn't have no woman in his life. Anything he got, he bought at one of the meat houses over across the border. And that description don't ring no bells. Course, it's not much of a description. No scars, tattoos, moles? Nothing like that?"

"No, at least not visible ones. Nothing stood out about her except she was very pretty and once had a great figure. I wondered at the time if she could have been pregnant. Sort of a round face. Mestizo features. Hazel eyes and long black hair hanging below her shoulders."

"I'll ask around."

After talking with Garza, I phoned the Hidalgo County Sheriff's Office as I drove toward Las Cruces to take another look at the crash scene where Liver Lips died. Deputy Nap O'Brien informed me Kurtz had no record and no reputation as a brawler, which led me to believe Bert went "off the reservation" to do his mischief. O'Brien knew Rael because of an arrest for fighting outside a local bar a few years back. The dustup involved no weapons of any sort, so the charges were dropped after an overnight stay at the jailhouse. The Lordsburg PD reported roughly the identical information.

There wasn't much to see at the crash scene, and I didn't think Detective Montoya's sharp eyes had missed anything. Nonetheless I pulled over, put on my flashers, and walked the area. Sometimes a crime scene—and this was one—talks to you. Martinson's didn't, but I took out my Minolta and took a lot of shots anyway.

As I got back into my car, my cell phone rang. I answered and heard a familiar voice ask if this was a bad time. My heart rate soared.

"It's never a bad time to talk to you."

Paul chuckled. "Maybe if I distracted you while you faced down a bad guy, that might be a bad time."

"Nope, I'd just tell him to hold on a minute. I had to talk to the greatest guy on earth."

"Yeah, right. How's it going? You ready to come home?"

"Not quite, but I hope it's not long now."

"Damn, this is a lonely place when you're not around. At night I just sit around listening to noises. Did you know your house creaks?"

"It's talking to you. Letting you know you're welcome."

"God, I miss you, Vince."

"Me too, guy. Me too."

The loneliness and the yearning in his tone almost set me on fire. I let him talk for a bit as I headed on to Las Cruces. The temptation to catch I-25 and keep right on going almost overwhelmed me. As the city traffic got heavier, I reluctantly closed the call.

Since my big breakfast had now been digested, I hunted up a restaurant and had a quick meal before finding a motel. I checked into the local Traveler's Inn and had just completed a rough sketch of the Lazy M Ranch headquarters from memory when Hazel called to tell me she'd sent a detailed e-mail report with the information I'd requested. Then she told me Charlie had completed a sensitive surveillance job on a member of APD for an attorney whose client claimed the guy had planted felony assault evidence on him. Nothing Charlie turned up supported such a contention.

After being out of the office for a protracted period of time on the Bisti Wilderness missing-persons/murder case near Farmington last year, I'd invested in a USB device that gave me access to the Internet on my laptop regardless of the availability of Wi-Fi. I opened Hazel's report and whistled. She'd been busy.

Although there was a host of material, it merely filled in blanks in my knowledge of the people I had interviewed—with the exception of a single item about Martinson. Hazel had come up with a nebulous contact for him across the border. A man named Hector Acosta. Apparently Acosta was a Chihuahuan rancher Liver Lips worked for in the past and used as a reference on a few job applications. Thorough as usual, Hazel provided contact information for Acosta. The address was in Palomas, Mexico, a town not far from Columbus.

A valid New Mexico driver's license gained a tourist entry into border Mexico—although beginning in June of next year, a passport would be required—but taking a car across the international border involved some preparation.

It proved unnecessary. When I phoned the number Hazel provided, the speaker informed me that Señor Acosta was in Las Cruces visiting two of his sons at NMSU. How convenient of him.

Chapter 7

I COULDN'T decide whether the TownePlace Suites on Telshor Court in the City of Crosses emulated a Swiss chalet or went for a look all its own. Nonetheless, it was a place worthy of the Marriott name once I stepped inside. A desk message from Hector Acosta—prompted by an earlier message I'd left at his hotel—invited me to join him on the first tee of the NMSU golf course or for a late dinner in the dining room of his hotel that evening.

As I wrote an acceptance of the dinner invitation, a uniformed bellboy with a sprinkling of pimples across the bridge of his nose came in search of my luggage. I allowed him to carry the overnight bag but kept a grip on my laptop. I tipped him and went directly into the bath to freshen up. Whether I traveled fifty miles or five hundred, I always felt scroungy upon arrival.

I had once served in the Marine Corps with a light colonel named James Guerrero, who came from the El Paso, Texas area. Upon retirement he had earned a PI license in case he got bored being a man of leisure. Colonel Guerrero had called me for assistance a couple of times, so I phoned him to ask for reciprocation.

He knew of Hector Acosta but wanted to get an update on him, promising to call before my meeting that evening. I also fed him the names of the rest of the people involved in the case and gave him an idea of my interest. I went a little defensive while telling him the case revolved around a kidnapped duck, but he didn't fall off his chair laughing. Maybe I was a tad oversensitive on that point.

I devoted the rest of the morning and part of the afternoon to seeing what I could learn about the players in the "Quacky Affair."

Guerrero got back to me later that afternoon. "Hector Acosta y Roybal is a heavy hitter."

"Roybal?"

"That's his mother's maiden name. Acosta is his father's name. You want physicals?"

"I've never met the man, so they might help."

"He's fifty-five, stands five ten, and weighs in at around one eighty, one ninety. Black, wavy hair, hazel eyes. The only known distinguishing mark is a round brown mole on his left cheek. Born in Ciudad Juárez, just across the border from where I sit. He comes from an old ranching family that went bust backing Pancho Villa in the civil war. Things got bad for the family after that, but apparently Acosta found a backer, because he earned a business degree from New Mexico State. Shortly after graduating, he ended up in Brazil, where they say he made a lot of money in emeralds.

"When he came back home, he had enough money to buy a spread called Rancho Rayo. It's a couple of hundred thousand acres west of Palomas, just across the border from the New Mexico Boot Heel. Somewhere along the way, he met and married an American girl, about ten years younger than he is, named Frances Simpson. They have four children—a daughter and three sons. The twin boys, Juan and Jesus, are at NMSU."

"He's supposed to be visiting them now," I said. "Rancho Rayo. That's something to do with lightning, isn't it?"

"Yeah, the Lightning Ranch. I gather his brand is a big lightning bolt."

"So everything sounds on the up-and-up?"

"Everything I told you is pretty much public record. When I tapped some sources in the local and federal police forces, I got a clean bill of health."

Something in his voice put me on alert. "But it doesn't feel right?"

"I'm not sure, but it looks too clean, like a whitewash. One of my best sources over there is a commander in the *Federales*. He's given me the scoop on some pretty big names, but he came damned close to denying even knowing Acosta. I don't believe it. That doesn't mean Acosta's dirty, but it sure put me on my guard. One other thing—I don't have an estimate of net worth, but I can tell you it is serious money. And that's unusual too. Most of the time there are records, or at least estimates of the worth of major players like Acosta."

Colonel Guerrero told me Paco Rael had no serious record—bar fights mostly—and was not presently wanted by the authorities. He apparently earned a living as an itinerant cowboy, including work on Rancho Rayo.

THE MAN who rose from an immaculately set table in the corner of the dining room that evening mirrored the mental picture painted by James Guerrero, right down to the mole. He wore a pale blue silk Guayabera shirt with sharply creased tan slacks and shiny, tasseled, cordovan loafers. The glittering pin affixed to his shirt collar was a platinum or white gold zigzag set with diamonds. His cattle brand.

"Mr. Vinson," he said in a deep voice.

Strong grip; soft palm. This rancher didn't ride the range with his vaqueros. He did his business in a comfortable office. Acosta was pudgier than I expected and a little shorter. He must fudge his official profile a little. Still, he was a handsome and impressive man, exuding an air of competence and confidence.

"Mr. Acosta. Thank you for making time for me."

"How could I not? When a private investigator wants to interview you, who can resist? I must admit, curiosity earned you the invitation."

I smiled. "It often does."

"It works well, no? Your targets either succumb to your call or run away from you, I imagine."

A curious remark. I had not mentioned Martinson's name when asking for the interview, but Liver Lips had done just that—run away. Based on Acosta's speech patterns, I would have thought him born on this side of the border. He spoke with no accent, merely the Latin custom of tacking on the word *no* to make a question out of a statement.

"I think you have my game figured out. Are you certain you aren't a licensed investigator?"

"No, although there have been times when I felt I was one. You know, trying to figure out men, motives, and maneuvers. At the moment I am engaged in something of the sort—a problem with one of my sons attending the university here. It seems there was a girl…." He lifted his palms in exasperation.

"Isn't there always?"

"My sons are identical twins, you see. And sometimes they like to play games with the unwary. The young lady predisposed to favor Jesus didn't take it well when Juan took his place. That occasioned some trouble, but it is all working out well. But enough of that. Here is our waiter. Do you need time to review the menu, or may I suggest a plate?"

"I'll have whatever you're having."

He ordered two filets mignons, rare, with potatoes lyonnaise and a vegetable, which he left to the chef's discretion. He ordered a pricey bottle of Bordeaux but had coffee in the meantime. I settled for hot tea and lemon.

"How was your golf round this afternoon?" I asked.

"I played up to my usual mediocre standards. A shame you could not join us. But you have piqued my curiosity. What could possibly be your interest in me, Mr. Vinson?"

"Please call me BJ."

"Gladly. I am Hector." He pronounced it the Spanish way with the *H* silent and the accent on the second syllable. "Of course, when I went to school here, I was most often called Heck. You know, I kind of miss that. Not too many of my associates deal with such familiarity."

"Well, Heck, I am investigating the theft of some valuable property by a man named Richard Martinson."

"Ah, poor Liver Lips. I heard of his accident." The name came out as "Leever Leeps," but I understood it to be a parody of his vaqueros' pronunciation of Martinson's name. "You're looking for Mud Hen's duck, no? Let's see, what did she call the bird? Quacky, was it not? Quacky Quack the Second." A glint of amusement lit his eyes.

"Exactly."

He shook his head. "Only Mud would go to the extreme of hiring a private investigator to find a duck."

"The insurance company hired me."

His eyebrows twitched. "She insured a duck? *¡Dios mío!* Am I missing the boat? I have some roosters on the ranch I should insure."

"I take it you know Mrs. Muldren."

"Ah yes. We have been neighbors for a long time. For years we bought and sold cattle at the fence line dividing our ranches—and our countries. Alas, those days are gone forever, I'm afraid."

"I came across your name while looking into Martinson's background. He used you as a reference on a couple of occasions."

"Yes, I allowed him to list me as a previous employer."

"What sort of work did he do for you?"

"A cook. A decent one, as a matter of fact. He used to take the chuck wagon out on the range to feed the vaqueros, uh... cowboys. At first he drove a mule wagon, but as time went on, we modernized and used a truck." Acosta laughed. "I think he rather preferred the mules."

"How long did he work for you?" I thought about the Immigration and Control Act of 1986 Millicent had mentioned, but that only covered hiring undocumented workers on this side of the border. Did Mexico have a similar law? I decided not to ask.

"Off and on for a number of years. He was merely a skinny kid when his uncle first sent him to me. I knew the uncle from various business dealings, so I hired Liver as a favor to him. But he earned his keep. He usually came around in the spring and again in the fall."

"For the gatherings?"

He nodded. "And sometimes at other moments. If things got too bad for him up here, he'd show up on my doorstep, and my foreman would give him something to do for a few days—whether I was in residence at the hacienda or not. I had the feeling he was perhaps fleeing the law when he showed up at those odd moments."

"The law?"

"Liver was not a bad man. Not a desperate criminal, but easily manipulated by others. He often found himself in your lawmen's sights, so to speak. Drinking. Fighting. That sort of thing."

"Why didn't he stay in Mexico if he had a ready home there?"

"He could take the solitude for only so long at a time. And even though he spoke our language well, in truth he was never completely at home in my country. He always went back to Deming when the pressure eased up."

"You mentioned an uncle?"

"Yes. An old Texas cowhand named Charles Martinson. He passed on a few years back. Shame. He was the only family Liver had."

"Can you think of any reason why he would steal Mrs. Muldren's property?"

Acosta shifted in his chair as the waiter delivered our order, the chef himself in tow. The two men made a production out of our simple meal. The platters were blue-and-white glazed pottery. A stemmed goblet rang when the waiter's ring accidentally touched it. Acosta greeted the chef by name. After introducing me, the two spoke briefly, reminiscing about other meals.

The filets were extraordinarily thick and so tender and delicious we both forgot to speak for a few minutes. As good as the beef was, the potatoes were better. They were done to perfection. The wine was full-bodied and went down smoothly, but I couldn't discern much difference between it and the ten-dollar Cabernet I usually drink. A connoisseur of wine I am not.

"You can order for me anytime," I said.

Acosta chuckled. "Let's see, where were we? Oh yes, Mud and Liver. They did not get along particularly well. He worked for her occasionally, but they had a falling-out over his unreliability, as I understand it. However, it would not be difficult to get on Millicent's bad side." He waved a hand. "To be fair about it, Liver could strike a number of people wrong too. He was not lazy but neither was he industrious."

"There's reason to believe he took the duck at the behest of someone else," I said. "You said he was easily manipulated. Do you know anyone who might influence him to do such a thing?"

"Perhaps he was paid. Nothing more than a job for him."

"I don't believe so. I spoke to him about the theft before he died. He admitted taking the duck, but he said he'd done it for someone who wanted to get back at Mrs. Muldren."

"I see. Did he say who this person was?"

"Not outright, but he let a few things slip. Things he probably hadn't intended to reveal." Sometimes a confidential investigator shades the truth in pursuit of a goal. Hell, sometimes he downright lies.

"I hope he told you enough for you to locate the missing duck. I am told Mud's ducks make excellent pâté de foie gras."

"So I understand." I leaned back in the chair. "I met a young man at the Lazy M named Paco Rael. I understand he is a Mexican citizen and spends most of his time in your neck of the woods. Do you happen to know him?"

"Him and his parents as well. The elder Raels were domestics on the ranch until Mud lured them across the border. Paco occasionally works as a vaquero for me. He seems like a decent young man."

"Yes, although I'm told he sometimes associates with some undesirable elements."

"I will have a talk with him the next time we meet. Perhaps I can put an end to that practice."

We passed another half hour in pleasant conversation. He ordered a small helping of flan, a Mexican-style custard, for dessert, and at that point I switched to coffee.

"A good cigar would be nice now." He sighed. "But the health police have dealt the deathblow to such pleasures after a meal."

"That is a striking pin you wear on your collar. Your ranch brand, I believe."

"Yes. A lightning bolt. My brand comes from the name of the ranch, Rancho Rayo. It is actually a tie tack, but I also wear it as a lapel pin or collar decoration."

"It's beautiful. White gold or platinum?"

"Platinum. Frankie—my wife—had the diamonds sent directly from Amsterdam. Her name is really Frances, but I call her Frankie. That has caused some amusement among our hands. They take enjoyment in calling her Doña Frankie."

After a short tussle over the check, we rose and said good-bye. To this point I'd merely made a few indirect connections radiating out from the ranch. But now I'd discovered a circle: Mud, Acosta, Liver Lips, Rael… and back to the Lazy M again.

And one of the heavyweights in the tableau—Acosta—was an interesting man. Charming, likable, and seemingly open and aboveboard. But there was an undercurrent I couldn't put down simply to cultural differences. Colonel Guerrero's inferred caution about his contact's reluctance to share information about Acosta raised my antennae.

Chapter 8

THE NEXT morning, Del called to say Hank Grass, the GSR vice president, had phoned wanting to know where we were on the case. What it boiled down to, of course, was he wanted me to tell him Millicent Muldren had her own duck kidnapped so they—or more to the point, *he*—could wiggle off the hook. I told Del he damned well knew I didn't work that way. Fire me and have the insurance company send in their own team, or leave me alone to collect the facts as they were—not as GSR wanted them to be.

Charlie Weeks called me next. I had asked him to check out a couple of duck races the woman at the Deming-Luna County Chamber of Commerce told me about.

"In a few of the races, contestants enter their own birds. Some had stakes a bit higher—by a couple of thousand or so," he said.

"That's not enough to warrant the expense of insuring Quacky for a quarter of a mil," I said.

"Not so fast," Charlie warned. "There's a betting syndicate in Ireland that actually handicaps the things."

He went on to say Millicent Muldren and Quacky Quack the Second—not to mention the first Quacky Quack—were no strangers to those racing circles. No one knew for certain the size of the betting that went on around those races, but if this involved the Irish syndicate, it was probably substantial. The largest race on the duck circuit came up later this month in Miami.

Was it possible the theft of Millicent's property had something to do with racing? I'd learned not to leap to conclusions before all the facts were in; nonetheless, this had to be given serious consideration. It might explain not only why Liver took the bird but also why no ransom demand had been made. Did someone want to make certain Quacky didn't race in the Miami Steeplechase—Duckchase—whatever? If so, why not just kill the bird instead of taking her? Perhaps they had, and Mud Hen had Liver Lips snatch the carcass in order to frustrate Hank Grass's inevitable claim the duck died of natural causes. At any rate, it was time I started taking this ducknapping thing seriously.

"Do we know if our duck was entered in this big race? And if so, what was… uh, the morning line on her?" I asked Charlie.

"Can't answer that. The deadline for entries is not until next week." His wry sense of humor surfaced. "I don't know what the odds are, but the Muldren colors usually do well."

"You keep nosing around down there. I'm going to head back to the Lazy M."

"You figure somebody stole the duck to keep her out of the race?"

"Makes as much sense as anything else."

AFTER CHECKING out of the Marriott, I headed west to drop in on the ranch—uninvited this time. Sometimes the unexpected shakes things loose. When Maria answered the door, a ray of sunshine reflected off the Impala's windshield and caught in her sleek hair. She smiled, called me by name, and graciously ushered me inside where she asked me to wait while she informed the señora a guest had arrived.

Millicent Muldren greeted me in her office in a Pendleton plaid shirt, faded jeans, and fuzzy blue house slippers instead of boots. Her gray hair lay close to her skull, lending prominence to small, diamond-studded earlobes.

"BJ." She offered the hand that wasn't cuddling a growling Poopsie.

"Millicent, I thought you would be getting ready for your trip to Miami."

She didn't miss a beat. "No reason to go without Quacky."

"Is that why Liver took her? To keep her out of the race?"

"I don't know. Is that what you've come to tell me?"

"I don't have any idea, but if you'd shared that information with me, I'd be a couple of days ahead of where I am right now. Why didn't you?"

"I don't go around broadcasting I run all over the countryside racing a duck."

"And making hefty bets on her, I imagine."

"I've been known to risk a dollar or two. Anything wrong with that?"

"Depends on the local laws, I guess. But why keep it a secret?"

She shrugged her broad shoulders and motioned me to one of the barrel chairs. "I'm a private person, BJ. And frankly, I wasn't certain what the insurance company's reaction would be. I had to lean on them hard to get them to insure the bird. Threatening to take my business elsewhere was the only way I could get them to do it."

Without another word, I removed my recorder from my belt and thumbed a button. My disembodied voice asked who would want Martinson to take the duck from her.

"No one. At least, I can't think of anyone. Can you, Bert?" came her taped reply.

"Not offhand."

She glanced up at me but said nothing.

"It's a good thing I work for the insurance company and not for you. If I did, I'd walk out of here right now and forget about Quacky Quack the Whatever. Look, I think we both have the same goal here, and that is to find out who took the bird and secure her return—if she's still alive."

Her hand flew to her throat, making me recognize her sincerity. She was obsessed with that damned white duck.

"She *has* to be alive," she half whispered.

"No, she doesn't. And it's time you faced that fact. Unless, of course, you know more than you're telling me. Have you been contacted?"

She shook her head. "No."

"No note. No telephone call. No message delivered from anyone?"

"No, nothing at all." She leaned back in her chair, looking tired. "I'm sorry I didn't deal straight with you before, but you made it plain you worked for someone else, not me."

"Do you intend to cooperate from now on?"

"Yes. Anything to get my sweetie back. I'll make it worth your while. I swear, I'll—"

"No. My paycheck comes from the insurance company. I don't do backroom deals. Now, is there anything else I need to know? For instance, if they took the duck to keep her out of the race, who would have the best motive? Whose interests would be served?"

"Anyone who enters the race. She would have been the favorite. She won two of her last three races."

"How many dollars are we talking about?"

"Is that necessary?"

I sighed. "I am not an IRS agent. I do not represent the Treasury. And I am not a blackmailer. All I'm trying to do is find that duck."

"Substantial."

"Twenty-five thousand substantial? Fifty? A hundred?"

She merely met my gaze and held it. I understood her reluctance. If she won that kind of money, it probably wasn't reported to the insurance company. And very likely not to the IRS either.

"Does anyone in particular stand to benefit?"

"A man by the name of Kenneth Hammond. He's a Miami commercial developer. More money than he knows what to do with and into racing in a big way."

"Is he capable of the theft?"

"Capable and willing. Anytime he's in the area, I keep my precious under lock and key."

"Does he have a reach this long? Could he arrange something like this clear out here in New Mexico?"

"Money reaches around the globe. Yes, he could arrange it."

"All right. I'll check him out. But something else occurred to me. If she… uh, Quacky is the future of your down and pâté business, could someone have stolen her in order to breed her with his own drakes?"

"Yes, that's possible."

"Who comes to mind in that case?"

"Lily Stropshire," she said without hesitation. "Up in the Lordsburg area. She's been trying for years to get a foot in the door with her duck down. It's horse-piss quality. If anyone needs my precious, it's Lily."

"What makes the difference between good down and bad?"

"Do you want to be educated or merely illuminated?"

I blinked. Was this the same Millicent I'd met the other day? Without waiting for my response, she proceeded to educate me.

"The best down in the world is eiderdown. But the eider is a sea duck, and they don't do well here. My ducks are domesticated descendants of mallards, as are many of the ducks these days. Mallards can crossbreed with sixty-three other species of waterfowl. At any rate, down is the fine, fluffy material gathered from the duck's breast. It is rated according to fill power—that is the number of cubic inches occupied by one ounce of down. The larger the fill power, the higher the quality. The down with high fill power is puffier, has more loft."

"Okay, loftier is better."

"Although the down is the most valuable part of the duck, it's by no means all. Many farmers—and when it comes to ducks, I'm a farmer, not a rancher—slaughter their birds pretty quickly. I prefer to let them mature. That way I get larger breasts, by far the most popular meat of the duck, and that also allows for the production of foie gras, which is a fattened liver product, as well as magret, the breast of a duck that has produced the foie gras. Both are considered delicacies."

"And your missing duck produces this kind of quality?"

"Her offspring, yes. When mated to the proper drakes, of course."

THE STROPSHIRE Duck Farm sat about a mile south of the highway on the sundown side of Lordsburg. The prosperous-looking white board fence fronting the place quickly gave way to tired barbed wire. The house dropped the value of the real estate even further. The outside walls were badly flaked, exposing chicken-wire netting beneath the stucco. But once past the house, I saw that Lily's ducks were better housed than she was. The sheds had been recently painted and were well maintained. The place sounded just like Millicent's: the endless quacking of the females and the somewhat weaker squawking of the drakes.

A short, broad-bottomed, thick-legged woman came out of one of the sheds and stood watching as I walked down the driveway. She had a green kerchief tied over her white hair and wore a man's shirt over a blue denim skirt. The hair turned out to be platinum blonde. Deep brown eyes didn't track with her hair. Contacts or bleached hair? I voted for the hair. Probably a shade under forty.

"Help you, mister?" she asked.

"Maybe. How long have you been duck farming?"

She moved toward the fence, scattering some of the birds congregated around her, and regarded me coolly. "Ten years or so. Why?"

"Trying to get the lay of the land. Domesticated mallards?"

She glanced at the white birds with orange beaks and legs. "Mallard strain. You a buyer?"

"No, ma'am, I'm a confidential investigator from Albuquerque. My name's B. J. Vinson."

"Investigator? What do you want with me?"

"I'm looking into the theft of a valuable duck—"

Lily Stropshire's laugh started way down inside her, split somewhere in her esophagus, and exited by way of her nose in a snort and her mouth in a donkey's bray. "Old Mud hired a private investigator to find her duck? I can't believe it. That woman's one of a kind, I tell you."

"Perhaps it's a laughing matter to you, but to the insurance company who hired me, it's serious business. As a matter of fact, it's a felony."

"Felony? I don't care if she does have a fancy name, she's only a damned duck."

"Let me put it this way. The property was insured for several thousand dollars, and that's a felony in anybody's crime book."

She gave her imitation of a burro and a boar again, this time wiping away a tear or two. "So what are you doing up here? I didn't have anything to do with that. Heard they caught the guy who did it, anyway. Get outta here. Get off my property."

"Very well, Ms. Stropshire, I'll honor your request. But I'll go straight to the county courthouse for a warrant. Then the sheriff and I will both be back. On the other hand, we can sit on your patio and have a glass of iced tea. I'll ask a few questions and go about my business."

"My cousin's the court bailiff over there, and you're not gonna get a warrant. Still, that tea sounds pretty good. I've got some steeping that oughta just about be done. Go on, I'll be there in a minute."

She disappeared back into the shed while I walked back to a small patio of flaking concrete outlined by a double row of crumbling red bricks. Her picnic table was one of those gigantic cable spools laid sideways. I settled into an aluminum frame chair with alternating white-and-green plastic support strips and switched on my recorder as she came up the path. She whipped off the kerchief covering her head and fluffed her brassy hair with strong fingers. Without speaking, she snatched a jar of tea from a sunny spot on the patio and entered the house through a creaky screen door. A moment later she yelled, asking if I wanted lemon or sugar. I settled for lemon.

The door screeched again, and she plopped into the chair opposite me, handing over a tall tumbler of tea and ice cubes. Two generous lemon wedges floated on top. The glass was already beginning to sweat.

"So I'm supposed to have Mud Hen's Ducky Duck or whatever her ridiculous name is?"

"I believe that's Quacky Quack the Second."

We both broke up, easing the tension.

"How come she sicced you on me?"

"She didn't. I just asked about others in the duck business, and your name came up. She said Lily Stropshire owned the Stropshire Duck Farm, her closest competitor."

"Yeah, I'll bet she did. Said it exactly like that, I imagine. Well, we've butted heads a few times. I got a contract with one of the slaughterhouses, and she tried to wreck it. Put out the word my ducks weren't any good." Lily shrugged. "And to be truthful, they aren't up to her standards. She's been raising ducks and developing her farm ever since she was a little girl—and that was a long time ago, I can tell you. That gives her a quarter-century head start. But I'll get there." Her jaw took on a stubborn set. "And I don't need to go steal anybody's duck to do it either."

"Any thoughts about who would?"

"Hell, Mud's probably made at least one enemy for every year of her life. She shaves her deals so close, nobody else can make any money. I'm not saying she cheats—no boot on the scale or filling up her calves with water at the sale barn or anything like that. But she drives a bargain that doesn't leave room for anybody else. Another thing, somebody comes down sick, most neighbors send over some help. Not Millicent Muldren. No helping hand. Course, she doesn't ask for help either."

She turned her gaze from the distant horizon to me. "Anyway, I'm working on my gaggle. This year's flock is better'n last year's." She waved a hand toward the pens. "I've got two good-sized ponds back beyond the incubating sheds. My ducks are waterfowl, like God made them. Mud herds hers to forage like they were a bunch of cattle."

"I remember a pond out by her pens."

"Yeah, but it's not big enough for a gaggle that size. No, she herds them, or has that Luis fella do it. As far as who took the duck, nobody in particular jumps to mind as a likely candidate. A lot of people'd like to squeeze her a little, but nobody'd resort to breaking the law."

"Not everyone would think of snatching a duck as a real crime. Probably nobody outside the family knew she had it insured for big bucks."

Her eyes twinkled. "How many bucks?"

"Plenty. Otherwise the insurance company wouldn't be paying me to sit here and have tea with you."

"Well, thank the insurance company for me, will you?"

I stayed for another half hour and another glass of tea, asking all sorts of questions, including a couple intended to trip her up. She didn't fall for it, and the wry smile on her pouty lips told me she knew exactly what I was doing.

When I stood to go, she asked if I wanted a tour of the place. "You can inspect every damned duck I have, if you want."

"They all look alike to me."

"Don't gimme that. They've got some way of identifying that duck if they rolled the dice on her. And if they didn't share that info with you, then neither one of you's very smart."

I laughed. "Yeah, they shared it with me, but I'm not too certain your assessment isn't accurate anyway. Insure a duck?"

"They insured Betty Grable's legs and Harry James's lips. You know, her trumpet-playing husband."

"And Millicent's duck."

"And Millicent's duck. By the way, I hear she races that damned thing. I hear tell there's big money thrown around at some of those races. You ever think about that?"

"Do you know where she races and who she races against?"

"No. I just heard things. Everybody around these parts knows about it."

"In other words it's a rumor."

"Maybe so, but that's big money." She indicated her farm. "This is just chicken feed, but you come out here to Lily Stropshire's pitiful little duck farm looking for valuable property anyway. What kind of private investigator are you?"

"A thorough one."

Yeah. Thorough. One of these days, Del would tell me to inspect every blessed duck on the Lazy M to make sure Quacky wasn't hidden somewhere among the flock. And being thorough, I'd end up taking advantage of Lily's semiserious offer to look at every damned duck she had.

Chapter 9

I CALLED Del with an update. He heard me out patiently enough and then summarized my report in a slightly exasperated tone. His buddy, the VP, must have phoned him again.

"So it boils down to three things—payback from somebody who holds a grudge against Mrs. Muldren, another somebody who wants to screw up a big-stakes duck race, or yet another somebody—this Ms. Stropshire, for example—who's looking to improve the gene pool of her herd of ducks."

"Flock," I corrected. "Or gaggle. Or brace. Or raft. And there are a couple of other names for bunches of ducks."

"Thank you for the day's trivia lesson."

"Don't feed me sarcasm. You called me in on this caper. I didn't ask for it. Besides, there's another possibility."

"Yes, I know. The one Hank Grass wants to hear. The duck died, and the owner is claiming someone took her."

"Right," I said.

"This went from a simple interview of a simple man—"

"Who is now dead. Most likely murdered."

"—to a range of individuals who wish Millicent Muldren ill," he finished.

"You have stated the situation perfectly. Charlie's contacting another investigator in Florida to look into a fellow by the name of Kenneth Hammond, who's supposed to be big in the duck-racing circuit. Still, do you know the odds against getting to the bottom of this? Probably something akin to winning the lottery. Nobody takes it seriously."

"Somebody does if Martinson was murdered."

"That assumes he was murdered because of the duck. It might have nothing to do with the theft. He wasn't exactly a sterling character."

The long and the short of our conversation? I was sentenced to spend more time hundreds of miles from home—and Paul. I suppressed the urge to call him. He would be at work now.

So I started over, beginning with Det. Manny Montoya, who told me that on the night of Liver Lips' fatal car wreck, a Deming police officer had spotted a black Firebird speeding west on I-10 near the city limits. By the time he found a turnaround on the interstate, he'd lost the car. At the time there was no alert out for the Pontiac, so the policeman's only interest was in issuing a speeding ticket. He wasn't certain but thought the car had Mexican license plates.

According to Manny, no such car left the country through the Columbus, the Santa Teresa, or the Antelope Wells POE. That indicated Martinson's problems might have arisen from his drug connections, not from stealing a duck, but I needed more information before zeroing in on that conclusion.

I ran down Officer Garza by phone and quizzed him about Paco Rael, who provided another tenuous connection between the Lazy M and Liver Lips. And to Acosta, for that matter. Did the Mexican rancher fit into this picture? Was he a gambler who bet heavily on duck races? He struck me as more of a thoroughbred man, but who knew? I contacted Colonel Guerrero in El Paso to ask about it. He didn't have an answer, but he agreed to ask around.

A phone call to the Lazy M revealed that Paco had left for home that morning. The querulous tone in Maria's voice told me she was dying to ask about my interest in her son, but she was too well trained to do so.

Perhaps Liver's boyhood buddy, Lopez, knew where to find him. It was a stretch but not much, because everything seemed to be a closed loop down here. Everyone seemed connected to everyone else in some manner or form. It took a little doing to find Elizondo Lopez. He wasn't at his shack, and the neighbors on either side claimed they didn't speak English—or Spanish either, when I pulled out a few words I'd learned in high school classes.

I spent the afternoon in my hot car parked around the corner from Lopez's place, sweating liberally and marshaling my troops by cell phone and laptop. Within the hour, I knew Hector Acosta frequented horse races, sometimes making large wagers, but there was no indication the duck-racing crowd knew him.

I was also aware, thanks to Hazel's efforts, no record existed of Paco Rael crossing into Mexico through any of the nearby POEs after my visit to the ranch. That didn't mean a whole lot since most people walk or drive across the border simply by flashing ID. Or maybe he didn't use the legal routes for his visits. He could simply hop the fence between the Lazy M and the Rancho Rayo. Of course, that would leave him with a long hike unless he had left a vehicle over there. I should have asked how he arrived at the ranch in the first place.

A little later in the afternoon, an old pickup short on paint but daubed with liberal globs of Bondo dropped Lopez off on the road almost directly in front of me. I got out of the Impala and intercepted him before he reached his dusty front yard. He recoiled slightly when I hailed him, but at least he didn't take off running. He stood in the middle of the dirt road and stared at me while I invited him for a drink. Judging from his eyes, that was a risky maneuver. Dilated pupils and dark shadows beneath them signaled a dope high. His agitated manner and instant nervousness when he recognized me confirmed my suspicion.

"Naw, man. I gotta rest. Up all night."

"Okay, we'll go talk at your place."

"Uh-uh. No good. Girlfriend's coming by later."

Yeah, like this guy had a girlfriend. "Okay, then we'll talk in my car."

"Cut me some slack, man. I need sleep."

"You need to get in the car, or else I'm coming to your place."

"You ain't got no right—"

"Do you really want to complain to the cops about rights in your condition?"

"Arright. Your car, but jus' a minute."

He stumbled as he turned to follow me but recovered and slouched along behind. I regretted the choice of the vehicle as a meeting place the moment he shut the door behind him. His body odor was foul. Sweat popped out on his forehead. He kept scratching at his arms. Classic symptoms of meth users. I started the car and turned on the air conditioner.

"All right, let's get this over with. What do you know about Paco Rael?"

He blinked rapidly but couldn't hide the sudden wariness in his red-rimmed eyes. "Nothing. Don't know—"

"You lie to me, Lopez, and I'll haul you down to Bill Garza. He believes you're a piece of shit, so what do you think he'll do when he sees the condition you're in? Paco Rael. How do you know him?"

"School. Went to school together. Down in Columbus."

"Is that where Liver Lips met him?"

"I dunno. Guess so." He scratched at his upper arm so hard he drew blood.

"Don't bleed on my seat covers. They have business together?"

He dropped his gaze to the left. "Naw. Just friends. Not buddies—not, you know—compadres. Just friends."

"You're lying, Lopez. Rael was Liver's meth connection, wasn't he? He's probably yours too."

He put both hands to his head and rubbed vigorously. Dust motes flew. "Naw, man. Don't know nothing about that. Don't know nothing!"

"Where'd you get what you're on now?"

"Had some around. Found it in Liver's place."

"Try another story. I was there when you went looking, remember? You didn't find anything."

"Went back," he said, eyes whipping around wildly. "Found it after you left. I gotta go, man."

"Lie to me one more time, and I'm driving straight to the police station."

Lopez hugged himself. His head drooped. I would lose him soon.

"Did Rael supply Liver with dope?"

"Okay, okay. So he scored some weed for us now and then. Just for old time's sake, you know."

Was that a breakthrough or just this guy's pathetic effort to get me off his back? "Where did Rael get it?"

"I don' know."

Suddenly his head snapped back. I caught his reaction and followed his stare. A low-slung black car approached from the east, slowing as if to make a turn. Instead it came to a halt a quarter of a block away. Lopez went crazy.

"I gotta go," he yelled, clawing at the door handle.

I grabbed for his arm, but he snatched it away and made his escape. My eyes were glued to the motionless car, so I wasn't even certain which direction he ran. The vehicle was a black Pontiac Firebird with red-and-white flames painted over the hood and across the sides. I wasn't sure if it was a '96, but it certainly had Mexican plates. I started trying to make out the numbers when the car suddenly shot forward, heading straight for me. The Impala idled in neutral, but I managed to get it in gear and jerk the wheel to the right. The Pontiac veered off at the last minute and sped down the dusty road. I ended up in the ditch.

It took me a minute to work my way back onto the roadway and get turned around. By then the Firebird had disappeared. I got on the cell phone to the state police, but Montoya wasn't available at the moment. I left a message about his missing murder vehicle, citing three numbers from the license plate I'd memorized before the car came charging toward me. Then I spent half an hour vainly searching for the car.

Although I knew Lopez would make himself scarce, I returned to his shack anyway. He didn't answer my knock, so I resorted to peering through the filthy windows to satisfy myself no one was inside.

I checked in at the closest motel, one called the Border, to be near Lopez's shack. The place was a row of cinder block rooms with a carport between each. The motel could have been lifted right off of an old Route 66 postcard. When I traveled on other people's money, I didn't stay in the priciest digs, but this was considerably beneath my usual standards. The room had a musty smell, and cranking open the old casement windows didn't help. The air conditioning was the evaporative type, which contributed to the mustiness, so I switched it off.

I stripped to my shorts and washed up in the stained bathroom sink. That gave me some temporary relief, but not a lot. Still in my skivvies, I sat on the creaky bed and brought my files and expense tickets up-to-date.

After about an hour, Manny Montoya called my cell and thanked me for the tip on the Firebird. He asked if there was anything else I could provide, like who was in the vehicle and how many? But the windows had been tinted far beyond the legal limit, so I couldn't help him out. Neither he nor the Deming police had had any luck in locating the Pontiac, which probably meant it was stowed in somebody's garage by now.

We hung up, and I prepared to go find a place to eat when my cell phone rang again.

"Where are you, Vinson?" Bill Garza's tone was gruff, unfriendly. I told him and earned a chuckle. Probably the only one I'd ever hear from the guy. "What are you doing in a dump like that?"

"I wish I could give you a rational reason other than it's the closest one to Lopez's shack I could find, but that's the truth."

"Funny you should mention Elizondo Lopez. Is that who you was talking to when you caused a dustup about that black '96 Firebird?"

"Yep. We were sitting in my car around the corner from his place. Why?"

"Was he breathing when you seen him last?"

"Breathing and running. Why?"

"Well, he ain't doing neither one of them now."

Chapter 10

A FIERCE bald eagle centered in a gold-trimmed blue shield adorned the door to the Deming PD. The flowing ribbon across the bottom read "Deming Police 1902."

Garza had paved the way for me, and I found myself escorted back to a bullpen of open spaces littered with desks, with a few cubicles around the perimeter. Garza occupied one of those semiprivate affairs.

He rose and shook my hand with a mean grip. I dismissed it as an unconscious display of strength from a very powerful man. His luxurious black mustache—speckled with touches of gray—was so thick I inspected it for clues to his last meal.

He motioned me to a chair and got right down to business. I decided what I had taken for unfriendliness was merely his brusque way of dealing with the world. "What time did you talk to Lopez outside of his house?"

"Must have been about two. You can pin that down, because I called Detective Montoya from my cell phone the minute the Pontiac raced by me. They'll have the call logged."

He tilted a tablet on his desk and took a look at it. "Two-oh-seven." His black eyes rose to meet mine. "You get run off the road by a car in Deming, but you call the state police?"

"The state police had a bulletin out on the car. I came into this thing in the first place because of Martinson's death. Why wouldn't I call them? And I didn't phone you because I knew they'd contact you. I spent my time trying to locate the car again."

"But you didn't have no luck."

"That's right. He'd put me in the ditch, and by the time I got out, he was gone."

"He?"

"That's an assumption on my part. The windows were tinted so dark I couldn't see."

"Hmmm. What did you want to talk to Lopez about?"

I briefed Garza on everything I'd learned, although I skimmed over some of the facts surrounding confidential information Millicent had given me. But I made a point of describing Lopez's condition. "You warned me he was a pothead. But he was on meth, not weed."

"Not surprising. Lopez used whatever he could get his hands on. Where'd you go after that?"

"I don't know how long I drove around looking for that Firebird, but after I gave up, I checked into the Border Motel."

"You didn't talk to nobody else?"

"No one can corroborate my story, if that's what you mean. Now you tell me something. How did Lopez die?"

He hesitated momentarily. "Albuquerque PD says you're okay, so I guess I can share information. A man walking home from the store found him in a ditch about five o'clock not half a mile from where you were parked."

"How was he killed?"

Eyebrows as thick as his mustache climbed. "What do you mean, 'killed'? You know something you haven't told me?"

"He was alive when I saw him. Now he's dead. Something or somebody killed him, right?"

"Overdose. If he was high when you talked to him, he must have been in outer space before his heart quit on him. I'm surprised he had time to pull the needle out of his arm."

"He injected the meth?"

"He injected something. The tox screen results aren't in yet, so we don't know for sure what it was. Could be horse."

"Did he have the needle on him?"

"Beside the body. I sent it for testing."

"It doesn't add up."

"Why not?"

"He was feeling no pain when he was talking to me. Lopez struck me as the kind of guy who scrambled for every dollar, every fix. He'd have waited until he came down from his high before using up another dose. And most users choose the drug because they don't need the needle to get a good high. Smoking does it just fine. Did he have tracks on his arms? I didn't notice them the two times I saw him."

"Nope, but there's a first time for everything."

"How are you going to treat his death?"

"I'll leave it open until I have the ME's report. Then we'll see. If I understand things, the first time you talked to Lopez, you were interested in Liver Lips Martinson. This time you were asking about Paco Rael."

"That's right. Rael and his relationship with Martinson. Martinson needed a drug connection somewhere, so I started asking questions."

"You think every Mexican is involved in drug running?"

"No, I don't. I have some very good friends who are of Mexican heritage, and they're fine people. But when I'm looking for leads, I pursue them until I'm satisfied they're dead ends. In this case I don't have any leads, so I'm casting a net to see what I catch."

He merely grunted, but his body language said he'd accepted my explanation. When he'd asked all his questions, I talked him into taking me to the ditch where Lopez died.

THE EXTREME southern edge of the city limits was semirural, with a few small residences interspaced with derelict buildings and vacant lots. The weed-littered ditch where Lopez died was a perfect place for dumping a body. On the other hand, it also served as a good spot for a junkie to hide while injecting his veins with poison. Garza lifted the crime scene tape and led me down into the channel. I removed the small Minolta from its case on my belt and took pictures—of weeds. Upstanding plants and crushed stems. Footprints here and there and discarded candy wrappers, paper scraps—the usual detritus of a place like this.

I asked if he would share the results of the autopsy with me as we made our way back to his cruiser.

"Don't see why not. You hanging around?"

"Yes. I'll probably switch motels tomorrow, but you have my cell, so you can always contact me. Has a canvass of the neighborhood turned up any information?"

He expelled a heavy breath of air. "The people around here are suspicious of cops. Yeah, I know, that's true up in Albuquerque too. But some of these people are undocumented or they're sheltering others who are. We asked all the right questions but got no answers. Except descriptions of your Impala. They're not so reluctant to talk about outsiders."

"Did the Firebird's tire tracks tell you anything?"

"Faxed the photographs to Manny. His shots of the tracks they found at the Martinson crash scene were pretty poor quality, but he thinks they're from the same car."

"That tells me this was murder."

"You probably right, but I'll wait for the autopsy."

On the ride back to the station, Garza pointed out a middle-priced motel on Pine east of the police station. It looked far superior to the Border, so I told him I'd be there starting tomorrow afternoon. I recovered my car and headed off in search of a meal. Sometimes I do my best thinking while eating.

I didn't make it to a restaurant. As I wheeled into the parking lot of a small neighborhood café, a distinctive clatter caught my attention. I looked up through the windshield to see a Bell bubbletop with one large upright *M* and another toppled on its side painted on the belly—the Lazy M's helicopter. I pulled out of the parking lot without stopping and headed for the local airport. Bert Kurtz might have an idea of where Paco Rael was. The bird would be on the ground before I could get there, but perhaps seeing to the tie-down of his craft would delay Bert long enough for me to catch up with him.

I arrived in time to see Paco Rael approach on foot as Bert gave instructions to a ground attendant. When the rancher turned around and spotted his buddy, a great grin split his lips. They talked animatedly as they moved toward the parking lot. They were so totally engaged in conversation they took no notice of me. Paco must have met Bert to give him a lift from the airport. Was he driving a black Pontiac Firebird?

Not today. The two men made their way to an old Plymouth Duster. The once-rich gold paint had faded to a sickly yellow, and there were dings and dents on the body. But when Paco fired it up, the motor had the muted roar of a powerful engine.

It's hard enough for one man to shadow a mark in a crowded city, but in a small town—forget it. Nonetheless, it would probably take them a while to figure out I was following them, maybe enough to determine where they were headed. And if they called me on it, I could truthfully claim I had gone to the airport to meet Bert in the hope he could tell me where to find Paco.

I pulled out of the airport lot and headed west, trailing along behind the Duster. A few blocks later, Paco parked in a lot in front of a small strip mall. Both men got out of the Duster and headed straight for me.

"BJ," Bert said, extending a hand. "You following us?"

"Trying to run you down, as a matter of fact. I saw the helicopter."

"Well, you caught me. What can I do for you?" He indicated a cantina at the west end of the mall. "We're going to have a beer. Join us?"

"I wouldn't mind a Dos Equis, if they serve it."

"Everybody serves Dos Equis around here. You remember Paco, don't you?"

"Sure." I turned and offered a hand. Shorter than I remembered—probably around five eight—his handshake was firm. "How are you, Paco?"

"Doing fine, Mr. Vinson."

"I'm BJ. Actually, it was you I'm hunting. I called the ranch this morning, but your mother said you'd left. I thought Bert might know how to get in touch with you, and sure enough, here you are."

A slight frown marred his sleek features. "Me? What you want with me?"

"A friend of yours died this morning, and I thought you'd want to know."

"You mean Lopez? Yeah, Bert told me. What happened to him?"

"It looks like an overdose, but I'm not so sure."

"Why not?" Paco's dark brown eyes studied me intently.

"It's a long story. Let's have that beer, and I'll tell you all about it."

As soon as we were settled at a table with chilled bottles of Dos Equis in front of us, both men turned to stare at me. My problem now was how to extract information without giving too much away. Ignoring the noise in the place, I thumbed on the tape recorder at my belt hoping it would catch something of our conversation.

"Do you live here in Deming, Paco?"

The question obviously took him by surprise. "Uh, no. I live in Palomas. South of here."

"On the other side of Columbus, right?"

"Yeah. Little ways. But what's this about Lopez?"

"The couple of times I met him, he claimed he was a weed man."

Paco snorted. "Yeah, right. A pothead. But he liked his grass boosted a little. He went for yerba mala or fry, and he'd go crazy for some bazooka."

I recognized the street terms for marijuana mixed with PCP and formaldehyde and crack cocaine. Any of them could have produced the symptoms I observed in the Impala. "How about meth?"

"Sure. I've seen him on meth. The ganja wasn't too bad, but I didn't like to be around him when he was on meth."

"Where did he get it?"

"Where does anybody get it? You just go out and find a source, man. There's some around."

"Do you know who supplied him?" Bert asked. And here I had pegged him as a MYOB kind of guy.

"Hell, I don't know. I don't use that shit." Paco turned back to me. "But if he was on meth, he could have overdosed, couldn't he?"

"Sure," I agreed. "How did he take his meth?"

The question got me a Latin shrug. "Burned it, I guess. I've never been with him when he was taking it, but I've seen him under the influence."

"Did he ever inject it?"

"I already told you I don't know. Could have, but I got the idea he didn't like needles too much."

"I got the same feeling. I didn't see any needle marks on his arms, except the one that killed him."

"Not everybody shoots up in the arm," Paco said.

"True. But I'm willing to bet the coroner won't find evidence of it anywhere. We were talking when a car drove up, and he about went crazy. Tore out of my Impala and took off running."

"What kind of car?" Bert asked.

"Black Firebird. Tinted windows. Red-and-white flames on the hood and sides. Mexican plates."

"I don't know it." He turned to Paco. "Do you?"

"Nope. I mean, I've seen black Pontiacs, some of them Firebirds, in and out of here, but it's not a car I know."

"You have any friends who drive Firebirds?"

"Probably, but I don't remember anybody in particular."

Paco spoke in the American vernacular. No inflection, no mispronunciation, and no unusual syntax to identify him as a Mexican citizen. But then, he'd been educated in the Deming school system, so that wasn't surprising.

"Paco, do you mind if I ask you some questions? You too, Bert. Sometimes you don't realize you know something until you're asked a question."

The men exchanged glances before Paco leaned forward with his elbows on the table and laid his hands on top of his forearms. Had he just closed his stance? But his eyes met mine as he spoke. "Sure. It's okay."

Bert grunted, and I took that as agreement. I pulled out my small recorder and put it in the middle of the table, pretending to flick the On switch as I did and hoping they hadn't noticed it was already running.

"I record all of my interviews," I explained. "Saves trying to remember everything people say."

When neither man objected, I went through the ritual of stating who I was interviewing, the date, time, and place, and then started asking questions. I was interested in learning who might have a drug connection in the area—who might have supplied both Lopez and Martinson with weed or meth or anything else, for that matter. Beyond learning the names of a couple of friends or acquaintances, I got little for my efforts. Then Bert leaned forward and spoke in a low voice.

"Look, a lot of the stuff—you know, the recreational stuff—comes right out of that place where Liver Lips used to work, R&S Auto Repair over on South Iron. Hell, the police know it. The state cops know it. Even the DEA knows it. But if you ever say I told you, I'll deny it."

Rael sat up straight and motioned toward the recorder. "Dude, you just taped yourself telling him."

"Oh shit!" Bert said. He reached for the device but pulled his hand back abruptly. "Forgot about the damned thing. All right, BJ, I'm at your mercy. You keep me out of this, okay?"

"Sure." I brushed aside his concern. If this turned into a real case— as it appeared to be doing—the tapes would belong to my client, not to me. "Why don't they bust the joint if they know that?"

"They've tried," Paco said. "This local cop named Garza would like to pin Rybald's ears back, but he hasn't had any luck so far. Zack's penny ante, but he's got a sweet setup. Just about everybody in the county goes in and out of that shop from time to time. They leave their cars and trucks and vans, and who knows which ones are carrying the shit?"

I agreed. "You're right, it's a natural. But the authorities must realize that too."

"Yeah, but they don't know how to handle it."

"I met your boss."

Paco's features froze for a millisecond. "Yeah, who's that?"

"Actually he was Liver Lips' boss too. Hector Acosta."

"No shit. You met Don Hector?" His Spanish roots showed in the pronunciation of the last two words.

"I'm a history buff. All my life I've read about the Spanish dons, but I didn't realize they still used the title."

"Yeah, for men who have some respect, some standing. You know, like the local banker or a big ranch owner. Where'd you meet him?"

"I had dinner with him the other day. I knew Liver Lips used to work on his ranch, and when I learned he was in Cruces, I asked for a meet. He's a pleasant man. Good company."

"Yeah, he's great. Liver used to come down and help out with the gatherings. For such a scrawny shrimp, he was a damned good cook."

"Mr. Acosta said you were a good hand too. A good vaquero."

"I do all right. Don't embarrass myself on a horse. But I do more than haze cattle. He trusts me to run errands for him. Take deposits to the bank. Make deals for feed and with the veterinarian. You know, stuff like that. He had me running all over the place for him."

As Paco reached for his bottle of beer, I got the distinct impression he felt he'd let his mouth get away from him. He wasn't comfortable talking about his *patrón,* and I wondered why.

Chapter 11

LATER THAT afternoon I had the meal I'd missed by chasing down Bert and Paco and decided not to spend the night in the Border, switching to the motel near the police station. I gnawed on a greasy hamburger and some surprisingly good onion rings while I worked the phone. By the time night fell, I had talked to two more area duck farms and the largest poultry processing plant in the state.

While everyone agreed Millicent's flock was the best around for its down and pâté, she also had a decent income from the sale of eggs. And buyers were free to incubate the eggs and theoretically upgrade their own gaggle. Therefore, I was close to eliminating the improvement of a flock as a reason for the theft. However, that didn't exonerate other duck farmers completely. Maybe someone thought the loss of Super Duck would degrade Mud Hen's quality.

Colonel Guerrero had confirmed Acosta was known to wager a buck or two on horse races and dog races, so why not duck races? Guerrero had dug deeper into the rancher's finances and learned Acosta had a lot of money to risk on such ventures. One of the richest men in northern Mexico, he invested in cattle, gemstones, gold, banking. Everything he touched seemed to prosper. His latest venture was said to be an attempt to rejuvenate some depleted oil fields in southern Texas by deep drilling.

As I planned my next day, Charlie called. He sounded tired.

"You're working late." I glanced at my travel clock. Eight p.m.

"Just like you, I imagine. If it's true there's no rest for the wicked, then PIs must be evil sons a' bitches. I just picked up an e-mail from the guy we hired down in Florida to check out Hammond."

"He come up with anything?"

"I guess Kenny—everybody calls him Kenny down there—is as happy as a mouse in a cheese factory. Seems like Mud Hen cleaned his clock two years running. Some people claim she took close to a quarter of a million from him. That's probably an exaggeration, but it's serious money, that's for sure."

"Interesting."

"And that's not all. They say the two of them already made a king-size bet for the race coming up. And there's supposed to be a forfeiture clause."

"So if one party doesn't race, he—or she—loses the wager?"

"You got it."

"That's odd. Millicent isn't planning on going to Florida. She said there's no point in it since Quacky's gone. I wonder why she doesn't race another duck? That gives her better odds than simply forfeiting."

"Because she's got to race that particular duck against Hammond's—uh, let's see—Hammond's Thunder Duck."

"How can sane people be so crazy? She's a hardheaded rancher and businesswoman. I assume this Hammond's got some shrewds too. If he's a big-time Florida commercial developer, he's bound to have brains. But here they are making crazy bets. You can't handicap a duck race, for crying out loud. You can't even train the damned things."

"They must know something we don't. The word is this year's bet is a quarter of a million."

I whistled. "That's a hell of a motive."

"Right, but who for?" Charlie asked.

"I see what you mean. It could be that Hammond had the duck stolen to ensure he wins the bet. On the other hand, if the duck became sick or disabled—"

"Or dead," Charlie said.

"—or dead, Mud Hen could have had Liver Lips break in and steal the duck so the insurance company would cover her loss."

"That's the way I see it."

"Who knows about this bet?"

"Half of south Florida, I'd guess. I don't know about down where you are."

"I haven't picked up any whisper of it. I wonder if Bert knows."

"That's a good question."

"Yeah, and he's here in Deming tonight. He flew in this afternoon. He said something about a boy's night off."

"If he's like the cowboys I know, find the nearest dance hall," Charlie said.

"Or cat house."

"Sometimes it's kinda hard to tell the difference."

I got off the line to throw on some fresh clothes and look for the local country and western place. My cowboy boots and Stetson were in my bedroom closet at home, but I had a pair of black Levi's. A pale blue dress shirt sans tie and a pair of cordovan ankle boots rounded out an outfit that wouldn't get me thrown out of most places around here. If they looked like they were going to reject me, I could always find the nearest pasture and smear cow pies on my boots to add a little ambiance.

A SERVICE station attendant gave me directions to Lena's Nightclub, the local version of Albuquerque's C&W Palace. About half the size of the Duke City joint, it occupied a red-painted wooden building that looked like a Midwestern dairy farmer's barn but without the usual gambrel roof. I pegged it as a rowdy honky-tonk. After avoiding a parking lot full of vehicles—mostly pickups—by parking on a side street, I elected to walk the long block to the front of the place.

Lena's smelled and sounded like every other roadhouse I'd ever been in—except more so. The atmosphere… funky. These were working people, and some of them had apparently come straight from the field without bothering to clean off their boots. Human voices, shrieks, and laughter vied with the band for dominance. Sometimes one prevailed, and sometimes the other. Two beefy individuals stood just inside the door keeping a wary eye on everyone who entered. Bouncers. One probably spoke English and the other, Spanish.

The tiny entryway opened directly onto the bar, a long, curved, polished mahogany affair staffed by two bartenders and a barmaid working at high speed to keep bottles served and glasses filled for the denim-clad customers bending their elbows.

I nodded a friendly hello to anyone who might be watching and stepped toward the main source of activity, the big hall on the far side of the barroom. Pausing at the top of the three steps leading down into the nightclub itself, I took in the dance floor to my right. The sight of a double row of line dancers prompted a deep yearning for Paul. He would have been right at home here.

I shook off my mood as I spotted Bert Kurtz's lanky form on the floor opposite a trim blonde dressed in cowgirl duds. Her skirt looked to be made out of black-and-white cowhide—Herefords, I think they called them. Steady or casual? Casual. Bert struck me as a man who preferred playing the field.

Paco Rael danced next to his friend, his attention totally devoted to the small, raven-haired woman who swiveled her hips like she was doing flamenco. There is something almost hypnotic about watching line dancers. The men do their own thing in unison—more or less—while the women perform their dance, which is often different from, but oddly complementary to, their male counterparts'.

I tripped down the steps and took a small table near the dance floor. A waitress caught my order of Long Island iced tea, and I settled back in the chair to watch the goings-on. Both Kurtz and Rael were accomplished dancers. When the music ended to a round of applause and a few *yippie-ai-yo*s, the foursome made its way across the floor to a table almost directly opposite mine. They drank and talked and laughed while I debated crashing the party.

Before I came to a decision, a busty brunette walked up behind Bert, leaned over his shoulder, and kissed him on the cheek. He stood and embraced her, after which she greeted the other three with identical busses. She stayed only a few moments before waving good-bye and walking off.

As she broke free of the crowd and walked past my table, the band struck up a lively tune. I lurched to my feet and tapped her on the shoulder. She turned and gave me the once-over.

"Excuse me, miss. Would you take pity on a lonely stranger in town? One dance is all I ask."

She gave a bemused smile. "I think I can spare one."

"Thank you. My name is BJ."

"Okay, BJ, but I won't dance with you unless you promise to tell me what BJ stands for."

I returned her smile. "Fair wages for such arduous work. I don't line dance, but I can handle the fast two-step the trio's playing. When we're on the dance floor, I'll whisper the awful truth in your ear so no one else can hear. After I swear you to secrecy, of course."

She gave a low, throaty laugh and allowed herself to be led onto the floor. As soon as we began to move to the music, she told me her name was Laura Dowlinger and demanded payment.

"BJ stands for Burleigh J."

"Good Lord! Did your parents hate you?"

I took that to be an involuntary response and laughed. "No. It was my granddaddy's name, and the granddaddy before him."

"Oh. A family name. I guess that makes it okay, then. But that's only half payment." She arched an eyebrow.

"Oh, you mean the *J*. Well, back when I had a military ID, it read MIO."

"Middle initial only. My brother's Army."

"Good for him, but he'd be better off in the Corps."

"You were a Marine?"

"Semper Fi. I'm surprised you accepted my invitation to dance." I gave her a spin, bringing her closer into my arms.

"Why? You're a handsome man."

"Thank you, ma'am, and you're right pretty yourself. But that's not what I meant. I'm surprised your dance card isn't all filled up."

She fluttered a hand on my shoulder. "In case you haven't noticed, we don't have dance cards around here. And if we did, these bozos would try to play poker with them. That's all they know how to do with cards— of any kind." She glanced up at me. "Albuquerque? Denver? You don't have a Texas drawl, so I'm guessing north."

"Right the first time. Albuquerque. I'm just down here temporarily on a job."

"What kind of job?"

"I work for an insurance company."

"Well, fair warning. I don't need any."

I laughed. "I don't sell it. But if you wanted a great big policy, I'd probably have to make sure you aren't a dangerous criminal or on your deathbed before they wrote it up."

"Oh my goodness."

"You saved my life, I want you to know." We did another spin. "I don't know a soul here except for those two guys over there." I nodded toward the Kurtz table.

"Who? You mean Bert and Paco? Are they buying insurance?"

"I know them from elsewhere." Did her muscles stiffen beneath my touch? "I spent a little time down on the Lazy M," I explained casually. It had not been my imagination. The tension went out of her at my explanation. Had she thought I was DEA? "I guess they're pretty well-known around these parts."

"Everybody knows those two."

"I'm surprised Bert doesn't go to Lordsburg to play. Or over the border."

"Oh, he does that all right. If he wants to go on a real binge, he heads for Palomas. When he's on his schoolboy behavior, it's Lordsburg. But if he's only feeling a little wild, he comes to Deming. He has that whirlybird, so it doesn't take much longer to get here than it does to the other two places."

"So he plays a calmer game when he's in his own backyard?"

"You got it, cowboy."

"If he's looking for a semiwild party, can we expect some fireworks tonight?"

"Not necessarily. I mean, he doesn't tear up the place every time he shows up."

After the dance, Laura agreed to let me buy her a drink. I had apparently turned on a switch when I mentioned Bert Kurtz, because that's all she wanted to talk about as we sat at the little table and sipped alcohol. Her bobbed brunette hair picked up the strobe lights as she spoke. Laura was a pretty woman with high, smooth cheekbones and a generous mouth. She told me she and Bert had dated a few years back, but the relationship went nowhere, so she broke things off. Reluctantly, I gathered.

She reinforced what I already knew of Millicent's son: a hard worker, a hard drinker, and a hard fighter with a love-'em-and-leave-'em attitude.

She knew a little about Paco as well. They had also gone out together a couple of times, but it didn't take. She attributed it to the fact she was as tall as he was, something that bothered him, although it didn't matter to her. She went light about providing personal details. She painted Rael as a cipher—everyone knew him, but no one knew much about him, especially his life across the border. I suspected this vagueness was behind the nervousness I noticed on the dance floor when we first talked about the two men. Maybe because of his border straddling, she mentally connected Paco with the drug business. Or perhaps she knew something.

I kept probing, trying to elicit that something, until she took her leave, pleading she had to go to work early tomorrow morning. I had the distinct impression she would have welcomed me in her home had I been interested. After she left I wandered across the floor to the Kurtz table. Paco spotted me first. His quick frown turned into a fast smile.

"Well, lookie who's here. Hello, Mr. Vinson."

"Hello, Paco. I told you to call me BJ."

"Right, BJ. This here's Babs. It's really Barbara, but everybody calls her Babs."

"BJ," the petite, dark woman said softly, acknowledging my existence. The *J* came out something like "Zhay." Cute rather than pretty. Pert nose, sparkling eyes, small ears, and a gently pointed chin.

Bert rose and shook my hand. "Howdy, BJ. This one's Veronica. She won't let me call her Ronnie, so I guess we're stuck with Veronica. Right, honey?" He gave her shoulder a squeeze.

Veronica, who insisted on remaining Veronica, was pretty. Something only a little short of lovely, actually. She reminded me of a Swedish blonde with golden skin. But her twangy acknowledgment of my greeting was pure Texas.

Introductions done, Bert offered me a seat and insisted on buying me a drink. I switched to a mug of the local lager. More than one Long Island iced tea would have put me in the danger zone.

The night stretched out longer than I planned, but after three or four more dances, the women decided to repair their makeup. Paco tagged along to make a stop at the men's room, leaving Bert and me alone.

"Okay, BJ, what's up?" He leaned forward over the table and fixed me with a brown-eyed stare.

"Can't put much by you, can I?" I touched the button on the recorder hanging on my belt without much hope it would pick up anything other than the noise of the nightclub. "I've turned up something kind of disturbing and wanted your take on it."

"What's that?"

"Did you know your mother placed a sizeable bet on a duck race down in Florida? A bet with a forfeiture clause. Do you know what that means?"

"It probably means the insurance company will claim she got rid of Quacky to cover her losses. But hell, she's made more money on that duck than she'll ever lose. How much is the bet?"

I returned his stare. "A quarter of a million dollars."

Even in the semidarkness of Lena's Nightclub, I saw the flush rise up out of his collar and creep over his startled features.

Chapter 12

A CONFIDENTIAL investigator's job is to collect facts, not to spin the meaning of them, although I've been known to violate that concept a couple of times. Once the $250,000 bet with the Florida real estate developer surfaced, I could have filed a report that would make Del's friend at the insurance company very happy and allow me to claim my assignment was over. But in my eyes that would be a job only half-done. I needed to talk to Millicent again, and I didn't want to do it by telephone. The mileage log on this case was beginning to look like the state's budget deficit this year.

I decided to undertake the trip without letting anyone know I was on the way. I took I-10 west out of Deming and caught Hwy 81 south at Hachita and headed down toward Antelope Wells—where there are neither antelope nor wells. I kept an eye out for the ranch helicopter but saw no sign of it. Either Bert got underway early, or else he had cut across Mexican airspace, but either way he was probably already home or well on the way.

His shock at my revelation at the club had been profound. A quarter-of-a-million-dollar loss would impact the family ranch operation in a significant way. Mother and son were headed for a showdown with blood on the floor. Hyperbole, of course. Hopefully.

At high sun, I turned down the gravel road to the ranch house. As soon as the house came into view, it was obvious something was going on. Vehicles littered the front yard, mostly pickups, some with extended cabs and dual rear wheels—vehicles made for hard driving over rough territory. Some sported ranch brands on their sides. It looked like a meeting of the local cattlemen's association.

On a hunch, I did not ring the doorbell but detoured around the side of the building toward the back. Halfway there I heard the growl of voices, angry voices. I rounded the corner and came to a halt. A broad, shaded patio spanned the length of the building. Approximately a dozen men and a couple of women perched on padded outdoor chairs and lounges.

Millicent and Bert sat at a glass-topped table littered with bottles of booze, apparently presiding over the group. Everyone's attention was centered on a stubby, pot-bellied man with wisps of white hair and a very big voice.

"I already spent ten grand on fixing the fences and cleaning up after the bastards. Before the year's out, they'll eat up all my profits and leave me in the hole… again."

Aha, this was a meeting to address the ranchers' problems with immigrants trespassing on their property.

"Tom, we're all in the same boat," Bert said. "That's why I asked everybody to meet here. We can't count on the Border Patrol. We can't count on any of the Feds. Locals either. We gotta take things into our own hands."

"Hell, Bert, what can we do? All my boys already tote iron, but that's just for protection. Ain't a man on my spread that ain't been shot at or threatened. On my own land!"

Bert spotted me and laid a hand on his mother's arm. As soon as her gaze focused on me, she bounced out of her chair.

"BJ, what are you doing here?"

"Needed to talk to you again, but I see you're in the middle of something."

She turned to her guests. "Folks, this is Mr. B. J. Vinson. He's a private investigator out of Albuquerque. Maybe he has some thoughts on this subject."

She introduced me around. The man who had been speaking turned out to be Tom Blackthorn, the owner of a large spread to the south of the Lazy M. The others were all ranch owners or managers as well. Then I listened while Bert explained.

The Boot Heel ranches bordering the state of Chihuahua were in a state of crisis. This area was one of only four major stretches of the US-Mexico border not fortified with electronically monitored steel fencing. As Millicent had noted on my last visit, the strands of barbed wire and the occasional obelisks actually marking the border were funneling the illegal smuggling activity right through their property. "Like herding cattle through a pasture gate," as Tom Blackthorn put it.

To a man—and woman—these ranch owners were facing ruinous expenses from fouled water supplies, break-ins and thefts, litter, rustling, and the slaughter of livestock—not to mention coming across the occasional corpse of some poor immigrant. Cut fences were an expected way of life now. One rancher reported a windmill toppled and another burned, acts of vandalism. Whenever confronted, the *traficantes* escorting these trespassers displayed weapons threateningly or actually fired on the cowpunchers. The flood of drugs and illegal immigrants upset the delicate ecosystem of the Chihuahuan desert. The heavy presence of the Border Patrol and militia groups that sometime showed up put an additional burden on the land.

Now the Lazy M and its neighbors were contemplating forming their own resistance group to fight the growing problem. One of the owners claimed to have enough influence to get cowboys from each of the outfits sworn in as county deputies.

"Gentlemen… and ladies," I said when they ran down and looked to me for a reaction, "this is outside of my area of expertise, but it strikes me that if you have enough influence to deputize your help, you surely have enough juice to get some official aid with the problem. Sometime back our governor, along with other border chief executives, sent troops from the National Guard to patrol the border. Perhaps you can prod him into doing it again. Your cattlemen's association likely has the ear of your congressional delegation. I'd be sure those avenues were fully explored before putting your help, your families, and yourselves at risk by armed confrontation."

"We've done all of that. Every last thing you suggested," Bert said. "We get a few more Border Patrol in the area for a while, and then it dies off again. We need something to let the bastards know we mean business."

"Now, Bert," his mother said, "maybe we should listen. There's a virtual war going on over there, and we don't need to import it over here."

One of the other owners, a man introduced as Pierce Chavez, spoke up. "Hell, Mud, if the Mexican Army and National Police are giving them fits down there, it's exactly the time to shut down the highway to the North Forty-Eight." Chavez, a portly man in his fifties with a two-day beard, looked more like one of his own cowpunchers than a prosperous rancher. He munched a dead cigar, perhaps from agitation. Or maybe it was his way of chewing tobacco.

"How are you going to compensate your hands' families when one of them gets himself killed in a shootout with the traffickers and coyotes?" Millicent asked.

Chavez stuck to his guns. "Same way we do it when they get killed for being in the wrong place at the wrong time. A little insurance and the rest out of our pockets. I'd sooner go broke that way than this."

"Well, speaking for the Lazy M, I don't want any part of it."

An angry murmur went around the group. Somebody uttered a particularly nasty vulgarity—the other woman present, I think. And then I understood. This wasn't Millicent's meeting; it was Bert's. He'd called the group together to discuss their mutual problem, and now his mother had sabotaged him.

"What're you planning on doing, then?" Blackthorn demanded.

"Mending fences, moving my livestock to acreage across the highway, and watching out for my own fanny until Washington gets the message and does what they oughta done all along."

"Mud Hen, you know full well what it'll take to get them assholes to moving. They'll wait until some poor rancher's whole family gets massacred," Chavez said.

"Any volunteers?" Millicent asked.

If she intended to break up the meeting, she'd found the perfect way. The group streamed into the house and out the front door like a herd of puckish buffalo. I heard Bert assure some of them his mother would come around. Within sixty seconds flat, Millicent and I were alone on the patio.

"Okay, what's going on?"

She leveled her opal gaze on me a moment before responding. "What are you going to recommend to the insurance company?"

"I don't recommend. I report facts. Can I take it Bert told you I've found the two-hundred-fifty-thousand-dollar bet with the forfeiture clause?"

"Yes, and when that shithead Hank Grass hears about it, you know he'll make a recommendation. My claim will be denied. I'll not only lose my sweetie-pie, I'll lose a lot of money too."

"You can always sue. You need an attorney before you do anything else."

"Even if I win, that'll just cut my losses in half. The lawyer will take the rest of it."

"Then—"

A tornado interrupted me. Bert stormed out of the house and stood in front of his mother, seriously invading her space.

"What the hell was that?" he demanded. "You agreed to the meeting. We've planned it for a week, and then in one minute, you cut me off at the knees. Why?"

Millicent motioned to me. "You heard what the man said. He made—"

"Oh no you don't! You can't blame this on BJ. He started off saying he didn't know what the hell he was talking about. You just latched on to his idiot suggestions to do what you wanted to do all along. What I want to know is why?"

Despite being called an idiot, I was interested in her answer. But she just rehashed the argument that it was too dangerous to pit their armed men against the smugglers' armed men. Then she firmly terminated the conversation and started inside.

"I'll have to talk to you again before I leave, Millicent. I have no interest in doing you harm, but I have to state the facts as I know them. Let's make sure your position is fully covered before I give my final report, okay?"

"Very well. I have to make a few phone calls, and then we'll talk." She turned and went into the house in that mannish yet somehow womanly stride.

Bert watched her disappear through the door, eyes smoldering. Then he turned to me, his face still flushed. "Look, I didn't mean to call—"

"Never mind that. Let's see if we can figure out what's going on. You said she agreed to this meeting with the other ranch owners. Why? She has a well-earned reputation of going it alone. She's not known for cooperating with anybody. If nothing else, my investigation has convinced me of that."

"Yeah, but this is bigger than anything we've ever faced. I'm not kidding, this thing has been building for quite a while, and it's about to boil over. What Tom Blackthorn said is absolutely true. Our people have been shot at. Somebody's going to get killed no matter what we do. If I've got to die, I'd rather do it defending my ranch. Everybody feels that way, even the hired hands. Hell, especially the hired hands. They're the ones out there stumbling across the smugglers and the drug mules."

I took a seat at a table and steepled my fingers. Bert sat opposite me. "When did you get back?"

"I left Lena's right behind you. I went straight to the airport and flew home. I wasn't planning on staying overnight anyway because of the meeting. But what you told me about that bonehead bet shook me up. Ranching has seen better economic times, and things get a little harder every year. That's why the damages the smugglers and the illegals are causing are so important. It could put some of us under. And the loss of a quarter of a million could do it to the Lazy M."

He leaned back in his chair and dry washed his face. "Damn, BJ, the insurance company's gonna use the bet to invalidate the policy. They'll claim the duck got sick or died, and she had the carcass stolen to trigger a payoff to cover her losses."

I nodded. "But it could also be someone else had the duck stolen to make sure the bet forfeited."

"You mean this Florida developer, Hammond?"

"That's a possibility. Or maybe somebody else has a stake in the bet. He could have put together a group of people to raise the money. Or there could be similar side bets. That's why I told your mother she needed an attorney for this. Tell me, did you see the duck the night Liver Lips took her?"

"No. I seldom go down to the duck pens. That's Mud's personal preserve. Luis is the only one who works the ducks with her, but you've already talked to him."

"No one else saw anything that day or night?"

"Hell, everybody saw something that night. When those ducks started caterwauling, every hand on the place turned out with pistols drawn. But I've questioned everyone on the ranch, and nobody admits to seeing anything out of the ordinary earlier in the day."

"Let me talk to Luis again, since he's down at the duck pens more than anyone else. Maybe I missed something when I interviewed him before. Look, the insurance company has to have a solid reason for denying the claim, and your mother's bet gives them a legitimate arguing point. I know I work for the other side, but I collect and document information fairly, regardless of which way it cuts."

Bert rested his elbows on the chair arms and mimicked my finger steepling. "Okay, talk to Luis. Ask him whatever you want. He's an honest guy. However it is, that's the way he'll tell it. But none of this explains what just happened."

"You mean Millicent sabotaging the meeting? No, it doesn't." I thought for a moment. "What if the duck wasn't stolen because of the race?"

"What do you mean?"

"Maybe we shouldn't simply assume the race was the motive."

His brow creased. "What other reason could there be?"

"How about a personal grudge? She's not the most popular rancher in these parts."

"True, but those guys get their pound of flesh by beating her to the market and making a sharper deal. I don't know anybody who'd try to sink the Lazy M this way."

"Maybe they didn't know about the bet. Or about the insurance. Besides, your mother is convinced someone could have taken the duck in order to upgrade an inferior flock or to degrade hers."

He shook his head. "That's a stretch, isn't it?"

"When you get right down to it, insuring a damned duck for quarter of a mil is the stretch."

Bert had no answer, so he went to find Luis Rael.

WITH MY statement from Luis, both written and taped, in my pocket, I found Millicent in her office standing at the window. She did not acknowledge my presence for a long minute. Finally she spoke.

"What do you want to know?"

"I have a statement from Luis Rael saying the duck was alive and well as late as 5:00 p.m. on the day Liver took her."

She dropped into her chair and swiveled to face me. "That ought to mean something."

"Perhaps, but he's a paid employee."

"That doesn't mean he'll lie for me. Luis is his own man." She fell silent as she brushed her blotter with the edge of her hand. Agitation or resignation? "I have nothing else to offer. If my word and Luis's statement aren't enough, there's nothing I can do. If we're finished, I have to attend to something."

"Have you been contacted?"

"About Quacky? No." She looked at the ring on her left finger and then rubbed the faceted diamond absently.

"What are you going to do about your bet with Hammond?"

"What can I do? I've talked to him twice. Told him what happened. Asked him to be a gentleman and release me from the wager."

"And?"

"He refused. Kenneth Hammond is no gentleman." She laughed bitterly. "Of course, he'd say I'm no lady."

"Oh, I think you are. I think you're a hell of a lady, Millicent."

A bit of spark came back. She straightened her spine and eyed me frankly. "That makes you a minority of one."

"You can refuse to pay the bet. I doubt a court would uphold Hammond's claim."

"I suspect he can find one that will. You see, the wager is in writing and witnessed."

"I'll need a copy of it."

She squinted. "You're asking me to sink my own ship."

"Now that I know it exists, I have to ask for it. You can give it to me, or you can give it to GSR's attorney."

She sat silently for a moment before taking a two-page document from the bottom drawer of her desk and running off a copy.

I thanked her as I accepted the paperwork. "For what it's worth, an illegal bet is hard to enforce legally."

"Believe me, Hammond will see that I pay—one way or the other. Just as I would if the tables were turned."

"Do you have anything else to tell me?"

"No. I have to go now, BJ." She glanced out of the window. "I see Luis has my gelding saddled. I have something to check out down at the City."

"The City?"

"Have you been to the City of Rocks State Park north of Deming?" When I shook my head, she continued. "It's something to see. As the name implies, it's a city made of stone, complete with streets and alleys."

At my doubtful look, she explained. "They say that about thirty-five million years ago, a big volcanic eruption called the Kneeling Nun spewed lava and ash and pumice for 150 miles. Over time, wind and rain and freezing and thawing have shaped it into what it is today, something that looks like a big damned city made out of solid rock sitting right out there in the middle of the desert.

"Well, when the Kneeling Nun blew, she threw some of that same stuff over on our patch of ground. It's not as big as the one at the park, but when my grandpa first laid eyes on it, he said it looked like a damned city made out of rocks. It's more the size of a village, of course, but Gramps always thought on a bigger scale, so he called it a city. The City of Rocks. When they made that place north of Deming a state park in 1952, my daddy thought about putting up a fuss since his family used the name first, but he never got around to it. So they've got their City of Rocks up there, and we've got our own down here. You should see it sometime."

"I will, but right now I need to head back to Albuquerque. I've got to wrap this thing up. Good luck to you, Millicent."

"Tell me something, cowboy. Do you think I had Quacky stolen because of the bet?"

"It doesn't matter what I think, Millicent, but for whatever it's worth—I don't."

"Good."

I stood at the window in the cavernous living room and watched as she mounted and rode off toward the southeast. She and the big piebald named Rufus she rode looked as if they were a single unit. Before they passed out of my line of sight, I noticed she had a rifle scabbard strapped to the saddle forward of her right knee. The boss toted iron just like the hands.

On the drive up to I-10, I called the office and told Hazel I was on the way back. I asked Charlie to get his hands on police and credit reports on Hammond and his ventures… anything that might warrant his stealing his opponent's racer.

For good measure, I asked Charlie to see if he could find out if the Florida developer did his high-stakes gambling on his own or with a group of cohorts. Unless I could find someone desperate enough to commit a felony to avoid a large loss, then Millicent's goose was cooked, and that was no pun.

As I pressed on north, the realization I would see Paul this evening made it hard to keep my foot off the accelerator. To combat the urge, I set the speed control, something I do not ordinarily do. I like the feeling of controlling things too much to rely on that equipment.

I inserted a fresh tape into my recorder and put my thoughts down for the record. I reviewed everything I knew. Something wasn't adding up. Millicent Muldren was a fighter, a brawler, a mud hen. She wouldn't stand for someone getting on her high side without putting up a hell of a fight. That resolve had shown quite clearly in my earlier meetings with her.

But today she seemed a different woman. She had agreed to a meeting with the neighbors and then poked a hole in the community balloon. She seemed almost distracted. I could come up with only two reasons for this behavior. Either she had given up, or someone had contacted her about her duck. And Mud Hen Muldren was no quitter. Had she lied to me again?

I had just picked up I-25 North at Las Cruces and left the city behind when I glanced into my rearview mirror and spotted a state police car roaring up behind me with lights flashing.

Chapter 13

I CHECKED my speedometer. Sixty-five right on the money, but there was no question the patrol car zeroed in on me. Then my hands-free cell went off.

"BJ," Hazel's voice filled the passenger compartment, "there's been a shooting at the Lazy M Ranch, and they want you to come back. The state police have been alerted to flag you down."

"One's on my tail right now." I signaled a right turn and pulled off onto the shoulder of the freeway. "Who got shot?"

"I don't know. Some woman called, but she was all excited, and her English wasn't too clear. All I know is someone got shot."

"That must have been Maria. As soon as I find out what's going on, I'll let you know. I left a message on Paul's phone saying I'd be home tonight. If I have to go all the way to the ranch, there's not much chance I'll make it back. Will you let him know the plans have changed?"

She agreed and hung up. I lowered the window as a black-uniformed patrolman got out of his unit and walked toward the Impala. Apparently he hadn't been briefed on the situation, because he approached warily, with his hand hovering near his pistol. I waited him out. Sudden moves made cops nervous on traffic stops.

"Mr. Vinson?" He halted at the side of my car, standing back slightly so I had to crane my neck to see him clearly. Young, probably no more than a few months out of the academy. His eager, earnest appearance would erode with a little experience on the job. His name tag read Dorman.

"That's right."

"Do you have some ID, sir?"

"Sure." I dug out my driver's and PI licenses.

"Thank you." He examined both carefully before returning them. "Sir, the Hidalgo County Sheriff wants you to meet one of his deputies at...." He leafed through a pocket notebook. "Uh, at the M Lazy M Ranch. That's—"

"Yes, I know where it is. I just left there a couple of hours ago. Did he say why?"

"All I know is there's been an incident."

"All right, I'll turn around at the next opportunity, or are you supposed to take me in the cruiser?"

"No, sir, but I'll lead you to the next turnabout a mile dead ahead. You stay on my tail until we get to Las Cruces, okay?"

"Lead the way."

As soon as we were headed south on I-25, he poured on the gas. We approached the City of Crosses at considerably more than the posted speed limit. He slowed somewhat at the I-10 junction but picked it up again on the way out of town. Just shy of where Liver Lips Martinson died in his pickup, the patrolman pulled to the side of the road and waved as I breezed past him.

Maria answered one of my repeated calls to the ranch, but she was hardly intelligible, so I turned down the road to the ranch house, still in the dark about what had happened. Bert's blue-and-white Corvette and Millicent's gray Lincoln Mark S sat between a Hidalgo County Sheriff's unit and an EMT emergency response vehicle. A black Ford Escort in the corner of the yard had a medical doctor's medallion on its rear bumper.

Maria answered the door and waved me inside, apparently too distraught to speak. A ruddy-faced man in his forties with bristly red hair, carrying about twenty excess pounds on his uniformed, five-ten frame met me in the hallway.

"I'm Deputy O'Brien, Mr. Vinson. I think we spoke on the phone the other day."

"Yes, I remember. Can you tell me what's going on?"

"It's Bert." Millicent came into the room, still dressed in the riding clothes she'd worn that morning. There were splotches of dried blood on her skirt. The hyper Yorkie yapped in the distance, obviously outraged at being penned up in the office. "He's been shot."

"How badly? I mean…."

"He's not dead, but right now I don't know much except he has a concussion from a near miss or even a grazing shot. He's lost a lot of blood. You know how head wounds bleed. The doctor's still in there with him. The old goat threw me out."

Millicent took a deep breath before filling me in. When she had arrived at the ranch's miniature City of Rocks that afternoon, she expected to meet someone, but the place was deserted. She dismounted from her gelding, Rufus, and waited for about half an hour. No one showed, but she heard Bert's helicopter off in the distance a couple of times. Just as she prepared to give up and return home, the whirlybird approached from the north and dropped down for a landing. She squinted against the dust storm it raised and fought to hold on to her skittish mount as her son killed the engine and scrambled out of the machine. She knew from his stiff-legged gait he'd spotted Rufus and come for a showdown.

Halfway to where she waited, he suddenly halted and looked to his left. Almost at the same moment, a gunshot rang out. Bert pitched over into the dirt. Rufus, already nervous because of the chopper, bolted for home as she rushed to her son. He bled from a head wound, but he was alive. She pulled off her bandana and bound the wound as tightly as possible.

After using her cell to phone the emergency operator for help, she called the ranch house to let Maria know what had happened. Then she cradled Bert's head in her lap until Luis arrived in a ranch pickup. Two of the Lazy M's hands showed up hard on his heels. The men lifted Bert into the bed of the truck before the cowboys took off for the City to search for bushwhackers. Millicent rode in the back of the truck, clutching her son to her breast as Luis raced for the house over the rough track.

"Will he be all right?" I asked.

"The doctor says he should recover in a few days."

"Millicent, I'm sorry to hear what happened, and I'm thankful Bert isn't seriously hurt. But I don't understand why the sheriff's office had me stopped by the state police and sent back here. I'm not involved in this."

I spoke to her but held the eye of the deputy, who responded to my question. "Mud insisted I get you back."

"Why?"

"Because of this." O'Brien handed over a clear plastic envelope containing a tatter of white paper.

"That note makes it your business," Millicent said.

The scrap of lined tablet paper was the kind every grade school kid in the country used. Printed block letters dug into the surface as if the pen had been pressed to the paper unnaturally hard.

YOU WANT SEE YUR DUCK. CALL OFF RANCHERS MEET. YOU DONT YOU BE SORRY. SOME BODY CLOSE TO YOU PAY. BE AT CITY NOON TOMORROW. ALONE. NO TRICKS OR SOMEBODY DIE. DONT TELL NOBODY.

"Do you recognize the handwriting?" I asked.

"No," Millicent answered.

"The language is awkward. There are missing words and some misspellings. The punctuation is nonexistent except for periods."

"Like a foreigner," Deputy O'Brien said.

"Or a semiliterate," Millicent said.

"Or more probably someone faking it to keep us guessing." I turned to the deputy. "I assume you have a lab that can process this?"

"Yeah. The state police will give us a hand."

"When was it delivered?"

"I found it yesterday afternoon," Millicent said.

"Yesterday?" My blood rose, but I tamped it down. "Found it where?"

"Pinned to a wall down at the duck incubation shed." She pointed to the hole torn in the upper left-hand corner. "It had been forced over a nail."

"No one saw a stranger on the property?"

She shook her head.

"That argues it was an inside job. Could Luis have put it there?"

"No! He wouldn't do that to me. He and Maria have been with us for years."

"I understand he's the only one you allow in the duck pens."

"The other hands shortcut through them occasionally. They catch hell if I see them, but they do it when they're in a hurry to reach the house from the corral behind the pens. Besides, it wouldn't be hard for an outsider to sneak onto the property."

"You didn't hear the birds put up a racket?"

"They don't always, especially if you move slowly and quietly. And the part of the shed where the note was pinned wasn't inside the fence with the ducks."

Millicent admitted both Luis and Maria could read and write English but insisted neither could have been responsible for the note. O'Brien offered to take writing samples from everyone on the ranch.

"Including Bert and Mrs. Muldren," I said. The deputy gave me a penetrating look. "To properly exclude them. It'll save time later in the investigation." I didn't know how much—if anything—Millicent had shared with the deputy about the bet or the insurance.

"Makes sense, but Bert's not gonna be writing anything for a day or two. Leastways, nothing that's gonna look like his writing."

"I'm sure you can find samples somewhere in his desk." I reread the note. "Millicent, this tells you to meet the writer at the City at noon. How many people know about this other City of Rocks?"

"A lot of people, I guess. Probably everybody in the Boot Heel."

"I heard about it as a little kid," O'Brien said.

"Millicent, you lied to me," I said. "Again. You denied being contacted."

"I know, and I apologize. But the writer said not to tell anyone."

"So you just rode off to meet a possible duck thief threatening bodily harm to someone close to you without a thought for your own safety?"

Her eyes widened. "Why would anyone harm me?"

"That depends on why the duck was stolen in the first place." I held up the glassine envelope containing the note. "So this is why you wrecked Bert's meeting?"

She dropped onto one of the big sofas in the living room. Her boots sank into the thick bearskin rug. O'Brien and I took the couch opposite her.

"Yes, it is. I encouraged Bert to take the night off in Deming. Usually I disapprove, but I halfway hoped he'd get drunk and oversleep. But you shook him up with your news, and he came back later that night. Before he did, I'd already called around trying to cancel the meeting. I managed to reach some people, but the rest were either out of touch and didn't get my message, or else ignored it."

"And I walked in on the meeting just in time to give you an excuse to back out of cooperating. What would you have done if I hadn't appeared?"

"I'd have found a way."

At that moment a tall, bespectacled man in his early fifties walked into the room. Millicent introduced him as Dr. Mullens, the family's longtime physician. He acknowledged me briefly.

"The EMTs left," he told Millicent. "I wanted Bert to go to the hospital up in Lordsburg overnight, but the mule-headed son of a gun refused to go. I practically told him he was gonna die if he didn't, but he just dug in his heels. Reminds me of his father. Ren was just as pigheaded." After venting, he turned professional. "Mud, Bert's not badly hurt but he's lost some blood. Not enough to worry about. He's got a mild concussion, so I don't want him to sleep too long until his headache goes away. He can nap off and on, but he needs to wake up now and then to keep from falling into a coma. I left some pain medication."

"What's the extent of his wounds?" O'Brien asked.

The doctor placed an index finger just back of his left temple. "There's some damage in this area. Don't think the bullet actually struck him, but came close enough to knock him silly. Might have hit his head on a rock when he fell. That would account for the blood. Kinda strange, really. Mud said he was walking toward her and suddenly stopped cold in his tracks and looked off to his left. I'm no expert on trajectories, but it looks to me like it wouldn't have done more than singe his haircut if he'd kept on walking. Wonder why he stopped?"

"Didn't he tell you?"

"I haven't questioned him. He hasn't exactly been coherent until now."

"You saying someone missed him on purpose?" O'Brien asked.

The doctor pulled a face. "I don't know what I'm saying. That's not my field. It's yours."

"I gotta go question him, Doc. I need some answers."

"Take it easy on him, O'Brien. Keep your questions to a minimum. You can always talk to him tomorrow. You oughta be out looking for the shooter, anyway."

"Got a man out there now. And three of the Lazy M hands to boot. They found the spot where the bastard fired from. It wasn't in the City, by the way. Off to the east."

"Mexican?" Mullens asked.

"Not necessarily," O'Brien said. "If it was me done the shooting, I'd hightail it for the border. None of our lawmen's gonna cross over there. I'd just hike up the fence a spell and reenter the US wherever I wanted."

"Damned fortified fence," the doctor said. "Either build the blessed thing from one end of the border to the other or else don't build it at all. It just herds the stampede right at us."

I suspect the good doctor spoke for many of the border residents.

When we trooped into his room, Bert lay on the bed looking strangely vulnerable for such a tough man. A startlingly white bandage circled his head, making the brown hair leaking over it appear almost black. His skin, however, had lost some of its robust color. His eyes fluttered a couple of times before he focused.

"Sneaking in a nap, were you?" the doctor asked. "Remember what I told you. Naps are okay, but for short periods of time until the headache's gone."

Bert took a look at each of us. His gaze stopped on me. "BJ, what are you doing here?"

"Sheriff hauled me back. Wanted to know if I'd ambushed you."

He winced as he shook his head. "Wrong fellow. Complexion's not dark enough."

"So you saw the bushwhacker?" O'Brien asked.

"No. But the shot came from Mexico."

"Damned near it. You up to telling me what happened?"

Bert had to stop to rest now and then, but the story slowly emerged. He had been furious with his mother about the meeting with the other ranch owners, and the longer he thought about it, the madder he got. When he finished checking on some of his hands who were moving cattle from a pasture abutting the border to one across the highway, he started back to headquarters. On the way he spotted Millicent's piebald gelding at the edge of the City. Puzzled over why she was there, he decided to check her out. Besides, it was a perfect place to have a showdown—nobody around to put a leash on their tongues.

He landed far enough away to keep from spooking Rufus, shut down the engine, and started walking toward the City. Out of the corner of his eye, he caught a flash of light bright enough to make him halt and look for the source. After that everything went blank.

"You think the flash he saw was the gunshot?" the doctor asked.

"How far away was the shooter?" I asked the deputy.

"My man figured a couple of hundred yards."

"At that range he wouldn't have time to see the muzzle flash. It was probably the metal gun barrel or sunglasses. Whatever it was, it may have saved his life." I reconsidered my answer. "Or damned near took it."

Chapter 14

MILLICENT AND I imitated Mexican jumping beans as a lanky cowboy with an East Texas drawl floorboarded the pickup across the flatlands southeast of the ranch house, jerking the steering wheel this way and that to avoid creosote bushes and clumps of mesquite but plowing right through broad swatches of wildflowers. The Lazy M driver, who had introduced himself as "Lynz"—which I took to be Linus—seemed glued to the seat.

More than once my cherry-red Lobo baseball cap tapped the roof of the compartment. The back of my head made regular contact with a Winchester .30-30 mounted on a rack over the back window. Millicent, riding in the middle, had less to hang on to than I did, but she sat as impassive as a bouncing block of stone. I expected her to call the driver down. She didn't. Apparently they drove this way down here. O'Brien and a crime scene deputy called Buck ate our dust in a Hidalgo County Sheriff's Explorer as we raced to the City of Rocks.

After five miles of torture, I spotted Bert's chopper sitting on the hardpan, where it would likely remain in splendid isolation until he was fit to pilot it again. Beyond the grounded bird, I glimpsed the City.

Although I had been prepared for the sight, it still startled me. From this distance the place appeared to be well named. It looked like a ten-acre cluster of buildings rising out of the desert floor. Not a city maybe, but a town—a ghost town. Linus ground to a halt, and once our trailing column of dust drifted past, I climbed out of the vehicle and checked to make sure all my various joints worked. A couple of doors slammed, and O'Brien and Buck joined us as we stood staring at the City. Then Millicent stepped forward.

With a Winchester under her arm, she brushed aside the wind-whipped crime scene tape supported by stakes driven into the dry earth and strode to a rusty stain on the ground fifty yards in front of the helicopter. Blood. Bert's blood. I glanced around. Linus also carried a rifle; Buck toted a shotgun. O'Brien had a large black semiautomatic handgun on his hip. I felt naked. My 9 millimeter rested in the trunk of the Impala.

"Best I can recall, the shot came from over that direction." Millicent pointed to the east.

"Little more to the south." Buck led us across the desert. "Here's where he stopped and took his shot. Wasn't a big man. Small boots, and his footsteps wasn't wide like a man Bert's size would be. I reckon him to be five nine or less." He indicated a couple of scooped-out spots where he'd taken casts of the prints.

There was little to see and less to find. The zephyr, virtually a constant in this open, exposed country, had obscured almost everything. If yellow tape hadn't marked the spot, I would not have been able to find where Bert went down. Nonetheless, we walked every inch of the place, following Buck—the entire forensics team, I gathered—as he explained what he and the Lazy M hands had found. He had taken photos before everything totally vanished beneath the force of the wind, so except for snapping shots of the blood-soaked spot, the helicopter, and a wide-angle view of the City of Rocks, my Minolta stayed on my belt. My recorder, however, played during the whole expedition.

"How do you figure it?" O'Brien's question took me by surprise.

"Did you ask Bert if he saw anybody besides his mother on his approach to the City?"

"Tried to ask him right after I arrived," O'Brien answered. "He said not, but I'm not even sure he knew the question. Too addled at the time. Haven't asked him since."

"Whoever was coming to meet Millicent saw the helicopter land and thought he'd been double-crossed. So he did what he'd threatened and tried to kill someone close to her."

"Makes sense to me."

I turned to Millicent. "The note tells us the writer knew about the planned meeting with the ranchers. But did anyone besides the people who were invited know it actually took place?"

"We're not exactly a closemouthed bunch. It's likely a lot of outsiders knew about it. Everybody on the Lazy M knew."

"Why does it matter?" O'Brien asked.

"Because if the shooter knew, he might have had an inside contact."

"Must not be too inside, or he'd have known the meeting fell apart," Millicent said.

"Has anyone checked out that rock pile over there?" I eyed the City.

"Yep," Buck answered. "The ranch hands and me went through it after we finished with the crime scene. Wasn't nobody there."

"Let's have a look." O'Brien hitched up his equipment belt and started walking. The rest of us trailed along behind.

The Lazy M's City of Rocks might have been smaller than the big one north of Deming, which measured about a mile across, but it was still impressive. Nature had laid out a tangle of fat, massive monoliths and slender pillars of stone precisely like a city or a town.

The brown and gray rocks had the look of weathered rhinoceros skin. Alleyways and streets and even a broad avenue meandered between buildings of solid rock with occasional stele that reminded me of Egyptian obelisks and Indian totems. Sporadic gusty currents whispered and whistled eerily across the frozen lava and hardened pumice, giving the air a dry, dusty smell. We found no sign of an intruder. The place was pristine—except for our own footprints.

Buck took us a quarter of a mile farther east to the fence where the shooter had slipped across the border into Mexico. I eyed the strands of taut barbed wire and turned to look back the way we had come. There seemed to be a faint trail in the sand, something more than just our recent passing.

"This wire looks new," I said.

"It is," Millicent answered. "It gets cut a lot. This is their highway, and we try to keep a close eye on it."

O'Brien shaded his eyes with his hand. "They likely cross and take shelter in the City before making their march to the highway, where somebody picks them up."

"It's got something else too. Water." Millicent waved toward a windmill a quarter of a mile to the north.

"Drug mules or coyotes?" I asked, meaning the humans who smuggle illegal aliens across the border.

"Both. Sometimes the Border Patrol will put a man in the City to watch for them, but then they just move up or down the line to another place. But this is their favorite."

I looked across the fence. "What's over there?"

"That's the Rayo. The Lightning Ranch."

"Hector Acosta's spread?"

She glanced at me. "Yeah. You know Heck?"

"Met him recently in Las Cruces. You?"

"Oh yes. Heck and I are old friends, old competitors." She rubbed the back of her neck, shifted the rifle under the other arm, and turned away.

Puzzled, I watched her walk back toward the vehicles, closely shadowed by Linus with his rifle at the ready.

O'Brien moved up beside me. "Mud has a long history with Acosta. Back in the old days, Acosta's daddy worked on the Rayo. There was a lot of across-the-border trading back then, so him and her sorta grew up together. There was talk at one time about those two getting hitched. That was before Ren, her husband, come on the scene, of course, and before Acosta went out and got rich and married that blonde show gal. They say he bought that ranch over there just because his papa used to work as a peon on it. Wasn't no vaquero; just worked digging ditches and cutting grass and the like. Acosta and Mud would've made a grand pair. Not sure which one woulda survived, but it woulda been a hell of a show."

"If they're old friends and rival ranchers, why don't they get together to keep the cartels from using their land? It seems like it would be easier to put a stop to it if both sides were plugged."

"The Mexican ranchers claim they're as helpless as we are to shut down the traffic. Maybe they are, and maybe they ain't. Or maybe they get paid to look the other way."

"Is that happening on our side too?"

"Not that I heard of. Our people are victims, not partners."

We piled into our vehicles and headed back to headquarters. Halfway there a small red-and-white Piper swooped overhead, wagged its wings, and nosed up to gain some altitude.

"Speak of the devil," Millicent said. "That's Heck Acosta's plane. Looks like he's come calling."

The craft circled over the ranch house once and then settled down. Apparently the wind sock I'd noticed near Bert's helipad had other purposes. The flat ground nearby served as a strip for small craft. As we drew closer, the bold streak of lightning painted on the Piper's tail left no doubt as to whose plane it was.

A khaki-clad Acosta stepped off the patio to greet us as we parked. He went straight to Millicent and engulfed her in a bear hug. "Mud, oh, Mud." He patted her gently on the back. "Now they're shooting our boys. How are you holding up?"

"I'm holding up just fine. Bert will be all right."

"Yes, I know. Maria tells me he grows stronger by the minute." He released her and turned to me. "BJ, we meet again. A pleasure to see you, but not under these circumstances, of course. I'm glad you were here to give Millicent some comfort." His eyes twinkled briefly. "Has anyone described you as a comforting presence before?"

"No, I'm mostly treated like a burr under the saddle."

"Deputy." He acknowledged O'Brien and nodded in Buck's direction. Linus had headed for the stables the moment we arrived.

"What are you doing here?" Millicent asked.

"I was in Cruces when I heard the news and came to see if I could help. Word has spread all up and down the state. Shocking! How did it happen?"

"Bert saw me out for a ride down by the City and landed his chopper to talk. As he was walking toward me, someone shot him—from over in your direction."

We moved inside, where Maria had prepared something to eat. Welcome news. I hadn't stopped in Cruces for lunch on the way to Albuquerque, and it now approached evening.

While Millicent went to change out of her bloody clothing, I snatched a moment to call Hazel at home. She put me on the speakerphone— so she could take notes, she claimed. She heard me out and promised to fill Charlie in tomorrow morning. Yeah, right. He probably sat right there listening to the whole conversation. They were still keeping their romance a secret—or so they thought. She agreed to call Del and give him a preliminary report.

Maria detained me a moment as I headed for the dining room. "You find my boy yesterday?"

"Yes. Caught him with Bert in Deming. I had a drink and a talk with them at Lena's."

Her broad mouth turned down, making her plump face almost comical. "*That* place."

The Lazy M's table was a little less democratic today. Neither of the Raels took a seat. Luis remained in the kitchen, and Maria, sporting a starched white apron, buzzed around serving everyone and showing Acosta undue deference. She called him "Don *Ector*." Linus and a couple of other hands wandered in to fill their plates and take them back to Bert's bedroom. A few moments later, we heard sounds of hilarity and good-natured ribbing from that direction.

"Best thing for him," Millicent said. "He sure as hell won't go to sleep while they're poking fun at him."

Heck dominated the dinner conversation. I suspected Millicent wouldn't have allowed that had she not been in a funk over her son's near-fatal shooting. The Mexican rancher gradually pulled her out of the doldrums by asking pointed questions about everything under the sun, including news about her prize duck. She shared neither the mysterious note nor the real reason she had been at the City that afternoon. The light from the wagon wheel chandelier caught in Acosta's lapel pin, periodically discharging rays like the bolt it represented.

I concentrated on my medium-rare steak and a boiled potato loaded with butter, chives, and sour cream. Chopped chili peppers spiced up the black beans. As I finished a helping of chocolate mousse, I realized I would need to take a long walk before retiring for the night. Millicent had offered a bed, and in view of the hour, I accepted.

After Acosta's plane lifted off in a blaze of bright lights, I walked through a black night eased by a canopy of impossibly brilliant stars and a moon lying low on the horizon. I slowed my brisk stride as a couple of shadows moved at the edges of my vision. Bruno and Hilda. Did the big Dobermans remember I was a friend?

Unless Millicent was capable of sacrificing the son of her loins for a damned duck—or more properly, for $250,000 she'd foolishly bet on a damned duck—then the theft appeared to be genuine. She was crafty but not venal. The handwritten note wasn't an outright ransom demand, but it looked to be the opening move in that direction.

What would have happened if Bert hadn't chosen to confront his mother at that exact moment? Would the situation have been resolved, or would Millicent be lying on an OMI slab up in Albuquerque right now? No. The note didn't threaten her, merely those close to her. Someone wanted something, and I suspected it was not money. What, then?

Whatever it was, the thing now pointed away from a duck race down in Florida. Although if the thief knew of the bet, he now realized he held five aces. Millicent would have to do almost anything demanded of her to avoid a quarter-of-a-million-dollar loss. I looked east toward a Mexico that lay invisible in the distance. The threat came from there.

But maybe the bushwhacker had just taken the Lazy M off the hot seat. If the note could be construed as evidence the duck had been snatched, then GSR would probably have to pay her claim. And Bert's shooting provided powerful evidence the theft was legitimate. I touched the jacket pocket holding a photocopy of the threatening message O'Brien had given me before he left.

When I returned from my walk, I looked in on Bert and contributed to the effort to keep him from falling into a coma until the danger of the concussion passed. He was having a hard time of it, especially since the pain pills Dr. Mullens had given him tended to make him drowsy. I put a fresh tape in my recorder and led him through everything before, during, and after the attack. Even though I gleaned little new information, I was satisfied on one point. Bert had known nothing about the mysterious note. Now that he knew of it, he cut his mother some slack about the ruined meeting with the ranchers.

After half an hour with Bert, I retired to my room to prepare for bed and to call home. The phone rang several times before a masculine voice answered. Not Paul's. Definitely not Paul's.

"Uh… is Paul there?"

"Yeah, sure, Mr. Vinson. He's coming in from the garage. He'll be here in a sec."

A moment later, Paul's throaty growl came across the line. "Hi, Vince. Thought you were gonna be home this evening."

"I sent you a message. Didn't you get it?"

"Yeah, Hazel called. But I'm still disappointed."

"Me too. Who answered the phone?"

"Oh, that was Niv. You know, Niven Pence, Mrs. Wardlow's great-grandson."

Gertrude Wardlow had lived across the street in a white brick for as long as I could remember. Tiny and in her seventies, she had an indomitable will. Both she and her dead husband, Herb, were retired DEA agents. She might look as if a puff of wind would blow her and her helmet of blue-white hair over backward, but she'd saved my butt when some thugs, unhappy with the way I was investigating a case, decided to shoot up my place. When she distracted them, they'd put a few rounds through her window, shattering the urn on her fireplace mantel and spilling Herb all over the living room carpet.

Then last year she had galloped to the rescue once again by yelling at a crazy man intent on beating my brains out with a ball bat in my own backyard. She and Paul had a special connection ever since she phoned 911 when she saw him kidnapped from in front of my place. On the few occasions she had been called upon to introduce him to someone else in our decidedly geriatric neighborhood, she'd judiciously called him my "boarder." I vaguely recalled her great-grandson, Niv, as a long beanpole with sandy hair and freckles.

"What's he doing over there?"

"When you backed out of coming home this evening, I promised Mrs. Wardlow I'd tutor him in English. He's a freshman at UNM this year."

"Oh." It came out flat.

Paul laughed. The bell tones of his baritone rang in my ear. "You're *jealous*! That's great. You're jealous of a freshman, yet."

"Not so loud. He'll hear you."

"He went back in the living room. I'm in your study."

"Anyway, I'm not jealous. Not much, anyway."

He turned sober. "Man, when are you coming home? I planned on wearing you out tonight."

"Probably tomorrow night. There doesn't seem to be much left for me to do down here."

"Hazel said somebody got shot."

"Yeah. A rancher by the name of Bert Kurtz. He's not hurt too badly, but it could have been fatal."

"You're not in any danger, are you?"

"Nope. They're not gunning for me this time."

We didn't chat for long, and after I hung up, I realized why—I wanted the English lesson over and done with and that skinny freshman out of the house as soon as possible. I trusted Paul implicitly, but it was impossible to rein in my galloping imagination.

Chapter 15

MY MOUNTING sense of anticipation crested at the sight of Paul's old Plymouth at the curb in front of the house on Post Oak Drive NW late Sunday afternoon. I'd been halfway afraid he would be gone, although he didn't have weekend classes at the U. I eased into the driveway and barely stopped long enough to retrieve my bag from the trunk before I mounted the back steps and let myself into the kitchen.

He was there, and like Maria last evening, he wore a white apron—albeit a more masculine one—and held a soup ladle in his left hand. The unmistakable aroma of green chili stew assailed my nostrils. My man had prepared a favorite dish to honor the return of his conquering hero. I registered the big, loopy grin on his face, dropped my bag, and rushed forward. We held one another close without speaking, taking comfort in the warmth of the act.

"Gotta let me go," he finally said. "The tortillas are browning, and you don't like them burnt."

I held him at arm's length and gazed into golden brown eyes filled with love and trust. "Man, it's good to be home."

And it was. I had lived my entire life in this house my father built and remembered every moment of it with ease and comfort. But it had never been as totally, as completely my home as in the past two years—after Paul became a part of my world.

When we sat down to Paul's stew, the words spilled out as we caught each other up on recent events. He won a freestyle race against the best athlete on UNM's swim team. Paul was great in the pool, but he seldom participated in organized aquatic events. Odd, because he was a competitive guy.

He claimed to have found the ideal dancing partner for his boot-stomping forays to the C&W Palace. A pert, vivacious blonde lesbian who loved dancing as much as he did. She had absolutely no designs on his lean, buff body. Perfect.

He was pumped by the approach of next Friday… his Emancipation Day. His second-session summer school classes ended that day, putting him that much closer to his master's degree. I'd hoped this would give him a little freedom for the rest of the summer, but he said he needed to work on his thesis. So little chance of that.

"Did you notice the paint job?" he asked as we pushed away empty stew bowls.

"I didn't take time to notice anything except your car out front."

He smiled. "There's a new coat of paint on the front trim and the fascia on one side of the house. The rest of it will be finished in a couple of days."

"I'm surprised you found the time."

"Not me. Niv Pence. When Mrs. Wardlow asked me to tutor him, I refused to take any money. But nobody gets out in front of that old gal, so Niv's painting all of the wood trim on the outside of the house. And doing a pretty good job of it too."

Finally sated with verbal conversation, we retired early to communicate in other ways, and I had the pleasure of studying the fascinating dragon tattoo on his left pec prowl with the movement of his torso.

"WELL, IT'S about time," Hazel announced Monday morning when I got to the office. I wondered if she referred to my being out of town longer than planned or to the late hour of my arrival. Probably both.

"Good morning to you too."

Hazel had been my mom's best friend—both of them were teachers—and my surrogate mother after my parents died in a car crash a few years back. She recently changed her hairstyle to something a little more… *puffy*… the only word I could think of. But it suited her. Her gold-framed glasses made her gray eyes seem bigger. The transition that began last year was now complete. She went from dowdy-dumpy to chic-dumpy. But perhaps a little less so. She'd lost a pound or two in the week I'd been away. I pecked her fondly on a powdered cheek.

Charlie peeked over her shoulder. "Welcome back. Everything all tied down on the Great American Ducknapping Case?"

"As tight as it's going to get." I handed Hazel my expense reports and asked her to prepare a bill for me to deliver with my final report to Del later.

"To Del? Don't you want me to send them to the insurance company?"

"No, this isn't the usual deal. GSR will probably end up paying our bill, but right now this seems to be a private arrangement between Del and the GSR VP. I'll give the report and invoice to him and let him sort it out."

"You want the bill or the report first?"

"You can start on the bill while I review the tapes and finish dictating the report. That shouldn't take more than a couple of hours. You can add that to the bill."

I was surprised they allowed me to go straight to my private office without assailing me with a myriad of details about other active cases. Maybe there weren't any other active cases. The question came into sharper focus when I found a couple of files containing completed reports and final billings. One, a missing daughter from Chicago, Charlie located living with a man in Old Town. The other was a background check on a potential upper-level manager for a public utility company. I read and signed off on them before settling down to work on the report to GSR.

Later, as Charlie and I sat in my office munching corned beef on rye sandwiches from the City Hall Deli, we talked over the current caseload while Hazel transcribed my dictated report. I was relieved to learn we had a full plate. Thanks to my friends at APD, I had plenty of referrals. So many, in fact, Charlie proposed bringing in Tim Fuller part-time. Tim, a retired APD sergeant with a PI license, helped us out now and then. I readily agreed to his recommendation.

When we finished, I left for my one o'clock appointment with Del at the Stone, Hedges, Martinez offices on the top floor of the Albuquerque Plaza two blocks down the street on Third NW. I stewed for a few minutes in their plush waiting room. The law firm had invested more money in the green travertine floor and the corded, overstuffed beige chairs and couches than I had in my entire office.

Finally, Del rushed in and apologized for keeping me waiting. The first sight of him always threw me. He never seemed to age. His sapphire eyes and fresh-scrubbed, boyish face seemed unchanged. Once we were seated in his elegant private office, rich with modern artwork and gleaming sculptures, we exchanged a few pleasantries before he speed-read my report. As he laid it aside and examined the invoice, his eyebrows climbed.

"What's this? A final bill? Isn't that a bit premature?"

"Why? The investigation's complete, as you can see from the report."

"But you haven't found the thief."

"So far as I'm concerned, I have. Liver Lips Martinson stole the duck on orders of one of the Mexican drug cartels."

"Why a drug cartel?"

"To intimidate Millicent and the other ranchers into allowing them free access."

"What about this Miami developer?"

"I don't believe he shoots people from the border. No, the cartels make more sense."

"Which cartel?"

"I don't know. And unless GSR is willing to pay a serious hazardous-duty premium, I'm not going to find out. The report is clear. It contains a copy of the extortion note Mrs. Muldren received."

"But that infers the duck is alive and presumably recoverable. Our client may be able to avoid a claim."

"I'll tell you what. You strap on a six-shooter and come with me, and we'll run those south-of-the-border banditos to earth. Del, these people were willing to kill her son just because they figured she double-crossed them by calling a meeting! What do you think they'll do to us if we go poking around on their turf?"

"You're sure the duck is across the border?"

"The duck or the duck's carcass. She's probably pâté by now. If it were you, wouldn't you take her where the American authorities can't reach you?"

He frowned as he aligned my invoice and report precisely in the center of his blotter. "I guess. Hank Grass isn't going to be happy."

"Even if the duck is alive, there is still no way to recover the insured's stolen property. So your good buddy, Hank Grass, is going to be held responsible for his own actions. Why in the world would he insure a damned duck for such an outrageous amount, anyway?"

"No idea. Oh well, I'll submit this to him and see what he says."

"In the meantime I will consider my assignment at an end."

He seemed inclined to talk, but I'd been away from the office for several days and needed to get some work done. I took the elevator down to the ground floor and exited the Plaza by the Third Street door. I turned left, and as I reached the corner of the Hyatt Regency, I noticed someone had tied a yellow ribbon around the outstretched finger of the construction foreman, one of the nine bronze statues of the Sidewalk Society. Had some of our boys returned from Iraq? Hopefully the whole cockeyed nonsense had ended while I wasn't paying attention.

I made another left and walked back to my office. It felt good to be home as I settled into my comfortable chair and picked up the file Hazel had left on my desk. So far as I was concerned, I'd be happy if another out-of-town job never crossed my desk.

The case Hazel had elected to give me was a personal-injury lawsuit filed by a fellow named Jordan Carl Vermillion, a fifty-two-year-old college-educated man who claimed to be unable to work due to a back and neck injury caused by tripping over some shoe boxes in Strother's Clothiers, one of Albuquerque's upscale men's shops. He had taken a tumble over the Independence Day weekend, an accident witnessed by several other shoppers and half the store's staff.

My problem with the case? This was not his first such accident. Hazel's online check of the state judiciary records showed he'd had a similar incident the prior year, that time in a big-box store. My natural paranoia came to the fore when I noticed the previous accident had occurred almost precisely one year ago.

I examined his bland, unremarkable face in the photograph the store's surveillance camera captured. It had a bloated look. Deep laugh lines framed the mouth, running from nose well down into the chin area. Pale eyes stared owlishly through thick, frameless lenses. He looked like your neighbor down the street or your slightly weird Uncle Oscar from Omaha. But he didn't look like a criminal.

Of course, most criminals don't look like criminals. They don't have a "look." They appear to be the neighbor or Uncle Oscar because they are the neighbor or Uncle Oscar. There are exceptions, of course: the bad boys, the down-and-outers, the street bums. But those are not the people who normally show up on my radar—they usually have a lot more in common with Jordan Carl Vermillion than the hard cases.

I hate surveillance jobs because they start early in the morning and go on forever. Even if you catch the subject with the goods or in the act—whichever applies—lawyers and insurance companies don't want a "gotcha moment"; they want a videotape of more than a single incident.

SOMETIME AFTER dawn the next morning, I parked down the street from Vermillion's brick-fronted stucco house on La Charles Avenue NE in a middle-class neighborhood with a mix of residents. Kids came and went from movies or sports fields or whatever summer vacation activities consumed them, while ripe old senior citizens puttered around in adjacent yards. The door to 4313 remained firmly closed.

According to Hazel's Internet research, license plate numbers on the red 2007 Toyota Corolla parked on the right side of the double driveway matched the vehicle registered to Vermillion. I took out my recorder and noted the time of my arrival, ticking off the exact minute. Lawyers and courts were big on precise times. Nothing happened until 7:07 a.m. when the front door opened and a man matching Vermillion's description and photograph stepped out onto the porch. He looked around carefully before marching out in his jammies and a robe to bend over and pick up his newspaper—without the aid of a neck brace or cane or crutches of any sort. He unfolded the paper and read the headline before going back into the house. I recorded it both visually and verbally.

Nothing more happened—and I recorded that into my log as well. As a matter of fact, I recorded everything except the pressed ham and cheese I had for lunch—until 12:14 p.m., when the postman stuffed Vermillion's box with several envelopes. At twelve twenty the front door opened again. As the subject went to the mailbox at the sidewalk alongside his driveway, I videotaped his walk, as well as his hearty wave to a next-door neighbor. Then I dictated another note for the log.

When my car began attracting attention as the neighbors came and went, I shifted to the other side of the street. I noted that in my log as well. I always bring a book or magazine, along with some snacks, to make it look like I'm a businessman on break or a salesman stealing time from my employer, when a stakeout in a neighborhood like this makes me vulnerable. The client tends to freak when a stakeout is busted. Of course, I bring a pee bottle as well, but I don't advertise that activity.

All remained quiet until 2:33 p.m., when the garage door opened and an older-model Mercury Montego that Hazel's notes said was registered to Bertha Vermillion backed out and pulled away. Since the garage door remained open, I moved my car directly opposite the garage, noted the events in the log, and settled down to wait—again.

Two hours later the Montego returned, nosed up the driveway, and eased into the garage. The driver gave a sharp tap on the horn before getting out and going to check the mailbox her husband had already emptied. I thought for a moment she had seen me, but once she had satisfied herself the box was empty, she walked back up the drive.

Then the interior garage door opened, and Jordan Vermillion, dressed in khaki walking shorts, a green golf shirt, and sandals, came out and waited until his wife opened the trunk. My cam caught him leaning over and lifting two large grocery bags out of the car. As a bonus he dangled a gallon of milk from the fingers of his right hand. I got it all on the cam. And I don't care what the lawyers said, it felt like a "gotcha" to me.

I stuck it out the rest of the day before terminating the surveillance at 10:14 p.m. I hummed the "Triumphal March" from *Aida* all the way back to the office. It seemed appropriate to the moment. I'd caught out a conniver in one working day, and now the insurance company's lawyers could handle the rest. An honorable job well done.

I HAD just finished dictating my report on Jordy baby the next morning when Hazel buzzed through a phone call from Millicent.

"BJ, have you made your recommendation to the insurance company on my claim yet?"

"I don't make recommendations. I merely present the facts my investigation has uncovered. I reported those to the attorney who hired me on their behalf yesterday afternoon."

"But you have experience in these matters. Do you think what you reported will support my claim or not?"

"I'm sorry. I can't give you an opinion on that."

"I understand. But has your legal obligation to the insurance company been fulfilled?"

"Yes. I've rendered my final report."

"Then I'd like to hire you."

"To do what?"

A lengthy silence grew before she spoke in a small voice, one that did not seem so mannish. "I don't know. I just need help."

"Look, if you're asking me to recover your property, I can't do that. We both know that duck—dead or alive—is somewhere over the border. I don't have contacts over there. There are good PIs in Las Cruces and El Paso and Tucson. Any of those can probably do you more good than I can. I'll be happy to touch base with some of them and make a recommendation."

"No." Her voice built to full throttle. Mud Hen was back. "I need less investigating than I do advising. I like the way you handled things while you were here. I think you're an honest man. Would it be asking too much for you to come back down here? To talk."

"Millicent, I don't come cheap. For the life of me, I can't think of any advice I can give that would be worth the cost. As a matter of ethics, I can't advise you how to handle the insurance claim; I've already admitted I can't recover the duck. So what possible value could I be to you?"

The line sputtered and crackled for a moment. "I may be forced to sell the ranch. And I've had an offer."

I spent ten minutes trying to convince her I had no special knowledge of ranches, ranching, or ranch real estate values, hence I could not properly advise her whether an offer was fair or not. In short, I could contribute nothing. Then I asked who had made the offer.

"Heck. Hector Acosta."

Chapter 16

"INTERESTING COUNTRY," Paul said. We raced down the stretch of road midway between Las Cruces and Deming. We hadn't spoken much since stopping for lunch in the City of Crosses.

I had agreed to visit the Lazy M provided my companion could take the weekend off and accompany me, making the trip pleasure rather than business—sort of a precelebration of his summer classes ending in a week or so. And in my opinion, that was all this would turn out to be—a vacation trip. I glanced over at the man beside me and decided that was enough.

I'd declined payment for my time because of the anticipated nature of the trip. Millicent's only obligation consisted of providing us with accommodations, nourishment, and a couple of mounts. Paul liked horseback riding; I tolerated it.

He had been born and raised in Albuquerque and never strayed far from his home grounds. On the other hand, fascinated by local history, I had wandered the length and breadth of New Mexico's hundred and twenty-one thousand square miles. Our state was rich in both geological and human history. Home to four Native American reservations and nineteen Indian pueblos, the tattered remnants of once huge Spanish land grants and old Hispanic family names brought over late in the fourteenth century littered the territory. We had an official aircraft, the hot air balloon; our own fossil, the Coelophysis; and an official question, red or green, which referred to the kind of chili you preferred.

A place of awesome sunsets, broad blue skies, sudden thunder squalls, and massive displays of brilliant and sometimes deadly lightning, it was the land of turquoise and roadrunners, of blue grama grass and the Lord's Candle—otherwise known as the yucca—and of Smokey Bear and Clovis Man. It had earned its name—the Land of Enchantment.

I pointed out where Liver Lips Martinson died in his pickup, and when we got to Deming, we took time to visit the real City of Rocks, the state park north of town, which dwarfed the formation on the Lazy M Ranch like New York City overwhelmed Albuquerque.

Just short of 8:00 p.m. we reached the turnoff to the ranch house. The dying sun silhouetted Big Hatchet Peak to the southwest, turning it into a black monolith haloed by reds and purples—the hot colors of the prism.

Maria opened the door to our ring, but it was Poopsie who greeted us with sharp yips and an excited dance, her hard little claws clicking on the flagstone entry. Millicent met us in the great room in a stonewashed denim skirt with a matching vest over a white cotton blouse. She wore sneakers instead of her usual cowboy boots.

"BJ, thank you so much for coming."

After that greeting and the introduction that followed, I watched Paul and Mud size one another up. I had merely told her I was bringing a companion without explaining further.

"Hope you haven't already eaten. Bert and the hands are still out, and Maria's holding dinner. I think she's prepared barbecued baby back ribs."

"Homemade sauce or out of the bottle?" Paul asked.

"Don't let Maria hear you ask that," Millicent admonished. "Her own recipe, of course."

"I can hardly wait." Paul smiled, dimpling his left cheek and making a conquest.

"Bert's back at work?" I asked.

"Oh yes. You can't hold that man down. He went out and got the whirlybird the day after he got shot."

"It's kind of late for them to be out, isn't it?"

"Some fences were cut last night. We had moved most of the stock west of the highway, but there were still a few head in that pasture. Some of them wandered across. Bert and the crew went to round them up."

My eyebrows climbed. "Across? You mean across the border?"

She nodded. "It happens occasionally."

"Is it all right? I mean, do the Mexican authorities get involved?"

"Our neighbor over there is a rancher. He understands." Her mouth tightened. "We need to talk after dinner."

"Whenever you're ready."

"I'd like Bert to be in on this. Paco Rael's here. Perhaps he can entertain Paul while we talk. He's out with Bert and the crew at the moment."

"Do you mind if Paul and I freshen up and then go for a walk around the place while we wait for the others?"

"Certainly. You have the same room as last time. Paul can have the one adjoining it on the east. Maria will show you the way."

I glanced out the window. A big black shape moved in the dying twilight. "Uh, are the Dobermans on the loose?"

"Yes, but we'll introduce you to them again. They won't bother you."

"Do you think the dogs know that?" Paul whispered as we followed the housekeeper up the stairs and down the hall.

After we washed off the road dust, Luis went outside with us to make certain Bruno and Hilda sniffed Paul and me in all the important places so they would know we were friends. At least that's what Luis claimed. A few minutes later, we were alone beneath a jeweled sky. The night was too impressive to waste in talk, so we crossed the oriental bridge and strolled aimlessly over the yard. The vast universe was silent except for the scuffle of our boots in the grass, the occasional grunt of one of the dogs, and a few crickets playing love songs on their back legs. Then a long, muted cry floated over the distance.

"I haven't heard a coyote in a long time," Paul said. "It gives me chills. I don't think I've ever heard anything lonelier."

The muffled padding of paws, a big dark shadow, and a cold, wet nose startled me. One of the Dobermans nuzzled my hand, begging an ear scratch.

"Jesus!" Paul exclaimed. "Frigging dog about freaked me out. This guy wants to be petted."

"This one too."

Trailed by our silent shades, we resumed our walk.

Paul's hand grasped mine. "It's so big and empty out here. Quiet. But you know what? I think I could get to like it. It was sorta like this in the South Valley when I was growing up down there."

A brilliant light suddenly blinded us. I blinked a couple of times and discovered we'd wandered out to the helipad.

"They've turned on the lights. Bert must be on his way. He travels by helicopter."

"To chase cattle?"

"He claims he can herd them better in the chopper than from horseback."

"Hell, I'd think it would stampede them."

Still night blind, we moved away from the concrete pad as the distinctive chop of a whirlybird cut the night. A moment later, Paul pointed out pulsing red dots approaching from the southwest. We watched in silence as the helicopter's landing lights came on prior to the machine gently settling onto its skids. The motor switched off. The rotors gave their distinctive whacking sound a few seconds longer before switching to a whine as they slowly ground to a halt. The hatches opened, and two men got out of the passenger compartment. Bert's weathered Stetson was shoved back, probably because of the bandage around his head. Paco was with him.

Greetings and introductions were made on the move; everyone was hungry and tired.

Maria was a magician, a *mágica*. No one could tell the meal had been held for hours. Her salad greens were crisp; the ribs, spicy and steaming hot. The potato salad just the way I liked it—red potatoes, not russet, and chopped small. I'll swear she even home baked the bread. Likely she churned the butter as well. The result was a feast that tasted like the meals of my childhood.

The spread's three cowhands arrived in the middle of the meal— horses are slower than helicopters—and livened up the atmosphere. The earthy cow talk they brought to the table seemed appropriate to the setting. As he had the last time, Paco Rael was part of, yet apart from, the group. He came in for his share of ribbing and responded to it well, but he remained more of an observer than a participant, unlike his parents, who were clearly members of this household.

Paul, with his interest in sports, fit right in and soon engaged in a friendly dispute with Linus over the merits of this year's Dallas Cowboys. Linus was pro; Paul, con. Would this easy camaraderie survive once they figured out our relationship?

The three Lazy M hired hands, plus Paco and Paul, adjourned to the bunkhouse for a friendly game of poker while Millicent, Bert, and I retired to the office for a talk.

"How are you doing, Bert? I'm surprised to see you're flying already."

"Clean bill of health." He touched the fresh bandage circling his head. "This damned thing gets in the way, though. My hat rubs my head sore."

"So don't wear the hat for a few days."

His mother gave a horselaugh. "Cowboys would rather be caught without their britches than their hat. And Bert's one hundred percent cowboy."

I turned to her. "What is it you think I can help you with?"

She picked up a string of amber beads from the desk and leaned back in the chair. Millicent caught me looking at them as she deftly rubbed each between her thumb and forefinger. She lifted what I had taken to be a rosary and dangled it from her hand.

"Ren bought them for me years ago when we were in Marrakech. They're worry beads, and believe me, I've done lots of worrying over them. They're a comfort." She got a dreamy look in her eyes. "We stayed in a little hotel with only a dozen rooms in the Medina, the old fortified city."

She rambled on about the sights and sounds and smells of the once imperial capital of Morocco. Bert brought it to an end by shuffling his feet and clearing his throat.

"Ah well. That was another time, another world. What I need to know now is what the insurance company is apt to do." She caught my frown. "Not what they're going to do as much as how they will do it? When we've had claims before, we usually got pretty prompt service. A check inside of thirty days or so. But I get the feeling this might not be a usual case." She stopped and awaited a response.

"I told you over the phone, I cannot ethically advise you on this matter."

"But you know them. You can give me some guidance."

"No, I don't know them. I know the attorney they hired. I've worked with him a lot over the years. He's a straight arrow, but he has no control over what his client—and that would be the insurance company—will do or how they will do it. I don't think it takes a lot of serious brainpower to conclude that somebody over there's got his tail in a crack by overinsuring a duck for a quarter of a million dollars. But that's internal politics."

"And it's the internal politics that may sink me. I'm in a jam, BJ. You know what's happening to the economy. It's tanking. I don't know a rancher around who expects to make a profit this year or next. Everybody's nailing the barn door closed. And it's not just the credit markets drying up. The environmentalists have been after the government to withdraw the leases on public land, or at least raise the rent on them enough to bankrupt us. Add to that the torrent of illegals and drugs coming through here and tearing up our land and improvements, and it spells economic disaster. Armageddon is more like it."

The amber beads clicked audibly. "And when you add the theft of Quacky to that, it's certain ruin."

I glanced at Bert. He sat immobile, holding his thoughts close.

"Then why did you make that bonehead bet?" I asked.

"It wasn't a bonehead bet. It made perfect sense, and it could have turned this year into a profitable one. I've beat that Florida peckerwood two times out of three with my precious."

I stretched my legs out in front of me. "Millicent, the first thing I tell a potential client is that if he lies to me, I walk away. My job is hard enough when I have all the facts. It's impossible when I'm only given half the information. Sooner or later almost all of them do lie, or at least shade the truth in their favor, but if I catch them doing it right off the bat, I'm gone. And you just lied to me for the third time."

She tossed the beads on the desk. "I didn't lie, but I didn't tell you everything either. I found out that scumbag intended to challenge me to a sucker bet by putting in a ringer. But he was wrong. I had *him* set up for a fall. I found out his racer got hurt. Leg caught in the coop so bad he had to take her to the vet. I not only accepted his bet, I insisted on a default clause saying the two named ducks had to race against one another. He accepted even though he'd have to race a substitute for Thunder Duck. When he did, I'd have called him on it, and he'd have been in default."

"I don't understand. One duck looks like another to me, but professional duck farmers can surely tell the difference."

"It's not always that easy. We mark our valuable birds—brand them, if you will. If he gave the stand-in Thunder Duck's mark, it might be virtually impossible to tell the difference. But I had an ace up my sleeve. Don't ask me how, but I got my hands on the vet's report, including X-rays. So I could have proved he cheated."

The world had just tilted again. Except for the ransom note—if that's what it was—Liver Lips could have been hired by a crooked duck owner to cover his fanny—although I did not believe anyone paid Liver Lips for the job. The shock on his face when I wanted to know who had hired him to steal the duck had been real. He hadn't realized the significance of the act he was recruited to perform.

"I'm not certain I should be hearing this," I said. "But the damage is done, so let's go on. Look, you ought to be able to get this fellow Hammond to call off the bet. Just let him know you're onto his game."

"Uh-uh. All he has to do is show up and I've lost. I don't care how lame his duck is, if she can make it to the finish line, my goose is cooked—and that's not a pun."

"Maybe he doesn't know she's been stolen."

"The whole state of New Mexico knows it. He knows. You can count on that."

"Once again, what can I do?"

"You can prove that shithead intended to cheat me."

"Intentions are impossible to prove. Actions are all that count."

"You give me reasonable intention and leave the rest to me."

I thought for a few minutes. They waited me out in silence. Finally I sighed. "Before I agree or decline, you said something about Hector Acosta offering to buy you out."

"Yep, and unless you can save my bacon, I may be forced to sell. The Lazy M is a pretty solid outfit. Like most mother cow operations, we borrow feed money and some of our operating capital, but we raise our own animals to replenish the herd, so we don't have to go out and buy livestock. I owe a hellish amount on a bull we bought last year, but even if this year turns out to be as bad as I think it will, we'd have survived without too much heartburn. But that two hundred fifty thousand dollars represents all of our reserves. I can liquidate some investments to buy us more time, borrow on life insurance policies and maybe squeak through. But I'm not sure it's worth it."

"How about borrowing on the ranch?"

"In this economy? Maybe, but this land's never had a mortgage on it. My people added to it as they could afford it. I'm not sure I'm willing to go that route. If it ever went into foreclosure, I might end up with less than Heck is willing to pay."

"Is he offering a fair price?"

The tightness around her lips appeared again. "Fifty cents on the dollar."

"Tell him to go to hell. Whoever sent you that ransom note and shot Bert did you a favor. Before that, I'm certain the insurance company would have denied your claim, but in light of those two events, they have to consider it seriously."

"But they'll drag it out as long as they can."

"I still don't see what the big deal is. Simply refuse to pay the bet. There's not a court in the land that will enforce that wager."

Bert grunted at that, but Millicent made a sour face.

"My Grandpa Muldren gave up his first ranch to pay a debt of honor. My pa never broke his bond once it was given, and I've honored my debts for almost fifty years. I'm not about to welsh now. If my word's no good, I'm finished—as a practical matter, as well as an ethical one."

"I have no contacts in Florida. I don't think I can do anything for you. Find a good investigator who knows the territory."

"You find him," she came back at me. "And then ride herd on him for me. Make sure he does his job."

We talked for another half hour, and in the end I agreed to make some calls on Monday to see what I could learn. But I made it clear to both of them I wasn't about to head out to Florida any time soon.

Paul sauntered into my room around midnight with a loopy grin and unfocused eyes.

"Did those slicks get you drunk and take you to the cleaners?"

The grin grew wider. He held up a roll of green. "Paid for our trip."

"I'm surprised. Those guys seem pretty sharp to me."

"Yeah, they are. But I put myself through my freshman year at the poker table. Range poker is not the same as South Valley poker."

Chapter 17

SUNDAY MORNING we rose with the rest of the household. Paul wanted to get in a horseback ride before we headed back to Albuquerque that afternoon. After breakfast—a duck-egg omelet with bits of ham, onion, and red chili peppers—Luis saddled an old mare named Lucy for me and a feisty palomino gelding dubbed Streak for Paul. I took it as payback for Paul winning at the bunkhouse last night. Maybe not. Streak seemed reasonably well behaved, although Bert warned not to let him "get his head." I don't know about Paul, but that warning prompted me to keep a tight rein on Lucy, and she was a plodding old gal well past her prime.

Before Millicent boarded the chopper with her son to check some distant pasture, she asked if I was carrying and offered one of the ranch's rifles. I declined, but after they lifted off, I went to the Impala and got my 9 millimeter from the trunk.

Thin threads of dirty-white cumulous clouds smudged the blue sky as we moved out under a light, cooling breeze. Wearing a borrowed Stetson, Paul looked to be a genuine cowboy on Streak's broad back. I probably appeared more like the tenderfoot I was. I learned to ride at a North Valley stable.

We set off in a southeastern direction, which I figured would take us somewhere in the vicinity of the City of Rocks. In light of yesterday's cut fences, my curiosity demanded to see if there was any sign it had been used to shelter anyone recently.

Paul surprised me by opening and closing gates from horseback as we went from one pasture to another. Of course, ranch-savvy Streak helped a great deal, but despite his claim to be a city boy, Paul admitted he'd spent a summer working on a spread in the far South Valley—a once small ranch now a housing development.

To many, the word *desert* called up images of barren sand dunes or the shifting gypsum mounds of White Sands National Monument farther to the east. But we were surrounded by an astonishing array of plants. The ubiquitous creosote bushes, locoweed, and mesquite were everywhere, of course, but between the two of us, we managed to identify some of the other plants.

I pointed to a handsome, long-spurred plant with canary-yellow flowers. "There's a golden columbine. You usually find them at higher altitudes."

"What are we here?"

"Something over four thousand feet."

"There's a plant even I know." Paul nodded at a low, greenish-white bush. "That's plain old poison ivy. I got into some when I was a kid. About itched me to death."

"Did you know a lot of birds and animals eat it?"

"Then they must have internal calamine glands."

We identified sage, rabbit bush, scarlet beardtongue, and buckbrush. I saw what appeared to be chokecherry, but it was out of bloom, so I couldn't be sure.

The horses set an easy pace. Paul kept a snug rein on Streak, who broke into a gallop at every opportunity. On the other hand, the farther Lucy got from the stable, the slower her gait became. After another hour, Paul pointed ahead of us.

"Is that it?"

"Yep. The Lazy M's own City of Rocks."

"Man, that looks weird out there all by itself. Even weirder than the big one up at the state park."

"New Mexico's full of weird. You think you're standing on the moon at the Bisti Badlands. And then there's Carlsbad Caverns, Tent Rocks, White Sands, and those eerie lava beds in the Malpais."

"I gotta get out of Bernalillo County more often," he said.

We went silent, falling increasingly under the spell of ghostly monoliths as we approached the City. The horses plodded between the first two hunks of mute rock on the north-northwest side. The "street" that opened up before us was a broad avenue strangely devoid of plant growth. I saw no human footprints, but wind whistling through the alleyways raised weak, wispy dust devils. Footprints in the sand would not last long out here. Our mounts' hooves no longer clopped; now they made a huffing sound. We could have passed through a portal separating two worlds.

"That big boulder in front of us looks like a hotel. An old western hotel."

I stared at the hulking mass. "Why? It's just a big rock."

"Come on, where's your imagination? It's a couple of stories high. It's kinda square. It looks like those pictures of a frontier hotel minus the balcony that runs around the second story. And that's Muldren City's saloon over there." He pointed to the right.

I fell into the spirit of the thing. "Okay, then that's the bank. And the telegraph office."

He laughed, obviously delighted I played along. "Let's go see if we can find the freight office. Then the town's complete."

"Oh no. Not without the jail, it isn't."

"Right. I forgot the sheriff's office and the jailhouse." He twisted in the saddle and pointed. "There it is, right across the square from the hotel." Paul dismounted and looked for a place to tether Streak. "They forgot the hitching rail. No western town's complete without a hitching post."

He tied his reins to the only bit of green in sight, a small mesquite bush. "Hope that holds. I'd hate to walk back to the ranch house."

I joined him on the ground and dubiously tethered Lucy to the same puny plant. While he scrambled up the side of the "hotel," I searched for evidence of human habitation.

"Watch out for snakes," he yelled, already out of sight atop the boulder.

In a natural alleyway at the side of the jailhouse, I found impressions like miniature buffalo wallows. The small lane was sheltered from the worst of the wind. People had rested here, smoothing out the dust and dirt to make a bed, probably for an overnight stay. A pile of debris and tumbleweeds lay against the end of the small passage where the rock walls met again. I nudged the garbage with my boot... all food related: greasy sandwich or tortilla wraps and crumpled Styrofoam containers for coffee or posole.

The human coyotes probably hid illegal immigrants here while they stocked up on water from the windmill in the distance. Then, before the morning light came, they would spirit their charges across the desert onto the highway where someone waited to pick them up. A natural—and obvious—spot. I was willing to bet the smugglers had not remained with their human cargo during that long, anxious wait. They probably camped somewhere in the near vicinity, realizing the Border Patrol would be aware of the City's potential for hiding illegal aliens and other contraband.

A muffled shout from Paul drew me out of the mental drama playing out in my head. I walked back to the plaza but found no sign of him.

"Vince," he said from above me. I looked up to find him squatting atop the hotel. "There are people out there."

"Where?"

"Walking across the hardpan. I think they're headed here."

"Keep out of sight. I'm coming up."

He guided me to a fold in the rock that provided easy toeholds. When I pulled myself to the top, he lay prone, holding his hat in front of him to shade his eyes. "There's ten, fifteen dudes out there. All on foot."

I lay on my belly beside him and looked where he pointed. The distant figures walked one behind the other, Indian style. The column spread out like a military unit. I wished for my binoculars. The man in front carried something I thought to be an automatic rifle. As we watched, he turned south, heading directly for the City. Two of the men separated and made north toward the windmill. The group probably planned on remaining here overnight.

I rolled onto my back and took out my cell phone. Dialing 911 reached the emergency operator, who put me in contact with the Border Patrol in Deming. Within a minute I was speaking to an agent named Ramirez. He heard my report and ordered me to get out of there—without being seen, if possible. As I turned to tell Paul to get back to the horses, he grunted.

"Uh-oh. They got company."

Two mounted outriders came in from the east, passing on either side of the column and halting to speak with the point man. After a brief conversation, they galloped straight for the City.

"They're gonna scout it out. They'll cut us off," Paul said.

The horsemen were coming fast. With no way to reach our mounts and get away, much less escape unseen, I decided on a bluff. As soon as they got close enough, I yelled a warning and planted a bullet in the sand twenty feet in front of the closest rider. They pulled up but didn't seem particularly worried. No wonder—my pistol shot sounded rather insignificant.

"This is the United States Border Patrol," I bellowed at the top of my voice. "Drop your weapons, dismount, and lie down on the ground. Hands behind your heads."

The two men looked at one another for an instant before raising their rifles and cutting loose. I ducked down, pulling Paul with me as chips of stone showered us. Automatic rifles.

When I risked a peek over the ledge, I discovered their mounts were not broken to gunfire. One man had been thrown; the other struggled to bring his horse under control. I aimed over his head and fired… an impossible shot as he was almost out of range of the pistol. But the bullet must have come close enough to divert his attention. He lost control of the animal, and the beast bolted.

The other man had regained his feet and scrambled to find the rifle he dropped. I loosed two more shots, forcing him to decide whether to recover his weapon or hold on to his panicked pony. He opted for the horse and raced after his companion. The column of men had dropped to the ground except for the leader, who pumped his arms and screamed at his flank guards.

I heard, rather than saw, Paul move. He was halfway off the rock before I reacted. He ignored my warning, so I turned my attention back to the intruders. The leader, still on his feet, held something to his ear, probably a satellite phone or a walkie-talkie. A moment later, Paul appeared on the desert below me. I watched helplessly as the coyote dropped his phone and lifted his weapon. The man was out of range of my peashooter but well within the reach of a rifle.

Paul snatched the abandoned AK-47 from the dirt and spun on his heels just as the coyote fired a volley. Sand geysers danced where Paul had been less than a moment before. He raced for the gate, weaving back and forth erratically. He slipped in a patch of sand and fell on his hip. Bullets tore out chunks of lava and ash from the stone over his head. He scrambled to his feet, grabbed the rifle he'd lost, and ran.

Enraged and terrified for my lover, I stood atop the stone monolith and screamed at the *traficante*, dropping as the man turned his weapon on me. Rock shards fell all around me as I cowered behind the parapet. The weapon fell silent. I gave a shaky gasp of relief when Paul slid up beside me a moment later. Busy checking him for injuries, I forgot to give him hell for his foolishness.

Panting from his exertions, he handed over the rifle. "Give me the popgun. You take the AK. I'm not much of a shot."

"Let's hope that's not the sniper who almost nailed Bert out there. I'm sure as hell not in his league." I checked the gun's clip. Almost a full load.

We risked a look. The men from the windmill had rejoined their leader. They dropped canvas water bags in a pile and milled around as he shouted orders. That gave me an idea.

I set the rifle for single fire, took careful aim, and squeezed off a round. Even from this distance, I saw the water bags jump. I quickly fired three more shots to make certain they were shredded. The windmill provided available water, but now they had nothing to haul it in unless they traveled with spare containers. Not likely. They'd have filled every bag they had. Now they would be forced to decide whether to make a run for the highway or hightail it back over the border before reinforcements arrived.

Or—I amended my conclusions—come at us for revenge. And it looked as if that's what they intended. Except it was likely much less personal than revenge; they probably figured we had a vehicle, and that would be quicker than waiting to be picked up by their own transportation.

"Oh shit, here they come!" I handed Paul two automatic reloaders for the revolver—all the ammo I'd brought—then scrambled to a spot thirty feet to the east, careful to keep out of sight.

My words were punctuated by a salvo of automatic fire. These guys were seriously defacing the Lazy M's City of Rocks. During a pause, I removed my hat and eased my gaze over the stone parapet. The leader walked in the middle of a skirmish line of four other armed men. They were much closer now. This was serious business. I aimed and fired.

The *traficante* I figured to be the leader clutched his shoulder and dropped. A fusillade of bullets smacked the stone where I sheltered. These guys were quick. I whistled at Paul and tossed him the rifle. He stuck his head up and took a quick shot. He slipped back behind the stone berm and shook his head. He had missed.

He threw the weapon back to me, and I shifted position again before sighting in on another target. He cried aloud as his leg crumbled beneath him. I took cover again.

"They're backing off!" Paul cried.

Intent on taking advantage of the situation, I raised my head. Mistake. These guys were military. Two men backed away slowly to cover their retreat while the third helped his two wounded companions. The rear guard let go at me with a vengeance. I ducked and scrambled to the far end of the hotel before I fired again. I missed this time, but I made the smuggler dance.

That ended the action for the moment, so I hit the 911 button on my phone and reported a firefight. Once out of easy range, the men huddled around their wounded leader, who sat on the ground and waved his good right arm furiously. Then, to my dismay, the three uninjured men separated from the group and formed a widely spaced skirmish line. What the hell was so important about facing us down? By all rights they should have scurried back over the border to safety and tried again later. Maybe it *was* a lack of water. Had destroying the canvas bags been a mistake?

"Let's go," I said. "Get to the horses before they get any closer."

When we scrambled down off the boulder into the plaza, both horses were gone. They'd uprooted the mesquite bush where they'd been tethered and bolted for home.

"What do we do now?" Paul asked. I was pleased to see he was calm.

"Find shelter on another rock."

"The saloon?"

"Nope. We'll make our stand at the jail, podnuh."

If Paul noticed my puny attempt at humor, he didn't acknowledge it; he merely took off across the plaza. He had scaled the boulder before I moved. I tossed him the rifle and then scrambled atop the rock. He gave me a hand up the last few feet.

Eons of wind and water had scoured the dome forming the jailhouse roof, leaving it slightly depressed in the center. The only problem was that the hotel stood taller. Anyone up there would have us at his mercy.

We watched and waited. The three thugs were taking their own sweet time getting here. I didn't blame them. The walls they faced were tall and straight and without handholds. I doubted they could scale the hotel from the outside even by standing on one another's shoulders. No, they would have to enter between the two towering rocks we'd called the city gate. For the first few seconds, they'd have no protection. Not an appealing prospect. Time stretched out; the adrenaline rush abated, leaving me slightly nauseated and allowing me to notice things that had eluded me before. My right thigh, where I'd once caught a killer's bullet, throbbed with phantom pain. The sun beat down on us mercilessly. I'd lost my hat somewhere along the line—probably somewhere up on the hotel. My tongue was thick with thirst. My sweat-soaked shirt clung to my back. We were no better off than the *traficantes*. Our canteens were on the fleeing horses.

"Don't have a drink on you, do you?" Paul asked. "Sure could use one."

"No, but there's a windmill about a quarter of a mile north of us."

"Probably water closer than that right under us, but I have the same problem with it. No way to get to it. Isn't it about time for the cavalry to arrive?"

"I don't know how the Border Patrol operates. I don't know if they show up in helicopters, vans, or by horseback. Shhh!" I laid a warning hand on his arm.

A shadow hesitated in the opening between the two monoliths forming the gate. Finally a stocky, bearded man slipped cautiously into the plaza. A large, battered hat almost hid his eyes as he scanned the clearing before turning to the hotel. Paul glanced at me, but I waited. If his compadres were coming, I wanted them all where I could see them. As the smuggler stood looking around warily, I watched the gate for another shadow. I would only get off one burst before they scattered.

Then he took me by surprise. He quickly backed toward the jail. Before I could react, he passed out of sight below us. Paul met my gaze, eyes wide. I pointed to the revolver in his hand. He nodded his understanding. If the man attempted to scale the boulder, Paul would deal with him.

Moments later, grunts and scraping noises confirmed the smuggler's intention. Muffled shouts came from somewhere out of our sight. His friends were trying to hold our attention while he got into position. Apparently they didn't realize the hotel loomed over the jailhouse.

A sliding noise. A low curse. More scraping sounds. Leather soles on stone. The man had almost reached the top now. At any minute I expected to see the brim of his hat. Paul slipped silently around me and positioned himself directly in front of where the man would appear. A left hand slapped the top of the boulder. An AK-47 appeared next, clutched in the right fist.

When the man's head appeared, his eyes went wide as Paul calmly pulled the rifle from his grasp and clubbed him with the butt of the revolver. Without a sound, the man dropped to the floor of the small canyon.

The next surprise was theirs. The horsemen had returned, or at least one had. His pinto bolted through the gate, its rider brandishing a pistol. Within a second he spotted his friend on the ground and glanced up. His revolver roared, and something hot passed near my right ear before I ducked out of sight. Paul's automatic rifle stuttered.

"Got him!" he yelled triumphantly. He blinked slowly. "Got... him. Oh God, I killed a man."

"No, but you still can, if you want to." I nodded toward the smuggler. He'd been knocked from the saddle and was trying to crawl to the gate. Unsure how badly the bozo was hurt, I pulled Paul down out of sight. "Let him go. We just have to survive this long enough for the BP to get here."

"If they even bother to come," Paul said dryly. "Maybe they don't do rescues on the Sabbath."

"Keep a watch for the coyotes. Especially on the hotel roof. If they get up there, we're in trouble."

I eased down out of sight and hit my Redial button to place another call to the BP. I got a different agent, but he knew about the situation. I reported the attack, including the live fire. He told me two teams were on the way, one by air and one by ground. I just hoped we were still alive and kicking when they got here.

As I closed the call, the sound of sustained gunfire startled me. What was happening? Had the BP arrived? I stuck my head over the parapet. Little puffs of dust peppered the sandy floor of the empty plaza—as if it were raining.

Oh hell. It was! It was raining lead pellets, and that deadly shower started to fall on the jailhouse roof. I grabbed Paul's arm, literally hauled him over me, and pushed him to the west end of the parapet. "Jump! For God's sake, jump!"

He didn't ask questions. He disappeared over the edge. As I followed, the top of the rock sounded like a roof under assault by a thunderstorm. Something stung my hand. A stone shard brought blood. Without looking, I slipped over the edge and slid down the side, landing in the dirt with a bone-crunching thud. My knees collapsed. I caught myself on my palms. Paul grabbed me and pressed us both against the side of the rock.

The little alleyway where I had found signs of a camp provided as much shelter as we would find in this barren, godforsaken place. The gunshots were less uniform now, more uncertain as clips ran out of ammunition.

"What the hell's going on?" Paul gasped.

"Letting that guy you knocked out of the saddle get away was a mistake. He told them we'd moved from the roof of the hotel. Now they're firing into the air, letting the bullets fall straight down. Not very accurate, but eventually one of them might find its mark."

"Shit, can you do that? Then let's give it back to them." He raised his rifle.

I yanked the barrel down. "No. Maybe they'll think they got us and go about their business."

The firestorm came to a ragged end. The men were closer now. We could hear shouted orders and answering voices. Then, over it all, I heard something else. The clatter of a chopper. The *traficantes* heard it too, judging from all the excited shouting.

Paul leaned his head back against the boulder. "I've seen this movie. That's John Wayne out there, isn't it? Wish I had a bugle. I'd play 'Charge.'"

I laughed. He sputtered and then burst out laughing. We snorted like a couple of hysterical hyenas. Abruptly we sobered and looked at one another sheepishly.

"You hear that?" Paul asked.

"Hear what?"

"Nothing. There's no shooting."

"The bad guys are headed for home."

"So why don't the good guys scoop them up? You know, shoot them, or at least take them into custody."

"They might catch the wounded guys, but the BP won't fire on anyone unless they're fired on first."

"That's a shitty way to fight a war."

"Let's try to get out of here without being shot by anybody. They might not fire on illegals, but I'm not so sure about how sacred our hides are."

We emerged from the shaded alley into a bright, sunlit plaza streaked with black shadows. The man Paul had clubbed still lay at the base of the jailhouse. I took a closer look. Dead. A victim of his fellow smugglers' blind firing.

"Hold it!" a loud voice ordered. "This is the Border Patrol. Drop your weapons. Down on the ground, face-first." Then he repeated the words in Spanish.

Chapter 18

WE FELL to our knees and went prone like a trained gymnastics team…
in unison.

Within seconds a group of very aggressive BP Special Ops in
uniforms and armor surrounded us and demanded to know who we
were. In the background I heard someone giving military-style orders
to the remainder of the men sweeping through the City. Without moving
from the prone position, I told them we'd made the call warning of the
incursion. A desert-camo-uniformed man wearing a first lieutenant's
silver bar instructed two of his team to take us to the Lazy M headquarters.
They promptly pulled us to our feet and deposited us in the back of a
large helicopter. The man riding shotgun kept an eagle eye on the ground
below us, his automatic rifle at the ready, as we raced back to the ranch
house.

Luis and Maria met us when we exited the chopper before it pulled
away and headed for the City. Even though their eyes burned with
curiosity, the couple said nothing except that Bert and the señora were
on the way back to the ranch headquarters. That was all right with me.
In a few minutes, we would be answering a whole host of questions for
the Border Patrol team commander. We took advantage of the delay to
go upstairs and clean up.

After washing away the worst of the dirt and grit, I met Paul in the
hallway outside our rooms. His first words told me he had come off his
adrenaline high.

"Are you sure I didn't kill that guy I shot?"

"I'm sure. And you aren't responsible for the one who got shot by
his own men, so don't give it another thought." I saw he hadn't considered
that possibility and was sorry I'd opened my big mouth.

A commotion in the foyer told me the reception team had arrived.
We went downstairs and met the BP team leader in the hallway talking
to Millicent and Bert. The agent's name tag read Ramirez. This must be
the man who took my initial call. In a quick, no-nonsense report, he let us

know the only people they'd netted were the frightened and bewildered illegal immigrants and one of the wounded coyotes. The rest, including the one who had acted as leader, escaped back over the border.

Millicent grasped my arm. "Are you two okay?"

"We're fine," I assured her. "Juiced up a little. But we're fine."

As Millicent ushered us into the big common room, I asked Luis if the horses had returned safely. He appeared pleased by my concern as he assured me they had.

I wasn't surprised to find Deputy Nap O'Brien talking to Bert in the sitting room, but why had no one from the state police showed up? DEA and ATF were also among the missing.

Paul and I took seats on the long divan opposite Millicent, who was flanked by two BP agents—the team leader and his second. I studied Ramirez as he leaned across Millicent to speak to the other agent. Short and stocky, Ramirez, in his midthirties, looked to be a tough customer carrying the entire weight of the border problem on his shoulders. He wore his coal black hair in a Marine-style whitewall. Brown eyes flashed as he scanned the room every few minutes. This was a cautious man who looked for trouble even when there was none. He had an X-shaped scar high on his left cheek that reminded me of the barbed wire that probably caused it. That accounted for the mangled appearance of the first two fingers on his left hand as well.

The other man was Senior Patrol Agent Chill Williams, an athletic black man probably ten years Ramirez's junior. If his boss represented caution, Williams stood for action. His suppressed energy and impatience surfaced occasionally in an unconscious lifting of his shoulders, almost as if he were twitching.

O'Brien occupied an easy chair at one end of the two facing sofas. Bert claimed a recliner at the other. As soon as everyone was served— iced tea for everyone except Bert, who had a beer—Ramirez kicked things off.

"You want to tell us about it, Mr. Vinson?" He laid a small recorder on the coffee table between us. Although not on a case, I pulled out my own and switched it on.

"Please call me BJ, Officer…. Sorry, but I don't know much about BP rank and protocol."

"We're agents. I'm a Special Operations Supervisor, usually referred to as SOS, but you can call me Randy." His manner was bluff but not unfriendly.

I led them through our morning in a fair amount of detail. No one spoke except when Paul added a point or two of his own. Ramirez listened, leaning forward on the couch, elbows on his knees. Other than periodically scoping out the room, he steadily stared at me. Williams twitched in silence. Everyone else held motionless other than taking an occasional sip. When I finished, Ramirez eased back on the sofa.

"Chill?" he prompted his companion.

"Mr. Vinson... uh, BJ, there's something that doesn't make sense to me."

"Let me guess. Why the sustained gun battle? Why not just retreat back across the border?"

"Exactly."

"Maybe shooting their water bags to pieces was a mistake. Perhaps they needed to secure the area and get free access to the well."

"They had access to the well. It was out of range of your rifles," Williams said.

Ramirez cleared his throat. "They didn't know how many of you there were. So far as they knew, you were in sufficient force to deny them water."

"Unless they were idiots, they knew there were only two of us long before all the serious shooting began."

"You're right," Ramirez said. "I don't believe water was the problem. There's another windmill less than ten miles from there, and it's safely back across the border."

"Did the Mexican authorities apprehend them from that side?" Paul asked.

"The Mexicans consider this our problem," Williams said. "They don't lift a finger."

"Sometimes we get cooperation," Ramirez said. "But they would have disappeared before anyone official showed up over there. We apprehended the illegals they abandoned—nine men and one woman. They were thirsty but not desperate."

"What about the wounded man you caught? Did he shed any light on things?"

"Hasn't said a word except to ask for medical treatment."

"How did they get horses across the border? Isn't there a fence?" Paul asked.

"Plain old barbed wire, which they cut on the way over."

"If it wasn't water that brought them after us, what do you think it was? Something in the City? Something hidden there?" Paul asked.

"Possibly," Ramirez said. "The rest of my team's checking it out right now."

"That has to be it," Millicent said. "What else would make them stand and fight? There must have been a load of drugs hidden there somewhere."

Ramirez transferred his gaze to me. "Did you recognize any of them?"

"Recognize them? I don't know anyone around here. How could I recognize anyone? Besides, they were too far away to identify."

"They probably thought you had binoculars. Are you saying you don't know anyone down here?"

"Just the people I've met on the ranch."

"But if I understand it correctly, you identified yourselves as Border Patrol," Williams said. "They thought you were us. Maybe somebody we know."

Ramirez shook his head. "Even more reason to retreat and try again later. We've had run-ins with people from the other side before, but that's never prompted a major gun battle."

"Maybe one of the big honchos came along on this run. Somebody who didn't want to be identified," Williams suggested.

"Possibly. But why would a big cheese accompany them? They were just bringing over some illegals. It wasn't like they were crossing with a heavy load of merchandise." Ramirez addressed his next question to me. "Were they laden down with packs?"

"No." I hesitated and reconsidered. "The coyotes weren't carrying anything except light packs. Were the illegal immigrants carrying?"

"They were acting as mules, all right, but there wasn't enough product to warrant a major figure leading them over. Unless, of course, he just wanted to enter the country without leaving a record. What about the horses? Did they seem to be packing?"

I thought that question over. "They had saddlebags, and they looked full. But that's all I can tell you."

"I didn't get a good look, but one had a tripod of some kind. Made me think of surveying," Paul said.

"I don't understand that shooting straight up in the air maneuver," Williams said.

"Indians used to do it back in the old days, I hear," O'Brien said. "Shoot up in the air, and let nature take it from there. Course, they done it with bows and arrows."

"You can see where arrows are falling, but you can't see where bullets come down," Williams said before correcting himself. "But in this terrain, you could see enough dust pimples to adjust your aim."

"BJ and Paul were costing them too much," Ramirez said. "So they tried anything they could think of to offset the advantage of their cover. Whoever was in charge had them point their rifles straight up in the air and unload."

"Waste of good ammo," Williams said.

"The smugglers had, what—eight or nine weapons?" Ramirez asked.

"Before we took two away from them," Paul said.

"That still left seven. The gang probably fired somewhere close to a thousand rounds during the whole engagement. Wasteful but effective. It flushed you from cover."

"Yep, chased us right off the roof... uh, the top of that rock," I said.

Ramirez grinned, revealing an unexpected sense of humor. "Were you on the hotel or the saloon?"

Paul chuckled. "Started out on the hotel, ended up on the jailhouse roof."

That got a laugh.

"I figured we were nuts identifying those rocks as buildings," I said.

Millicent waved a hand. "Everybody does it. As a child I named every rock in that place. I even gave the ones I called 'houses' family names."

The phone at Ramirez's waist rang. It appeared to be a satellite, not a cellular, phone. He got up and excused himself to walk off toward the windows and answer his call.

"You fired first?" O'Brien asked.

"Yes, but not at them. Kicked up dust well in front of the two horsemen."

"And you claimed to be BP agents?"

"It seemed the prudent thing to do when I saw armed men who obviously didn't belong on the ranch coming straight toward us."

"You coulda hid. Likely they wouldn't have found you."

"They'd have seen our horses and rooted us out. Besides, the City looked like an overnight place to me. I found trash where people had eaten and wallows where they sacked out. Didn't want to be trapped there. What are you trying to say?"

"Nothing. Just trying to understand the situation."

Paul addressed Williams. "How come you didn't catch any of them except for the undocumented workers and the wounded man they abandoned?"

"They were doing what we wanted them to do—running for the border. It didn't appear we would interdict much in the way of drugs, so the best thing for everyone was for them to go back where they belonged."

"Ever since Ramos and Compean, the BP's been mighty skittish about shooting at Mexicans," O'Brien said.

He referred to the February 2005 incident when Border Patrol Agents Ignacio Ramos and Jose Compean shot a Mexican driver while trying to run down a van in Fabens, Texas. After the smuggler escaped back over the border on foot, the agents discovered about 750 pounds of marijuana worth around a million dollars in his vehicle. Despite a widespread public outcry, the US attorney in El Paso prosecuted and convicted the two agents for several crimes committed during the altercation. Both were presently serving time in federal institutions.

O'Brien's comparison didn't track for me. "As I understand it, those two agents were accused of shooting an unarmed man, although plenty of us don't believe that was the case. These people today were obviously armed and had shown a willingness to use their firepower aggressively."

Ramirez returned to claim his seat, sparing Williams the pain of responding.

"My team found nothing at the City. We brought in a K-9 unit, but the dogs didn't find anything either. No drugs. No fugitives. No weapons caches. Nothing at all. SPA Williams and I have to get back to headquarters. Are you hanging around in case we need to talk to you again, BJ?"

"No, we need to get on the road too. Paul has to go to work tomorrow." I handed him a card with all my contact numbers.

"Confidential Investigator," he read. "A PI. Are you on a case?"

"Nope, this was supposed to be some relaxation time."

We all walked the agents and O'Brien to their vehicles. One of the BP teams had come by land, and Williams returned with them. Ramirez headed for the waiting helicopter. After we watched them out of sight, I turned to Millicent.

"We'd better get moving too. It's going to be late by the time we get home, and I need to get started on your problem first thing tomorrow. I know an investigator in Florida, but I want to locate one who has an in with the racing crowd down there. We need some leverage on this Hammond guy."

Luis brought our overnight bags down, and we said our good-byes quickly. Just before we took off, Maria brought us a big picnic hamper.

Once we were on the road, I expected Paul to be full of talk, but he rooted around in the basket and came up with a couple of pieces of homemade fudge. After he polished those off, he grew quiet again. I glanced over and found him drowsing. I understood the phenomenon. Lethargic episodes often followed periods of high excitement and danger due to the release of tension and reaction to adrenaline. I let him nap. He roused after we picked up I-40 out of Las Cruces and offered to drive. Instead I found a rest stop where we pulled off to explore the contents of Maria's hamper.

As we munched on thick slabs of roast beef between a rough rye bread and devoured coleslaw with a tangy sauce beneath a peaceful canopy of early stars, the armed assault of this morning seemed far in the past. Not so for my companion.

"That thing this morning, you do that much? Get in shootouts?"

"Naw. That's rare."

"What about getting shot in the leg? You know, when you got that intriguing scar." He smiled, his teeth bright in the gathering darkness.

"I was in the APD back then, and my business there was catching crooks and killers. My work now is to gather information. There's a world of difference."

"Still, it happens now and then," he insisted.

"Well, it did this morning."

"Sort of exciting, wasn't it?"

"I wouldn't call thinking you'd killed a man exciting. More like frightening."

"Well, okay. There's that," Paul admitted.

Chapter 19

As I left the house the next morning, I eyed Paul's old Plymouth at the curb. And by old, I mean *old*. I couldn't even tell you the year, but it had to be a late seventies or early eighties model. He'd named the rattletrap the Barrio Bomb, but it wasn't much of an explosive threat any longer. It merely wheezed along. He'd refused my offers to buy him a new—or at least a newer—car, saying he'd get one when he could pay for it himself. Paul made decent money for the limited hours he worked, and his living expenses were minimal, although he insisted on donating something for the groceries each month. But he was bound and determined to finish his education debt-free. Admirable, and an accurate measure of the man I treasured, but I had to admit the faded purple wreck brought down the neighborhood a bit.

Upon my arrival at the office, I started looking for a competent and trustworthy PI in the Miami area. My search eventually led to a man by the name of Bob Cohen, whom I pictured as a heavy, florid chain smoker, a judgment prompted solely by his raspy voice and quick, breathy speech. Nonetheless, he had a reputation as a careful investigator with high moral standards and contacts in racing circles. I wasn't certain if that included duck races.

"Yeah, I know Kenny Hammond," he said after I briefly explained the situation.

"Know him or know of him?" If he knew the developer personally, he might not be the man for the job. Personal loyalties might get in the way.

"Everybody in the state knows him by reputation. I know him casually from occasional Kiwanis meetings. Nothing that would prevent me from doing the job. But I'm not sure I'm up for helping someone blackmail the guy."

"If that were the game, I wouldn't touch it myself. No, if my client's right, Hammond tried to set her up for a quarter-of-a-million-dollar fall. She tumbled to it in time to protect herself, but now that protection might come back and bite her in the fanny."

"That default clause you mentioned?"

"Right. If—and I say if—he had anything to do with the theft of her racer, he was trying to defraud her. I'm convinced the duck is across the border in Mexico, so that's a dead end from here. Since Miami has a large Hispanic population, I thought Hammond might have contacts in that community who could help him with something like this. All my client is looking for is something to level the playing field again."

"All she's looking for is something to hang over his head and make him back off." He stopped to reconsider. "Well, that's close enough to being on the right side of the ethical line, I guess. Hammond's pretty thick with the Cubano community, so you could be right. Let me check out a couple of things, and I'll get back to you this afternoon to let you know if I can do it."

He probably wanted to check me out. He was careful, and I liked that. I liked that very much.

After I got off the phone, I invited Hazel and Charlie into the office to bring them up-to-date on the situation and endure Mother Hazel's lecture about being careful. She always delivered one after a close shave, and I guess a hail of gunfire qualified. Once her rebuke was out of the way, we settled down to discuss some of the other cases. I began to get the feeling things were getting away from me. We had two new cases I knew nothing about. They were ordinary assignments, tracking down a long-lost heir to a small estate and conducting a background check on a potential hospital administrator, but I'd always been the one to accept or reject cases. Now it seemed that responsibility had fallen to Hazel by default.

That shouldn't have bothered me, but it did. I had a world of confidence in my office manager. She knew the way the place operated better than I did. She knew me and my capabilities and interests and standards, so there was little danger she would accept something inappropriate. I'd be more likely to cave in to some poor soul's pleading and take on a disastrous case than she was.

But things seemed to be growing more than I ever expected—or wanted. Charlie put in full days now, and it was past time to make his job permanent. Hazel spent more time sleuthing from the office than she did acting as administrator. She regularly called in a discreet temp to do the transcribing and run down things at the courthouse. She also called in Tim Fuller from time to time to give Charlie a hand. All this would have pleased most businessmen, but I didn't consider myself an entrepreneur. I was a cop. A cop without a shield, but a cop nonetheless. I investigated.

Charlie hung around after the meeting and asked if I had a minute. I invited him to join me at the small conference table in the corner of my office. He claimed the chair to my right. Odd. He usually took a seat directly opposite me so he could watch my expression, an old cop's trait. He spent a few seconds twisting the worn gold Albuquerque High ring on his right hand. I waited him out.

"BJ, we might have a situation here."

"What kind of situation?"

"Well, personal, I guess you'd call it." He studied the tabletop a moment longer while I held my tongue. "How do you feel about office relationships?"

"Relationships?" I struggled to hide a smile. "You mean office romances?"

His rangy shoulders rose and fell. "I suppose. Romance seems kinda strong, though."

I let the smile loose and beamed at him. "Hell, Charlie, it came to that last year while I worked that case up in Bisti."

He ducked his head and looked like a craggy sixty-year-old schoolboy owning up to being smitten for the first time. "You might be right. How do you feel about that?" He lifted his head and fixed me with his blue-eyed gaze. A lock of gray hair fell over his forehead.

"I think it's great. You two are made for one another."

His lips twitched. "I'm talking about Hazel, you know."

"I know. I've known for quite a while. Probably before you did."

"Well, back in my cop days, two people on the job getting involved was frowned on."

"You're labeling us, Charlie. I don't think anybody looks at office romances like that any longer. Of course, it's Hazel, and I meant what I said. I think it's great."

The man actually blushed. "Well, thanks for being so understanding. I'd rather you didn't say anything to Hazel. You know, wouldn't want to embarrass her."

"Are we talking about the same Hazel? But, okay. I won't say anything if you don't want me to."

"It's not formal. I mean, I haven't asked the question or anything like that."

"Enough said. You have my blessing, if that's what you want. But let me know when I can put a dozen red roses on her desk."

"I'm going to do that this afternoon. Then I'll tell her we had this little talk."

BOB COHEN phoned shortly after lunch to accept the assignment. He made a point of stating he worked for me and no one else, which made clear how close to the ethical edge he felt the case skirted. Personally I had no such qualms. Hammond had intended to use underhanded means to take Millicent's money, and I saw nothing wrong with finding a way to prevent him from doing so.

Cohen gave us some "go-to" Internet addresses for public information on the Miami developer and faxed some other data. After reading the material, I was struck by the developer's absolute pettiness. Hammond, a man with a personal net worth in the high eight figures, dealt in hundreds of millions of dollars on a regular basis. That he would resort to cheating to win such a paltry amount—by comparison, admittedly— proved what an egomaniac he was. Win at all costs. Consequences be damned.

Reviewing that information carried me into the afternoon, when Charlie's promised roses showed up—pink, not red. The color perfectly matched Hazel's powdered cheeks. I walked into the outer office to find her holding a small black box in her hand and muttering, "Charlie, you old fool."

He took a ring from the box and held it up. She blushed brighter but held out her hand. He slipped the circlet on her finger.

"Congratulations," I said. "It's about time."

"BJ, are you sure it's all right?" Hazel turned toward me but continued to gaze at the modest diamond and sapphire ring on her finger.

"Of course it's all right. If he'd waited much longer, I'd have bought the ring myself and claimed it was from him. When's the wedding?"

"We haven't talked about a date. I didn't even know he'd bought a ring."

"Had it for a month," Charlie said. "Just waiting for the right time."

I clapped each of them on a shoulder. "Well, I'm going to settle the date right now. You two are getting married in my living room on New Year's Eve, just before the ball drops in Times Square. Agreed?"

"I guess so." Charlie gave Hazel a look.

Her pudgy cheeks dimpled in a smile. "Sounds good to me. But I want a small affair. Nothing elaborate."

I went home that evening happy for two of my favorite people, but as I walked into the kitchen and found Paul throwing together a quick meal, my world turned bittersweet. Hazel and Charlie could sanctify their love in a public ceremony—and more power to them—but that privilege was denied us. Why? For the millionth time, that question came to mind, and I did not like the ugly answer that rose in response.

THE NEXT afternoon, as I harvested some additional information on Hammond from the websites Cohen had provided, Hazel announced a phone call from my old comrade-in-arms, James Guerrero.

"I don't know if you're still interested in that fellow you called me about the other day," he said, "but I ran across something interesting this morning on Hector Acosta."

Despite the fact the GSR investigation had closed and my present assignment was Hammond, I assured him I was.

"Do you remember I told you Acosta supposedly made a lot of money in Brazilian emeralds? Well, there's a little bit of a stink about that. Not in Mexico but down in Brazil. The former mine owner, who's also the landowner, claims he's been defrauded."

"What kind of fraud?"

As Guerrero related the tale, the owners—a family named Guzman— knew the mine was pretty near played out when they leased it to Acosta and his associates. They had sold the mineral rights for a pittance but insisted on a royalty provision. The modest monthly payments they were receiving satisfied the family until a write-up in the Mexican press extolled the exploits of Don Hector Acosta. The article made a big point of the millions he had made on Brazilian emeralds. Supposedly enough to bankroll everything else—the ranch, some commercial developments in Mexico City and Veracruz and Durango and elsewhere. Old man Guzman read it and immediately contacted his lawyer to file a suit claiming a million in unpaid royalties and nine million in damages.

"I take it from your tone of voice that doesn't sound right to you," I said.

"Nope, it sounds like money laundering to me. That's conjecture... not a conclusion. It would be a hell of a way to wash dirty money."

"If that's the case, you'd think they'd take the mine owner into their confidence."

"I damned sure would have. If that's what was up, the last thing they need is a squeaky wheel. And a loud squeaky wheel, at that."

"You said Acosta has some commercial developments in several places. That might tie into something else that's related. See if you can find any connection between Acosta and a man named Kenneth Hammond or Hammond Development, Inc. out of Miami, will you?"

I gave him the particulars on the Florida developer before we did some Corps reminiscing and hung up. Acosta and Hammond were both into commercial development. Maybe they knew one another, had joint business interests.

The Brazilian lawsuit required a bit of thought as well. It might provide a chink in the Mexican rancher's armor that could be exploited. If Acosta felt some pressure, he might be inclined to help Millicent with her wager problem as a public relations ploy. Providing he had ties to the Miami Cuban business community and Hammond, of course.

I gave Acosta's name to Cohen so he could check for a Miami connection while James nosed around his contacts across the border. Then I phoned Millicent to see if she knew of any association between the two. I expressed surprise when she answered her own phone.

"I do that quite often, actually. But Maria isn't here today, so I'm it."

"Where's Maria?"

"She and Luis had to go home. Or at least, they had to go to the Lightning Ranch. Paco was breaking a bronc and it fell on him. Broke his shoulder, they say."

"Will he be all right?"

"Oh yes. But Maria needed to see for herself, so I told them to take a week off. They should be back by the weekend. Have you made any progress?"

I told her about Bob Cohen and filled in some of his background, including the fact he knew Hammond slightly.

"I have him looking for Hispanic contacts," I said, "because I believe your duck disappeared across the border after Liver Lips took her."

"I see." She sounded distant, distracted.

"Is everything all right?"

"Yes. Except for maybe losing the ranch that's been in my family for a hundred years, everything's peachy. Hector's made another offer. Sweetened it by about half a spoonful of sugar."

"But it's still not an acceptable offer?"

"No."

"If you do end up having to sell it, why don't you put it on the market?"

"That's what I'll probably do."

"If we aren't successful in getting you out from under this, do you think Hammond will take a mortgage on the place and let you pay it off?"

A bitter laugh came across the line. "A rational man would. If I failed to pay up, he'd have a ten-million-dollar ranch for two hundred fifty thousand dollars. But I'm not certain Hammond's rational when it comes to me. We've battled over the ducks several times, and I've absolutely humiliated him. He's not accustomed to losing. Who knows, greed might triumph over vengeance, but I'm not about to broach the subject until I know it's necessary."

I rooted around in my memory and came up with nothing. "When did you say the race is scheduled?"

"Saturday, August the twenty-third. You've got nine days to pull my fat out of the fire, BJ. I'm counting on you."

"You've got more time than that. Even if that's the default date, you can stall while we do our investigation. By the way, do you know if Hammond and Acosta are acquainted?"

"Wouldn't surprise me. Hector attends some of the horse tracks in Florida, although I've never seen him at duck races."

"Do you know of any joint ventures they've undertaken as commercial developers?"

"No, but Heck's got his fingers in as many pies as Hammond does, so it wouldn't stretch the imagination too far to make that connection. Are you suggesting Hector had my precious kidnapped?"

"I have no proof of that, but as you said, it wouldn't stretch the imagination too far."

"That low-down son of a bitch! And now he's trying to steal the Lazy M."

"Hold on, now. We don't know that."

"No, but it makes sense. I'll shoot that bastard the next time I lay eyes on him."

"Wait a minute, Mud." That name just came out of my mouth, but it seemed in character at the moment. "You can't let him know we suspect there might be a connection. Don't put him on his guard."

"I'll be sweet as pie. Rhubarb pie."

"Have you heard the latest news about Acosta? He's being sued for ten million."

"Pesos?"

"Dollars, I assume." When I briefed her on the situation, she jumped to the same conclusion Guerrero had.

"He's laundering drug money."

"Maybe. Have you ever suspected him of being in the drug business?"

"They use his ranch to traffic the stuff, but they use ours too, so that doesn't mean anything. No, if that's what it is, I suspect he's just cleaning their money for them."

"Could be."

"Just a minute, BJ, I've got another call coming in." After a lengthy pause, she returned. "It's him. Hector's calling."

"Take it, and then call me back. I'm curious about what he wants."

"I'll do better than that. I'll hook you in on a conference, but don't say anything. I'm not going to tell him."

I hit the Mute button to block out any ambient sound and waited. A moment later I heard Millicent speak.

"Heck, how's Paco?"

"That's why I'm calling, *chiquita.* He's going to be fine. Merely a hairline fracture of the scapula. They've bound him up, and he'll be uncomfortable for a while, but he will recover. Maria and Luis wanted you to know they're returning to the Lazy M in a couple of days."

"Tell them to stay as long as they need to."

"The boy will be fine. He's up and around and already back in the saddle. This morning he and his father took a short ride out to one of the line shacks where Luis and Maria used to live. We've both had worse accidents. The biggest problem Paco has is not physical—it's romantic. He had to delay his wedding for a few weeks."

"Wedding? I didn't know he was getting married. Maria and Luis haven't said a word. Usually they speak quite openly about their family. And they know we're fond of Paco."

Acosta cleared his throat. "They didn't know about it."

"What? Why not?"

"You'll have to ask Paco that. He met Madelena—that's the young lady—about a year ago, but no one realized they were getting serious until just recently. I only learned of it when he asked if he could take a week off for his honeymoon."

"Oh dear. Are his parents upset with him?"

"Surprised is more like it. But she's a likable young lady, and they'll grow fond of her. That's what parents do, no?"

"Yes, it's our lot in life. Madelena, you say?"

"Yes, Madelena Orona, a Palomas girl. I know the family quite well."

"I see. Please let me know what their plans are. I'd like to send a wedding gift."

"Of course. I hate to grow crass on the heels of something like that, but have you thought over my offer?"

Millicent's tone remained casual. "No, not really. As I said, I'm not inte20rested in selling the Lazy M, and if I were, I'd put it on the market."

"I heard there was some urgency in the matter. The rumor mill, you know."

"Oh, you must mean the bet I've got with someone on a race. I wasn't aware the news leaked out. And speaking of the rumor mill, I heard you were being sued for ten million dollars. Something about Brazilian emeralds?"

"It's nothing. The Brazilian has no valid claim. As a matter of fact, the suit has been dropped. There was a death in the Guzman family. One of his sons, I believe. They have the killer, by the way. A mere child of thirteen, if you can believe it. A vendetta between two families, no doubt. At any rate, old man Guzman decided he had more important things to attend to than pursuing frivolous claims against me."

Chapter 20

MILLICENT'S CONVERSATION with Hector Acosta triggered something in the back of my mind, but I wasn't certain what it was. After I hung up, I dialed my El Paso contact. James Guerrero was a one-man shop, so when his voice mail informed me he wasn't in at the moment, I left a brief message.

My desk clock snagged my attention, and I bolted out of my chair. If I didn't get a move on, I'd be late for lunch with Lt. Gene Enriquez. My old partner at APD and I tried to meet regularly. That kept me abreast of Duke City goings-on and got him a free lunch.

I left my building by the Copper exit, crossed Fifth, and walked past the block-long pedestrian mall that closed Fourth to vehicle traffic. Then I headed north on Third on the latticed-shaded sidewalk along the east edge of Civic Plaza. The intermittent shade was welcome on this sunny August day.

The DoubleTree dominated the 200 block of Marquette NE, rising as a white monolith for fifteen or so stories—I'd never actually counted them. Our usual lunch place for the past few years had been Eulelia's in the historic old La Posada Hotel on Second and Central, but, alas, Conrad Hilton's hotel—the first he built outside of Texas—had been sold once again and was closed for repair and renovation.

I arrived first and sat at our table for five minutes before Gene arrived, looking harassed—as usual. He had me by about five years, and if I remembered correctly, his forty-first birthday was coming up pretty fast. I'd have to call Glenda to see what the plans were for the event.

He plopped his stocky five-seven frame down in the chair opposite me and snatched the menu a waitress left. "Haven't heard from you in a while. You must not have needed me to solve your cases for you."

"Gene, Gene, Gene. How many times do I have to tell you, confidential investigators don't solve cases, they merely collect facts and turn them over to clients."

"Yeah, right. Like we collect facts and turn them over to the DA. If we left it to those bozos to solve cases, we'd all be in deep doo-doo. Let's order before you start picking my brain. I might not have any left by the time you get through." He waved an arm in the air, and our waitress materialized.

He ordered a T-bone rare with reduced-fat cottage cheese, asparagus spears, and beets. Either Glenda had him on a diet, or he was taking it easy in order to pig out at whatever birthday shindig the family planned. Or maybe his promotion to lieutenant last year had turned him into a sedentary desk cop fighting the calories harder than ever. I settled for a BLT with baked potato chips. We both had iced tea, his with enough lemon wedges to effectively convert it into lemonade.

As we waited to be served, I filled him in on the situation. Then I listened to his ideas on the case with interest because Gene was a good, intuitive cop. Plus he had roots and family in Mexico. Maybe he had some idea of how things operated down there.

He agreed the Brazilian mine was probably a money-laundering operation and showed no surprise over a kid killing one of the Guzman family. Some of the most vicious gangs in Mexico and the rest of Latin America had taken to recruiting from the growing ranks of orphaned and homeless children.

When our platters arrived, we dug in and shifted to updating one another on our lives. I asked about the family, and he gave me the news on Glenda and his five kids. He asked about Paul. He'd been aware I was gay all during the time we partnered together as detectives. He had no personal problem with it, although he endured a few barbs about riding with a queer. He'd handled it, and after he learned he could trust me, we'd been one of the most effective teams on the force.

GUERRERO CONFIRMED what Gene told me when he called back later. "Oh yeah, BJ, the story's all over the press down there. And let me tell you, it wasn't any family feud that got Guzman's oldest son killed. Someone sent that kid to do a job, and he got it done."

"That's hard to believe. It seems risky to use children to commit murder-for-hire. How can anyone trust a youngster not to rat him out when the authorities catch him? It doesn't make sense."

"Not to you, maybe, but it makes perfect sense to the goons who use them. There's an explosion of homeless children in places down there, many of them orphans or simply abandoned. Although most of the drugs in the US come up from south of the border, until recently drug use in Mexico itself was manageable. That's started to change. Some of the youth gangs and cartels are deliberately getting these kids hooked on narcotics so they can use them as mules, runners, spies, even as gunmen. They use them up and throw them away. Orphans are expendable."

"But don't the kids give them up when they're caught? The law of self-survival seems pretty basic to me."

"Who can they turn in? Just the man who gave them the assignment. And that guy is a low-level hit man who's probably already on the run. As far as the kid who does the deed is concerned, he's a minor who won't do a lot of hard time. Of course, that doesn't protect him from retribution from the victim's gang or family, but nobody cares if that happens. That's an oversimplification, of course, but there's no question in my mind that's what happened in Brazil."

"So Acosta put out the contract?"

"I didn't say that. Acosta might not even be in the drug business—beyond the laundering. Or he might be on the fringes of it. He may have had no knowledge somebody planned to take care of the Guzman problem in that manner. In fact, it's possible—barely—that he didn't even know the Brazilian emerald operation was being used to launder money. A couple of crooked mine executives could have cooked the books so production appeared to pay an adequate return to Acosta and his investors with most of the money going to the drug cartels."

"Come on, do you really believe that? If Acosta didn't know, he had to suspect."

"A lot of people close their eyes to suspicion when there's money like that involved. Who's to say what he really knew? At any rate, that's the argument his lawyers will make if it ever comes to that. Which it won't."

"Unbelievable. Have you had any luck connecting Acosta with Kenneth Hammond?"

"Not yet, but I've got some feelers out. This killing will make my sources a little more cautious, but eventually someone will tell me what we want to know. If there is anything to know, that is."

I told him what had happened to Paul and me at the City of Rocks. He said the likelihood of fingering a couple of gangsters shot up in a gunfight was remote, but he agreed to make some inquiries.

After that I got Deputy Nap O'Brien on the line. He hadn't heard about the Acosta suit and murder, but as I laid it out for him, that elusive thought struggling to break loose in my mind came to the fore.

"You said a woman might have left the impression in the sand out at the City the day Bert got bushwhacked. Do you think it could have been a kid instead?"

"Yeah. Coulda been a big kid. Or a woman. Or a smallish man. But he had to be a pretty good shot. I just don't know, BJ."

After that downer, I turned to the computer to check criminal records in Texas, New Mexico, Arizona… and for good measure, Florida. Hector Acosta's name came up once. An old drunk-and-disorderly misdemeanor case in Las Cruces during his NMSU days. After that, nada.

Why was I so interested in Acosta when all the signs pointed to a ducknapping by a Florida man about to lose a quarter of a million on a bum bird? Because Acosta benefited too. He wanted the Lazy M, or at least he made an offer for it, and the theft of the duck was forcing Millicent to do what she would never have done otherwise—seriously consider his offer.

Chapter 21

BOB COHEN phoned the next morning to inform me he turned up a connection between Kenneth Hammond and Hector Acosta. A search of the Florida Associated General Contractors' trade journals and the local newspapers revealed four articles linking the two developers at a meeting of general contractors and investors held in Miami the previous spring. The stories contained photographs of some of the principal players, among which were Acosta and Hammond. Three newspapers—the *Miami Herald*, the *Daily Business Review*, and *Diario Las Américas*—covered the meeting, and two of them mentioned a collaboration between the two men on some commercial developments in Little Havana.

"From what I can find out," Cohen said, "they've known each other for years. One of the articles refers to them going deep-sea fishing together sometime back."

"Anything about mutual racing interests?"

"Nothing in the articles, but they're both known as horse racing enthusiasts. Hammond's duck racing is well-known down here, but there's no mention of Acosta as a duck man. However, he could be backing Kenny's play."

"So Acosta might even have a piece of Millicent's bet."

"There's no evidence of that, but a cop acquaintance of mine has some leverage on a man in Kenny's office. He's pretty low-level, but he might know something."

"Chase it down, will you?"

I took my tape of the conversation to Hazel for transcribing and then tried to get Manny Montoya on the phone. He was out, but the state police dispatcher agreed to run him down and deliver my message. He called back within half an hour.

I asked if he'd made any progress on the Liver Lips Martinson murder. "You have declared it murder, haven't you?"

"Homicide by vehicle. We got another sighting of the '96 Firebird, but it disappeared again. I have everyone at all the border stations within a hundred miles keeping a close look out for it, but I'm willing to bet it's still on this side of the line."

"Anything turn up on the radar screen about Liver Lips himself?" I asked. "Like for instance, what he was doing up in Albuquerque where I ran into him? He didn't come all the way up here to get his scratched arms treated. Maybe he delivered the duck to someone in Albuquerque."

"I don't think so. I traced his movements backwards. He'd dropped somebody off in Barelas." Barelas south of downtown Albuquerque was once called the barrio.

"Do you know who?"

"No, but I know where. The Six Pack. You know it?"

"Yeah, I know that dive from my APD days. The sheriff's office had to take a run out to the roadhouse at least twice a week. But that's not in Barelas. The Six Pack's out on the old Belen highway."

"From what I hear, they should have shut it down," he said.

"They did, more than once. But the owner had good connections up in Santa Fe."

Ramon Ruiz Parnewski had managed to hang on to the liquor license every time the county shut him down because he leased the bar to some relative. When things died down, he installed another son or nephew or cousin as the owner and opened up under the same name. He'd been playing that game since the sixties.

According to Manny, Liver Lips had given someone a ride up to the old man's house, which *was* in Barelas. The description of the passenger proved worthless, and nobody admitted to having an out-of-town visitor within the last few weeks.

"You read anything into that?" I asked.

"Hell, no. They wouldn't tell me if it was the parish priest coming up to baptize somebody's baby."

"So Liver could have been hauling an illegal alien or making a drug delivery or turning over the duck. Or all three, for that matter. The bird could have been in a coop in the bed of the truck."

"I don't think so," he said.

Manny found where Liver stopped for gas and a bite to eat. The owner of the truck stop saw him pick up a hitchhiker as he left and recognized the man climbing into the back of the pickup as a local by the names of Sills. Manny interviewed him. Sills claimed the truck bed was empty except for a toolbox. He said the passenger up front with Liver was Mexican. At least he heard them speaking Spanish.

"Do you know where Liver picked up his passenger?" I asked.

"Apparently at his house in Deming. Neighbors told us a young couple came to his front door two days before his death."

"A couple? A man and a woman?"

"Yes, and we figure one of them was the passenger he delivered. Other witnesses at the truck stop confirmed there were only two men in the truck, so they apparently dropped the female somewhere."

"Or she never left with them. Do you have a description of her?"

"Yeah. Mexican with long hair. Long black hair. One kid we talked to said she was *muy linda*."

"Very pretty, huh? He have any comment about her curves?"

"Yeah. Little disappointed there. Said she shoulda taken better care of herself. Carrying too much weight around the middle."

"Like she was pregnant, maybe?"

"Who knows? Our informant's a fourteen-year-old kid with hormones on steroids."

I told Manny about the closemouthed woman who answered Liver's door the morning after his death. He promised to look into it more deeply.

AT A standstill for the moment, I looked for another case to help me work off some nervous energy. The job Hazel handed me was one I didn't want but probably deserved because I'd been the one to accept it.

Chance LeGrande, or Chancy as he preferred to be called, qualified as a chump. Worse, he was a jerk and had been for all the years I'd known him. After his father left him twenty or so million dollars, Chancy bought a 2007 Bentley Azure soft-top convertible simply because no one else he knew drove one. He liked to imagine the lower classes *ooh*ing and *ahh*ing as he drove down the road like the second coming in the elegant car—or *the motorcar*, as he called it when he put on airs. That wasn't just my opinion; it was shared by most of our mutual friends. As soon as his pricey play-pretty went up in smoke—so to speak—he crawled all over APD to find his stolen vehicle. When he felt they weren't responding appropriately, he turned to me for help.

I tried to tell him APD had better resources than I did, but he refused to listen. He claimed to know who took the car, and he just wanted me to go get it back for him. Well, he didn't *exactly* know who stole it, but he'd narrowed it down to two people: his ex-wife, Shelley, a pistol in her own right, and his ex-boyfriend, Armando, both of whom he had chased off with his outrageous—read *sexual*—demands. Again, not just my opinion.

I did a quick search of the records at MVD and NICB, the National Insurance Crime Bureau, looking for title transfers of the Bentley's VIN. Wasted effort, of course. Anyone stealing a three-hundred-fifty-thousand-dollar automobile would at least falsify vehicle identification numbers and license plates, but it was a place to start. The car was probably across the border by now. Well, maybe not. People would remember a flashy Bentley showing up at some point of entry.

The convertible had been taken from the big circular driveway in front of Chancy's west side "estate house." More of his elitist attitude, and here I'd thought LeGrande was French, not class-conscious English. The theft occurred sometime after he took a cab to the airport to fly to Taos for an art studio opening. Apparently he didn't want to leave the car in a public lot but hadn't put it in one of the estate's three attached garages because he thought it gave the house—a scaled-down castle—class. He figured because the elaborate wrought iron gates were closed and locked, the car was safe. Anyway, the vehicle had simply vanished. Nobody in the neighborhood noticed the luxury automobile driving down the road.

I got in the Impala and drove over to Rio Grande Boulevard and started ringing doorbells and pounding on doors. Occasionally at one of the fancier places—those like Chancy's—I had to speak to someone through a box on a locked gate. The residents of Rio Grande Boulevard considered themselves the cream of the elite, and not too many of them were inclined to invite a confidential investigator in for a cup of tea and a quiet talk. But my poking around revealed that a family had been moving into a large home a quarter of a mile down the road. Consequently there had been moving vans in the vicinity the morning of the theft. Now a household of that size might require two such vans, but midway through the afternoon, it dawned on me that I was hearing a description of three different vans. After that it didn't take much time to come to the conclusion that despite Chancy's locked gates, the thieves had simply

loaded the Bentley into a van and driven away. I asked Hazel to check
with local moving companies and truck rental outlets.

Any physical evidence, such as tire tracks, had long ago been
windswept and driven over, but this scenario argued someone close to
Chancy had engineered the theft. Someone who knew he would be out
of town at that particular time. Perhaps he was right. It might be one of
his exes.

Shelley proved difficult to find, but it was relatively easy to locate
Armando Alderete. A couple of calls to gay friends who kept up-to-
date on the lavender handkerchief scene in town sent me straight to his
mother's home in Los Lunas, south of Albuquerque. She ordered her
son outside to talk to me, by which I concluded everyone tended to walk
all over the guy. I contemplated using the opposite approach, cajoling
him a little, until I saw the protruding lower lip. The sight of a forty-
year-old man sulking like a teenager convinced me bulldozing was the
way to go.

He studied the card I had given his mother. "What do you want with
me?" His high, thin voice set my nerves on edge. The puffy flesh beneath
the smooth skin of his face and the saddest eyes I'd ever seen on a human
reminded me of a hound dog begging a treat.

"What I want is Mr. LeGrande's motorcar." I might as well put on
airs myself. "And I don't want to spend all day finding it either."

"I don't...." He swallowed. "I don't have it. What would I do with
a car like that?"

"I don't know what you would do with it, and I don't give a damn.
He knows you took the car, and he hired me to get it back. Any damage
to it, I'm to take out of your hide."

"You can't.... Uh, I want a lawyer."

"Hey, bonehead, I'm not the cops. They might get you a lawyer,
but I sure as hell won't. If you didn't take the Bentley, you know who
did. Either way, I want the car back."

"I didn't! I swear on my mother's grave."

"I just met your mother. She doesn't have a grave."

"Well, you know what I mean. Maybe that bitch Shelley took it.
That would be just like her."

I resorted to trickery... all right, a lie. "You know, that's exactly
what she said. 'That bitch Armando took it.'"

"You talked to Shelley? And she blamed me? I wouldn't know how to do something like that. And what would I do with a car that everybody on the street stops to stare at?"

"Even at ten cents on the dollar, that Bentley would bring you thirty-five thousand. Now that your free ride with Chancy is over, thirty-five would help cover your expenses while you look for another sugar daddy."

Armando's eyes took on a wild look, and he repeated himself. "I wouldn't know how!"

"No, but Shelley would, wouldn't she? All you did was help her, right? If that's true, helping me recover the car will go a long way in buying you some consideration from the district attorney."

The sad doggy eyes went crazy. "District attorney? I don't want anything to do with the district attorney. Or... or the cops either. They were mean to me when they asked me questions before. Just trying to get Chancy's goat. You know, to scare him. Payback for the way he treated us. Oh God," he moaned.

Shelley, she of the iron will and vengeful nature, shouldn't have chosen such a weakling as a collaborator. Within an hour, Armando confessed everything to the detectives working the case down at APD. All he'd done was give her a set of keys he'd made while still in Chancy's good graces and let her know when her former husband planned on flying to Taos. She took care of the rest.

The cops located her at her sister's house in Madison, Wisconsin. By the next morning, they had found the Bentley in a rented self-storage unit in Albuquerque. Hazel added something extra to the bill for recovering the vehicle undamaged. Of course, the police would have eventually taken the same route I did and found the car, but Chancy didn't need to know that.

I took the rest of the day off and dropped by the country club pool, hoping Paul would show up even though I knew he had a late class. He didn't, so I did the therapy I'd been ignoring lately. I hit the water and wore myself out swimming.

Chapter 22

BOB COHEN checked in early the following morning with news he had talked to a junior accountant in Hammond's office named Jackman. This was the man Cohen's contact had on a leash. He seemed privy to at least some of the developer's personal affairs. He knew, for example, his boss had put together a group to fund the bet with Millicent but didn't have names. He'd reluctantly promised Cohen to see if he could learn more details.

A call to the Lazy M Ranch went to voice mail, so I left a message. Apparently Maria and Luis had not yet returned. It had been two days since I eavesdropped on Millicent's conversation with Acosta, and he'd said there would be a delay before the pair came home.

Despite a workout in the pool yesterday afternoon, my right leg felt stiff. Would that old bullet wound ever give up and leave me alone? Probably not. After telling Hazel where I'd be, I headed to the North Valley Country Club without much enthusiasm. Swimming, once a pleasure, was now simply a chore unless Paul sat in the lifeguard's chair. Today someone else occupied it. But on the bright side, Paul's summer classes were almost over, and we planned on getting away for a few days after finals.

I hit the water and gradually got into the swing of the thing. My muscles loosened, and my mind went into neutral as I concentrated on each stroke, each kick. Tired but feeling pretty good after a quick shower, I made a round of the clubhouse. The card room was semibusy, as it usually was, but few other members had made an appearance this early in the morning except for golfers already on the course. I headed back downtown to the office.

Hazel had James Guerrero on the line when I walked through the door. The El Paso investigator confirmed the information Cohen gave me earlier. He'd verified most of the details with a separate source and added the fact that Hammond, Acosta, and a few others were partners in a large Veracruz shopping center called Plaza Rayo, or Lightning Square. James had also picked up rumors of trouble in paradise. Gossip hinted at some sort of strain—if not downright rift—between the Florida developer and the Mexican rancher, but no one knew the cause or how deep it ran.

He had heard snatches of talk about the shootout at the City of Rocks. Wild tales claimed ten smugglers from a northern Mexico cartel were killed, or perhaps fifteen US Border Patrol agents. At any rate, all the yarns were bloody. Hector Acosta was kicking up sand because his ranch had been used as the launching point of the supposed raid. When I asked what that meant, James replied, "Nothing."

He also told me the kid who killed the Guzman son in Brazil had been thrown into a crowded adult prison, where guards found him two days later with his throat slit. That, James claimed, ended that. The authorities would never identify those responsible for the murder. When I asked if he knew a good investigator in the Palomas area who could poke around in Acosta's affairs, he expressed doubt. Acosta was too powerful for locals to mess with. Nonetheless, he agreed to keep his ears open.

Hazel occupied the next couple of hours going over a number of administrative issues. Last year I had finally convinced her to add her signature to the firm's general business account, but she occasionally asked me to sign checks to keep my finger on the pulse. I did it solely to placate her. She was far more careful with the company's money than I was.

Millicent returned my call shortly after lunch, sounding tired. No doubt she felt the absence of her domestic pair. All the duck-farming chores now rested solely on her back because she trusted no one with them except Luis. Not to mention cleaning and cooking for the ranch. Apparently the ranch had no bunkhouse cook, although Linus was a decent hand with cowboy fare. She heard my report without comment. When I finished, she asked what it all meant.

"It means your childhood friend Heck Acosta could have been responsible for stealing your prize duck. Actually, that makes sense for two reasons. He might have felt the need to support his business partner—Hammond—by buying part of his bet with you. If so, he certainly didn't want to lose his money. Did you ever discuss the Hammond situation with Acosta? For instance, did he know you'd discovered the fraud?"

"Switching his racer, you mean? No, I never discussed that with anyone. Not even Bert. You said there were two reasons. What is the other?

Oh, I see, the ranch. Heck wants the Lazy M, and a quarter-of-a-million-dollar loss makes me vulnerable."

"Exactly. He benefits more than Hammond does."

"Not if you put Hammond's ego into the equation, but I see what you mean. Heck benefits doubly."

"That's the way I read it."

"Do you think they were in cahoots on the theft?"

"No idea, but it really doesn't matter."

"If the rumors are true, do you have any idea what the trouble between Heck and Hammond is?"

"None at all. It could be nothing more than gossip. James Guerrero's trying to find out, although he admits it's a long shot."

"Can I call you back, BJ? I've got to think this over."

"Sure. I'll be here the rest of the day. If not, Hazel will know where to find me."

I had not heard from Millicent by the time we closed the office for the day, but she had my cell number if she needed to reach me.

I MET Paul at Applebee's on San Mateo and Academy at six. Before he left this morning, he'd expressed a desire for one of their chimichangas—a fried flour tortilla filled with cheese, shredded beef, *carne adobada*, and served with guacamole, sour cream, and salsa. After we were seated at one of the tables along the windows at the front of the restaurant, he ordered a "thingamajig," which is supposed to be an approximate translation of chimichanga. I dithered over the menu before ordering the same. Then we sat quietly and contentedly until the waiter brought our mugs of beer.

Paul took a deep sip and leaned back as he set the heavy glass on the table. "Well, it's all over on Friday."

"Great. Did you ask about getting some time off at work?" I asked.

"I've got two weeks of vacation time coming, but they asked me to take only half of it." He shrugged. "I said okay. We'll save the rest for the holidays." He grinned. "How much time is Hazel going to let you have?" He must have read something in my face because he frowned. "You haven't told her you're taking some time off, have you?"

"Well, not exactly. But that's the beauty of being the boss. I don't have to clear it with anyone."

"This is Hazel we're talking about, you know. You might own the joint, but she believes she runs it."

"And she does. Don't worry, I'll clear the decks."

The waiter delivered our order, and for the next few minutes, we devoted ourselves to eating, cleaning greasy lips and fingertips, and then smearing them all over again. The chimichangas were an excellent choice.

MILLICENT DIDN'T call until Friday morning. "I'm sorry to be so long getting back to you, but it's been hectic around here without Maria and Luis. They're coming back tomorrow. Heck is flying them in. He says he has something he wants to talk to me about."

"Get ready for some more pressure to sell. Who knows, maybe he'll up his offer to a reasonable level."

"Maybe, but I'd like you to be here, BJ."

"You need a lawyer for that discussion, not an investigator."

"Maybe, but I'd feel more comfortable with you here. You have some insight into the situation a lawyer doesn't."

"I don't know, Millicent. I have other plans."

"Please, BJ. I need you."

Painfully aware I was committed to Paul, I hedged. "Let me see what I can do. But no promises."

Before making any decisions, I reached Bob Cohen to see if he'd heard of any breach between Hammond and Acosta. He hadn't, but he got Hammond's accountant on the line with us. At first, Jackman was reluctant to speak with a stranger on the telephone, but under Cohen's patient prodding, he gradually loosened up, confirming he had been present when Hammond took a call from Acosta. By the time the conversation ended, the Florida developer had been extremely upset. The accountant had caught references to "the bet." Probably Millicent's bet.

"Did you get the feeling Acosta backed out of covering his part?" I asked.

"It sounded more like Kenny wanted Acosta to back off, and Acosta refused."

That made sense. By now the whole duck-racing world knew Quacky Quack the Second was missing. Regardless of who took her or why, the bet was now a cinch. Either man would benefit from a larger share of the wager. The accountant could add nothing further.

I procrastinated in reaching Paul until well after his last class but was spared trying to run him down when I heard his voice in the outer office. I stepped to the doorway in time to see him give my secretary a bear hug.

Hazel made no secret she wasn't fond of my gay lifestyle—no, that wasn't quite right. She had come around to ambivalence by now—but she held a genuine fondness for Paul. He was younger than I was, so if anyone "corrupted" anybody, I was the bad guy in her eyes. Of course, she had liked Del too, until he betrayed me while I was laid up with a gunshot wound.

She held him at arm's length. "You're too thin. You're not eating enough."

"Swimmers are supposed to be thin. You ever see a chubby swimmer?"

"Lots of them. Just take a look at any municipal pool."

"I'm talking about swimmers, you know, racers."

"Whatever. Are you eating enough?"

"Enough for both of us. I just burn it off."

"I worry about men who live alone... uh, about bachelors. They don't take care of themselves properly."

Paul's laugh was pure silver. "We need a woman for that, huh?"

Hazel sniffed. "Well, some of you do. What brings you here, anyway? We don't see much of you in the office."

"Just finished finals for my summer classes, and I thought I'd see what Vince is doing."

"I'm standing here watching the two of you," I said.

"Hi. Hope I'm not interrupting anything. I just wanted to know what I should get prepared for. You still wanna head for Los Alamos and play a couple of rounds on the municipal course?"

Hazel's gaze bounced back and forth between us.

"We're taking a few days off," I said hastily. "Or, at least, we were."

Both of them frowned at me. I tried to put the best face on the situation. "How would you feel about another visit to the Lazy M?"

Hazel gave me a frosty look. "Getting shot at once isn't enough?"

"What kind of ambush are we walking into this time?" Paul asked. "I thought you said Los Alamos was the best public course around."

"It is, and we've played it before. But the client just called and asked me to come down for a meeting. And I can guarantee there'll be no gunplay on this program. I just arranged that demonstration last time to impress you."

"A little comedy would have been fine, but that was high drama."

"Seriously, how do you feel about going down there for a couple of days? Then we could head over to the Gila Wilderness or go to Mexico for a little while."

"I don't have a passport."

"You don't need one until next year. Your driver's license will work just fine for now."

"Well, I guess so. At least it's a change from school."

I called Millicent and told her Paul and I would be down sometime tomorrow, probably early afternoon. She offered to send the helicopter to pick us up, but I told her I wanted my car since we were taking a few days off.

When she offered the use of her Lincoln, we compromised. I promised to get Jim Gray, the private pilot I usually use, to fly us down in his Cessna. That spiced things up for Paul a bit. He had flown to Farmington last year during the Bisti murder business, but soaring around in a small craft still gave him a thrill. I made up my mind to have Bert gave him a spin in the whirlybird. That was a whole other experience.

Chapter 23

PAUL AND I departed Albuquerque from the Double Eagle Airport early Saturday morning. Jim Gray, a lanky fixed-wing jockey with a small potbelly, got us off the ground and into the air with his usual efficiency. Although we approached the end of our monsoon season, dark thunderheads to the west announced rain over the New Mexico-Arizona border. Exercising his customary caution, Jim got on the radio for a final weather report. He knew I didn't speak radio—all that static and the special lingo pilots and controllers use rendered it incomprehensible to me—so he obliged us with an interpretation.

"Gonna be okay. The front's drifting off to the northeast. It won't even come close enough to give us a bumpy ride. We're gonna have a good flight."

We circled to the west and settled on a south-southwest bearing, passing over the old mining town of Grants and the El Morro National Monument, a huge, castle-like sandstone monolith rising from the scrubby desert plateau. A reliable water hole hidden at the foot of a bluff had made it a popular campground since pre-Columbian times. A succession of Indian, Spanish, and Anglo passersby had left inscriptions: names, dates, messages, and rock art, all carved into the stone to create a gigantic historical billboard. Somewhere nearby lay the desert Ice Cave. Farther to the west, the lava beds of the El Malpais Badlands cast an ebony shroud across the land.

As promised, the trip was uneventful. Jim set the Cessna down on the Lazy M's dusty strip with hardly a bump and turned to taxi back toward the house. On the way we passed a parked red-and-white Piper with an XE fuselage number, which Jim recognized as a Mexican registration. This plane looked larger than the small Piper Acosta flew last time, making me wonder if he had a fleet of aircraft. Did he check in through the nearest international airport or simply make an illegal hop over the border? In the latter case, did that raise any hackles at the Border Patrol?

Jim was in a hurry to salvage some of his weekend, so he kicked us out, revved the engines, and immediately took off for Albuquerque. I experienced a brief feeling of abandonment as the Cessna rose into the blue, leaving us in the middle of New Mexico's Boot Heel country without our own transportation. The sensation passed as Millicent, trailed by Acosta, came out to greet us. She wore a broad smile, but I saw the strain behind it.

After warmly acknowledging Paul, the Mexican rancher turned to me. "Nice to see you again. Millicent tells me she invited you down to prove that every visit doesn't end in a gunfight."

"That's what *she* tells me, but can you confirm that?"

He grinned. "I see. Since the *pistoleros* came from my side of the fence, you want to know if I can guarantee they won't come over and shoot up everything again, no?" His mood darkened for a moment. "We must all work together to put an end to that kind of thing."

I stepped to Millicent's side and gave her a peck on the cheek. Paul added a small embrace to his. She looked spectacular today in a fringed buckskin skirt and a white blouse with short, puffy sleeves and a bit of lace at the throat. Large silver earrings with bits of coral, shell, and turquoise dangled from her lobes. On many large women, the outfit would have looked ludicrous; on her it was becoming.

"Come on in," she said. "We ate quite early this morning, so Maria has whipped up a light brunch for us."

"Lead me to it." Paul rubbed his hands together. Maria, standing in the shade of the patio, flashed him a smile.

Millicent patted his arm indulgently. "Bert's out in the back pasture. He'll be here soon, but we don't have to wait. He and Paco can pick through our leftovers." She led the rest of us toward the portico, where covered dishes were laid out.

"Paco's here?" I asked.

"He decided to accompany his parents home," Acosta said.

"His fiancée came along so we could meet her," Millicent said. "Charming girl."

"Yes, but she wanted to visit an old school friend in Deming," Acosta said. "You will meet her later. Madelena is a very nice young lady."

"Luis drove her over in one of the pickups," Millicent explained. "They'll be back later."

If Maria's homemade tamales, *carne adobada* burritos, refried beans, and guacamole were "light," I'd hate to see a heavy meal. Delicious. Paul went back to the serving trays at least twice. Bert and Paco had better hurry up.

As if my thoughts had conjured them, the whack of rotors heralded Bert's small helicopter. He came in from the south and set the chopper down gently. Bert strolled toward the patio before Paco made it out of the cabin. I saw why when he finally came into view. His left arm was cocked against his torso, held motionless by a denim sling and strips of tape. He moved as if his cracked scapula gave him fits.

"BJ, I see you made it." Bert slapped his hat against his pant leg, raising a small cloud of dust. He gave me a firm handshake and winked as he turned to Paul. "You came back for the showdown, huh?"

"I thought last time *was* the showdown. But your mom claims there won't be any more."

Paco, moving up behind his buddy, merely nodded to me, although he clasped Paul's hand and murmured *"Con mucho gusto"* when Bert introduced the two of them.

"I see your wing's still clipped." I nodded to the heavy sling.

Paco moved his shoulder gingerly. "Yeah, but it's getting better. Pretty soon, Don Hector will put me back to work."

"Let's not rush things," Acosta said. "The time will come when it truly arrives."

A curious remark. Was it an old Mexican adage? "I'm looking forward to meeting your fiancée," I said.

"She's in Deming right now. She'll be back later."

"You fellows better dig in before Paul cleans out the pantry," Millicent said. She smiled and patted his arm. "That's all right, honey. I like a man with a healthy appetite."

"I ASKED BJ to join us for our talk." Millicent settled behind her desk. Bert took a seat at his own, leaving the two barrel chairs in the middle of the room for Acosta and me. "BJ's not only an investigator, he's a lawyer as well. So please feel free to discuss anything you wish."

If my client wanted to fib to her adversary, who was I to object? I nodded in a manner I imagined worthy of a doctor of jurisprudence and held my tongue.

He glanced at me before facing her again. "I wondered if you have given my proposal any thought."

"I've thought of little else."

"I can imagine. There is one element I can add to the deal. I am aware of your wager with Kenneth Hammond. Kenny and I are old friends. We have some investments together on both sides of the border, so we talk occasionally. I believe I can promise he will release you from your wager should you decide to sell the Lazy M to me."

"Get him to forget the wager, and we won't even have this conversation."

"I'm afraid I cannot do that. A man does not give up a quarter of a million dollars easily. Even today, that is a considerable amount of money."

"Which simply means you can do it, but you won't. Not unless I sell you my home."

"Millicent, be reasonable. We are business people, no? Favors one can do for friendship's sake, but business is business. Accept my offer, and you can retire comfortably."

"What do you think, BJ?"

"I've already given you my opinion. The wager does not have the force of law. No court in the land will prosecute Hammond's claim. Refuse to pay it, and it will only cost some of your pride."

"I agree," Bert said.

"What do you say to that, Heck?" she asked.

"What I say or what I think on the matter isn't important. But the Millicent Muldren I know, the Mud Hen of my acquaintance, honors her word."

I saw his devastating argument strike home. Millicent almost physically recoiled. Then she squared her shoulders. "Even so, the legal advice BJ provides must be given some consideration."

Acosta shifted his weight in the chair. "Let us put our cards on the table. The wager will be forfeit in less than two weeks. If I am to persuade Hammond to forgive it, I have to do it before that happens. I might have to engage in some… subterfuge, shall we say. I don't have much time. *You* don't have much time."

"How much of that bet do you hold, Heck?" I asked.

He didn't flinch. "I own a piece of it, and I'll gladly surrender that portion to you in any case. But I doubt that ten percent of two hundred fifty thousand dollars will ease your burden very much."

"I understood it to be considerably higher than that. Of course, rumors are often inaccurate."

Millicent waved a finger at Acosta. "That son of a bitch was going to pull a switch on me, Heck. He was going to—"

I interrupted her. "That's water under the bridge. Since you are a longtime friend of the Muldren family, I'm going to tell you something. I have investigators working in Florida right this minute to confirm the fraud Hammond planned, and when I do, the situation changes considerably. The bet might be technically forfeit in less than two weeks, but payment is certainly not going to be made until I am satisfied every legal avenue has been exhausted. And if a fraud was being perpetrated, the court system may have something to say about that. Hammond could find himself in some legal difficulties. He may find it easier to cancel the debt than to fight the claim and counterclaim for the next few years."

"You have never met Hammond, have you?" Acosta said, clearly unimpressed by my bluff. "Such arguments might sway many men, but not one with such a monumental ego."

"I know a little about the man, and he did not make his millions by taking unreasonable risks. Business risks, maybe. But not taking on the courts in a hopeless cause. It's not out of the question we can prove who stole Millicent's racer in the first place."

"You believe Kenny did that?" Acosta's black eyebrows twitched.

"Hammond or one of his associates. Someone who has a piece of that bet, for example. And I am reliably informed several individuals share in the wager."

Acosta faced Millicent. "Is he speaking for you?"

"If you pay a man for his advice, you are at least obligated to seriously consider it. Yes, Heck, I will let him proceed with his investigation until he brings it to a close."

"I see. Since I can add nothing further, I will take my leave."

"You are welcome to stay the night."

"Thank you for your hospitality, but I must get about my business."

"You can't leave until Madelena returns from Deming," she said.

"I will have Paco contact her and tell her we'll pick her up at the Deming airport."

"A shame. Maria delights in cooking for you, you know."

"And I take pleasure in her talents. It is not only your ranch I covet, Millicent. I would like Maria's cooking as regular fare."

Acosta rose and gave Millicent a kiss on each cheek before rearing back and taking a long look at her. "The years have been kind to you, my dear. You look just like the muchacha who stole my heart so many years ago."

"You go to telling whoppers like that, and I'm gonna wonder what else you're playing fast and fancy with."

He laughed aloud, said a quick good-bye to Bert and me, and bustled through the doorway, calling loudly to Paco in Spanish. We followed them outside.

Minutes later the Piper rose and circled back to the northeast.

"Well, that was quick." Bert stared at the departing plane.

"Too quick," his mother said. "I haven't seen Heck in such a hurry in a long time."

"We must have given him something to think about," I said. "Too bad. I hoped Paco's girlfriend would get back so I could take a look at her."

Paul's voice surprised us. "That wasn't going to happen." We all turned to look at him. He stood under the patio cover with a leftover tamale about halfway to his mouth.

"What makes you think that?" Millicent asked.

"When he came through the doorway and collected Paco, I heard him ask if Madelena would be at the airport yet."

"You must have misunderstood," Bert said. "He planned on having Paco call on the cell and tell her to meet them at the airport."

"No. I heard him clear as day. They'd already agreed to pick her up there."

"Son of a bitch," I swore. "Acosta didn't realize you spoke Spanish. Millicent, was he aware I intended to be here for the meeting?"

"Not until he arrived early this morning."

"With Paco and his lady friend in tow."

"That's right."

"Does Madelena Orona happen to be pregnant?"

Her look of surprise gave me the answer I needed. "How did you know?"

"I believe I've seen the lady before. At Liver Lips Martinson's house the morning of his murder. Bert, how fast can that helicopter get us to Deming?"

"Not fast enough. The Piper's got better air speed, and Acosta has a head start. But we can try."

"Let's do it," I said.

"Do you have room for me?" Paul asked.

"Yeah, it's a three-seater."

We ran for the helipad.

Chapter 24

BERT GOT us aloft without delay. We arrived at the Deming airport in time to see Acosta's red-and-white craft rise off the runway and circle east toward Las Cruces. We landed so Bert could refuel and I could ask a few questions of the airport personnel. Acosta's arrival and departure had seemed entirely routine to them, if a little rushed. He'd had the ground crew top up the gas tanks, filed a flight plan for the El Paso International Airport, took on a female passenger, and went airborne in record time. Had he been expecting us to follow in the chopper?

Half an hour later, we took off again, following I-10 west until we spotted Luis Rael's pickup on the highway below us. After that Bert veered southwest, and for a few minutes we were in Mexican airspace. As the Lazy M headquarters came into sight, I asked Bert to buzz the City of Rocks to give me a visual layout from the air.

Most of the "city" part of the stone pile centered in the area we had already visited. One "street" appeared to penetrate the formation from front to back. Bert confirmed it as a way out of the City to the south. There was no sign of life in the area beyond a coyote—the four-legged kind.

LUIS RAEL dry-washed his face in evident exasperation. "No, no, Señor Vinson, I did just as I was instructed. I am told to drive the girl to Deming to see a friend of hers. Then I am to do some shopping for Doña Millicent. After that I am to pick up Señorita Orona at the house where I left her and bring her back to the ranch."

"Those were your instructions, but that's not what you did. What happened?" I asked.

"I drop her off like I am told to. I go to the leather shop to pick up tack gear they were repairing for us, but it is not ready. So I do some more chores and come back to the saddle shop later. Now it is ready, so I pick it up and go back to the house for the señorita. She has me take her and her lady friend to one or two stores. Then we take her friend home." He

seemed to run out of steam. Luis was not accustomed to long speeches…
at least not with an interrogator.

"And then?"

"And then she has me take her to the airport. She tells me I can
return to the ranch, but I cannot leave her alone like that. She says Paco
and Don Hector were coming for her. Still, I wait until they arrive."

"What did they say?"

"Don Hector, he said I should go home. Their plans had changed,
and they were returning to the Rayo."

"Did they say anything else?"

"Not to me, Señor. I heard nothing more than talk about getting
back home."

"Did you speak to your son? Ask him why they were leaving so
abruptly?"

"Only to say good-bye."

I leaned back in the chair behind Bert's desk as Luis stood before me
with his head bowed, hands clasped in front of him. He looked like a man
who knew he had done wrong but hadn't yet figured out what it was. I asked
for the name and address of the friend Madelena had visited. He provided
the address but only knew the name Elena. I dismissed him with my thanks.

After the door closed behind him, I looked at Millicent, seated at
her desk opposite me. "Do you believe him?"

"Of course. Why would he lie about his instructions? Besides, he
did exactly what I told him to do. I assure you that Maria and Luis are
both entirely loyal."

"Why? They've known Acosta—hell, they worked for him—long
before they came here."

"They have never done or said anything to violate my trust. They
are discreet, faithful friends and employees. Heck or Paco must have
called the girl and told her to go straight to the airport. Why is this such
a big deal, anyway?"

"Acosta knows we're putting two and two together, and he's still
hoping we'll come up with five," I said. "My investigation turned up the
fact Paco knew Liver Lips, but it appeared to be no more than a casual
acquaintance. The presence of Paco's fiancée at Liver's house on the
very morning he died ties her—and by extension, him—to the murdered
man. And that leads us closer to the idea that Acosta had the duck stolen.
It's possible he's responsible for Liver Lips' death."

"I find that hard to believe. I've known Heck since we were children. At one time… well let's just say that at one time everyone thought we might get married."

"But you didn't, and there was a reason for not marrying the man. Like maybe you sensed he wasn't what he pretended to be."

"You think he's involved in the drug trade, don't you?"

"I thought you reached the same conclusion when I told you about the emerald mine suit."

A retort formed on Millicent's lips, but she let it go and leaned back in her chair. "I guess it would explain why he's so hell-bent on getting the Lazy M."

"Gives him back-to-back properties spanning the border. Total control of what's rapidly becoming a four-lane highway for drugs and illegals."

"Undocumented workers, you mean."

"Okay, undocumented workers. Call it what you want, the act itself is illegal, so they're illegals in my book."

"Humans aren't illegals," she said.

"By that logic there are no felons, just people who perpetrate felonies. Millicent, if this does nothing else, it ought to put some starch in your backbone." My choice of words went down wrong, but I ignored the skin tightening around her eyes. "It ought to make you put aside your pride and announce to the world you're not going to honor the bet with Hammond. If he wants to sue, fine. Go to court with a good lawyer, and you've got a shot at coming out all right on the other end. To put it crudely, these people are planning on screwing you."

She came around—partially. "I'll consider it, BJ. I'll think about it."

The thwack of the helicopter drew us to the window. Bert had been called to one of the more remote pastures to look at a sick animal, and Paul decided to tag along for the ride. He had been impressed by our flight to Deming that morning, but now I wondered if Bert had engaged in enough aerial antics to dampen his appetite. Apparently not. The two men got out of the machine laughing. Millicent opened the outside door and invited them into the office.

"Vince," Paul said, "that was a hoot. That contraption's better'n any roller coaster I've ever been on."

"Paul flew the bird," Bert said.

"Yeah, for about two seconds. Bert had to save us from landing upside down."

"This guy knows a little about cowboying, Mud."

"Great, when we turn up shorthanded we'll know where to look."

It was good to see Paul so pumped. I'd been worried he'd be disappointed because we hadn't headed north for some golfing, but he clearly enjoyed himself in this environment.

Bert turned serious. "What do you figure that was all about? You know, spiriting Madelena off and keeping her away from BJ?"

We all found seats as Millicent settled behind her desk. "It looks as if Hector might be behind all of our troubles, including the loss of Quacky," she said.

"What do you mean? I thought this fellow Hammond was the one. He stands to gain a quarter of a million bucks now that she's disappeared. How does Heck figure in?"

His mother directed her gaze at me, so I answered the question. "We know Acosta has a piece of that bet."

"Ten percent," Bert said. "And just this morning he offered to surrender it. In fact, he offered to get Hammond to forget about the whole thing."

"Our investigation has picked up some kind of rift between the two men. According to one source, it concerns the bet. We're not exactly sure what the problem is, but I believe Acosta wants a bigger share now that Millicent can't meet the terms of the wager."

Bert waved away the comment. "So he tried to get a bigger share to surrender. Tried to put himself in a position to deliver on his promise."

"But remember, that promise is conditioned on your mother selling him the ranch. Are you in favor of selling?"

His eyes bugged. "Hell, no! I grew up here. I like running this ranch."

"Maybe Acosta will let you run it for him," Paul suggested. "You know it better than anyone, other than your mother, that is."

"I don't think so." I shook my head.

"Why not?" Apparently, Bert had given that possibility some thought too.

Millicent straightened up in her chair and answered with a question. "Why do you think he wants the Lazy M?"

"That's easy," Bert said. "It's the best working ranch in this part of the country. We've made money in years when other people have lost it. Good climate. Good land. Decent water. But most of all, we've developed a herd of prime mother cows. It takes years to do that."

"The Lightning is half again as big as we are. And Heck runs a yearling operation. He doesn't know squat about a cow-calf ranch," Millicent said.

"And what's a good way to get into that business? Buy the best one around, that's how."

"That's true," I agreed. "If ranching is his real interest."

"Of course it's his real interest. I know he's into lots of other things, but what else would he want with the Lazy M?"

"Think about it, Bert. You've been having a lot of trouble with drug gangs crossing your territory. Where's the trouble coming from?"

"Mexico. Oh, I see. It's the Lightning over there. But that argument says Heck's in the drug business." The room went dead silent until he shifted in his chair and gave each of us a pointed look. "You think he's in with the cartels?"

"It's possible," I said. "Things make more sense if he is. When he gets the Lazy M, he controls both sides of the border. And the highway bisects the ranch, so he would have undisputed control of a drug- and alien-smuggling route from Mexico into virtually any point in the US. And don't forget, the Lazy M has a landing strip as well. That makes dispersal of the goods even easier."

"Mud, this is the guy you grew up with. From what I hear, he was almost my papa. Come on!"

I spent the next fifteen minutes reviewing everything I had learned. I took them step-by-step through the investigation, considering and then dispensing with each of the other possible reasons for the theft of Millicent's prize duck. I led them through the Brazilian emerald mine business as a probable money-laundering scheme and the murder of one of the owner's sons, as well as the subsequent killing of the accused murderer. Inevitably we came back to Liver Lips and his fatal wreck.

After I finished, Bert sat with his elbows on his desk, his head cradled in his hands. Finally he lifted his chin and fixed me with a stare. "You haven't answered my original question. About spiriting Madelena away like that."

"I have. You just haven't heard it."

He recoiled as if struck by a rattler. "You mean you think she and Paco are mixed up in this? You think they work for a cartel?" He shook his head. "No way! Paco's been my buddy since grade school. He wouldn't do something like that to me."

I shrugged. "You mother's been pals with Acosta since *she* was in grade school. Doesn't look like that's given her much protection. And who does Paco work for?"

Bert went red in the face. "You're nuts, BJ. Hell, we've worked cattle together, slept out under the stars together, gone hunting. Man, we've romanced women and got drunk together."

I caught Millicent's look of despair and saved her the effort of responding. "Grow up, Bert. Not everyone shares your moral and ethical standards—or your definition of friendship."

For a moment he looked like an overgrown kid about to take on a schoolyard bully. Then he blew air through his nostrils. "I know that. It's just that...."

"I understand. You hear about things like this every day, but when it happens to you, it hurts."

"Hurts like hell!" Then he squared his shoulders. "Where's your proof? This is all speculation."

"It is speculation. But it's informed speculation."

"So you think Acosta sent Madelena to check out Liver's shack after he was killed in a wreck."

"Just so we're clear on this, Sgt. Manny Montoya of the New Mexico State Police considers it death by vehicular homicide. And yes, she went to make certain Liver hadn't left anything lying around that tied them to the theft of your mother's duck."

"Why her? If Paco's mixed up in this, why didn't he go?"

"My guess is she's not as well-known in Deming as Paco. Every time I described her to anyone, they came up blank. Only two things really stood out about her—she was very pretty, and she was carrying too much weight around the middle, probably meaning she was pregnant. Unfortunately— from their standpoint—I was already on Liver's trail and got to his place while the state police were still considering his death an accident."

Bert took the same approach as his mother. "I gotta sleep on this. But for argument's sake, let's say you're right. What do we do now?"

"First, you and your mother have to be careful. Very careful."

"You're saying they might try to hurt us?"

"Haven't they already tried? You've gone hunting with Paco. How good a shot is he?"

"Very good." Bert's complexion mottled. His hands on the desk clenched. "Are you saying Paco tried to shoot me out at the City the other day? You've gone off your rocker. This is the guy who's watched my back in a dozen fights. Hell, he faced down a thug with a big-assed knife for me once."

"He had no reason to turn on you then. He does now."

"You're insane or else you're some kind of racist."

My own gorge rose, but I held it in check. "My partner at APD was Hispanic, about one generation removed from Mexico. I'd trust him with my life. In fact, I have, more than once." I nodded toward Paul. "And the man I chose to make the most important person in my life has Mexican blood. No, I'm not insane or a racist. I'm a realist."

Bert glanced at Paul. "Sorry. But this is a shock to the system. It's like being told a member of your own family tried to kill you."

"After the sheriff's men found where he'd set up his ambush, O'Brien said the shooter appeared to be a small man or a woman. Paco's, what? Five eight? Slight build. Good shot. Knows the layout of the ranch."

"Yeah, but if he was the one meeting Mud at the City that day, then everything would have come out in the open."

"Maybe he just watched someone else's back."

"Did O'Brien find any sign of anyone else out there?"

"No, but the area was pretty windblown." A thought came to me. "And consider something else. The BP agents couldn't figure why the *traficantes* didn't simply back off when we challenged them at the City. Although I didn't catch it at the time, one of the agents said something significant. He said the traffickers might have thought we had binoculars. If I'd had a pair, I could have easily seen their features, enough to identify them later."

"So you think Paco led them to the City because he couldn't afford to be identified."

"Right. It didn't take him long to figure out we weren't BP, so we had to be locals. Someone from the ranch."

Bert's face closed up. "Oh my God, you shot the guy in the shoulder, and...."

"And right after that, Paco had the riding accident that broke his arm," Millicent finished.

Bert looked like he'd been clubbed. His features sagged. "All right, same question. What do we do now?"

"I haven't been to Miami in years. You up for a quick trip, Paul?"

Chapter 25

As SOON as we broke through the cloud cover, Paul glued his nose to the 747's window to stare at the massive metropolitan complex spread out beneath us. "Man, that's big. What's all that green over there?"

"That's the Everglades."

"Where all the alligators are?"

"Not all of them. The Biscayne National Park is over on the east side. Did you know Miami's the only major city in the United States founded by a woman? A local citrus grower, I believe, named Julia Tuttle."

He turned to me with a grin. "You and your trivia. When's hurricane season around here?"

"Right about now. The rainy season is roughly the same as the hurricane season."

"Shoulda brought my raincoat. I've got my bathing suit, sunglasses, and sweats. That's all I need." He turned back to the window. Paul never went anywhere without a swimsuit. I, on the other hand, would have to purchase one.

I had spoken to Cohen yesterday afternoon, and when he confirmed Hammond was in Miami, Bert got us to El Paso in the chopper. We had to charter a flight to the Dallas Fort Worth International Airport and then wait half the night before boarding the American Airlines jet that deposited us at Miami International. We'd grabbed sleep when and where we could.

As we prepared to land, I glanced at my father's Bulova strapped to my wrist and moved it ahead two hours to five thirty local time.

We only had carry-on luggage, so we immediately started off in search of our ride. As we hiked to the American Airlines counter, I heard my name on the loudspeaker. A nearby white courtesy phone connected me to the message center, where they steered me to Bob Cohen. He stepped forward with his hand out and introduced himself.

"Nice to meet you in the flesh," I said. "This is my friend, Paul Barton."

He offered his hand to Paul as well.

Cohen had a thick torso, but his limbs seemed a bit foreshortened. Steel-gray hair at the sideburns thinned out on top. His eyes, also gray, had a no-nonsense glint above loose pouches of flesh. His husky voice and the nicotine-stained fingers of his left hand confirmed my opinion he was a heavy smoker.

"My car's outside. Where are you staying?"

"The Ritz-Carlton in Coconut Grove."

"Nice choice. It's close to the financial district. Hammond's office is on Brickell. You have an appointment with him tomorrow morning at ten thirty."

"Good. Did Hammond put up a fuss?"

"I never spoke to him. I dealt with his executive secretary, Josefina Morales. She asked the purpose of the visit, of course, but I said exactly what you told me. You'd been referred by Mrs. Millicent Muldren."

It was overcast, but no rain fell as we exited the terminal and made our way to the short-term parking area. We stowed our bags in the trunk of Cohen's black Malibu sedan and sat back as he maneuvered his way out of the sprawling airport. Keeping to the left, he took the on-ramp of SH-953 south toward Coral Gables. After that I quit paying attention. Paul rode in the back seat, craning his neck this way and that.

"Man, it sure is flat down here," he said.

"About the highest it gets is around forty feet above sea level, and that's over on the west side," Cohen said.

"Sounds like one good wave would drown us all. And this is hurricane country too."

Cohen laughed. "Sure is. Although we've never had a serious hurricane strike the city. Affect us, yes, but not hit us directly. And with the warm Gulf Stream to the southwest and the cold Atlantic current to the east, you'd think we'd be ground zero."

"Is it always so hot here?"

"Muggy, but not really hot. The temperature doesn't hit a hundred very often, but the humidity makes it seem hotter than that. By the time you get settled into the hotel, we'll get some sea breezes, and things will ease up."

I spent the rest of the twenty-minute drive bringing Cohen up-to-date on the situation. He listened without interruption. When I finished, he chewed his upper lip before speaking.

"Kenny's a cutthroat bastard, but he'd only cut your financial throat. I've never believed he had that damned duck stolen. I can see him taking advantage of it by showing up with a bird that couldn't beat a crippled snail in a foot race. But that's about as far as he'd go."

"Would a two-hundred-fifty-thousand-dollar loss hurt him?"

"A quarter-of-a-million-dollar loss would hurt anyone. Especially now. Construction's in the tank around here. I imagine he's hurting some, and a loss that size wouldn't be easy to swallow."

"So the threat of a serious lawsuit might make him stop and think?"

"Maybe. Is that your strategy?"

"It might come to that before the interview is over, but I just want to see his reaction when I mention a couple of related murders."

"Murders? Who got iced besides the fellow who took the duck? I know about the emerald mine owner down in Brazil, but that one's a little far-fetched to tie into this mess, isn't it?"

"A friend of Liver Lips Martinson named Elizondo Lopez was fed a drug overdose right after he was seen talking to me."

"Somebody's serious. This Acosta fella?"

"That's what I believe."

"You want me to come with you to see Hammond tomorrow?"

"No, but I'd appreciate any feedback you can get from Jackman after my interview. I'll touch base with you later in the day."

Cohen dropped us in front of the Ritz-Carlton, a hotel posing as an oversized Italian villa on Biscayne Bay. We passed into the clutches of a doorman, who summoned a bellboy to handle our meager luggage. One wall of the marble-studied lobby where I registered was a huge pane of glass that looked out onto a garden courtyard. When we arrived in our room, Paul walked straight out onto the balcony to take in the view of the bay. One of those sea breezes Cohen had promised showed up to ruffle his hair.

Traveling, even in a sealed container with filtered air like the Boeing, always made me feel gritty, so we shared a shower and played around a little before grabbing a badly needed catnap. We'd only snatched sleep where we could in airports and planes over the past twenty-four hours. Paul slept a couple of hours before starting to get restless, so I dragged myself out of bed. We dressed and headed downstairs to the Bizcaya Grill.

I chose the caprese salad for my antipasto; Paul settled on ricotta potato gnocchi. The salmon milanese served as my *principale*; he went for the certified Angus filet. We both passed on wine in anticipation of some club-hopping later. Paul ate with gusto and declared it a feast. I agreed. After the meal I pulled up the Gay Miami website on my laptop. We decided to try Club Sugar on SW 32nd.

When the taxi dropped us at what appeared to be a liquor store in a primarily residential area, I wondered if he hadn't made a mistake. But once through the doors, we were assaulted by loud music, blinding strobe lights, and a blast from a locomotive air horn. We learned later the DJ alternated between the horn and a police siren, as the mood hit him. The place was essentially one big room with two separate bars and a stage built around a dance floor. Although it was almost eleven thirty— late by my standards—the place was only semifull. The show, advertised as a transvestite dancer, wasn't scheduled to begin until 2:00 a.m.

The crowd consisted of an eclectic group ranging from shirtless young men to gussied-up mixed couples to flamboyant queens in feathers and glitter. We claimed a table near the dance floor and ordered a couple of six-dollar beers.

I'm not much of a salsa dancer, but Paul coaxed me out on the floor to try a couple of numbers. After that he gave up on me and accepted offers from guys, gals, and a few who pretended to be one but were probably the other.

I sat at our table and watched him indulge in the second grand passion of his life. Swimming, of course, claimed the first. But he was also a great dancer, moving like water over smooth rocks, undulating with the rhythm of the pulsing music. I watched a couple of his partners put the moves on him, but he declined with a nod in my direction. It made me proud.

"Your friend's the hottest thing in the club." I turned to face a well-dressed Hispanic about my age. The type I called "slick," mostly because of his black hair pomaded flat against the sides of his head. He sported a pencil mustache. "I saw you come in together," he explained. "May I sit?"

I indicated a chair and nodded. "Sure. My name's BJ."

"Carlos." Neither of us offered to shake hands. He glanced at the dance floor and smiled, revealing large white teeth. "You had better keep an eye on him. He's exactly what most people here are looking for. The Cubanos desire him because he looks Anglo, and the Anglos will fight over him because he appears Latin. He's a charming blend of the two, no?"

Discussing Paul like a commodity, which, of course, he was to many here, made me uncomfortable. "Yes, he is… in addition to being a fantastic human being."

"You are a visitor to Miami?"

"Yes. And you?"

"Born here, although not long after my parents arrived from Cuba. May I ask what brings you to Miami? Tourism? Business?"

Simple paranoia, a trait many investigators consider mandatory, put me on guard. "A combination. I'm on business." I inclined my head toward the dance floor. "He's on vacation."

Although the club wasn't crowded, the loud music made it seem so. A conversation was difficult without leaning close to one another, which made me uncomfortable. Nonetheless, I was as curious about this Carlos fellow as he appeared to be about me. He asked his questions, and I asked mine.

Within fifteen minutes I knew he had been put on my tail by Hammond. Furthermore, he knew that I knew. That cleared the air considerably. By then he had ordered two rounds of drinks, but I still sipped on the first, letting him know I had no intention of getting drunk and careless.

During a break in the music, Paul returned to the table, escorted by his most recent dance partner, who clearly wanted to join us but was discouraged by Paul's casual "Thanks, man." I introduced him to Carlos.

"¡Con mucho gusto!" Carlos said.

"Same," Paul responded. "You come here often?"

"No, not often. It doesn't quite live up to its name. I can recommend some clubs, if you wish. Some more… uh, interesting places, perhaps?"

"This one's fine. Just looking to do some dancing. Nothing more," Paul said.

"Then you will break the hearts of most of the muchachos here."

He gave the man an innocent stare. "I doubt that, but thanks."

Carlos wasn't going to give me any more than I was going to give him, so I brought things to a head. "Look, if your boss thinks he can lean on me because we visited a gay club, tell him he's out of luck. Half the state knows I'm gay. I'm fireproof on this."

He spread his hands. "Why would one man in a gay bar try to blackmail another man in that same gay bar?"

"I can think of a couple of reasons, but it won't work."

"I can see I am interfering with your night out on the town. I'll excuse myself now, if you don't mind."

"Not at all."

He rose, gave us a smile, and took his leave. We watched him walk out of the club.

"What was that all about?" Paul asked.

"Hammond put a minder on our tail."

"How? I mean, how would anybody find us in the middle of millions of people?"

"All you need is a starting place, and they knew we started at the Lazy M. They just followed the trail from there."

"Why?"

"Hammond doesn't know why I'm coming, and he wants all the ammunition he can gather."

"Well, hell, that puts a damper on the evening."

"Sorry. You want to try another place?"

"I'm kinda tired, but I'm charged up too. I'd just as soon go back to the hotel room. Be with you."

I matched the smile on his lips. "All right by me. But I need to do something first."

I made my way to the bar and caught the eye of a bartender, a cute Hispanic who appeared to be a little older than most of the other servers. He finished a drink for a man on a stool midway down the counter and came over to give me his full attention.

"I need to buy a couple of rolls of quarters."

His expressive eyes narrowed. "Something going down?"

"Nothing definitive. Just a feeling."

He motioned me around to the end of the bar. "I'll sell you the coins, but if you're right, this'll work better than a roll of quarters." Leaning forward to shield his movements, he opened his hand to reveal a small leather blackjack. It looked mean and ugly.

"Okay, but I'll still need a roll for my friend."

"Nah. I got another one of these." He reached under the counter and then slid both hands across the bar toward me. When he moved back, napkins covered two lumps on the counter. I slid them into my pocket and handed him two $100 bills. "Thanks. We don't allow anybody to hassle our customers. Let me know when you're ready to leave, and I'll have one of the bouncers keep an eye on you."

"Thanks. We're leaving now."

"Give me a minute, okay?"

I nodded and returned to the table. Paul rose and glanced at me in surprise when I pressed the sap into his palm.

He glanced at it quickly. "You expecting trouble?"

"I didn't like the way Carlos said good-bye. Might be nothing, and that's probably exactly what it is. But we need to be ready if trouble comes. Let's go. Keep your eyes open."

A six-foot-four bouncer nodded as he held the door open. Then he followed us outside. I expected the night air to be cooler—as it would be back home once the sun went down—leaving us with a balmy Florida night.

"You guys have a car?" the bouncer asked.

"No. We need a taxi."

"There's usually one around. You stay put, and I'll see if I can get you one, okay?"

Our escort stepped to the curb, looked in both directions, and then headed off to the left. Paul moved out onto the sidewalk to watch his progress. After hesitating for a moment, I started to follow.

They came at us like shadows out of the night. I caught a blur of movement and shouted a warning a second before the thug reached Paul. Then I had an assailant of my own to deal with. A thick, squat man lunged with a blade in his hand. I sidestepped and brought my hand up under his extended arm. The blackjack caught him squarely on the chin. He staggered but didn't go down. I pivoted and landed another blow to his temple. He dropped to his knees and toppled over.

I whirled to see Paul in a desperate dance with his attacker. He struggled to hold on to the man's knife arm with his left hand while his right fumbled in his pocket. I darted forward, but before I reached him, Paul popped the sap against the man's throat. The hoodlum grunted. Paul slammed his knee into his opponent's groin and then calmly thumped the man's noggin with the weighted leather, sending him facedown on the sidewalk.

"Shit, shit, shit!" Paul yelped.

Alarmed, I rushed to his side. "What is it? Are you all right?"

"He slashed my shirt. My best shirt."

"There's blood on it. Are you hurt?"

"Just a scratch. But, damn, it's my favorite shirt."

The bouncer came running up and took in the situation with a practiced eye. "You guys get outta here before somebody calls the cops. There's a taxi coming down the street. Don't worry about these guys. I'll take care of them."

I thanked the bouncer and shoved a sizeable bill and the two blackjacks into his hand. The taxi had stopped short of us, and I was afraid the sight of two men sprawled on the pavement would send the driver racing away. But he held on while we bundled into the backseat. He appeared nervous until I told him to drop us at the Ritz-Carlton. Apparently nobody from the Ritz-Carlton would be involved in such shenanigans, because he settled down and drove away at a leisurely pace.

"Are you sure you're okay?" I asked.

Paul gave me an irritated look. "I'm fine. How about you?"

"Mine didn't even get a piece of my clothing." My crack broke the tension.

"That's because you saw them. I was blindsided."

"You did okay for a blindsided hick from the hinterlands."

"BJ, was that a gay bashing? Or was there more to it than that?"

"I think it's more than that."

"Man, Millicent's duck must be one hell of a bird to kick up this much trouble."

We were silent the rest of the way, each nursing his own thoughts. Paul waited until I paid the cab driver and then trailed behind me as we entered the lobby. He was, I gathered, trying to keep anyone from seeing his slashed shirt. We made it to the room without incident, although we entered cautiously.

After snapping on the light, I made a careful search of the room, including the closet and shower in the bath. Upon finding no intruders, I closed the door behind us and pulled the shirt over Paul's head. He had a small cut on his left side. A mere scratch, as he said. Nonetheless, I got a first-aid kit from my bag and applied some antiseptic. He balked at covering it with a patch, preferring to stand bare-chested on the balcony and take in the lights from the boats on the bay while the medicine dried. I went out to stand beside him.

After a long, comfortable silence, he spoke. "Life sure gets interesting around you."

"Just trying to prepare you for a life of investigative reporting, that's all."

His laugh, like a velvet fog, floated through the tropical night.

Chapter 26

THE NEXT morning, Paul tried out the hotel's blue-tiled swimming pool while I went to meet Hammond. I'd called Bob Cohen last night and reported our adventure. Although he expressed doubt the developer would stoop to doing us physical harm, I couldn't separate the attack outside Club Sugar from the earlier appearance of Carlos at our table, so I was a little nervous over Paul's safety.

Still on edge, I presented myself to the receptionist at the Kenneth G. Hammond Development, Inc. offices on the tenth floor of a high-rise on Brickell Avenue, in the midst of the city's international banking center. The curvaceous redhead behind the desk immediately picked up a white phone and informed someone on the other end I was waiting.

A busty woman of forty fighting to look thirty-five showed up a minute later. Her makeup—while thick—was so professionally applied you noticed it only up close. Pretty but not spectacular, in part because her hair made me think of a tiger: black roots, blonde dye job, and rusty tips.

"Mr. Vinson, I'm Josefina, Mr. Hammond's executive aide. Will you follow me, please?"

Attaché case in hand, I trailed her deeper into the entrails of the building. The impression I wasn't being shunted off to some reception area to await Mr. Hammond's pleasure proved premature. He had a waiting room in his private suite. Josefina indicated a seat, offered me a choice of coffee or tea, and when I declined, abandoned me to a stack of professional and news magazines. Ten minutes later the place exploded into activity with the appearance of a large human dynamo through an obviously private entryway. A six-foot-three, sunburned, sandy-haired man, whom I assumed to be Hammond—trailed by a couple of minions in white hard hats—began issuing orders left and right. He paused at Josefina's desk and learned I sat not fifteen feet away.

He immediately dismissed everyone and came over to offer a beefy hand. From his grip, I knew he had spent many of his sixty-odd years out in the field doing hard labor before building his construction company.

After the introductions, he begged five minutes to get settled, which I, of course, granted.

Precisely 300 seconds later, Josefina ushered me into one of the largest private offices I had ever seen. One entire wall was floor-to-ceiling windows, giving glimpses of both the city and the bay. A massive desk anchored one end of the room; a small conference area with easy chairs and a coffee table occupied the center. The far end held a drafting table and some sort of computer setup that I associated with architectural drafting and design.

Not even a blotter marred the gleaming teak surface of his desk. The usual pen and pencil, calendar, and other accessories rested on the credenza behind him. Still wearing the neatly buttoned double-breasted coat of an ivory linen suit, he rested his elbows on the naked desk and leaned forward. A lock of white-blond hair falling over one of his hazel eyes gave him the look of an oversized, aging pixie.

"How is Millicent these days?"

"She's fine. She asked me to give you her regards."

"Please convey mine to her."

"Certainly. I propose we skip the pleasantries and get down to business."

"That suits me." He glanced at his watch, as any busy nabob would have at this juncture. "Why are you here?"

"I thought that would be obvious. I've come to secure your agreement to cancel the duck-racing bet."

"And why would I cancel a bet I am assured of winning?"

"Possibly to avoid becoming involved in a criminal investigation regarding the theft of her racer."

"Why would that bother me? I didn't take Quacky. Nor did I have a hand in her theft."

"Personally, I'm prepared to believe you. I don't think you took her, but one of your associates did, and in doing so, he committed a felony."

"Ah yes, the insurance company. I imagine the size of the claim would lift an otherwise inconsequential act to the level of a felony. Have they agreed to pay Mud's claim on the duck?" Apparently Millicent's nickname had migrated all the way to the Gulf Coast.

I'd touched base with Del last night and learned no decision had been reached. That meant a debate raged within the insurance company over it, which I considered a positive development. Now I chose to interpret it in the most favorable manner possible, as a pending approval. "That is expected momentarily."

"Excellent," Hammond said. "Then this will be a zero-loss situation for my old friend. I collect on the bet without loss to her."

"I don't believe she would agree with you on that. She's still out the most valuable duck in her flock. One she insured for two hundred fifty thousand for a valid reason. That duck was crucial in maintaining the quality of her farm's pâté and down business."

"Even so, she won't take a quarter-of-a-million-dollar loss in one fell swoop. And Mud's resourceful. She will find an adequate replacement."

"Easily said, but more difficult in practice. I strongly urge you to consider my request to cancel the bet."

"Unfortunately, I'm in no position to do that."

I sat back in the Moroccan leather chair across the broad desk from him and steepled my fingers. "Are you aware an associate of yours is attempting to use the bet to pressure her into selling him the M Lazy M Ranch at a ridiculously low price? In fact, he's offering to get you to cancel the bet as a part of the deal."

"Rubbish."

"I have a tape recording of the offer."

"Well, whoever it is doesn't speak for me."

"You know who it is. It's the man who's taking a bigger and bigger share of the wager. Hector Acosta is attempting to steal the ranch by using your duck race—after someone made certain she couldn't meet the terms of the wager. Just as you couldn't if her racer hadn't disappeared."

"I don't know what you mean."

"Please don't take me for a fool. I have the veterinarian's reports on Thunder Duck."

"Impossible!" His ruddy expression turned even ruddier.

I reached into my attaché case and pulled out a folder. "Here is a transcript of the recording of Acosta's offer and a photocopy of your vet's report."

"And are you recording our meeting too?"

I indicated the small recorder on my belt. "I am."

He gave a cold smile. "That's okay. I am too. All of this means nothing, Mr. Vinson. My Thunder Duck will be there on the day of the race—two days hence, as a matter of fact. If Quacky is not, that means the bet is forfeit. End of discussion."

He made as if to rise, but I held up a hand. "I met your man last night."

"What man?"

"The man who tailed me to Club Sugar. I hope he delivered my message."

"What message?"

"That I won't be blackmailed because I visited a gay club."

"Mr. Vinson, I set no one on your trail and have no interest in attempting to blackmail you. Why would I?"

"To keep this meeting from happening."

Even as I uttered the words, a light went off in my head. Perhaps it did in his as well, because he appeared a little more interested.

"Describe the man."

I did and provided the name Carlos as well. He rocked his chair back and stared at the ceiling a moment.

"I have lived here my entire life, Mr. Vinson. And during that time I've learned a few things about pressure and intimidation. I will even admit to having resorted to them over the years. But let me tell you one thing. Before I go after someone, I do my homework. Then I use people who are professional at that sort of thing. What you have described seems very heavy-handed."

"And I haven't even told you the worst of it yet." I went on to describe the attack outside the club.

"Gay bashing, perhaps? It does happen, you know." He thought over what he'd said. "Knives? Both of them had knives?"

"Not only had them, they were seriously trying to use them."

"Let me assure you I arranged no such reception, but I can tell you one thing with certainty. That was no attempted gay bashing. People like that get their satisfaction from beatings and humiliation. They are attacking something they fear or don't understand, trying to prove their superiority. But a knife attack is something entirely different."

"My sentiments exactly. Give me another ten minutes, Mr. Hammond. I think you're entitled to know what my investigation has uncovered."

Actually it took more like fifteen minutes to go through the entire thing. I gave it to him in greater detail than usual because I wanted him to understand what was really going on. By the time I finished, I understood Carlos and the two hoods weren't his. It wasn't only his reaction to my story. His earlier question rang in my ears. Why would Hammond go to such lengths to avoid a meeting he could have refused to attend in the first place?

"If what you say is true," he said at length, "then I'm not certain it is in my best interest to cancel the bet with Millicent. Perhaps it's healthier for me to ensure it remains in play."

"Can you tell me how much of the bet Acosta holds?"

He cleared his throat. "Forty percent. He started out at ten but bought out the other stakeholders." He shifted uncomfortably. "Now he's pressing me for the sixty percent I hold."

"And that's what caused the rift the construction community is talking about." The more he thought I knew, the better off I was.

"So there's talk of that, is there? Well, frankly, yes. Heck's being rather persistent."

"Let's count the bodies again, Mr. Hammond. The Brazilian miner's son, his killer, Martinson, Lopez. All dead."

"You're making my argument for me."

"Not quite. A couple of things appear obvious to me. One, you're perfectly willing to accept your partner's perfidy. Two, with nothing more than what I have at present, I could make a very good argument that a conspiracy exists between you and Hector Acosta. It might not rise to the level of criminal proof, but it's a good civil case, which will get Mrs. Muldren off the hook in the matter of the wager. I haven't even begun to investigate you or Hector Acosta, not seriously. And guess what? It's going to be much easier to gather information on you than it is him— except, of course, to link you together."

"I believe that was a threat. One that I have on tape."

"No threat, simply a notification of how we intend to proceed. And we both have it on tape, remember? Mine will not be electronically altered, and I trust yours will not be either. That's rather easy to prove with today's technology, by the way."

Hammond flushed, but he controlled his anger. "If I agree to cancel the wager, Heck will be on my back to proceed. And even if I refuse, he can still demand payment of his forty percent share."

"Not if your racer doesn't appear at the prescribed place on Thursday."

"Now you're attempting to involve me in a conspiracy on the other side of the equation."

"Not at all. Criminal acts have been committed, and you were intending to commit one yourself by substituting your racer until Millicent discovered your intent."

"She can claim that, but proving it will be difficult."

"I think you've just put your finger on the solution. Make the vet's report on Thunder Duck public—at least in the racing world—and declare that since neither of the ducks can race, the bet is moot, canceled. If anyone wants to put another interpretation on it, proving it will be difficult."

"But Thunder Duck can finish the race," he protested. "Not in very good time, I'll admit, but she can cross the finish line."

"Simply say it's a matter of honor. Your opponent's racer was mysteriously stolen, and the man who took her was killed. You cannot take advantage of a situation like that, so you do the honorable thing and tear up the wager agreement."

He wiped his mouth with a palm. "That would satisfy Mud but anger Heck Acosta. And it appears to me he's the one I need to pacify."

"Are you afraid of him?"

"I grew up in the construction business. I can take care of myself. And I don't believe he would come after me for forty percent of a quarter of a million."

"The stakes are much greater than that. He wants the bet to force Millicent to sell him the Lazy M for something other than ranching."

"For his drug-running activities, you mean. Providing your assumptions are correct, of course."

"That makes perfect sense to me. Do you find it so hard to believe?"

He leaned forward and straightened his spine as if it were cramping. "Frankly, no. There have been rumors for years. But rumors aren't proof, and he has good contacts inside the government down there. Our association has been profitable."

"And now it's dangerous."

"So you claim. But I will give your proposal some thought. I assume you will be returning home, so how do I reach you?"

"I'm remaining in Miami for the next two days, at least. You can reach me on my cell phone." I handed over my business card.

"Very well, I'll give you a call. Probably tomorrow."

I FOUND Paul with his arms hooked over the edge of the pool, talking to a young couple on nearby lounges. I chuckled inwardly. Paul projected interest in the world, and the world returned his attention.

He waved me over. "Hey, Vince, this is Sam and Suzie." We managed to nod to one another as he rushed on. "They tell me there's a great public beach out on Key Biscayne. It's called Crandon Park Beach. You can drive there from here. Over a causeway, I guess."

Judging from his enthusiasm, that was where we would spend the afternoon.

Paul got out of the water and headed to the room to shower and get ready for the excursion. I checked my laptop for e-mail messages and tried to reach Cohen to brief him on the meeting. He was out.

During a quick seafood lunch at the hotel's lobby lounge, Bob Cohen returned my call. As Paul and I were in a secluded corner booth, I put the phone on speaker and filled both of them in on the Hammond interview. Cohen had no feedback from Jackman yet.

By the time we finished eating, the rental company delivered a car. I'd requested an Impala because the automobile was familiar to me, and they brought a silver one with all the bells and whistles.

Dressed in casual clothes and bearing totes full of swim gear we'd bought at a local shop, we pulled away from the hotel. I drove while Paul fired up the navigation system and got directions to the Rickenbacker Causeway and thence to Key Biscayne. After we were well on the way, he brought up my meeting with Hammond.

"Do you believe him? About having nothing to do with the ducknapping?" Curious how that word was no longer funny.

"I don't believe he had a hand in it, but he's bound to have figured out Acosta was behind it all, especially when his partner started buying up pieces of the bet."

"And you don't think he orchestrated what happened last night?"

I automatically checked the rearview mirror at the mention of the attack, but a horde of vehicles trailed behind us, any one of which could be full of men bent on revenge for being taken down by two queers—which is the way they would frame it.

"No, that was Acosta too. But now that Hammond and I have talked, Acosta may not feel the need to try anything like that again. Whatever threat such a meeting represented is over now. There's nothing to gain by trying it again."

"You're sure about that?"

"Absolutely. So watch my back, and I'll watch yours."

He gave his golden laugh and settled back in his seat to take in the scenery as we approached the causeway.

I'm a good, careful driver, but I'm not accustomed to narrow bridges spanning long, open stretches of salt water, so my anxiety level crept up appreciably before we exited the bridge. Shortly thereafter we parked in a lot big enough to accommodate half the vehicles in south Florida. After retrieving our totes from the backseat, we entered the park.

Paul observed they had a golf course. "We should've brought our clubs."

"We can rent some, if you want."

"I'd rather spend the time in the water."

But first we strolled the long beach on the Atlantic side of the key. I plodded through the sand; Paul took off his shoes, rolled up his pant legs, and walked in the gently rolling surf. His excitement was contagious. He'd expected the ocean to be colder. He'd never seen water quite that color—turquoise. Were those coconut palms? Could we try the kayaks? How about the jet skis?

"Hey, man, now there's a real lifeguard's chair." He pointed to one of the elevated towers strung out over the beach. "Makes me feel like an amateur."

The bayside nature trails affected us differently. The Miami skyline lying just across the flat stretch of water reduced him to a gawking tourist, and it took a lot to render Paul speechless. Soon enough, though, he'd had his fill of dry land.

We changed into our suits and hit the water. The sea floor sloped gently, so we waded quite a distance before it was deep enough to swim. Then he suddenly disappeared and surfaced again ten yards ahead of me as he used a steady overhand stroke to quickly carry him away. Then I lost sight of him. Seconds later something brushed my belly. He surfaced behind me, laughing aloud.

"This is great!" He punched a hand into the air. "Man, let's move the whole state of New Mexico to the Gulf Coast."

I puffed from exertion, all the while keeping a wary eye on the now-distant shore. "Then we'd lose the mountains."

"Yeah, the mountains are great, but this is the ocean! I'll catch you later, man. I gotta swim."

"Don't overdo it. There are currents, you know."

"Yeah, pops. I know." A gentle reminder he was his own man.

"I saw some wheelchairs for rent back there. Look for me with the rest of the geriatric set."

He laughed again and headed for deeper water. Resigned to the reality I wouldn't be able to keep him on a leash, I settled into my therapeutic routine, alternating between various strokes. There were no laps to swim, so I kept to one set until tired and then switched to another. I headed back to the shore on the backstroke. It took longer than expected.

I found our totes and pulled out a big beach towel. After drying off, I spread it in the shade of a palm—not close enough to be bopped by a falling coconut—and settled down to wait and maybe catch a few zzz's. I couldn't see Paul, he could have been any of a number of dark heads bobbing out there in the Atlantic, but I had enough confidence in his ability and good sense not to worry—much.

I got in a nap before I woke to spot a familiar lanky, finely muscled body trudging my way. A giggling, sun-bleached blonde nymph walked at his side. She looked disappointed when he waved good-bye and headed in my direction. I tossed him a towel. "Good swim?"

"The best. Man, I could get addicted to this."

He managed a short rest, but he soon prowled the beach again. Before the afternoon faded away, he had us kayaking out to a lagoon where we snorkeled down to a 1,500-year-old fossilized mangrove reef. We saw spotted leopard rays, a huge puffer, countless angelfish, and something called a damselfish. He was disappointed we didn't spot a bottlenose dolphin. Someone had told him they inhabited the area.

I wore out a good hour before the park closed at twilight but dragged my carcass around in his wake out of sheer determination. My major concern, however, was burning to a crisp under the bright sun. Even Paul's bronzed skin soon took on a rosy hue.

He had some energy left, so he drove back to the hotel while I played navigator. Halfway across the causeway, my phone rang.

"Mr. Vinson, this is Kenneth Hammond."

"Unexpected pleasure. I didn't think I'd hear from you until tomorrow."

"We need to talk. Someone just tried to kill me."

Suddenly I wasn't so tired anymore.

Chapter 27

WE HEADED straight for the construction site in North Miami, where a uniformed police officer flagged us down. Two police vehicles, an EMT unit, and an ambulance sat near a spidery skeleton of steel girders rising behind a long white trailer—probably the field office. Flooring had been poured on a few tiers of the high-rise, but the upper levels were open to the sky. Cranes and other equipment littered the fenced and gated site.

We were expected. After checking with someone over his radio, an officer directed us to a parking area in front of the trailer. As we got out of the Impala, the door to the field office opened. A dark-haired man in a business suit came down the wooden steps and introduced himself as Det. Tony Padilla. He offered a broad hand with a strong grip. I judged him to be about forty years old and forty pounds overweight.

"Is Mr. Hammond okay?"

"Yeah, he's inside. He told us he called you, but we need a private talk before you go inside. Best I can offer is my car."

"My Impala's closer. Let's use it."

He beckoned, and his partner came over to escort Paul elsewhere while we had our chat. The dying day remained warm and humid, so we left the car doors open. The dome light would make it easier for him to observe my body language. That was okay; I could read his as well.

"First, I gotta tell you I'm recording this. Okay?" Padilla said.

"Sure. I didn't know I'd be working tonight, or I would have brought my own so we could both have a copy."

"I'll give you a duplicate of mine," he said. I took that with a grain of salt. "I've already listened to Hammond's recording of your meeting this morning. But first let's go through the formalities."

He directed me to repeat my name and contact information, as well as my driver's and PI license numbers. He confirmed I was staying at the Ritz-Carlton and then asked the purpose of my visit to Miami.

I gave him the entire story, step by step, providing names, dates, and times as well as I could recall them without my notebook, which remained back at the hotel with my recorder. That took twenty minutes, and then he spent another twenty asking questions to clarify certain points. He was justifiably upset we hadn't called the police after the attack at Club Sugar. I apologized and pointed out our visit had to be low-key.

"That might be so, Mr. Vinson, but you're a former lawman and a licensed private investigator. You, of all people, oughta know when to involve the authorities. And we shoulda been called."

"Mea culpa."

"So you got a good look at this Carlos character?"

"He sat at my table and drank with me for twenty or thirty minutes."

"How about the two thugs who came at you outside?"

"It all happened so fast I didn't get as good a look at them. I can tell you they were Hispanic. I saw that from the glimpse I got of the one who came at me, and I heard the other one cursing at Paul in Spanish. He speaks the language better than I do, so he might be able to tell you more."

"My partner will get all of that. Would you recognize the guy who tried to knife you outside the club if you saw him again?"

I wiggled my right hand back and forth. "Iffy, Detective. I might be able to pick him out, but a lineup would be risky."

"Don't need a lineup."

I assumed he meant they had the man who'd made the attempt on Hammond. We went over things a second time, with him asking the same questions in a different way, a familiar technique. He was pretty good at it too. Finally he asked for opinion, not fact.

"You think this Hector Acosta's behind the attack on you and your buddy?"

"Yes. I have no proof, but my investigation led me to that conclusion."

"An investigation that started over a stolen duck, huh?" He had a sense of humor.

"Or as they're calling it, the ducknapping of Quacky Quack the Second." That brought an outright chuckle. "Now that I've answered all your questions, will you tell me what happened?"

He waved toward the building under construction. "Mr. Hammond and his superintendent were inspecting that structure over there about four this afternoon. When they reached the fifth floor, he sent the superintendent to check on something. While he was gone, a man—a stranger—walked up and clubbed him with a length of two-by-four. If Hammond hadn't been wearing a hard hat, he'd have gone over, but he caught himself and managed to grab on to the man. The old man's in pretty good shape for his age and probably put up more of a fight than the other guy expected. Anyway, the superintendent heard his boss yelling and came running. He grabbed Hammond and managed to save him. Unfortunately the other guy went over the edge."

"Dead?"

"Absolutely and irrevocably. I'd like you to take a look at him. The medical examiner's people have him over there in the meat wagon. You ready?"

"Let's go."

Paul and the other detective materialized just then and trailed us to the ambulance. The rear doors were open, and by the interior light, I could see a stretcher covered by a blanket.

"The medics were about to leave when you showed up, saving you a long trip downtown." Padilla stepped aside and waved me into the back of the vehicle.

The body wasn't pretty. The man had landed on his face, which distorted his features. I gave it a good look and shook my head.

"It's not Carlos."

"Are you sure? He's pretty banged up."

"Yeah, I'm sure. This Carlos character had a full head of black hair plastered over his ears with pomade. I remember thinking he must have used grease to hold it in place. This guy's haircut almost looks military."

"Some of the gangs around here go for that look. How about the joker with the knife?"

"Not so sure about that call. He's the right build, but I can't be certain. Any ID on him?"

"Name's Abner Walczek according to his driver's license. I suspect the name's as phony as the union card he's carrying. This guy doesn't look like a Walczek to me. Looks like he came right out of Central America."

"You might check Brazil. Acosta had a money-laundering operation down there until a couple of people got killed."

"We'll print him and see what we can find. You think your buddy's up to taking a look? He seems a little wet behind the ears, but maybe he'll recognize the guy who tried to knife him."

Paul and the other detective replaced us in the ambulance. Paul shook his head. He couldn't identify the man either. Even in the semidarkness, he looked a little pale as he climbed out of the vehicle.

"Okay if we go see Hammond now?" I asked. "How's he holding up?"

"I get the feeling this wasn't the first dead body he's seen. He's a tough old bird."

"Any record?"

Padilla hesitated a second. "You haven't checked? In his younger days, he got into some trouble busting unions. That's probably where he got the seed money to start his own operation. He put together some goons and got paid for busting up strikes. But he always managed to stay clear of any serious charges."

That pretty well matched the jacket and records Cohen had sent me.

Padilla rubbed his eyes as if they were tired. "There's some civil suits, but that's par for the course in the construction business. He's inside. You can go on in."

Hammond sat at one of the two desks in the trailer. A white hard hat lay on the surface in front of him. He'd shed his linen suit for dungarees and a blue denim work shirt with sleeves rolled halfway up his arms. He seemed no worse for the wear from his recent near-death experience. A man about three inches shorter and four inches wider, whom I took to be his foreman or superintendent, sat opposite him.

"Mr. Vinson, thanks for coming."

"That's okay. I'm just glad you're not hurt."

"It was a near thing, I can tell you." He nodded to the other man. "If Tom here hadn't come running, I'm not sure who would have taken that swan dive. Probably both of us."

"How did the man who attacked you get on the premises? The site has lockdown capabilities."

"You mean a fence and a gate? The gate is left open during the workday. People come and go all the time—subcontractors, vendors, city inspectors, and people looking for work."

"Who knew you were going to be inspecting the job today?"

"Anybody who wanted to, I guess. My schedule's not a closely held secret. Look, I haven't had anything to eat. Can we go somewhere and get a bite?"

"We can if Detective Padilla's finished with us."

The detective got the location of the duck track in the Glades from Hammond. After saying he'd have someone at the race site Saturday morning as a precaution, he told us we were finished for the moment. "When are you planning to return home, Mr. Vinson?"

"Not for a couple of days."

"Appreciate it if you'd check with me first, okay? Are you both certain you've told me everything you know about this situation?"

"I've told you everything pertinent, Detective." Hammond snagged a large envelope from the desk and stood.

"I can't think of anything else," I said.

Because no one was dressed for a fancy club or restaurant, we headed for the Ritz lounge for something to eat. Paul and I rushed upstairs to scrub off the sun block and change into fresh clothing while Hammond secured a table in the lounge.

As we started back to the lobby, I asked Paul if he wouldn't prefer to go do something else. He broke stride to give me a look.

"No way. This is exciting. Being around you goes way beyond Journalism 101. It's like Journalism 1001."

Judging from the empty whiskey glass on the table, Hammond was on his second drink by the time we arrived at the lounge. He waved for a waiter as soon as he saw us. I ordered iced tea with lemon, and Paul followed my lead.

The contractor lifted his tumbler. "I guess delayed reaction is setting in. That guy almost killed me." He took another gulp and put down the glass. "Despite what I said back there, I'm not hungry. I just needed to talk to you, Mr. Vinson."

"Please call me BJ."

"Okay, I'm Kenny. After you left this morning, I talked to Heck Acosta. When I laid everything out for him, he started a song-and-dance routine. I told him to cut the bullshit. It was time to get serious. I didn't want anything to do with drugs or drug running, not even peripherally, so I intended to cancel the bet with Millicent."

"His reaction?"

"He asked me to reconsider. Said he owned a good part of that bet, and it would be personally embarrassing for him if I called it off. And then I made a tactical error. I agreed to reconsider, but I did it too quickly. Heck's a shrewd man, and he's known me for a long time. He'd expect me to bluff and bluster and then end up horse-trading with him. I didn't. I just threw him a line about thinking it through and got off the phone. I think he suspects I simply won't show up with my racer tomorrow morning."

"Then why would he try to kill you?" Paul asked. "Wouldn't that guarantee your racer won't show up?"

"That's exactly what I thought as I hung up the phone. Another mistake. Heck knows where I keep my racing duck, and he knows the people who take care of her."

"So he might snatch the duck and see that the race goes on," Paul suggested.

"Exactly. I'm widowed, so he wouldn't have a wife to contend with. My two children are grown and pretty well estranged, so he knows I wouldn't have taken them into my confidence. He would either pay over my sixty percent share of the bet to my estate or forge some sort of document showing I'd sold it to him."

"Let me get this straight," I said. "Do you intend to cancel the race?"

He picked up the envelope he'd carried out of the field office with him and shoved it across the table. "Here's my signed and notarized agreement to cancel the bet, along with my original copy of the wager."

"You're sure about this?"

"I wasn't until about four this afternoon. I didn't even write it up until after that fellow went over the edge. I rushed right down to the trailer and scribbled the cancellation agreement. The field secretary notarized my signature. The original of the bet I already had in my briefcase."

I tapped the envelope. "This written cancellation of the debt is important, of course, but it—"

He held up a hand. "Yes, I know. But it could be challenged by any of the stakeholders. As Paul indicated a few minutes ago, the really important thing is to see that Thunder Duck doesn't show up at the racing channel tomorrow. That's the only sure way to put an end to it."

"What time is the race scheduled?"

"Ten o'clock."

"Do you have any objection if an associate of mine picks up your racer for safekeeping?"

When he agreed, I got Cohen on the line. He said he'd go for the bird right away. I put Hammond on the phone so they could work out the details. Once that was over, I asked if anyone besides Acosta would protest the cancellation of the race.

He toyed with his empty glass. "Ours is a small group. It grew out of a couple of us going to the rubber ducky charity races. After attending the Waddle, Walk, and Run race, where live ducks are dropped off in the ocean and the first one ashore wins the race, we got started joking about 'thoroughbred' ducks. One thing led to another, and we set up a place out near the Glades. We invested a few dollars in straightening and lining a fresh-water channel on some property one of us owned. It caught on but has always remained a small, intimate group. We will typically have six or seven racers and no more than two dozen owners and spectators.

"If you're thinking about side bets, I gave that due consideration before deciding on a course of action. I am not aware of any and have no responsibility for them if they exist. Besides, the people in my group are all long-standing friends and associates. I'll make some calls tonight to let everyone know the race is off."

"Acosta has a different motive. What if he comes after you again?"

"He won't. I've already taken steps to let him know what I've done. Now he has no motive to harm me."

"Except for revenge, of course."

Hammond nodded over my shoulder. I turned to see his superintendent sitting alone at the bar. "There are two more outside, keeping an eye on my car. I'll be safe until this blows over."

"It might not blow over," Paul said. "Some of those *patrones* carry a grudge for a long time."

"That's true, but Heck is driven by the dollar. We have several projects together, and my death might cause some problems for him. I'll watch my back until he cools off. But what he tried to prevent by sending that goon is now an accomplished fact. I'm willing to take my chances." He paused significantly. "However...."

"However, the danger may now lie back in New Mexico," I said.

Chapter 28

As SOON as Hammond left, I got a Federal Express envelope from the desk clerk, addressed it to Del Dahlman's law firm, sealed the wager documents inside, and left it with the night manager for pickup by the carrier. Then Paul and I returned to our room, where I called Del.

It was after 7:00 p.m. in New Mexico, but he was still at the office. He agreed to hold the envelope until I could pick it up upon my return. I gave him a little of the backstory, soft-pedaling the afternoon's violence, and explaining anyone wanting to get their hands on the envelope would be more apt to look for it in my office than in his.

Hazel had given me a good letting alone the last few days, doubtlessly so I could enjoy my vacation time with Paul, but I called her next—before she caught wind of trouble in paradise. She was home, so the shoptalk was short. When she asked after Paul, I handed him the phone so he could work some of his charm on her.

I hadn't wanted to talk to Millicent until I made arrangements for securing the envelope Hammond gave me and confirming Thunder Duck wouldn't somehow appear for the race tomorrow morning. When I reached her, she expressed shock over the attempt on Hammond's life, but a sense of relief crept into her voice I didn't want to hear.

"So it's over?"

"If you mean is the bet canceled and the race called off, yes. But don't make the mistake of thinking this thing is over. It's not. Acosta wasn't successful in preventing those two things, but that doesn't mean he's any less determined to get your ranch. He wants it for some reason, and it goes deeper than just getting stateside land that abuts his Mexican property."

"But that was your premise all along."

"He wants it all right, and he's committed to getting it. But it's more than just acquiring an easy walk across the border. Millicent, does Bert ever fly over the Lightning Ranch?"

"He flies over a piece of it quite often, especially when he's going to Deming."

"Has he seen anything suspicious lately?"

"Not that he's mentioned. I'll ask him when he comes in."

"Has Acosta been in touch? Or Rael?"

"Heck hasn't contacted me, and Bert hasn't said anything about Paco. He's still smarting over what he considers a betrayal by his best friend. Frankly, I'm not certain what's going to happen when they come face-to-face."

"So he's accepted that Paco tried to kill him?"

"I don't think he knows what to believe. I'm having trouble accepting it as well."

"Both of you had better believe it until we know otherwise—and act accordingly. This afternoon someone tried to kill a prominent Miami contractor in the middle of his own construction crew. Think how vulnerable that makes you out in the hinterlands."

"Why would Heck harm me? I'm the one he's trying to buy the ranch from."

"What happens to it if you and Bert are both dead?"

"It goes to my daughter, Penelope."

"Is she capable of running the ranch?"

"No. She grew up on it, but she always drew and painted, not hazed and branded. Now she's an artist living in Dallas with her lawyer husband."

"So she'd probably sell it if it passed into her hands. Does she know Acosta?"

"Of course. She's known him all her life. Calls him Uncle Heck."

"And have you shared any suspicions of Uncle Heck with her or her husband?"

"No."

"I think you should. Right away. You know, if I wanted something as badly as Acosta seems to want the Lazy M, I'd make an offer for fair market value. He's a wealthy man. Why would he try to steal it from you at half price?"

"You'd have to know Heck. He's well aware I wouldn't even consider selling the Lazy M unless I was forced into a corner. And if I died, Bert wouldn't either. But once Heck learned of my vulnerability—my foolishness—he saw an opportunity. And it's his nature to take advantage of something like that, both to push me into a sale and to get it at bargain-basement rates."

"And now that he's lost that advantage?"

"He might come back and offer me a fair price."

"And when you turn him down again?"

"Thirty minutes ago, I'd have said that would be the end of it. Now I don't know."

"Good, that means you've heard what I said. You and Bert have to be especially careful."

"All of our people are armed and alarmed."

"But they don't carry automatic weapons, and there's not an army of them. I think you should contact the authorities and express your concerns. The county sheriff, the state police, the border people, everyone."

"BJ, are we making more of this than there is? This is my childhood sweetheart we're talking about. The man I virtually grew up with."

"You need to consider that man as dead and buried. The Hector Acosta of today isn't the same man. If you don't accept anything else I've said, just believe one thing. He's a killer. He kills for profit, and your ranch represents profit."

"That's so cold-blooded. And there's no proof. No real proof."

"I'm not claiming everything is documented and tied up in a pretty package. It's not. But there's enough on the table to support what I believe. You don't need absolute, legal proof to protect yourself and those under your care from potential harm. All of this brings up another question. The Raels."

"No way. They're loyal, BJ. They won't betray me."

"That's what you said about Acosta. And Paco is their son. Do you honestly believe they spent time with him on Acosta's ranch and don't know he was shot, not injured by a bucking bronc?"

"How would they know? The effects would be the same or similar."

"Any mother I know would want to see the wound with her own eyes."

"You don't understand the mindset over there. Heck is the *patrón*. His word is law. If he says Paco fell off a horse, then Paco fell off a horse. Besides, Heck has supported their family for years. He got them their green cards and recommended them to me. He saw to it they had a job and a better life over here."

"That could have been out of friendship… or by design."

"You just don't know them. They're dear, gentle people."

"Or they're vipers in your own nest."

"BJ!" Real outrage tinged her voice.

"Sorry, but you have to consider the possibility. This is serious, Mud." Her hands called her that out of respect for her toughness and tenacity, and she needed to be reminded of that. "Someone could be plotting your and Bert's assassinations as we speak."

When she didn't reply, I asked if she'd had any word from the insurance company.

"I spoke to them this morning. I think they might end up doing something after all. The police reports you provided nudged them our way. Next week I'm going to have my lawyer start bugging them."

"So you think the duck's dead?"

"No, I don't. The more you convince me Heck's behind all of this, the more I believe she's being cared for over on the Rayo. He knows how I treasure that bird, and when he gets his way, I believe she'll come back to me."

"And if he doesn't get his way?"

"I don't know."

"I'm going to stay here until tomorrow morning. I want to be at the track to make certain Acosta doesn't try to present a ringer and claim you defaulted. After that I'm heading back to the ranch. Can Bert pick us up in Las Cruces?"

"Paul's not getting much of a vacation, is he?"

"That's all right, he understands." I glanced across the room to where he listened to my end of the conversation. He gave a smile and a shrug.

"It's kind of busy here," Millicent said. "We'll start the fall gathering in a few weeks, and there's work to be done before that. But you just tell us when, and he'll pick you up."

After I closed the call, Paul and I tried to salvage what we could of our remaining time in Miami. We caught a late dinner and the tail end of a comedy routine at the famous Improv on North Bayshore Drive. After that we returned to the Ritz, turned the car over to the doorman, and walked over to Biscayne Bay for a stroll along the shore.

Chapter 29

PAUL AND I were arguing when the airliner landed at the airport in Las Cruces late the next afternoon. I wanted him to take a flight home, but he insisted on coming with me to the Lazy M. He was having too much fun watching this adventure unfold to let it go now. He stood right beside me when Bert met us at the terminal in a pickup he'd commandeered from his flying service. By the time we arrived on the far side of the field, his bird had been serviced and was ready to go. We had little time for conversation until we were in the air. After chatting with the tower for a minute, he motioned to earphones. They made communication easier.

"Sorry to rush," he apologized, "but Mud called to tell me Paco showed up right after I left."

"Who's watching your mother's back?"

"Linus is sticking close with his trusty Winchester. He's been briefed and is on the prod. He's never liked Paco much anyway. O'Brien from the sheriff's office is at the ranch too."

"Bert, you've got a reputation for flying off the handle. I know you're hurt because Paco lined up with the other side, but you have to keep things under control."

"I want to see how the son of a bitch tries to spin it. And if I don't like it… well, no promises." He adjusted the mike in front of his lips. "Is it really over? I mean, is the bet thing settled?"

"Paul and I were at the duck track this morning, and the only people who showed up were Hammond and the police detective who caught the attempt on Hammond's life. The race didn't take place, so the bet was moot. The cancellation agreement Hammond signed is in my attorney's office in Albuquerque. So all the bases are covered."

"Thank God! Man, that's a load off our backs."

"I hope your mother made it clear the danger isn't over yet."

"Yeah, she did. But we can take care of ourselves now."

"Don't get overconfident. You almost got your wings clipped once." I glanced at the ground rushing below us. "How illegal would it be to fly over the Lightning Ranch?"

"I do it all the time."

"I don't mean skirt the corner. I mean fly over the ranch headquarters before heading to your place."

"I could lose my license if they catch us." He shrugged. "But if we stay below the radar, we oughta be okay. What the hell, let's go for it."

"Can you make it without stopping for fuel along the way?"

Bert tapped the instrument panel. "This is a Bell 47G-3B. It's got a maximum range of about 214 nautical miles. That's 250 road miles, give or take. Yeah, I can make it. Help me watch for the Mexican air patrol."

That remark set our heads to swiveling constantly.

A few minutes later, Bert dropped the bird's nose, and Interstate 10 meandered off to our right. He took us south of Palomas and then circled back to the north.

"You want to go in low?" he asked.

"No, I don't want to alert anyone. How high will this thing go?"

"Record's 18,550 feet. A Bell 47G was the first bird to cross the Alps back in '50."

"We don't need to go that high, but get us high enough so they might not notice us. You have a pair of binoculars?"

"On a harness back where Paul is."

Paul handed them up, and I adjusted them to my eyes.

"Here we go."

The bird lurched upward, leaving my stomach somewhere below. When Bert leveled off, he pointed dead ahead. The Rayo headquarters made quite a spread. Don Hector was at home—at least, his two Piper aircraft sat on a small strip. The main house—actually, it looked more like my idea of a gleaming white Moroccan royal palace—was flanked by rows of what appeared to be accommodations for the ranch's vaqueros. Almost every building sported antennae of some sort. I likewise saw what looked suspiciously like a radar dish but was probably only a TV satellite receiver. The entire place appeared to be deserted.

Ten miles to the west, we found the center of activity. A couple of dump trucks hauling loads of something covered by tarps bounced along rough ranch roads heading south.

"Does Acosta do any mining on the ranch?" I asked.

"Not that I know of."

A couple of miles farther, we saw a number of men and machines congregated at the foot of what appeared to be a small bluff.

"What the hell are they doing?" I handed Bert the glasses.

After studying the scene for a moment, he shook his head. "I don't know. That's not any ranch activity I recognize."

"Can I see?" Paul asked. Bert handed the glasses over his shoulder. "Could they be drilling for water?"

"I don't see a drill, just earth-moving equipment," Bert replied.

I made a circling motion with my left hand. "Make a run back over. I want to see if my phone camera will take a decent picture."

"Uh-oh," Paul said. "Aircraft coming in from the northeast. About five o'clock."

"Get us out of here, Bert, but don't go straight to the ranch." I snapped as many pictures as possible, although they probably wouldn't show any meaningful detail. "How fast will this baby go?"

"Cruising speed's seventy-three knots. Max is ninety-one. That about 105 mph. But that's not enough to outrun any fixed-wing craft I know of."

Paul and I kept eyes on the distant plane while Bert laid down the hammer. The other craft didn't seem to make a serious effort to catch us. The plane lagged far behind by the time we crossed the border.

"I'm going for the Hachitas Range and circle back to the ranch," Bert said.

"How are we on petrol?"

"Doing okay. We'll make it home with no sweat."

Bert headed west-southwest, riding the contour of the terrain below us. My stomach dropped again as he buzzed up the side of a mountain. He laughed at my reaction.

"Don't worry. This thing can climb at a rate of 860 feet a minute. I've hopped the Hachitas lots of times."

We topped Big Hatchet and dropped quickly down the other side. We hadn't seen the other aircraft in several minutes, so Bert turned north and circled around to approach the ranch as if coming from Deming. A quarter of an hour later, we dropped down onto the helipad at the ranch.

As we got out of the craft, Paco strode across the grass, heading in our direction with a big smile creasing his lips. His arm hung free of the sling he'd worn the last time I saw him.

"Bert," I said in a low, warning voice.

"Don't push me."

Millicent stepped through her office door onto the patio. Linus, his rifle cradled in his arms, uncoiled from a chair nearby. Maria emerged from the great room still wiping her hands on a white apron. Luis Rael came in from the barn area.

"Paco, you son of a bitch, you've got some nerve!" Bert yelled. "What're you doing here?"

Paco halted in his tracks. The grin slid from his lips.

Chapter 30

PACO RAEL'S face shut down. "Hell of a way to greet a buddy."

"You've got some explaining to do."

As Bert advanced on him, Paco spread his legs and set his stance.

"Why'd you turn on us?"

Paco's complexion went darker, but his eyes were neutral. "What do you mean?"

"Did you kill Liver Lips?"

This was more than Maria could stand. With a cry, she retreated into the house. Moving slowly, Luis made for the front of the building. I elbowed Paul. He followed my eyes, grunted, and moved to intercept the man.

"Why would I kill that guy? He was a nothing, a nobody. He didn't mean any more to me than he did to you. Did you kill him?"

"Did you try to take me out at the City?" Bert halted five feet in front of Paco, balled fists on his hips. I moved up beside them.

"How can you ask me that? You're my best friend. *Mi compadre.*"

"You didn't answer my question."

"Fuck no, I didn't try to shoot you. If I wanted you dead, you'd be dead. You know me well enough to know that."

"Somebody tried to shoot BJ and Paul out there the other day. Was that you? Were you leading that gang?"

"Come on, man—"

"BJ winged the leader, and the next day you ended up crippled." Bert's hand shot out so quickly, we were all taken by surprise—even Paco, who was prepared for some sort of physical confrontation. Bert practically tore the man's shirt from his shoulders. Paco gave a grunt but otherwise didn't flinch.

If Bert had hoped to expose a gunshot wound, it didn't work. White bandages wound so tightly they appeared to cut the flesh covered Paco's brown chest. Appropriate treatment for cracked bones, but the tape not only circled his torso, it also snaked up over his left shoulder, effectively hiding any puncture—such as a bullet wound.

Bert wasn't fazed. "Take off the bandage."

"What?"

"Take it off, or I'll cut it off."

Millicent stepped forward quickly. "Now, Bert, this has gone far enough. Think of his mother."

"I'm thinking of mine." There was a bite to his voice. "Where's O'Brien?"

"I sent him home an hour ago. Paco's just here to let his parents know his wedding's been rescheduled."

"He coulda told them that on the telephone." Bert glared into Paco's eyes.

Paul stepped out of the great room onto the patio with a long-barreled pistol dangling from his hand. I motioned him back inside. That house held more than one gun.

"Guess I better be going now." Pain tinged Paco's soft baritone. "I don't hang around where I'm not welcome."

"You're not going anywhere until I get some answers."

"What brought this on, man?"

"Why did you and Acosta run out of here the other day before BJ got a look at Madelena? I'll tell you why. Because you knew he'd recognize her as the woman he met at Liver's house the day he died."

"That's loco. She's never been to Liver's place. She wouldn't dirty her shoes in that shack."

"Paco," I said. "I'm sure you have a photo of your intended in your wallet. Why don't you show it to me?"

He shifted to face me. "Why? So you can tell more lies about us? So you can say she was there that day when she wasn't?"

"You seem to think I lie rather easily. What lies have I told?"

"Lies about Don Hector. Every time you come down here, you stir up trouble. Bert, you know me better'n you know this gringo. How come you take his word over mine?"

"Stop pussyfooting, Paco. Show him the picture. Show him, or by God, I'll whip your ass and take it off you."

Paco lifted his half-naked shoulder. "Don't let this fool you. You come for me, you'll have your hands full."

"Nobody's going to come for anyone." Millicent moved between them. "Everyone just cool down. BJ, did you tell the police about the woman?"

"Yes."

"Did they investigate? Try to identify or find her?"

"I don't know, Millicent, but I'm going to find out."

"Good. Maybe they got fingerprints or something from Liver's house."

Let her think what she wanted, but Bill Garza probably hadn't gone to that extreme. At the time I spoke to him, he still believed Liver Lips had died in an accident. And right after that, Lopez's murder would have claimed his full attention. But I had also told Detective Montoya about the mystery woman. Perhaps he had been more thorough.

"Maybe they got something," Paco said. "Hope so, so we can put this shit behind us. But, Bert, this is gonna be hard to forget." He pulled his torn shirt up over his shoulder. "I'll get my things and be out of here in five minutes. Any objections?" He turned his back on us and walked away. Millicent, trailed by Linus, followed him inside.

Bert slapped his hat against his leg and shook his head. "Are we just going to let him walk out of here like that?" he asked.

"Not if you have some proof?"

"Hell, the proof's under that bandage."

"You were the one claiming your friend wouldn't betray you. Now all of a sudden you're convinced he did. What changed?"

"Paco changed."

"What do you mean?"

"You'd have to know him like I do. Back when we were kids, if you accused Paco of something, he'd react one of two ways. He'd either get his dander up and explode, or else he'd start giving you reasons why it wasn't him."

"And if he blew up, it meant—"

"He hadn't done it. But if he went logical on you, then you could bet your bottom dollar he had a hand in it."

"So when you got out of the chopper and confronted him—"

"He went oily. He came back to see how we'd react to him. Mud tried not to let her suspicions show, but I guess I let the cat out of the bag. Hope I didn't mess everything up, but I needed to know."

"That's okay. When I went to Florida and laid everything out for Hammond, I knew he'd contact Acosta. But sometimes when a case isn't moving along, you have to stir things up. That's what I intended to do in Miami, and that's exactly what you did here."

As often happens, this one had unintended consequences. We went inside to find Millicent practically in tears.

"What is it?" Bert asked.

"It's Maria… and Luis. She's packing their things. They're leaving."

Understandable. If they'd thrown Paul off the ranch, I'd have gone too. And Paco was their son, after all. This wasn't the time for reasoning with her, but I couldn't help feeling she'd be better off with them gone.

Paul walked over and handed a pistol to Bert. "Luis got it out of a drawer while you were out there facing down Paco."

"You think he'd use it?"

Paul shrugged. "I just think he was afraid for Paco. But if a ruckus had started, who knows what he'd have done? He kept saying Paco was hurt. Guess he thought it wouldn't be a fair fight."

"Where's Linus?" I asked.

"Back in the bedroom area, keeping an eye on Paco," Paul said.

"Bert, why don't you take your mother to the office and calm her down. Paul and Linus and I will keep an eye on things in the meantime."

After the door closed behind mother and son, I headed for the front of the house to see what kind of car Paco had arrived in. I was mildly disappointed to see his Duster parked between Bert's Corvette and Millicent's Lincoln. Of course, he was too smart to show up in a black Firebird.

Remaining outside where I had some privacy, I called Hazel and asked her to contact both Officer Garza of the Deming Police Department and Sgt. Manny Montoya of the state police to see if either had searched Liver Lips Martinson's shack for forensic evidence. She promised to get on it right away.

She hadn't called back by the time the Raels came through the front door, lugging several pieces of luggage. Millicent and Bert trailed along behind.

"I'll send the rest of your things to the Rayo, Maria. But this is totally unnecessary. You are welcome to stay. You know how much I depend on you here in the house and on Luis in the pens."

Maria, diminutive and dignified, turned to face her employer. "You have been good to us, Doña Millicent, but I cannot do my job when things are like this between our families. And Luis can't either. *Lo siento.* I am sorry. *Perdóneme.*"

"Very well, but you are welcome here at any time. I don't intend to tell anyone you've left, so you'll be free to come back any time you wish."

"*Gracias.*"

We watched Paco's Duster and his parents' Ford pickup disappear down the long drive to the highway. Once they were no more than a distant trail of dust, Millicent turned and swept us with a hard glint in her eyes as she stomped into the house. "I hope you two are happy!"

Bert stood with a wounded look on his face.

"Don't worry," I said. "She'll transfer her animosity to me until she thinks things through a little better. And then she'll forgive us both."

"You saved her ranch but cost her two friends and companions. And right now that cuts deeper." Then he showed a crack in his armor. "We are right about this thing, aren't we?"

"I don't have any doubts. Do you?"

"I guess not."

"Look, I'm not very popular here right now, so I think Paul and I had better leave. But you have to be very careful for the next few days. Acosta is going to have to think things through and plan his next move. Keep in touch."

"I'll take you to Las Cruces."

"No, you stay close to home as much as you can. I'll call Jim Gray to pick us up in the Cessna tomorrow morning. You mother will have to put up with us until then."

THE REST of the ranch hands came in bellyaching about being shorthanded because both Bert and Linus hadn't been out in the pastures, but they really fired up the trash talk when they discovered Maria gone and their supper prepared by Linus. Frankly, I thought the home-butchered pork chops and fried potatoes were pretty good. Paul polished off two plates before heading off to the bunkhouse with the cowboys for a round of poker.

Millicent hadn't joined us for the meal, so after the rest of the crowd disappeared, Bert took a plate to his mother and spent a quarter of an hour with her. I watched the news on their satellite TV system, the first time I'd caught up on current events in several days. The sound bites on the state of the economy and the progress of the wars in Iraq and Afghanistan could have been recycled reports from a week ago.

When Bert returned, I lowered the volume. "How's she doing?"

"She's worked her way through most of the stages of grief. I think she's past anger now. I expect she'll show up before the night's out."

As if summoned by his prediction, Millicent appeared on the threshold of the great room and eased into the recliner reserved for her. She raised the footrest, giving me a good view of her worn, wool-lined buckskin house slippers. Her eyes were puffy, her hair in slight disarray. At the moment she was Millicent, not Mud Hen.

"BJ, I owe you an apology. You go out of your way to save my ranch, and I pay you back by blaming you for losing Maria and Luis. It wasn't fair, and I'm sorry. Bert, we'd better look for a cook the first thing tomorrow. The Lord knows Linus tries, and he's a better cook than most, but we've spoiled our hands when it comes to the supper table."

She looked over at me. "BJ, what do you figure's coming down the cattle chute at us?" Mud Hen was back.

"A stampede."

"How come? Heck will just make a decent offer, and when I tell him to go to hell, he'll drop the matter. They don't seem to have a problem getting their stuff over the border without owning the Lazy M. Why cause trouble over this particular stretch of land?"

"Because he's built his plans around this ranch. It's perfect for him. It abuts his spread. It's isolated. A year-round paved highway runs through it. It has an airfield for small craft. What more could he ask?"

"That's true, but what does it have that a couple of others in the area don't?"

The answer came in a flash. "The City. The only thing the Lazy M has the others don't is the City of Rocks."

Chapter 31

A BLEARY-EYED Paul knocked on my bedroom door the next morning on his way down to breakfast. He dug Maria's cooking, so he appeared as unhappy I'd chased her away as Millicent had been yesterday. He cheered up when I asked how he'd fared at the poker table.

"Those guys can't believe I'm cleaning their clocks fair and square. I had to pass the deal to prove I wasn't doing the South Valley shuffle."

"I take it you won."

"Money, yeah, but not sleep. They wouldn't quit until about three this morning. I don't know how they cowboy all day long on no sleep. They claim they snooze in the saddle, and they might be telling the truth."

Hazel called in the middle of breakfast to report Bill Garza had not checked out the Martinson shack because that was a state police case. Fortunately, Manny Montoya had. He'd picked up half a dozen sets of prints, which he identified as Liver, Lopez, a couple of local junkies, and Zack Rybald, the owner of R&S Auto Repair. The final set remained unidentified.

"Ask him if he can run those unknown prints through the system across the border. Jim Gray's on his way down to pick us up. I should be back in the office by noon."

"Good. We can use some help."

Paul stacked zzz's on one of the couches as I went in search of Bert. I found him in the office with his mother. Millicent intended to stay close to headquarters, although I suspected the decision was more a matter of taking care of her ducks than one of being cautious.

"We need to find something Madelena touched that hasn't been wiped down," I said.

Millicent shook her head. "Good luck with that. Maria was a meticulous housekeeper. She wiped everything down."

"Not everything," Bert said with a grin. "Come on."

We followed him to his bedroom, where he opened a bureau drawer and held up a bolo tie by its strings. "I took this off and handed it to her when she admired it. You know, acting goofy and saying she could have it if she liked it so much."

I could easily picture Bert doing his routine for a pretty woman, even if it was his best friend's pregnant fiancée.

"When she gave it back, I slipped it into my pocket. So I've handled it, but maybe there are still prints on it."

"Worth a try. I need to borrow it."

The sound of a motor overhead drew us outside. Jim's silver, cherry-trimmed Cessna Skycatcher circled the headquarters. A UNM alum and avid Lobo fan, Jim had painted the craft with his school's colors. He made good time. It was only eight o'clock. We watched him set the craft down smoothly and swivel to return to this end of the short runway.

Paul and I said quick good-byes. I was still urging them to be careful when Jim secured the cabin hatch. Moments later we were airborne and headed for Las Cruces to deliver Bert's bolo to Montoya's office. As we circled over the City of Rocks, which appeared deserted, I saw no sign of movement on a well-worn trail leading straight to the international border. The thought of scouting out the Rayo tempted me, but I wasn't willing to involve Jim in an illegal incursion into Mexican airspace.

As Deming appeared in the distance, I pointed to a column of gray smoke riding the morning breeze. "Dime to a donut that's Liver Lips' shack."

"And right after we talked about incriminating fingerprints," Paul said.

"We might as well have lit the torch ourselves." I grabbed my phone and got Bill Garza on the line.

"Yeah, it's Liver's shack. I get a call from your office about fingerprints this morning, and two hours later, his place is burning to the ground."

"Fortunately, Detective Montoya of the NMSP did the forensics work. Like you said, Liver was his case. Is it arson?"

"I'd say so. I can see the tire marks where somebody stopped and peeled out again. I figure they tossed a firebomb."

"You're at the scene?"

"Yeah, they put you through to my cell."

"I'm in the plane circling overhead. We're going to land, and I'll join you as soon as I can find a car."

"Don't bother with the car. I'll pick you up."

Paul wanted to come with me but agreed to return to Albuquerque with James when I gave him the responsibility of delivering the bolo to Montoya in Cruces.

Garza waited as I exited the Cessna and waved me over with his customary scowl. "If witnesses hadn't seen a car tear out this morning just before the fire, I'd accuse you of dropping a Molotov cocktail on that shack."

"I plead not guilty. Do you have a description of the car?"

"Would you believe a black Firebird? Get in. Let's go see what's left. Firemen got to the shack pretty quick, but it wasn't nothing but dry kindling waiting to go up. Not much they could do."

"Any sign of the car?" I asked.

"It's in someone's garage by now, probably within twenty miles of where we are."

"Detective Montoya said one of the prints he lifted in Martinson's house belonged to Zack Rybald."

He smiled. "Let's go pay that gentleman a visit. What could be better than finding that Pontiac in his shop?"

As we pulled into a parking space down the street from the R&S, Garza removed his black ball cap with a DPD logo and scratched his grizzled skull. "I'll bet my badge and throw in my pension more drugs go through that place than a Walgreens pharmacy."

"So shut him down."

He gave me a disgusted look and crawled out of his unit. "Don't think I haven't tried. But we haven't been able to find any probable cause to raid the place."

"Maybe the prints Montoya lifted will help."

"Doubt it. Liver Lips used to work for him. His lawyer will think up a dozen reasons why Rybald's prints would be there."

No one manned the customer-service desk when we entered the shop, but we saw Rybald down in one of the bays, working with a mechanic. He grimaced when he spotted Garza's uniform but continued working for a minute before he walked up three concrete steps into the public waiting area. Without offering to shake, he wiped his hands on a soiled red rag and leaned forward. An unconscious sign of aggression?

"Bill, what can I do for you?" His gaze moved to me. "You're that Albuquerque PI... uh, Vinson. Right?"

"Right. Good memory, Mr. Rybald."

"This about Liver Lips again?" He applied the same rag he'd used on his hands to his sweaty face. "I seen the smoke. Heard the sirens. A customer said somebody torched his place."

"You know anything about that?" Garza fixed him with the glare he gave friend and foe alike.

"Kids. Vandals. Anything that's abandoned around here is bound to get trashed."

"We're looking for a car. A black '96 Pontiac Firebird. You seen it?"

"The same one Montoya asked me about? Naw, we don't get many cars with Chihuahua plates in the shop."

"How'd you know it had Mexican tags?" I asked.

"Montoya told me."

"Didn't have to be in the shop," Garza said. "Coulda seen it on the street. One of your mechanics coulda worked on it on his own time."

"Hey!" Rybald yelled over his shoulder. "Any of you guys worked on a black Firebird with Mex plates? Anybody seen one?"

Denials came from the three bays at the rear of the shop.

"Guess not. I see anything like that, I'll let you know. Vinson, anytime you want that Impala of yours serviced, give me a call, and I'll give you a deal."

Garza's contemptuous stare followed Rybald as he tripped down the steps to the bays.

"I take it you don't like Mr. Rybald very much."

He turned and made for the door. "I don't cotton to smug sons a' bitches."

We drove from the shop to what was left of Liver's shack. The fire truck had departed, but one fireman hung around to make sure the ashes didn't flare up again. Smoke still rose from the pile of ashes and charred timbers. Half-burned four-by-fours stood at each corner of the small structure; everything else had collapsed. The shed out back stood untouched.

I mentally measured the distance from the dirt lane to the front stoop. "Firebomb, you said?"

"Firemen figured a Molotov cocktail."

"That was quite a throw. Whoever tossed it probably had to get out of the car. Somebody around here should have seen them."

"Several somebodies probably did, but only one would even admit to seeing a car."

"Hold on, I have an idea." I called the Lazy M and got Paco's cell number from Millicent. As I handed it over to Garza, I related the events of yesterday afternoon, including the fact I'd confronted Paco with my belief his fiancée was the woman I met at Liver's the morning of his death. "Can you run down any calls made from this number? Calls made yesterday afternoon or this morning?"

"You're thinking Rael called someone to torch the place?"

"Makes sense to me. If it wasn't the gold Plymouth Duster he left the ranch in yesterday the witness spotted, he probably didn't do it himself." Garza asked for the plate number, and I recovered it from my pocket notebook.

"So you think he set the place on fire to keep us from identifying his girlfriend's prints. How would we do that unless she has a record over here?"

"I don't think he knew the state police had already dusted the shack. And I have something with her prints on it. My friends should have delivered it to Montoya's office in Cruces by now."

I rode with Garza to the fire department, where a lieutenant informed us there wasn't anything to report yet, although he believed the fire was arson. The burn pattern supported the theory of a Molotov cocktail tossed through a window, but that was all he knew at the moment.

After that, I asked Garza to drop me at Sunrise Car Rentals on Airport Road, where I rented an Impala. After filling out the appropriate paperwork, I cruised the streets of Deming in the vain hope of spotting a black Firebird. After an hour I gave it up as a fool's errand and headed down I-10 for Las Cruces. On the way I called Millicent and gave her the latest news. Then I let Hazel know I wouldn't be home by noon after all. I closed the call, realizing how much I missed Paul... and he'd only left my side a few hours ago. The price of true love, I guess.

Chapter 32

TAKING A set of fingerprints isn't the same messy, awkward procedure as when I was a cop, at least in properly equipped metropolitan areas. More often than not nowadays, they are digital prints. Checking them through the system's more efficient too. And when you're comparing one set directly against another, it's even faster. The sky-blue turquoise stone in the bolo tie we'd delivered to the state police was huge, and the sterling silver backing held a print.

By the time I arrived, Montoya's people determined it matched the unidentified print found in Liver's shack by eight points. Eight points were good enough for me. Madelena Orona was the woman I'd seen in Martinson's shack the morning of his death.

I spent an hour giving Montoya the details I gathered in the course of my investigation. When he asked me to dictate a formal statement, I handed him the tape from my recorder. I'd switched it on as soon as we sat down at his desk. Then we went to a nearby café for a late lunch while someone transcribed our conversation. I settled for a BLT on rye with a fruit cup. He went for the menudo and a warm flour tortilla dripping with butter.

As we ate he shared what little he'd learned about Liver's murder. Using the three numbers from the Chihuahua license plate I'd given him, he'd determined the tags were a set stolen off a car in Guadalajara. The Firebird hadn't surfaced again until this morning's firebombing of Liver's shack. It probably now had a stateside plate taken from some vehicle in Colorado or somewhere else far from the Boot Heel country.

The state police's forensics team had discovered traces of heroin in the wreckage of Liver's pickup, fueling the suspicion his last trip to Albuquerque wasn't solely for the purpose of delivering a passenger to Ramon Parnewski. Liver had likely handed over a drug package to the Six Pack bar owner as well.

"Have you tied Liver to Paco Rael?" I asked.

"They knew one another. Both of them grew up around Deming and in northern Mexico, but there's no direct tie."

"The Orona woman was in his shack for a reason."

"Yes, and if we ever get our hands on her, we'll ask her what it was. In the meantime we've alerted the border stations. If she comes back over the line, we'll snag her."

"If she comes back as Madelena Orona and if she uses a manned border station, you might. What about Rael? Do you have enough to detain him if you locate him?"

"Only to question him about his girlfriend. Then he'll be free to go. We have better resources than the Luna County Sheriff's Department, so maybe we can run down calls made from the cell number you gave Garza. If so, it might lead us to the Pontiac and the arsonist. Then we'll have a serious talk with him."

My cell phone interrupted us. Hazel's excited voice caught my attention. "Bob Cohen just called. Kenneth Hammond was murdered this morning."

"What? How?" I pressed the speakerphone button.

"Apparently shot to death from long distance while he inspected one of his construction sites."

"Have they caught the shooter?"

"Not according to Bob."

"Hazel, this could be payback, or it could mean Acosta's cleaning up after himself. If that's the case, all of us need to be careful. Call Paul and give him a heads-up, will you? He's probably home by now, but even if he isn't, he has his cell phone with him."

"What about the people at the ranch?" she asked.

"I'll phone them as soon as we hang up. In fact, I'll probably head back down there. They're the ones in real danger."

"The murdered man was Hammond, the Miami developer," I told Montoya after I closed the call. "Can you alert the district office closest to the Lazy M?"

"That would be District Twelve in Deming. I'll let them know, but we might be overreacting. Maybe Acosta's just settling a score with the man who double-crossed him. Assuming he's the guilty party, of course."

"Maybe, but if Millicent and Bert both die, the ranch goes to her daughter, a Dallas artist with no interest in running a cow spread."

"So Acosta might pick it up after all. The benefits to a drug runner snagging the Lazy M are obvious, but are they strong enough to warrant all of this killing?"

I cleared my plate away and leaned over the table. "Liver Lips and Lopez were killed to prevent us—me—from learning something. In Liver's case, who got him to steal Millicent's duck. I'm not sure what Lopez knew, but let's suppose he knew who put his friend up to the snatch. The attempt on Bert was to show Millicent the threats were serious. Plus he showed up unexpectedly at the site where a meeting was supposed to take place, and the extortionist might have believed he had been betrayed."

"Hammond was payback for canceling the debt with Mud and preventing his bird from showing up for the race," Montoya said.

"And possibly to keep him from telling anything else he knew. If this thing breaks open, he'd have been called to testify."

"I hate to state the obvious, but if Acosta's cleaning up after himself, you could be next on the list."

"That thought has crossed my mind. Let's see if Cohen has any more details."

Bob could add little to what he'd told Hazel. Hammond had been inspecting the same North Miami project where the earlier attempt on his life had been made. He'd been standing on one of the exposed upper floors when a marksman caught him with a headshot. The police located the shoot site atop a building about 400 yards away. There were no leads to the shooter. I gave Cohen the same caution Montoya had given me before ringing off.

While Montoya hauled us from the restaurant to District Four headquarters on East University, I got Millicent on the phone and let her know what had happened in Florida. I also told her I was on my way back to the Lazy M. She agreed to try to reach Bert and call him back to the house.

As we entered the SP headquarters, another officer hailed Montoya. "I heard you were trying to run down a girl named Orona. I may know her. Hey there! It's Mr. Vinson, isn't it? Remember me?" I recognized the fresh-faced rookie who'd stopped me the day Bert was shot. "I don't think I introduced myself. I'm Hank Dorman. Hope you made it to the ranch and everything worked out okay."

"Close, but it worked out."

Montoya waved a hand impatiently. "How do you know her?"

"I used to go with a girl named Elena Corazón over in Deming. She had family and friends in the Palomas, Mexico area, and one of them was a girl named Madelena. Madelena Orona. I remember because I'd met lots of Coronas but never an Orona, and I always wondered if somebody just forgot to put the *C* at the front end." The young officer colored as he caught Montoya's exasperated look.

"Can you describe her?"

"Sure. Pretty as a picture. Tall, maybe five nine or so. She'd be about twenty-five now. Wore her hair long the last time I saw her. Black or real dark brown. No distinguishing marks."

"When is the last time you saw her?" Montoya asked.

"Couple of years ago. I broke up with Elena last year, and Madelena hadn't been around in a year or so."

"The Corazón family over here legally?"

"Elena and her brother are natural-born citizens. I don't know about their folks. I saw Elena a month or so ago, and she said her parents were back in Mexico. I didn't ask if it was permanent or a visit."

"That might be the girl Madelena went to visit in Deming," I said. "Do you have an address?" He cited one that matched the street number Luis gave me. "Tell me about her brother."

"His name's Latido Corazón." Dorman chuckled. "That's a play on 'heartthrob.' You know, *Latido* means throb and *Corazón*—"

Montoya interrupted. "Yeah, Corazón means heart. I get it. Age, occupation, description?"

"About a year older than Madelena, say twenty-six. Five ten, one fifty. Clean-shaven. Black hair, brown eyes."

"He have a record?"

"I wasn't an officer back then, so I never checked them out."

"Do it. What does this Latido do for a living?"

"He's a mechanic. Worked at a place called—"

"R&S Auto Repair," I said. "Does he still work there?"

"That's the place. No idea if he's still there."

"Find that out too," Montoya said. "And be careful how you do it. Don't scare anyone off. Get in touch with Captain Masterson in Deming and have his people do it."

"Before you go, do you know of any connection between the Corazóns and a man named Paco Rael?" I asked.

"Paco? Sure. He used to date Madelena. As a matter of fact, he used to date Elena too. He's a real ladies' man, that Paco."

"How well do you know him?"

"Played ball against him when we were in school. Knew him as well as anyone, I guess."

Montoya leveled a glare at the officer. "You know of any connection between him and Liver Lips Martinson?"

Dorman looked as if he'd just figured out his sergeant might believe he held out on a murder investigation. "Just a casual one. We grew up together down in the Deming area, so we all knew one another. That's all there was to it. If there was anything else, I'd have come to you, Sarge."

"Okay. Go take care of those two things for me."

Dorman all but saluted before rushing off.

Montoya exhaled and led the way to his office, where I read and signed the transcription of my tape.

Dorman rapped on the door and handed a file to Montoya. "Latido does have a record. Got busted a couple of times with marijuana, but it wasn't enough to charge him with a felony. He claimed personal use."

"Anything else?" I asked.

"Drunk and disorderly. Public fighting. That kind of thing."

"Gang activity?"

"No indication, sir," Dorman said.

"He do any time?" I asked.

Montoya browsed the record. "A couple of overnight stays in jail." He looked up at Dorman. "Is this address current?"

"It's the one where I used to pick up Elena. They've lived there for years."

Montoya handed the sheet to me. The mug shot, now a few years old, showed a slender young man on the rough edge of being attractive. He would have relished being called "Heartthrob." His profile shot revealed a prominent nose and Adam's apple.

Montoya asked Dorman if he'd contacted Deming.

"Yes, sir. They're working on it for you."

"Come on, Vinson, let's pay Heartthrob a visit."

I intended to go on to the Lazy M after we interviewed Corazón, so I trailed Montoya's cruiser on the sixty-mile drive back to Deming. He turned on both lights and siren, dragging me along in his wake at something like ninety miles an hour. He must have radioed ahead as a matter of protocol, because another unit waited for us at the Corazón residence. A DPD cruiser with Garza filling up the front seat sat directly in front of the state police unit. Montoya acknowledged the other officers but didn't bother with introductions. I gave Garza a nod.

The house was rough stucco painted a lively pink. No cars occupied the driveway or sat in front of the house. While the other lawmen marched up and banged on the door, Dorman headed to the back. I followed him behind the house. While he peered through windows to the house, I found something more interesting. A detached, single-car garage. Three small rectangular windows spanned the door, which faced an alleyway in the back. The glass panes, set about eye level, were useless for anything except admitting a little light. I rattled the Yale padlock securing the door before cupping my eyes and trying to see inside. I made out a dark shape. There was a car in there, but I couldn't tell what kind.

"Manny," I yelled. "Do you have a flashlight in your unit?"

"I've got one," Garza called. A minute later he and the other officers rounded the corner and handed over a big five-battery torch. The light barely penetrated the accumulation of dust on the inside of the glass, but it was enough.

"Bingo!" I said.

Chapter 33

WE PEERED in every window of the house but saw no one. The place had an abandoned air. Either Latido and his sister were gone, or they were doing a superb job of hiding inside. The state patrolman from the Deming office took off to get us a warrant to examine the Corazón house, the garage, and the Firebird locked inside. While we waited, Montoya and I brought Garza up-to-date. His interest was the Lopez murder, but since everything began to tie together, he was entitled to all the facts.

Garza went on the computer in his cruiser and came up with a license plate number. "According to DMV, the only car registered to any Corazón at this address is a green 2004 Chevy Camaro. It's registered to Latido."

"Let's get a bulletin out on it," Montoya said. "And we need to check the records for the house phone or any other telephone listed to the Corazóns. I want to know if there were calls from the cell number BJ gave us."

As Garza radioed in those requests, Montoya shook his head. "If only I'd talked to Dorman earlier."

"Don't beat yourself up. We didn't have enough information to piece this all together before today. I'd say Dorman was a lucky break for us."

He looked at me through tired eyes. "The Corazóns are across the border by now. They headed out as soon as Latido torched Martinson's place this morning."

"You're probably right," I said. "He couldn't risk neighbors identifying his personal vehicle for the firebombing, just as he couldn't chance driving the Pontiac on his run to the border. So he had to switch cars back and forth. Maybe he's the one who drove the Pontiac the night somebody ran Liver off the road. Or maybe he just provided a hidey-hole. Perhaps we'll find something in it to tie Liver and Latido together besides R&S Auto Repair."

"I'm sure Bill's going to jump on that one quick enough," Montoya said.

"You bet your ass," Garza rumbled. "This might be what I need to get past Rybald's armor."

I glanced at my watch. Coming up on three o'clock. "Latido's had plenty of time to get to the border. I wonder if his sister was in on it too."

"The cultural tendency is not to involve females of the family," Montoya said. "I know Paco Rael slightly. I've been at roadhouses when he and Bert Kurtz were drinking and womanizing—and fighting. It's hard to see Paco mixing up his fiancée in this, but she seems to be involved in some way."

Garza agreed but suggested perhaps she was already involved by the time they got together.

After the warrant arrived, the three law enforcement officers asked me to wait on the porch until they'd gone through the house. When Montoya finally called me inside and gave me free rein, there was little to see. The family had lived quite comfortably. The furniture, an eclectic mixture of thrift shop and upscale, gave the place no real style, although they apparently favored heavy Mexican pieces. Everything was neat and stowed in its proper place, no doubt a testament to Elena's housekeeping skills.

We hit pay dirt in the garage. Not exactly a mother lode, but enough marijuana and meth rested in the trunk of the Pontiac to earn someone a stretch behind bars. All this made Bill Garza happy. He might finally get a look inside the R&S Auto Shop. Montoya was more pleased by the crumpled passenger-side door and front fender of the Firebird. He called for forensics to perform their magic and perhaps come up with some paint from Liver's pickup on the vehicle.

Montoya answered a blast of static on his car unit and returned to inform us Latido Corazón's Camaro had passed through the border station at Santa Teresa an hour ago. We'd found Acosta's muscle on this side of the border, but it had shut down before we arrived.

After extracting a promise to keep me in the loop, I headed west on I-10, anxious to get to the ranch where the greater danger lay. Ten miles outside of Deming, I thought of a better way and pulled off onto the shoulder to phone the ranch. Bert agreed to come get me in the chopper. I couldn't get the image of all that earth-moving equipment on the western side of the Rayo out of my head and wanted another look at it.

I turned in the car at the rental agency and lugged my travel bag to the flying service across the field from the airport tower. Before the ranch helicopter put skids to the ground, I learned from a quick phone conversation with James Guerrero in El Paso that the rumor mill had Acosta crossways with some of his associates. Bert filled the machine's twin saddlebag fuel tanks, and then we lifted off before exchanging anything more than perfunctory hellos.

When we were well clear of the town, I spoke into the headset. "Bert, I want another look at the area where Acosta was moving all that dirt. You game?"

Bert nodded and turned south, staying low enough so as not to attract the attention of Border Patrol radar installations—or so we hoped.

The trip wasn't worth the risk. The entire operation had been shut down. The only sign of life was a ranch pickup headed west on one of the dirt roads. The gaping black hole in the side of the bluff, now devoid of equipment and men, gave us no clue as to what the project had been.

We circled the place once while I took photos and then made straight for the Lazy M. Millicent stepped out of the house onto the patio as we touched down. She came forward and gave me a big hug when I got clear of the chopper's slowly spinning rotors.

"BJ, thank you for coming. I was afraid I'd chased you off with my behavior."

"My skin's thicker than that, Mud." She seemed to enjoy being called that by her familiars, and I felt like one of them now. "Where's Linus?"

"I had to send him to the field when I called Bert back in. But I stayed close to the house and kept my .30-30 handy while Bert was gone. And I've got my babies." She indicated Bruno and Hilda. The Dobermans sat on alert a hundred feet away. "Of course, the real tiger's inside. If somebody gets past the Dobermans, they won't be able to set foot inside the house without Poopsie letting me know. Let's go to the office, and you can tell me everything that's happened."

We followed her into the great room, where the feisty little terrier ran circles around our feet while giving excited yips and yaps, some of them so shrill they came out as squeaks. After grabbing coffee, we retreated to the office. Bert paced the floor, and Millicent clicked her amber worry beads while I laid out everything that had happened since we last spoke.

"Acosta's run into some bad luck. James Guerrero, the PI in El Paso I work with, told me a few minutes ago the word is Acosta's on the hot seat. He got arrogant and made a few mistakes. It started with the lawsuit from the Brazilian mine owner and the murders of the owner's son and his killer. Our snooping around in his affairs hasn't helped his situation any. There's talk over there of a project gone wrong that's put him at odds with others in his cartel."

"Some project with Kenny?" Millicent asked. "Is that why they killed him?"

"In a way, but not the construction ventures they shared. I think the project that went wrong was the bet Hammond canceled, the bet that gave Acosta the leverage to pry you off your land. You and the Lazy M are right in the middle of Acosta's troubles. And we've seen how he takes care of his problems."

I gulped coffee. "This ranch has become tremendously important to Acosta and his associates. His next logical step is to try to buy the ranch for a reasonable price."

"No way," Millicent and Bert answered in virtual unison.

"Have you heard from him?" I asked her.

"No, nothing since he left in a hurry that day."

"Then he'll eliminate you two and allow Penelope to inherit."

"That won't be so easy," Bert declared.

"But not impossible. Desperate men do desperate things. Acosta's recent moves feel like desperation. There was no real reason to kill Hammond—except for revenge—unless he was afraid their stateside affairs were about to come under scrutiny. Hammond may have known something Acosta didn't want to come out during formal interrogation. Millicent, you need to tell your daughter and her husband what's going on, if you haven't done so. He's a lawyer—maybe he'll have some ideas."

"He's a tax attorney," Bert said. "He's not going to help much."

"Nonetheless, they need to know the details."

One of the Dobermans let out a bark.

"That's Hilda." Millicent got up and went to the window.

Bruno's deeper voice echoed the other dog. They stood at the fence beyond the helipad, barking and dancing.

"Acosta's making his move quicker than I thought," I said.

"I don't think so." Millicent moved to the french doors. "That's not an alarm, it's a greeting. They recognize whoever's coming."

"They'd recognize Rael, wouldn't they? And Acosta too. Mud, get away from that door."

She ignored me. "I see them. Two people walking."

Bert and I joined her. I could make out distant figures.

"Mud, where are your binoculars?" Bert asked. She indicated a case hanging on the wall. He fiddled with the lenses. "Hell, it's Luis and Maria."

"Walking across the desert? Get the pickup and go get them, Bert."

"Wait a minute," I said. "It may be a trap."

"Not those two. They wouldn't do anything like that."

"Maybe they wouldn't, but Acosta wouldn't have a problem using them as bait."

Millicent gave her son a scorching look. "If you don't go, I will."

"Lend me a rifle, and I'll go with you," I said.

"There's one in the pickup. Come on."

"Mud, arm yourself. And no matter what happens, don't leave the house. In fact, call O'Brien when we leave."

She didn't answer as I followed Bert on his dash to the pickup parked in front of the house. I piled in as he kicked over the starter and sprayed gravel getting around to the back of the house. He ground to a halt at the rear gate and had it open before I could react. The Dobermans dashed out, but he ordered them to stay and put them on guard.

Bert about tore the springs out of the pickup covering the quarter-mile to the Rael pair. He bathed us all in dust as he skidded to a halt ten yards in front of them.

"Bert! Oh, Señor Vinson! *¡Gracias a Dios!*" Maria appeared distraught and disheveled but didn't seem to be suffering from what must have been a miles-long walk across the Boot Heel desert.

"Get in," Bert ordered. "We need to get out of here fast."

"But Paco needs—"

"Get in!" He grabbed her elbow and shoved her into the cab.

"Bert," Luis said, "you must listen—"

"When we get back to the house." I pushed him into the truck and piled into the bed, hanging on for dear life as Bert whipped around in a big circle and drove like a wild man. He halted at the gate and yelled for me to lock it behind us. As soon as I jumped out of the truck, he raced to the house. I turned and faced the two Dobermans he'd put on guard. Had I made a gigantic mistake? I froze. Bert gave a whistle, and the two brutes trotted away to settle in a patch of shade on the patio.

Dragging along in their wake, I itched to run but feared the dogs might take it wrong. With every step I expected to hear a shot. Would I feel it when my head exploded? On second thought, I probably wouldn't even hear the shot… if it came.

Chapter 34

ALTHOUGH MARIA usually spoke for the pair, she was almost incoherent. Luis finally had enough. "*¡Cállate!*" Maria hiccupped and fell silent. "Señor Vinson, Paco wishes to speak with you. Now, please."

"Me? Why?"

"I do not know. When he brought us here, he told us to ask Doña Millicent to find you and have you to meet him. It is very important."

"Where does he want me to meet him?"

"At the City of Rocks. He is waiting for us to call him." Luis turned to Millicent, his head held high. "Doña, I beg you to allow us to stay here. Please consider it for my wife's sake."

"Of course, you may stay. This is your home."

"Luis, what happened?" I asked. "Why did you walk across the desert instead of driving here in your own truck? What's going on?"

"Bad things." His throat seemed to close up. "Paco will tell you everything."

"Bert, see if you can reach him on his cell," I said.

He yanked his cell phone out and punched up the number. "Paco? What the hell's going on?" He narrowed his eyes and listened for a moment. Then he handed the phone to me.

"Mr. Vinson. Thank *Dios* you're here. I need to see you. Now!"

"You can say whatever you need to say over the phone."

"I gotta show you something. Then everything will make sense to you. I know you have no reason to trust me, but I swear before God, I don't intend to harm you."

"Why this change of heart? Your parents are frightened out of their minds."

"They're afraid for their lives. And mine too. Some things have happened. My Madelena is dead. My son too. Don Hector is cleaning house."

"All right, Paco. Leave any weapon you have behind and come to the house. We'll hear what you have to say."

"No!" His voice rose. "You have to come to me. To the City."

"All right, we'll pick you up in the helicopter."

"No! If the helicopter comes, I'll disappear. I don't want Bert here. He knows I shot at him. When Bert gets mad, he does things he's sorry for later. I'll face him when the time comes, but first I need you to understand what is going on."

I pressed him further, but he stubbornly refused to say more over the telephone. When I heard the anxiety level in his voice rising, I acquiesced. "All right, I'll come in the pickup. But first I'm calling the authorities. And I'll be armed."

"Call them if you wish, but don't wait for them. Come now. I don't know how much time we have left."

I hung up and asked Bert for his pickup.

"You can't go out there. It's a trick."

"Maybe, but it doesn't feel like it. These people are frightened for their son. Anyway, why would he want to harm me?"

"Payback, maybe. Remember Hammond. Poking around in Acosta's affairs has stirred things up."

"If that's what he had in mind, he'd insist you come along so he could take care of both of us."

"All right," Bert said. "The rifle's still in the pickup, and it's loaded. There's a round in the chamber. Just pull back the hammer."

"If I don't like the look of things, I'll turn around and come straight back. Is O'Brien on his way, Millicent?"

"He's out on a call. They'll try to reach him as soon as they can."

Maria whimpered. I touched her shoulder. "Paco told me I could call them before I came." I turned to her husband. "Luis, when we returned to the ranch a while ago, I saw a pickup driving toward the border. Was that you?"

"Yes. Please go, Señor. Paco will explain everything."

Bert tossed me a key ring, and I headed for the front door. The temptation to call Paul and speak to him one last time pressed me, but I shook it off. If I believed that, I'd be a fool to go out there. But I was going, and I wasn't a fool. What the hell kind of logic was that?

The engine stuttered before catching. An omen? I threw the truck into low gear, popped the clutch, and prayed I still remembered how to operate a manual shift. I made it to the back gate without much trouble. Bert sprinted out back to open it for me. He left it ajar to expedite my return, and I was grateful for that note of optimism.

Within half a mile, I saw fresh tire tracks. They came from the southeast, did a U-turn, and headed back. Paco had driven his parents as close to the ranch house as he dared before dropping them off. He must have cut the fence and driven across the border. I followed his tracks to the Lazy M's City of Rocks.

I slowed to a crawl and glanced around, alert for danger. My right thigh cramped. Damned thing always acted up at the wrong time. I thumped my leg with a fist.

I hit the clutch and the brakes when a sudden flash of light from atop the stone pile startled me. Binoculars or telescopic rifle sight? Probably Paco letting me know he was there. Otherwise he was terribly inept, because the sun hovered just above the Hachitas on the western horizon. Forgetting to shift into low, I stalled the truck when I eased off the clutch and fed gas. The motor ground again but caught. I eased forward, my leg throbbing fiercely.

Feeling increasingly vulnerable as the tall gray walls of the City neared, I reached behind me and pulled Bert's rifle from its rack. The slightly oily feel of the metal restored some of my confidence. He took good care of his weapons. Still traveling slowly, I passed through the gate to the City. Disoriented by the sudden shade, I blinked until I could see again. I eased to a halt. The brakes squealed—sand in the linings, no doubt. Cautiously I opened the door and got out of the vehicle, cradling the rifle against my chest, one thumb on the hammer.

"Paco?" My voice floated across the silent plaza. Somewhere in the distance, I heard the caw of a crow.

"Up here."

He stood atop the jailhouse with an AK-47 held loosely in his right hand. I fingered the switch to the recorder on my belt.

"I wasn't sure you'd come," he said.

"I guess we both have trust issues. Why am I here?"

"Head down the avenue toward the back of the City." He moved out of sight.

"I don't like that idea. I'd rather stay close to the truck."

He reappeared and climbed down from the rock, favoring his left side. "I can't bring it to you, so I have to bring you to it."

As he stood in front of me, I asked if his bullet wound still bothered him. He hesitated a moment and then admitted it did.

"Is that why you wanted me out here alone, because I shot you?"

"No, you didn't ambush me or anything. You gave fair warning before the lead started flying."

"Let's get this over with." I motioned for him to precede me down that strange avenue.

He set his hat more firmly on his head and began walking in a graceful, confident stride that ate up the distance rapidly for a man no taller than five eight. The farther we walked, the deeper the shadows became. I figured we were almost at the rear of the City when I noticed something wrong. I glanced up. A sand-colored tarpaulin spanned the space overhead.

He must have heard my steps falter. He turned. "Neat, huh? From the air it looks just like solid rock. We're almost there."

In another fifty paces, I realized the wall to my left was no longer a rock wall. It had been replaced by another natural-looking heavy canvas tarp. He faced me again.

"This would eventually be metal cargo doors plastered with adobe to blend in with the real rock. Anybody walking by wouldn't have noticed a thing."

"Son of a bitch! It's a tunnel."

"Better than that, it's a highway. It has everything except traffic lights." He swept the canvas aside, revealing a massive ramp rising out of a deeper tunnel. A distant glow let me know it was lighted, probably from one end to the other.

"So this is why Acosta wanted the ranch."

"Needed the ranch. Last year, when Don Hector got wind of the bet Mud made with Hammond, he started planning this. He was sure he could get her ranch because he could make her lose the bet by stealing Quacky. He's put fifteen million dollars of the cartels' money into a rush job on a paved, lighted, five-mile tunnel capable of handling semis. Neat, huh?"

I shook my head. "Unbelievable. He can simply drive his drugs and his illegals right across the border any time of the day or night."

"Not immigrants. If he started driving workers across, too many people would know about it. This was for his drugs. But he fucked up. This isn't just for his organization. He made deals with other cartels to bring their good across too. When the idea caught on, he had to start showing some results. Instead of waiting until he got the ranch, he started building the tunnel... with the cartels' money.

"Everything was fine until you showed up and tried to talk Millicent out of paying up, or at least into stalling. He could handle that, but when you scared Hammond out of going through with the race, he got desperate."

"So he tried to kill Hammond, steal his racer, and show up at the race," I said. "How do you know so much about his affairs?"

"I was his number two, at least at this end. I mean, I wasn't number two in the cartel. Just in his part of it."

"Are you saying Acosta isn't the top man in his organization?"

"No. He's number two. And number two has to try harder, no? He tried so hard he got his dink caught in the door."

"So he's in trouble with the cartels?"

"If doesn't get his hands on the Lazy M, he is. And they're not happy about the hit on Hammond either."

"Why did you try to kill Bert the day Millicent came to meet you out here? Things hadn't started falling apart at that point."

"She wasn't meeting me. I was just a guide. Acosta had some *gran queso* from the home office come for the meeting. You know, to give him some cover."

My limited Spanish told me *gran queso* meant big cheese. "Millicent waited well past noon, but nobody showed up."

"Yeah, Don… uh, the guy stayed on the Mexican side of the border until he was ready to go meet her, but we kept hearing Bert's helicopter buzzing around, and that made him nervous. When Bert landed, he figured he'd been double-crossed, so he gave me instructions over the walkie-talkie to shoot the pilot. I couldn't refuse, and I had to make it look good. Bert almost fucked himself when he stopped dead in his tracks."

That explained why Buck and the Lazy M hands had found only one set of footprints, but I wasn't certain I bought that glib business about missing the shot on purpose. It seemed more logical Bert would have walked into the bullet if he hadn't stopped. But even a good marksman's aim can be off.

"Paco, why are you betraying Acosta by telling me this?"

Paco's eyes went to slits, and he tightened his grip on the weapon in his hand. Then he slumped against the rock wall and told me his story.

Acosta used to be a good man. At least, according to Paco and his family. He took care of the people who worked for him. But money and power changed him. When he overreached and things started to go wrong, he handled it like the rest of the drug lords. He settled his problems by killing. He had Paco arrange for Liver Lips to steal Mud's duck, but when I told Liver the law had a warrant out for him, he'd called Acosta for help. Instead of helping, Liver's *patrón* sent Latido Corazón to run him off the road.

"Was that Madelena I saw at Liver's place?"

He nodded. "We needed to make sure Liver hadn't left anything behind that would tie Acosta to the duck's kidnapping. Madelena wasn't well-known in Deming, so Acosta sent her."

"How did they know Liver talked to me at the hospital?"

"They didn't until he called after he gave you the slip. You must have given Liver some big ideas. He demanded money."

"Why kill Lopez?"

"That was Latido too. Liver and Lopez used to party together. Acosta didn't know how much Liver had blabbed, so he couldn't take a chance."

When Latido and his sister showed up at the Rayo one step ahead of the law, Acosta handled that loose end personally. He shot Latido with his own pistol. Killed him right in front of his sister and Paco and Madelena. Elena went crazy, so he shot her too. Madelena tried to stop him and got a bullet as well.

Paco drew a deep breath and pushed away from the wall. "Then Acosta turned his pistol on me and asked if I was going to be a problem. I said I was cool. He did what he had to do. But he saw something in my eyes. Just as I saw something in his. He'd take care of me too, after I'd disposed of the bodies for him. I… I had to carry away the corpse of my fiancée and my *niño*, my son. At that point I didn't much care if he shot me or not. But I realized that once Acosta killed me, he'd have to take care of my parents too. I couldn't let that happen."

"And now what?"

"Now that you know what happened, I am walking back to my truck in the middle of the tunnel and returning to the Rayo."

"That's suicide. Come with me and tell the authorities what you've told me."

"That will accomplish nothing."

"It will save your life."

He shrugged. "For today. And perhaps tomorrow. But he won't forgive my treachery. I will be the son who turned on him, and he'll hunt me down on either side of the border."

"That may be so, but why voluntarily return for the slaughter? He probably already knows you and your parents have disappeared. You'll walk right into a bullet when you go back."

He shook his head again. "He's not at the ranch. He's in Mexico City getting a dressing down from the cartel bosses. He'll be distracted for a while. Maybe long enough."

"Won't the others at the ranch have missed you by now?"

"I told them I needed to take my mother and father to visit family in Guadalajara."

"Why didn't you just come through the tunnel and drive your parents to the ranch house?"

"Mud and Bert were expecting trouble, and I didn't want to risk my folks' lives if shooting started. Bert has a hair trigger. It was safer to let them walk in."

I regarded the determined man standing in front of me. "Paco, I know what you're thinking. You can't just shoot Acosta down in cold blood."

"Mr. Vinson, you're holding a rifle in your arms. If a rabid dog ran at you, what would you do? Shoot it, no?"

"What do I tell your folks?"

"Never to return to Mexico again. No matter what, they never set foot over that border. And you can tell them I love them." He gave a wan smile. "You've got that recorder going, haven't you? *Mamacita. Papacito. Te amo. Te amo mucho.*"

Chapter 35

I DROVE away in a quandary. What was my moral obligation? I knew one man planned the cold-blooded assassination of another. Some might argue it was justified, but that didn't fit my code of ethics. On the other hand, if I tried to prevent the killing by warning Acosta, the playing field would tilt, and Paco would be on the receiving end of a bullet. I hit the brakes, stalling the truck when I forgot to use the clutch. I fumbled in my pocket, came up with Paco's cell phone number I'd written down for Garza, and dialed it.

No answer. I hung up and tried again. He'd said the tunnel ran five miles long, and he had to walk back to his truck, so he was likely still underground, where his cell wasn't receiving a signal. I waited five minutes before trying again with the same results. Suddenly feeling very tired, I put the pickup in neutral and turned the draggy ignition. It caught. Remembering to use the clutch this time, I threw it in gear and headed back to the ranch house.

Bert met me at the gate, locked it behind me, and hopped into the truck bed. I parked near the duck pens and hit the Redial button on my phone as I got out.

"*¿Quién es?*"

"Paco, it's B. J. Vinson. I can't let you do this. This is suicide. Throwing your life away for nothing."

"You can't stop me."

"I'll tell you exactly how I'm going to stop you. There's a PI in El Paso I work with who's very connected in Mexico. I'm going to call him and have him alert the authorities. You told me Acosta is in Mexico City, so you won't be able to get to him."

"Why didn't you just shoot me when we were in the City?"

"I don't want you dead. I want you healthy enough to help put that bastard in prison."

"Won't happen."

"It won't if we don't try. Turn around now, Paco, or I make the call."

He didn't answer, but the road noises lessened. He had stopped and was thinking it over. "What do you have in mind?"

"Come to the Lazy M so we can brainstorm the situation. When is Acosta due back?"

"Later tonight."

"What's it to be?"

"I will come. Perhaps Bert will shoot me and end all of this mess."

I had to laugh. A nervous laugh, but a laugh nonetheless. "Good."

"But first I have to do something."

"Now, Paco—"

"Listen to me, gringo. I know where he put his pistol. The pistol he shot my… my friends with. It still has his fingerprints on it. I know where their bodies are. When I get that revolver, then you can call your friend in El Paso."

"The pistol means nothing. Even if the authorities can match bullets from the bodies to the weapon, they still couldn't prove Acosta did the shooting. Hell, the gun will be in your possession, not his."

"But it does not have my fingerprints on it. No, I know Don Hector. He will consider the pistol a weapon against him. If nothing else, it will be enough to keep him off my family's backs."

"Can you get it and still get away?"

I could almost hear him shrug. "I can try."

"You've got two hours, Paco. Then I make the call. Do you have my cell phone number?"

"I do now. It's stored in my phone."

"Put it on speed dial. If you get in trouble, call."

"If I get in trouble, any call will be to say adios, Mr. Vinson."

The phone went dead.

I filled Bert in on the part of the conversation he'd been unable to hear as we walked over the oriental bridge across the man-made creek. We were met by a reception party larger than I expected. Luis and Maria stood to one side of Millicent. Linus and two other drovers, all bearing rifles, flanked her on the other. Linus set the other cowboys on watch as the rest of us trooped inside.

"We need the Border Patrol. Will you get them on the line, Millicent?"

As soon as she reached them, I took the phone and asked for SOS Randy Ramirez, the officer in charge who'd responded when Paul and I were penned down in the City. Ramirez came on the line and listened quietly while I related every detail of what I had seen and what Paco had told me. I had my recorder going and assumed his was as well. Military style, he repeated a condensed version back to me, and I confirmed his understanding.

"And Paco's going to try to get back to the Lazy M this evening?" he asked.

"He's going to try, but there will be people on his back if he runs into trouble."

"If he makes it to this side, we can help, but if he doesn't...." He left the rest unsaid.

"How about friendlies over the border? Is there anyone you can alert over there?"

"Hard to know who to trust in a situation like this. We might just be calling more trouble down on his head. I know one National Police commander, but he'd have to call on others I don't know."

"It's worth the risk. We can use some help down here," I said.

"We're on our way."

I hung up and caught Bert's look. "So he admitted shooting me, huh?"

"Admitted shooting *at* you. Said he had to make it look good."

"You believe him?"

"Yes." No point in sharing my doubts at this moment.

Bert rubbed his eyes with a callused hand. "Me too."

"*¡Gracias a Dios!*" Maria exclaimed.

"So what do we do, just sit here?" Millicent asked. Then she turned into Mud before my eyes. "We need to get out to the City. Paco might need help when he comes back. Is he going to use that tunnel?"

"Yes. Look, the light's going fast, and we're not going to do him any good stumbling around in the dark. Let's wait. He'll let us know what's going on as soon as he can."

"Fine," Mud said. "In the meantime, let's eat. Maria, rustle us up something, please. And Luis, go put the ducks to bed. Keep busy. Besides, we might all need a belly full of energy before this night's over. Bert, better put Bruno and Hilda in the kennel. They'll go nuts with the crowd we're going to have. Might as well put Poopsie in my bedroom too."

The household came alive with a burst of activity for a short while before settling into a period of anxious waiting. I don't know how Maria managed it on such short notice, but the scent of warm food soon flooded the entire house. After everyone ate, including the hired hands who came to the table in shifts, O'Brien showed up. Hard on his heels, Randy Ramirez and his senior patrol agent, Chill Williams, arrived in a helicopter with two other men. Maria and Luis fed the new arrivals while O'Brien and the two senior BP agents joined Mud, Bert, and me in the office. By the time I finished laying everything out for them, it had been an hour and a half since I last spoke to Paco. I glanced out the french doors. Night had fallen when I wasn't looking.

"I couldn't reach the NP commander I mentioned, BJ, and I don't trust anybody else. I've left a message for him to call me. What do you expect to happen?" Ramirez asked.

"I'm hopeful Paco makes it back across the border without incident. But he might have company. If he roars up out of that tunnel with others on his tail, I expect an invasion. Acosta may come across and solve his problem the way he's taken care of others."

"You mean by killing Mrs. Muldren and Bert. Well, my men and I ought to get out to the City. We need to be in place if and when D-day arrives. You'll show us the tunnel?"

"If you know where to look, a blind man could find it. They haven't finished constructing the camouflaged door yet."

Ramirez looked pensive. "How much of that tunnel do you figure's stateside?"

"Bert, how far is the border from the City?"

"Couple of miles."

"Okay," Ramirez said. "That means at least that much is our sovereign territory. You have any dynamite on the ranch?"

"Yeah. Got some in a shed out back of the horse barns. We use it to clear stumps, break rocks, clear out arroyos," Bert explained for my benefit.

"Way back of the horse barns," Mud said. "You gonna blast that damned mole hole?"

"That might be the best way to go, ma'am."

"Not until Paco gets through," she said. "He risked his life to let us know about the tunnel, and we owe him every opportunity to let him use it for his escape."

"That'll be cutting it awful close," Ramirez said. "Bert, show Chill where the dynamite's stored. Chill, borrow one of the ranch vehicles and take two men to that rock pile out there. Locate the tunnel entrance and begin wiring the explosives. Don't go in over a mile. I want to make certain any explosion takes place on US soil. Understand? I'll follow in the chopper as soon as we know what's going on."

"I'll go with them," O'Brien said. "I've got some demo experience."

"Good. Come on, Bert." Williams stood and went to the french doors.

I tossed Bert the keys to the pickup, and the three men left in a rush. The rest of us watched through the windows as Bert drove around behind the barn. A few minutes later, the vehicle reappeared. Bert turned the truck over to O'Brien, Williams, and two other agents. They immediately headed for the City.

After Bert rejoined us in the office, we had a spirited discussion over whether we were handling this right. Our voices died in our throats when my cell phone rang. Everyone watched as I opened the flip phone and put the call on the speakerphone.

"BJ, I got a problem. Don Hector is back. I'm not sure I can get away tonight." Paco's voice sounded calm—a little strained, but calm.

"Do you have his pistol?"

"Yeah. I put it in a bag, but I picked it up by the barrel. So his prints are still on it."

"Then you have no choice. You have to get away. If he discovers it's missing, he'll tear the place apart looking for it."

"Yes, and he's on the prod. The cartels must have ripped him a new one. He's like a volcano ready to blow."

"Get out of there, Paco. Deputy O'Brien and four BP agents are here. They plan on salting the tunnel with dynamite." I glanced at Ramirez. "They'll let you through before they blast the tunnel. What are you driving?"

"I'll be in my pickup, a dark blue Ford F-150."

"Stay in contact. Let me know when you leave."

I heard a noise on the other end of the phone. "He's here. I think he's found his gun is gone. I'm gonna try to get out now. Talk to you later."

The line went dead. I resisted the impulse to hit the Redial button. Paco didn't need a ringing telephone to give him away.

"How far away is he?" Ramirez asked.

"The Rayo headquarters is between fifteen and twenty miles from the City," Bert said.

"I've traveled those roads over there," the BP agent said. "They'll do good to hit thirty miles an hour. That gives us less than half an hour. I've got to get going."

"I'd like to hitch a ride."

"Sorry, no civilians on an operation like this."

"I'll take you, BJ." Bert jumped to his feet. "What's your radio frequency, Ramirez? We need to be able to communicate."

I halfway expected the agent to object, but he recited the frequency and said he intended to remain in the air, where he would have a good view of what happened on the approach to the border. Then he rushed toward his helo.

"That sounds like a good plan for us too," I said. "Bert, are your tanks topped up?"

"Always."

"BJ, take my rifle." Mud started for the gun cabinet in the corner of the room.

As we lifted off into a clear, moonlit night, I saw the running lights of the BP helicopter in the distance. Bert fiddled with his radio dial to put us on their frequency.

"Bert, can we go dark?"

"Yeah. There's more of a danger the other bird will run over us, but I ought to be able to stay out of his way."

Another quarter hour elapsed before we saw anything. Then we spotted a weird, bouncing glow in the distance.

"That's gotta be Paco. Man, he's really putting the hammer down. It'll be a miracle if he doesn't roll on that rough road."

I pointed to another set of bobbing lights behind him. "And there's why he's hitting the accelerator so hard."

"Yep, they're on his tail. Uh-oh, here comes another one."

A second set of headlamps appeared about half a mile behind the first. Paco led the front vehicle by about a quarter of a mile. As we watched, little dots of red winked on either side of the truck closest to Paco's vehicle.

"Oh hell, they're shooting at him," Bert said.

I grabbed the mike, and forgetting all radio etiquette, I blurted Ramirez's name.

"I see them."

"Can you give him a hand?"

"Sorry. That's Mexican airspace. My hands are tied."

"How far do you figure he is from the Mexican side of the tunnel?" I asked Bert.

"That's five miles from the border, at least. That puts him about two and a half miles from the tunnel entrance."

"That other truck seems to be gaining on him."

The lights on Paco's vehicle suddenly reached skyward. Then they went wobbly for a second before resuming their undulating motion.

"Whoa! He hit a hell of a bump. Almost went over," Bert said.

"Yeah. He lost some ground to the one on his tail. And the other driver's now warned about the bump in the road."

I hit the button on the mike again. "Ramirez, isn't there something you can do?"

"Pray, man, pray." Then I heard him raise Williams. "Chill, you ready on your end?"

"The demo guys are still in the tunnel, but I hear them coming out."

"Let me know as soon as you're certain."

"Wilco."

"Well, shit! There's something I can do," Bert yelled. "Hold on."

The Bell suddenly leapt forward, drawing an involuntary gasp from me. At the maximum speed of 105 miles per hour, we headed straight for the border. The lights of the racing trucks drew closer, larger. Paco had lost ground but still led by a couple of hundred yards.

Bert shoved the stick forward and sent us plunging toward the earth at a breathtaking rate. Even in the dark, I could clearly see the shape of the vehicles racing along a rough, dusty road. The first of the pursuers was now close enough to be enveloped in Paco's thick dust trail.

I yelped as Paco raced right beneath our skids. Then Bert suddenly flipped on his landing lights. I clearly saw the panicked expression on the driver's face as he twisted the steering wheel frantically. His passenger groped for the door handle. The gunman in the bed simply stared up, mouth agape.

At the last moment, Bert hauled back on the stick, and the agile little bird went into her steepest climb.

"Incoming!" I screamed as I saw those telltale red pinpricks coming from the second truck. This time they seemed directed at us.

"Don't worry. They can't hit a thing bouncing along like that. They're wasting their ammo."

A metallic clang put the lie to that statement.

"Think it just hit the strut work behind the cabin." Bert killed the lights and did a corkscrew turn that put us behind the vehicles. "She's acting okay, so I guess they didn't hit anything vital."

Apparently the men in the truck lost us in the darkness. Either that, or they were as stupefied as we were at what we saw when we came around. The first chase truck slid on its side, turned over on its back, and came to an abrupt halt. It must have struck an embankment. The other pickup managed to avoid the wreckage and keep on Paco's tail, but it had lost ground.

"Nice," Ramirez's voice came over the radio. "Too bad I didn't see that."

Bert and I grinned at each other.

"Chill, the first vehicle's our guy. He's only got about a half-mile lead on the thugs chasing him, so you can't wait until he reaches the entrance. I figure he's going about forty mph. Blow it as soon as you figure he's clear of the charges."

"Wilco."

Suddenly Paco's lights disappeared.

"Ramirez! Paco's in the tunnel."

All too soon the lights of the other vehicle dimmed and disappeared.

"The other truck just entered," I yelled.

I expected Ramirez to relay the information, but the radio remained silent. Then I realized we were all on the same frequency. William's voice started the countdown; I prayed he was good at math.

"Uh-oh," Bert muttered.

Flying around in the darkness after a shootout, "Uh-oh" was just about the last thing I wanted to hear.

"What is it?"

"She feels a little mushy."

"Oh crap! Get us back over the border. I'd like a decent burial."

We made it to the fence line. In fact, we made it back to the City in time to see the tarp spanning the walls over the tunnel entrance rip apart and billow into the air. Dust and bits of rock exploded from the entrance, expelling a pair of bright headlamps. Then the lights abruptly died.

"The explosion shoved Paco out of the tunnel too fast. He rammed into the other side of the wall," I said.

"We got our own problems." Bert flipped on the landing lights and grabbed the mike.

"We're going down, Ramirez. Keep your bird out of our way."

"Hard?"

"No, think I can bring her in okay. I'll steer clear of your people."

No one said anything for the next couple of minutes. Bert had his hands full trying to control a crippled bird. I got busy praying. "Hit our oil line," he said, more to himself than to me.

The earth rushed up to meet us. Twenty feet above the ground, he hauled back on the stick. The machine tried to obey, but the working parts were dry and freezing up rapidly. He almost made it to the ground, but the rotors suddenly quit before touchdown. We landed hard. The impact drew grunts from both of us.

"Get out, fast!" Bert yelled.

I didn't ask why. I just bailed. Fifty yards from the chopper, he turned around.

"What was that all about?" I asked. "You got her down okay."

"Fire. You always have to worry about fire in an emergency landing. But we were lucky. She might even live to fly another day."

"Let's go see what happened over there."

We set off in the darkness and found our way to the avenue at the rear of the City. We arrived in time to see three BP agents, working by the light of powerful portable lanterns, pull the limp form of Paco Rael out of the twisted cab of his Ford.

Epilogue

ACCORDING TO television and news reports, northern Mexico mourned the death of Hector Acosta, who—it was claimed—died in a tragic vehicular accident on his ranch. I wondered who or what had been in the casket displayed so prominently at his fancy funeral, since Acosta was more likely already entombed beneath the City of Rocks.

Three weeks after the BP agents blew the tunnel, Paul and I returned to the Lazy M for a postmortem and a hefty check for our services. Paul claimed he wanted to see what a royal princess of Duckdom looked like. Paco snatched Quacky Quack the Second at the last minute before racing for the tunnel, and she'd survived the truck crash better than he had. Also, we were both curious to see if the City had suffered any damage from the massive dynamite blast—even though Millicent had assured us it came through unscathed except for one toppled rock tower.

We gathered in the imposing great room at the Lazy M headquarters. Millicent looked impressive in her stonewashed denim skirt and vest, heavy with strands of turquoise and heishi. Bert was a dusty cowboy in from the range, while Maria and Luis seemed never to have left.

Paco, his crutches leaning against a nearby wall, was still recovering from his crash injuries. He looked slightly heroic in a chair at the far end of the long Navajo rug. Most of his bandages were gone, but a cast on his broken left leg and a big patch on his forehead gave him a vulnerable, yet rakish look.

He was under threat of indictment on drug-trafficking charges, but Millicent had gone to bat for him and he hadn't been arrested yet. The shoulder wound was the principal evidence against him, but the authorities didn't have the bullet that caused it. Neither Paul nor I could positively identify him, so he was probably home free.

We made a convivial group, and the meeting had a celebratory air. Everyone else had already heard details of Paco's flight, but this was Paul's and my first opportunity to hear the tale from his own lips. He took a deprecating tone, making it sound little more than an ordinary day. He'd turned over Acosta's pearl-handled pistol to the authorities and indicated where its victims had been buried. He'd also applied for asylum in the United States, and given the special circumstances, it would probably be granted.

After he'd answered all our questions, I sat back and watched Bert pull on a beer and engage in conversation with him. It appeared their friendship had survived—not intact, but clinging to life and likely to recover.

I had a different take on things. Maybe Paco started out as a decent human being, but just as power and money had changed Acosta, the drug culture had affected him as well. He'd shot Bert, and he could argue all he wanted that he'd had to make it look good. But to my way of thinking, he could have missed by a mile, and some guy standing a couple of miles away would never have known how bad his aim had been. But that was for Bert and Millicent to decide for themselves.

But I couldn't forget he'd made a determined effort to kill me during the shootout at the City. Worse, he'd tried to kill Paul, the one brilliant shaft of sunlight penetrating the clouds of my life. I harbored no doubt he'd have executed both of us without thinking twice about it if the BP hadn't shown up when they did. To my mind, he was nothing more than a handsome, charming killer who one day would be turned loose on the Boot Heel country.

Exclusive Excerpt

The Lovely Pines

A BJ Vinson Mystery

By Don Travis

When Ariel Gonda's winery, the Lovely Pines, suffers a break-in, the police write the incident off as a prank since nothing was taken. But Ariel knows something is wrong—small clues are beginning to add up—and he turns to private investigator BJ Vinson for help.

BJ soon discovers the incident is anything but harmless. When a vineyard worker—who is also more than he seems—is killed, there are plenty of suspects to go around. But are the two crimes even related? As BJ and his significant other, Paul Barton, follow the trail from the central New Mexico wine country south to Las Cruces and Carlsbad, they discover a tangled web involving members of the US military, a mistaken identity, a family fortune in dispute, and even a secret baby. The body count is rising, and a child may be in danger. BJ will need all his skills to survive, because between a deadly sniper and sabotage, someone is determined to make sure this case goes unsolved.

Coming Soon to
www.dsppublications.com

Prologue

A FIGURE watched from the edge of the forest as blustery night winds raced through undulating boughs to brush evergreens with feckless lovers' kisses and oppress the grove with ozone raised by a rainstorm to the west. Ground litter, heavy with fallen pine needles, trembled before gusts—as if the Earth itself were restless.

Advantaging a cloudbank obscuring the half moon, the intruder picked up a heavy duffel bag and breached a four-foot rock wall. The prowler crossed the broad lawn, pausing briefly before a brick and stone edifice to scan a white sign with spidery black letters by the light of a small electric fixture trembling in the breeze.

THE LOVELY PINES VINEYARD AND WINERY
Valle Plácido, New Mexico Ariel Gonda, Vintner
Established in 1964 Fine New Mexico Reds

Prompted by the rumble of distant thunder, the wraith made its cautious way to a large building at the rear of the stone house and removed a crowbar from the bag to pry a hasp from the heavy door. Unconcerned over triggering an alarm, the black shadow vanished into the depths of the deserted winery.

Chapter 1

Thursday, June 11, 2009, Albuquerque, New Mexico

I WAS reading an *Albuquerque Journal* article about the recent assassination of Dr. George Tiller, one of the few doctors in the US still performing late term abortions, when my secretary, Hazel Harris Weeks, tapped on my office door before ushering a dapper gentleman inside.

He held out his free hand—the other clutched a small bag—and spoke with a slight European accent. "*Grüezi*, Mr. Vinson, I am Ariel Gonda. It is good to finally meet you."

Taking *grüezi* to be a German word for "hello" or "howdy," I stood to accept the proffered handshake as my mind grappled to place him. Then a memory dropped into place. Ariel Gonda was the corporate treasurer of Alfano Vineyards in Napa Valley. I ran across his name during what I mentally referred to as the Bisti Business, but I'd never actually met the man before. If I recalled correctly, he was a Swiss national, so the word in question was likely Swiss German.

"Mr. Gonda, how are Aggie and Lando doing?" I referred to the Alfano brothers to let him know I'd made the connection.

"They are well, thank you. At least, they were when last I spoke to Aggie. I am no longer with the organization. I am now one of you. That is to say, a bona fide citizen of New Mexico."

I smiled inwardly as he neatly covered his tracks. It's best to be precise when drawing comparisons to a gay confidential investigator. "Welcome to our world, Mr. Gonda."

"Please call me Ariel. As you can see, I have become Americanized. In my native Switzerland, we would never have arrived at first names so swiftly. I find the informality refreshing."

"With pleasure—if you'll call me BJ. Please have a seat and tell me what I can do for you. Unless this is a social call."

"Would that it were. Unfortunately, it is your services as an investigator I require at the moment."

He settled into the comfortable chair directly opposite my old-fashioned walnut desk and glanced around the wainscoted room. I detected a gleam of approval in his pale blue eyes as he studied pieces of my late father's cowboy and western art collection adorning the light beige walls. He brought his attention back to me, a clue he was ready to discuss business.

I took a small digital voice recorder from a drawer and placed it on the desk. "Do you mind if I record the conversation?" With his consent, I turned on the device and entered today's date and noted the time as 10:15 a.m. "This interview with Mr. Ariel Gonda is done with his knowledge and consent."

I lifted my eyes to meet his and asked him to identify the name and location of his business. He limited his response to "The Lovely Pines Vineyard and Winery, Valle Plácido, New Mexico." After that was properly recorded, I asked the purpose of his visit.

He cleared his throat. "The matter that brings me here is a break-in at my winery precisely two weeks ago today."

I consulted my desk calendar. "That would be May 28. What time?"

"Sometime during the night before. I learned of it when I went to work that morning."

"How was entry gained?"

"The hasp was forced, rendering the padlock useless."

"What was taken?"

"Nothing that I can determine."

"Vandalism?"

"Merely some papers in my office and lab disturbed. But nothing was destroyed or taken, and there are some quite valuable instruments in the laboratory."

"Tell me a little about your business."

I examined Gonda as he spoke. During my involvement in the Bisti affair, I'd built up an image of a rotund, stodgy European bean counter, but the man sitting across from me was rather tall—probably my height, an even six feet—solid but not fat, and darker than I pictured Europeans from the Swiss Alpine regions. His striking aristocratic face ended in a high forehead. Light brown hair brushed the collar of his powder blue cotton shirt. He might consider himself Americanized, but his pleasing baritone hadn't yet mastered the art of speaking in contractions.

"The Lovely Pines is located northeast of here, just outside the village of Valle Plácido. Do you know it?"

I nodded. "The area, not the winery."

"I began negotiations to purchase the business from Mr. Ernesto C de Baca last summer. However, he passed away before we arrived at an agreement. In January of this year, I completed the transaction with his heirs."

Gonda lifted the small bag he'd placed on the floor beside his chair. The two glass containers he extracted looked to be green, hippy Bordeaux bottles often used for reds. The gold seal covering the cork was quite eloquently done.

"I brought samples. Please enjoy them with my compliments," he said before continuing his narration.

I listened patiently as he described the operation in his pedantic manner. The winery was located on ten acres fronting the north side of State Road 165 running out of Valle Plácido east toward Sandia Peak. A three-story stone and brick edifice housed the public rooms, offices, and family living quarters. The winery and the cellar sat some distance behind that building. A hundred-acre vineyard lay to the east, bordered on the south by a fifteen-acre lake or pond. Roughly one-fifth of a square mile in total land area.

I tapped my desk blotter with the point of a gold-and-onyx letter opener fashioned like a Toledo blade. "Valle Plácido doesn't have a police force, so I assume you reported the break-in to the Sandoval County Sheriff's Office."

"I did. However, since nothing was taken, the county officials decided it was a case of adolescent mischief and closed the investigation— such as it was."

"Apparently you disagree with that conclusion. Have there been other incidents?"

"Certain small things have occurred. Things I would not have noticed were it not for the earlier break-in." He leaned back in the chair and crossed his legs in a less formal manner. Covering the lower portion of his face with a palm, he pulled his hand down over his chin and neck as though smoothing a nonexistent beard. "I suppose I can best explain by telling you that two days following the actual burglary, if that is the proper terminology, I noticed some of my tools and equipment had been moved."

"How many employees have access to the area?"

"We have a viticulturist and two field hands working the vineyard. I am the vintner and have three assistants in the winery. Marc, my nephew, acts as my outside salesman and assistant manager. My wife, Margot, is responsible for the operation of the office. Then there is our chocolatier, Maurice Benoir, who is invaluable in making our chocolate-flavored wines. His wife assists him in running a kiosk in the entry hall. She acts as cashier for all of the various profit centers and sells handmade sweets she and Maurice concoct. And, of course, we have a cook and waitress for the bistro."

"A total of thirteen people, if I counted correctly. And all of them have access to the winery?"

"Most of them. Our viticulturist's wife is also on the premises, since they live at the vineyard. She does not work for us but has the run of the place."

"So the total is actually fourteen individuals. Let's be clear. All of them have access to the winery?"

"Throughout the day, anyone other than the cook and the girl who waits our tables will be in and out of the winery numerous times. But I refuse to believe any of them were involved in what occurred."

"I see. I must tell you in all candor, there is probably little I can do for you except to conduct background checks on your people. Chances are that a search might reveal something, but there's no guarantee. You might end up spending a lot of money for nothing."

He performed the palm-over-lip-and-chin maneuver again as he thought over what I'd said. "At least I would be assured of their honesty and would not walk around harboring darks suspicions about the people with whom I work."

"Mr. Gonda... Ariel, anytime you do a thorough background check on that many people, any number of moles and wens and warts are going to surface. They might have nothing to do with your problem, but be warned. You will likely not look at some of your employees in the same light as before. All of us have secrets."

"True. But I would appreciate your undertaking this task for me. I will gladly pay your going fee. It will be worth it to clear any lingering doubts from my mind."

"Any exceptions? Your nephew, for example?"

"Please look into the history of everyone. Except my wife and me, of course."

"Very well. I'll need a complete list of employees with as much information as possible. Anything you give me will be held confidential. By the way, you didn't mention your own children."

"Margot and I have only one. A son. Auguste Philippe came rather late in our lives. He was born here, actually. He entered this world in Las Cruces in August of 1990 while I was working with the European Wine Consortium. He is presently a freshman at UC Berkeley pursuing a degree in chemical engineering."

"Are there individuals from your former life—either here or in Europe—who would cause such problems for you?"

"I have made my share of mistakes with people during my career. But I cannot conceive of anyone so aggrieved he would come like a thief in the night." Gonda gave a very European shrug, "Anyone who leaps to mind would certainly be more aggressive. The place would have burned down, for example." He pursed his lips before honing in on precise details, which I suspected was his nature. "Of course, the building is brick and stone. But there are ample flammable materials on the inside."

So there was someone. But was he willing to reveal enough of himself to name him or her? Or them? "You could be making a mountain out of a molehill."

That comment brought a brief smile. "A charming analogy. I have worried over this for fourteen days before coming to see you. Deep down inside, something tells me not to ignore this. To get to the bottom of it quickly. And there have been two other incidents."

"Tell me about them."

"I am experimenting with a sparkling wine—what is commonly referred to as a champagne—using an imported grape, of course. My cabernet sauvignon varietal produces reds, not whites. At any rate, I have a small, temperature-controlled room adjacent to my laboratory with a special wine rack used in the *remuage*, what you here call riddling. Are you familiar with the procedure?"

"You'll have to forgive me. I am not a wine connoisseur. I enjoy a glass with my meals occasionally, but that's about it."

He nodded acceptance of my words. "After the second fermentation, champagnes or sparkling wines are racked upside down at a forty-five-degree angle so that sediments—mostly dead yeasts—settle in the neck. At regular intervals, usually every three days, the bottles are given hard twists so the sediment doesn't solidify. At the proper time, the bottle necks are frozen, the offending plugs removed, and the wine is corked. That procedure is not, of course, limited to sparkling wines."

He must have recognized he was lecturing, because he got back to the point. "I do the riddling in that room myself. The last time I performed the chore, I noticed a disturbance in the slight film of dust on the base of one of the bottles."

"Did the sheriff's deputies take fingerprints?"

"I noticed the disturbance only after they closed their investigation. But it bothered me enough to pay you a visit."

"Has anyone handled the bottle since?"

"I picked it up before I understood the significance of the dust."

"You mentioned two incidents."

"At least one bottle of our chocolate-flavored wine has gone missing. And a bit of food stored in the place as well."

"I'd guess several of your bottles go—"

He held up his hand and straightened in his chair. His posture and body language became formal again. "It is not what you are thinking. I have a very liberal attitude with my employees. I like them to enjoy the fruits of their labors. Each receives a ration of wine, and he or she is free to make special requests. I seldom refuse any reasonable petition."

After submitting to another half hour of questions, Gonda executed my standard contract, handed over a check for the retainer, and made arrangements for me to visit the Lovely Pines. Then he took his leave.

"Such a distinguished gentleman," Hazel observed when she came to collect the contract and the check. And the two bottles.

"You're just a sucker for an accent." I handed over the digital recorder for transcription as well. Earlier this year, Hazel had threatened rebellion if I didn't do away with the tape recorder I'd used for years. I'd probably have ignored her except the thing was virtually worn out. Might as well join the twenty-first century, right?

My formerly dowdy office manager scoffed. "I can take them, or I can leave them."

She had blossomed since she and Charlie Weeks were married in a civil ceremony held in my living room last New Year's Eve. Like me, Charlie was a retired cop. But he'd put in his time at the Albuquerque Police Department, whereas I was medically retired by a gunshot wound to the thigh. Last year he earned his way into a partnership as the only other full-time investigator in the firm. After the legal documents formalizing this were signed, I made a big deal out of having the gold lettering on the outer office door redone to read "Vinson and Weeks, Confidential

Investigations," but Hazel insisted I'd only done it because someone scratched a hole in the paint on the letter *C*.

"There will be a lot of background investigations on this one," I told her.

"Deep?"

"Record checking for the most part, I imagine. Unless that turns up something that needs to be pursued."

"Hmmm." She left for the outer office.

I swiveled my chair to the window and took in the view that anchored me to my third-floor suite of offices in a renovated downtown historic building on the southwest corner of Copper and Fifth NW. I enjoyed looking out the north-facing window and imagining I could look down on my home at 5229 Post Oak Drive NW. By craning my neck to the west, I could almost see Old Town where the twelve original families settled the new Villa de Alburquerque in 1706. Day or night, the scene outside that pane of glass always grabbed me.

Like a lot of confidential investigators, I preferred working for attorneys. They understood the limitations of my profession. We were fact collectors, not sleuths in the popular sense of the word. Movies and TV programs and novels had skewed the public perception of my trade to the point that private citizens often suffered an unrealistic expectation of what our job really was. I worried that the dramatic outcome of that nasty Bisti business might have led Ariel Gonda to the same misconception.

Turning back to the desk, I picked up the file I was currently working. Local attorney Del Dahlman—who was my significant other before I was shot while serving with the Albuquerque Police—had hired me to look over the shoulder of the city's fire department as they conducted an arson investigation. One of his client's warehouses burned to the ground in a spectacularly stubborn blaze a few days ago. Del was concerned about where the inquiry might lead. I was beginning to think the case was heading precisely where he did not want it to go.

After phoning the lieutenant heading the arson investigation, I drove out to meet him at the scene of the fire for another walk-through. Like most cops—and ex-cops—I wanted to see the scene of the crime up close and personal. More than once.

That walk-through took the remainder of the day, so I headed straight for home from the South Broadway site to clean off the soot and mud. With any luck, the cleaners could salvage my suit pants. If not, I'd add the cost of a new pair to Del's bill.

I was surprised to find Paul home when I arrived. In his second year of a UNM graduate program in journalism and holding down a job as a swim instructor and lifeguard at the North Valley Country Club, Paul Barton carried a lot on his plate. Although we'd been together for almost three years now, I sometimes felt we were ships passing in the night. The nights were perfect, of course, but our schedules didn't allow us much time in between.

I'd offered him a job at the office, but he was an independent cuss and turned me down. He was still driving his ancient purple Plymouth coupe, even though he could have afforded a newer model. But he was determined to finish his education without any debt hanging over his head.

I returned his smile as he stood up from the kitchen table where he'd been studying. After a gentle but stimulating kiss, a pot of his very special stew percolating on the stove captured my attention. The savory aroma of green chili and chicken and potatoes sent my sudden hunger wandering back and forth between the gastronomic and the carnal.

"With warm flour tortillas?" I asked.

"And butter." He grinned. "After dinner, I'll expect a reward for my culinary efforts."

I beamed like a smitten teenager. "Abso-fucking-lutely."

DON TRAVIS is a man totally captivated by his adopted state of New Mexico. Each of his B. J. Vinson mystery novels features some region of the state as prominently as it does his protagonist, a gay ex-Marine, ex-cop turned confidential investigator. Don never made it to the Marines (three years in the Army was all he managed) and certainly didn't join the Albuquerque Police Department. He thought he was a paint artist for a while, but ditched that for writing a few years back. A loner, he fulfills his social needs by attending SouthwestWriters meetings and teaching a weekly writing class at an Albuquerque community center.

Facebook: Don Travis
Twitter: @dontravis3

THE
ZOZOBRA
INCIDENT

A BJ VINSON MYSTERY

DON TRAVIS

A BJ Vinson Mystery

B. J. Vinson is a former Marine and ex-Albuquerque PD detective turned confidential investigator. Against his better judgment, BJ agrees to find the gay gigolo who was responsible for his breakup with prominent Albuquerque lawyer Del Dahlman and recover some racy photographs from the handsome bastard. The assignment should be fast and simple.

But it quickly becomes clear the hustler isn't the one making the anonymous demands, and things turn deadly with a high-profile murder at the burning of Zozobra on the first night of the Santa Fe Fiesta. BJ's search takes him through virtually every stratum of Albuquerque and Santa Fe society, both straight and gay. Before it is over, BJ is uncertain whether Paul Barton, the young man quickly insinuating himself in BJ's life, is friend or foe. But he knows he's stepped into something much more serious than a modest blackmail scheme. With Paul and BJ next on the killer's list, BJ must find a way to put a stop to the death threats once and for all.

www.dsppublications.com

THE
BISTI
BUSINESS

A BJ VINSON MYSTERY

DON TRAVIS

A BJ Vinson Mystery

Although repulsed by his client, an overbearing, homophobic California wine mogul, confidential investigator B. J. Vinson agrees to search for Anthony Alfano's missing son, Lando, and his traveling companion—strictly for the benefit of the young men. As BJ chases an orange Porsche Boxster all over New Mexico, he soon becomes aware he is not the only one looking for the distinctive car. Every time BJ finds a clue, someone has been there before him. He arrives in Taos just in time to see the car plunge into the 650-foot-deep Rio Grande Gorge. Has he failed in his mission?

Lando's brother, Aggie, arrives to help with BJ's investigation, but BJ isn't sure he trusts Aggie's motives. He seems to hold power in his father's business and has a personal stake in his brother's fate that goes beyond familial bonds. Together they follow the clues scattered across the Bisti/De-Na-Zin Wilderness area and learn the bloodshed didn't end with the car crash. As they get closer to solving the mystery, BJ must decide whether finding Lando will rescue the young man or place him directly in the path of those who want to harm him.

www.dsppublications.com

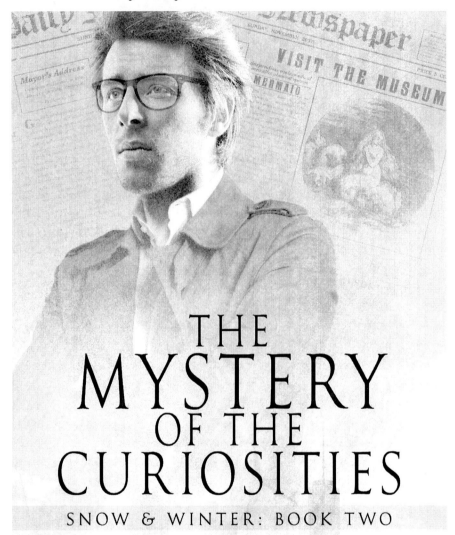

THE
MYSTERY
OF THE
CURIOSITIES

SNOW & WINTER: BOOK TWO

C.S. POE

Snow & Winter: Book Two

Life has been pretty great for Sebastian Snow. The Emporium is thriving and his relationship with NYPD homicide detective, Calvin Winter, is everything he's ever wanted. With Valentine's Day around the corner, Sebastian's only cause for concern is whether Calvin should be taken on a romantic date. It's only when an unknown assailant smashes the Emporium's window and leaves a peculiar note behind that all plans get pushed aside in favor of another mystery.

Sebastian is quickly swept up in a series of grisly yet seemingly unrelated murders. The only connection tying the deaths together are curiosities from the lost museum of P.T. Barnum. Despite Calvin's attempts to keep Sebastian out of the investigation, someone is forcing his hand, and it becomes apparent that the entire charade exists for Sebastian to solve. With each clue that brings him closer to the killer, he's led deeper into Calvin's official cases.

It's more than just Sebastian's livelihood and relationship on the line—it's his very life.

www.dsppublications.com

More Mystery from DSP Publications

S.A. Stovall

VICE CITY

Vice City: Book One

After twenty years as an enforcer for the Vice family mob, Nicholas Pierce shouldn't bat an eye at seeing a guy get worked over and tossed in the river. But there's something about the suspected police mole, Miles, that has Pierce second-guessing himself. The kid is just trying to look out for his brother any way he knows how, and the altruistic motive sparks an uncharacteristic act of mercy that involves Pierce taking Miles under his wing.

Miles wants to repay Pierce for saving his life. Pierce shouldn't see him as anything but a convenient hookup… and he sure as hell shouldn't get involved in Miles's doomed quest to get his brother out of a rival street gang. He shouldn't do a lot of things, but life on the streets isn't about following the rules. Besides, he's sick of being abused by the Vice family, especially Mr. Vice and his power-hungry goon of a son, who treats his underlings like playthings.

So Pierce does the absolute last thing he should do if he wants to keep breathing—he leaves the Vice family in the middle of a turf war.

www.dsppublications.com

CPSIA information can be obtained
at www.ICGtesting.com
Printed in the USA
LVOW10s1507170717

541644LV00011B/155/P